THE HUNTER'S GOODBYE

JASON LANKTON

Copyright

Cover Design by Deranged Doctor Design

DEDICATION

To those who told me I could to this,
and those who believed it.

Chapter One

All I really wanted was a good cup of coffee and these second-rate vampires were keeping me from it. By the time I got them cornered in the dank basement beneath an old repair shop, I was pretty worked up. Putting three down was a good start, but the remaining two were being a pain in my ass.

They led me headlong on a pursuit through nearly every abandoned building along St. Louis Avenue and had finally stopped to make a stand. I don't know how many abandoned buildings we crashed through before that, stirring up homeless people, stray dogs, and rat colonies. After a while, they were just a blur of bricks and bodies.

For some reason, the handful of squatters in the building with a faded "Mort's Repair" sign hadn't been scared off by the sudden appearance of five low-grade vampires in their midst. That changed as soon as I exploded through the poorly barricaded door. I'm a big guy—like pro wrestler big—and I'm covered in tattoos that sometimes glow, depending on the situation and my state of mind, so when I make an entrance, people tend to panic and run away. Generally, those that don't run are monsters of some variety. In this case, they were low-grade vampires.

Sunrise was less than an hour away, meaning these undead hooligans would be desperate to finish me off fast, so they could go find a dark hole to hide in. It also meant my morning wasn't gonna get any easier. I become a big grumpy jerk when that happens.

Their ambush was frantic and aggressive but also sloppy and predictable. I saw it coming and reacted with the degree of brutality fitting a man whose job it is to kill monsters. It was a violent but brief scuffle, the kind I'm built for. Two vampires went down quickly without much of a fight. The third put up a fight but still went down, messily. Four and five were hurt, desperate, and angry. Imagine you have an injured badger cornered in a basement, except the badger won't die unless you take off its head or destroy its heart in some epic way. Now imagine there's two of them and they're each the size of a young man and they want to drink your blood. Now you're up to speed.

So here we were. Me and them. Me, a mortal man—albeit a big one—tired, frustrated, and bloody. And them. Two undead bottom-feeders, also tired, frustrated, and bloody, but also a little worse for the wear. I had already removed a generous portion of number four's right arm, leaving a disgusting stump above the elbow, thanks to my aggressive machete skills. The nasty bastard still had his left arm though. Number five had a length of rebar protruding from his chest, close to the heart but not close enough to finish the job. The skin smoked and sizzled like a grilled steak on a hot skillet where the rebar met flesh. Most vampire varieties have a terrible silver allergy. But there ain't silver in rebar. Rebar is mostly iron and generally useless against vampires. The seeping blood around Sirloin's wound crackled and bubbled with each labored breath. That was interesting, but I'd have to ponder that later.

All five of these creepies had been male and were probably in their twenties when they died but had probably been around a while. Their skin was ivory white, indicating they hadn't been gorging on victims. Newly turned suckheads usually do. The young ones don't have any discipline and tend to be prolific killers before they learn restraint and discretion. Eighty percent of the vampires that get killed by Hunters, get killed in the first year of having been turned. Apparently, a euphoria comes on and sparks a feeding frenzy, and the vampires have at it like crackheads. It's my job to disabuse them of that behavior.

Bright red blood flowed from Lefty's ragged stump, a sharp contrast against its pale skin. Sure, that was distracting, but what really had my attention was the fact that sonofabitch held my machete in its right hand. My machete. The same one I had used to cut off its arm not one full minute ago and killed its three other companions before that. It was my fault of course. The walnut handle had gotten slick with gore and I dropped it in the ensuing melee. Mr. Machete—I don't pick the names—was one of the simplest of the enchanted weapons in my modest armory, but it was also one of my favorites, for its brutal simplicity. Yes, the added silver and iron in the steel were great amplifiers for the bulk of my applications and yes, the etched runes ramped up the weapon's natural properties to eleven on the Kill-O-Dial. But essentially, Mr. Machete was simply a sturdy blade with a wooden handle. Brutal simplicity. You swing it at the right thing and something either dies or wishes it had.

Sizzling Sirloin snarled and bared its jagged, chipped, and criminally dirty at me; the rebar heaved up and down in an exaggerated, silly motion. Some vampires have pointy fangs like you see in the movies. This variety didn't. Just jagged and nasty. It came from being so ravenous. They end up biting into bones and belt buckles and whatever. Given time, they'd learn even better self-control. Well, I wasn't going to give them that time.

Lefty lunged, swinging Mr. Machete wildly at me. At the same time, Sirloin rushed at me from the left, flailing its nasty fingernails. Not claws. Nasty, crusty, untrimmed fingernails, with caked-on blood and dirt. I stepped hard toward Sirloin, lowered my shoulder, and rammed into its torso. As I said, I'm a big guy, and I'm built like a freight train, so there was a lot of mass behind that shoulder. We both toppled out of Stumpy's path, Mr. Machete missing me by a breath. Sizzler snarled and grabbed at my hair. Fortunately—because of times like this—I kept my hair cut short, so there wasn't anything to grab onto. Lefty's momentum carried it a few steps past Sizzler and me. It growled and spun. I worked my arm under Sizzler's chin and shoved, keeping its teeth away from my face. With my free hand, I grabbed the rebar and yanked it free from the creature's chest drawing a disgusting *slurp* sound. Sirloin roared with renewed agony and thrashed wildly. I rolled from on top of its body just in time to miss another strike from Lefty. The blade missed me entirely and sunk deep into Sizzler's shoulder. It screamed again as the rune-etched blade burned into its flesh. Stumpy bellowed in frustration and anger and yanked the blade free, then spun to launch at me again.

"My turn," I said, swinging the rebar still in my hand. It cracked against Lefty's head with a satisfying ring of metal on bone. The nasty bugger staggered back a step and lost its grip on Mr. Machete. I scrambled forward and caught the weapon before it hit the floor.

"You're using it wrong," I said and swung the blade in a wide horizontal slash. Lefty's anger turned to sudden confusion as its head fell off and tumbled to the floor.

"That's how you do it," I said between breaths and pushed the now lifeless body over.

Sirloin screamed and I caught it as it jumped at me. Again, we went to the floor and rolled among the blood and gore and scattered vampire parts. The young vampire chomped and clawed at me viciously, while I held it back, beating at its head with the bottom of Mr. Machete's grip. My elbow jostled against Lefty's fresh corpse and I lost my grip on the weapon. Dammit. Not again. The blade clattered to the floor and I lost track of it in the jumble of vampire carcasses. Sizzler kept biting at me, both of his hands dug into the lapels of my jacket in a death grip. I pawed around with my free hand and found something that wasn't too heavy to pick up. I dug my fingers into a handful of matted hair and swung. Lefty's severed head smacked hard against the side of Sizzler's. I swung again. And again. A fourth time, cracking skull against skull. The bloodsucker's grip finally loosened slightly. That was all I needed. I let go of the severed head and rolled away two full somersaults before staggering to my feet.

Sirloin tossed the gruesome head aside and got to its feet before rushing at me. I was ready. This time, I stepped forward and extended my arm. I punched the disgusting creature squarely in the throat with all my strength, which is considerable. With my mass, a punch like that is devastating. Undead or not, a solid throat punch does some severe damage, and hurts like hell. Five staggered away from me, clutching at its throat, rasping, and gagging in pain and anger. With a moment to finally act, instead of reacting, I pulled my coat aside and yanked my gun free of its holster.

It was a .44 magnum revolver, silver-plated—of course—with faintly glowing runes etched along its barrel and cylinder in hues of blue, green, red, and yellow. Something like what Dirty Harry would carry if he was a badass monster hunter like me. The bullets were cast from a combination of lead, iron, and silver and were each enchanted by the same guy that imbued the gun. Paired with this gun, these bullets inflicted some special damage on vampires. The Holy Handgun was a force to be reckoned with—again, I don't pick the names.

The creature's angry eyes flashed with faint realization as I raised the gun and thumbed back the hammer.

It shrieked angrily and leapt. I squeezed the trigger. The gun barked and jumped in my hand. The report was deafening in the closed space. The bullet exploded into Sizzler's skull and its head snapped back. Smoke and light, flashing like a welding arc, poured from the gaping hole in the vampire's head. It spasmed for a few seconds and dropped to the floor, like a puppet whose strings had been cut. Limp. Lifeless. Disgusting.

I holstered the Holy Handgun and took a minute to catch my breath. I rubbed absent-mindedly at one of the glowing rune tattoos on my left arm while I tried to collect myself. Not an easy thing to do when you've got a variety of ichor on you and are surrounded by several vampires in varying states of disassembly. There among them, I spotted Mr. Machete's polished blade, reflecting a glint of the morning sun breaking through a cracked basement window. I stooped and picked it up.

I was alive and relatively unharmed. Five vampires were not. Still, my work wasn't done yet.

"God, I hate this job," I sighed and began removing hearts and heads from all the corpses. In my trade, we call that the Hunter's Goodbye.

Chapter Two

My name is Bill Kemper and I'm a professional monster hunter.

You could say it's an honest trade, albeit a dicey and terrifying one. I perform a necessary service and get paid well by the secretive Nine-Fold Council to do it. But don't get too excited, you won't find help wanted signs for my job, and really, you don't want it. Chasing the undead through tetanus-laced fun houses and rolling around in dark basements among infectious body parts ain't all fun and games. Those on the receiving end of my services tend to reject my advances in hazardous and malicious ways.

Although the precept is rejected by modern society, monsters exist. Regardless of what you've heard or believe, there are indeed creatures to go bump in the night. I'm the guy that bumps back. I can't stand by and do nothing while supernatural creatures prey on innocent lives. I can't, and I don't.

The Nine-Fold Council agrees with me and pays me to do what I do. The pay is great, but that's just because the life expectancy of a Hunter is equivalent to that of a sanitation worker at the height of the black plague in 14th century Europe. It ain't good.

I don't know why, but St. Louis is a hotbed of supernatural activity. It ain't the only one of course, but it's my city. And that makes it personal. So I Hunt. I find the things that people don't wanna believe are real, and I ask them firmly to vacate the land of the living, and I show them the way out.

And afterwards, I go get some coffee.

My encounter at Mort's Repair Shop had me running well behind my preferred routine and unfortunately, the job wasn't even done yet. But I hadn't heard from my informant yet, so I had some time to kill before I had more monsters to kill.

I'm a big, intimidating man who kills big, intimidating creatures—most of them straight out of the original scary versions of Grimm's Fairy tales—for a living. Predictable and uneventful pursuits are the guideposts for my free time. All I really wanted was to spend the rest of my day drinking some coffee and maybe read a book. There was a place not far from my house that had great coffee.

Of course, I couldn't go there looking like I had slaughtered five uncooperative vampires in a dank basement. On the way, I stopped at a truck stop and used one of their rent-a-showers for a quick clean-up to change into the spare clothes I kept in my car. There was always a need for fresh clothes.

The Blue Sky coffee shop sits between a used book shop called Lazy Day Books and a tanning salon called Sunny Sides. It was built on the kind of simplicity that spoke to my uncomplicated mind. Exposed red brick walls, simple furnishing, quiet people. It was one of the few places the employees didn't look at me like I was an ogre and the only place that served the Bill Kemper special. Unlike those chain shops that leaned heavily on brand recognition, product placement, and popular corporate logos the Blue Sky relied on good coffee and good service.

The owner, a widow from Mexico named Sarah, had built the shop up from nothing through hard work and determination. She treated everyone that came into the shop like family, even me. That dose of humanity was what kept me going most days.

Since the shop isn't close to the interstate or any of the trendier areas in St. Louis, the Blue Sky regulars are usually locals, like me. Well, nobody was like me but that's beside the point. They were familiar to me, and I was familiar to them. That didn't mean they understood me. It just meant that I hadn't tried to eat any babies or grind anyone's bones, so I was an acceptable oddity.

The little brass bell above the door chimed as I opened the front doors and I was immediately treated with the heavenly aroma of freshly brewed coffee and pastries straight out of the oven. The few customers waiting in line for their orders ignored me. They were far more interested in whatever they had on their phones than me, which is saying a lot. Regular or not, I stood out like Dave Bautista in a school lunch line.

The old hardwood floor creaked under my weight, barely audible over the chattering baristas and the soft hum of jazz piped in through a hidden speaker. A chalk sign above the register announced in colorful, curly, and flowery letters that today's lunch special was a pumpkin spice latte and a tomato panini.

I headed on autopilot for my usual table in the back corner. It's positioned just right, so I can look out the large window or toward the counter to see the baristas at work. It also puts me with my back to a wall and a clear view of all the entry points. I'm told it's what some veterans get in the habit of doing, especially those who'd seen combat. I wasn't an old vet but being on high alert is a habit that has saved my ass more than a few times. Sometimes, the Hunters become the hunted. It's a side effect of the trade, one for which paranoia is actually useful.

My table was little, round, and undersized for a man of my stature—as were all of the table at the Blue Sky—but it was *my* table and I took a sad bit of comfort in that fragile two-foot circle of familiarity. The top was covered with broken-up pieces of colorful tiles covered with a thick coat of clear epoxy. I used to try to make out patterns or pictures in the random mosaic, but there were none, just familiar shapes that kept my mind occupied if I let them.

I kept my head down and avoided eye contact with the customers as I weaved my way toward my table then stopped a few paces short. A little old lady wearing a hairdo from 1952 and thick glasses with one of those thin retaining chains dangling from either side was sitting there. In my spot. At my table, my chair. Just pecking away at a small piece of lemon cake. I didn't recognize her; she wasn't a regular, but she sure had made herself right at home in my happy place. There was an empty table next to her. Why hadn't she taken that table? It was a nice table too, pretty colors, bathed in the sunlight streaming in through the large storefront window; most importantly, it wasn't mine.

I thought of vampires and werewolves and demons and goblins and how much I deserved this one little thing in return for my reluctant services to an ungrateful and unknowing world. I imagined this little old lady thanking me and getting out of my seat and offering me my table as a gesture of gratitude like a person would for a soldier returning from war. But I was no soldier, and I was fighting battles decent folk would never hear about or believe. I was a secret monster, fighting secret monsters. God, I was a pitiful martyr.

I nodded politely at the lady then eased myself onto one of the small chairs at the unoccupied table. She watched me for a moment, with haughty indifference. I was used to it. Didn't like it but was used to it.

I rested my arms on the table and it wobbled. Come on, really? I took hold of it gingerly with my meaty hands and wiggled it. Yep. The legs were uneven. The old lady peeked at me through her schoolmarm's glasses as I repeatedly confirmed the table's lack of stability. There was nothing for it, I'd have to suffer through this tribulation. I glanced at the lady, who was not trying to hide her disapproval of whatever I was. I grumbled a muted apology for whatever I'd apparently done and smiled without showing my teeth. That scares people. When a gorilla shows its teeth, it ain't smiling.

I leaned on my elbows, hoping the unfamiliar table and the untested chair would hold me, and waited for someone to bring me some coffee.

This wasn't the type of place where servers came to your table to take your order or brought your order to you. Customers went to the antique wood-topped counter, order what they wanted, and waited there for it. I didn't do that anymore. Not that I was something special or anything like that, it's just the baristas knew my order by heart—it never changed—and I imagined some of them would prefer not to have me in line scaring the normal folk. The regulars were used to me, but I still make people nervous.

Somebody would get around to me eventually.

The usual day crew was working today. Besides Sarah, who seemed to never leave, there were three other baristas working the pre-lunch crowd. Alex couldn't make a sandwich to save his life, so he manned the register. Due to his red hair and prominent freckles, some of his co-workers called him Opie. He didn't seem to mind. Simone had come to town from New Orleans for college and was famous in the neighborhood for her pastries. Between helping fill orders and keeping fresh baked goods in rotation, she never seemed to stop moving. Jonas, who looked like he belonged in a clothing advertisement instead of a coffee shop, kept the coffee orders flowing and never got one wrong.

I watched them work with casual interest. Eventually, Sarah noticed me and raised one finger, mouthing "one minute." I nodded.

"God, I'm tired," I mumbled quietly to myself. The old lady glanced at me suspiciously.

"Long night," I added quietly.

"Indeed," the lady said with a sour-lemons look and returned to her cake.

A couple of minutes later, Sarah approached with a light blue coffee cup and a small saucer with a piece of buttered toast on it. She had an attractive face that she didn't bother hiding under makeup, and she didn't need to. She had a natural beauty that came easily for people like her who smiled a lot. Her dark brown hair was about shoulder length, but she usually kept it up in a loose ponytail. Her brown eyes had a joy of their own when she looked you in the eyes—Sarah was one of the few people who willingly made eye contact with me. She looked everyone in the eyes when she spoke to them. She was the closest thing to a completely "good" person I had ever met and if I'm being honest, that was probably what kept me coming back to The Blue Sky. I get an unhealthy portion of badness on a daily basis, but I also get paid for that.

"Good morning," Sarah said. She had a hint of an accent when she spoke but her English was probably better than mine

I grunted, "It is still morning, isn't it?"

"For a while longer, yes," she said as she placed the drink and dish gently on the table in front of me. "One Bill Kemper Special?" Coffee, Americano, black. Wheat toast with cinnamon butter. Wheat because that's good for you or something. Right?

"Thanks," I said and sipped from the scalding coffee. God, I love a strong cup of coffee.

"We missed you this morning," she said. "Did you have a busy morning wrestling badgers?"

The little old lady looked up suddenly from her pastry.

I grinned. Sarah had been guessing wrongly for weeks what I did for a living. I had come in looking pretty rough a few times, twice recently with new visible scars. She never pressed but she had a genuine concern for people's well-being.

"Nice try," I said, "no."

She said, "Has it been a tough day, so early?"

"You could say that," I said, and wrapped my hands around the mug. It was too hot to hold for very long, but I liked it. "Hard morning."

Sara didn't speak. She just stood there and watched me for a minute while I studied my coffee.

Finally, I said, "A guy can take a lot of punishment when he don't have a choice."

"Ah," Sara leaned close as if sharing a secret, "We call that being human."

My God, how did she stay so positive?

"That's what they call it?"

She nodded, "That's was what we call it. Us humans. That includes you, mister."

"I am human I guess," I said and met her eyes.

"As far as I can tell."

I let the corner of my mouth curl, "Nice to be reminded."

"Anytime," she said then added, "Literally. I'm here all day... and all night."

I raised my eyebrows at that.

"I'm pulling a double."

Alex hollered for Sarah, he wasn't keeping up with the orders, few as they were. She held up one finger at him.

"Another one?" I asked.

Sarah shrugged, "Val wants to go out for her birthday tonight, she's turning 21, so I took her shift. She'll regret it in the morning, but enjoy it tonight."

"You're a saint," I said.

"I'm a businesswoman," Sarah corrected, "and my business needs people in it."

"Shrewd."

She laughed, "Practical. And it will give me some time alone to study. The night shift is quiet here."

"Study?"

"Si. Did I not tell you? I'm taking some online courses," she said triumphantly. "I'm going to get my degree."

"Nice," I said and nodded my approval, "Good for you."

"Thanks," Sarah said, practically bubbling with pride. "I'll be the first in my entire family."

"You're a trooper," I said.

"That's what my Abuela used to say," Sarah said, and her smile faded. "You look tired. Are you sure everything is ok?"

"Tired covers it," I said and set the mug on the wobbly table. My hands were getting too hot. "Just did a double shift too."

Sarah raised an eyebrow, "Oh yeah? Are you saving up for college?"

I shook my head, "I just work too hard."

"Well, don't steal my thunder," Sarah said, "I'm the official workaholic around here."

"Thunder's all yours. I'm just saving for retirement."

"Retirement?" she put her hands on her hips, "You're a little young for that aren't you?"

Young. I hadn't been called that in a long time.

"I'm old beyond my years," I said.

Sarah laughed, "I think that's supposed to be 'wise beyond your years.'"

I shrugged, "I missed the wise part. I just got the years."

"Sarah!" Alex called again, on the verge of panic.

"I have to go save Alex before he freaks out."

I nodded and picked up my coffee cup again, its handle dwarfed in my meaty hand, "Thanks for the table service."

"The coffee is on the house," Sarah said as she headed for the register. "You owe me a dollar thirteen for the toast."

"No charity," I called after her.

Sarah looked over her shoulder, "It's not charity. It is just me being nice. Say thanks and live with it."

"Thanks," I grumbled.

I sipped gingerly at the hot coffee for a moment, luxuriating in the simple perfection of fresh-brewed, un-doctored coffee.

After I had gotten about halfway through the cup, a pale grey tattoo at the base of my skull began to itch. Without really thinking, I rubbed at it for a few seconds in a counter-clockwise motion, then felt a slight chill in the air around me. The chill seemed to swirl and fade away, then a ghost sat down in the chair opposite.

Technically, Leonard Albert Johnston was a disembodied spirit. I didn't know how that was different from a ghost, but he has insisted on the distinction.

Ghost or spirit, to me, he looked like a monochrome hologram of Jimi Hendrix wearing a Jedi robe.

A few years ago, a frightened psychic came to me and told me that the late Leonard Johnston wanted an official introduction. We've been associates since then, Leo and me. The magic tattoo on my neck—courtesy of my Norwegian tattoo artist and the psychic's careful instruction—was tuned to Leo. I don't know the specifics of that kind of magic. It just works, sometimes without my consent. As a result, it made me the exclusive inheritor of Leo's consultations and the only mortal person who could see or hear him.

"Hey, Leo," I said quietly as I bit off a chunk of my toast. The old lady looked up at me with open curiosity. When she realized I wasn't talking to her, she returned to her own tedious pecking.

"Oh man that looks good," Leo said, eying my toast.

"It's just toast," I mumbled.

"It's just toast to you, my friend. Me? I'd eat a horse's ass right now if I had real teeth."

I almost spit out my bite as I choked off a laugh.

"Want some?" I asked quietly after regaining my composure.

"Mighty generous, Bill," Leo said without malice, "If only it was possible. No, I will continue to dine upon the feast of knowledge and enlightenment until the end of the universe."

"What's that taste like?"

"A lot like empty promises," he admitted.

I let out a grunting chuckle.

"You look like you've had a hard morning," Leo whispered as if sharing a secret.

"You ain't the first person to notice."

"I'm not a person," Leo said, "and I can see things, astral planes, you can't comprehend."

"You talking about my body or my soul?"

The spirit shrugged, "One mirrors the other."

"So, you say," I took a deep swig of coffee. It was still too hot, but it was so good. "I've had rougher days."

"Yes, I recall most of them. You know you'll have rougher ones still," Leo stated.

"Yeah," I leaned my elbows on the table, and for a moment I wasn't sure it would hold my weight. It probably wouldn't for very long. "But that's the job."

"The job," Leo repeated ominously, "You say it as if it's a prison sentence."

"It ain't a picnic."

"But you keep doing it?"

"True."

"Why?"

I shrugged.

"Come on Bill, spill it. What do you get out of it?"

I didn't answer right away. I tried to think of something clever or snarky, but nothing came. Instead, I thought of the unstable table trying to support my incredible weight. When would it give? What was its breaking point? The point where it had taken everything it could possibly take and just fell apart.

"Why do you always ask me that?"

"It's part of the deal," Leo said looking into my eyes. "You get my services. I get to dig into the deep corners of your soul with profound and probing questions.

"It ain't profound," I said lifting my elbows off the table and it didn't fall apart. "Always the same damn question."

"It's profound because it's the question you always ask yourself," Leo said and leaned back in the chair, steepling his fingers like a philosopher expounding on the mysteries of the universe. "I've existed without a body for a long time, long to me at least. I forget what being a human is like. I like to hear it from the horse's mouth."

"I ain't the best reference for a regular human," I grumbled.

"You're more human than you give yourself credit for. Anyways, I exist simultaneously between two universes." He held up two fingers, which also looked like he was giving me the peace sign. "It's a form of existence without solid mortal anchors. If I'm not careful, I can lose track of what humanity is supposed to be like." He lowered his index finger, now giving me the bird, and laughed at himself. "That's why I ask, so I don't forget what humanity is. You're my baseline."

Two universes. The mortal universe and the Otherside. Leo moves freely between them, partly because of his magic connection to me. The Otherside is not only for disembodied spiritual guides, though. They aren't all Jedi specters over there. It's where a bunch of the really nasty things come from. When I say really nasty, I mean the things people refuse to believe in. Some nights I'm glad the way is shut.

"I ask again," Leo said pointed at my forehead. "What do you get out of being a Hunter? Why do you do it?"

I shrugged after a couple of seconds digging for the answer, "I dunno, to make the world a safer place?"

"Is that a question or an answer?"

"Hell if I know!" I said, too loudly and gestured at the world at large. I bumped the table and sloshed some of my coffee on the mosaic top. The old lady scowled and shook her head.

"Sorry," I whispered and dabbed at the spilled coffee with a tiny napkin.

"It's difficult for me to embrace selfless enlightenment when I don't understand those for whom I am being selfless."

"Deep Leo."

"I agree," he agreed, "I'm a virtual abyss of philosophical insight."

I dropped the coffee-soaked napkin onto the table. There was still spilled coffee, the little disposable rag wasn't enough to clean up the mess I had made.

"Who else is gonna do it?" I said finally.

"There are other Hunters."

"Dead ones, mostly."

The old lady mumbled something about decency without looking up from her snack.

Leonard studied her for a moment then looked at me, "You want me to possess her body and freeze that sour look on her face?"

"Can you do that?"

"I don't think so. I've never tried."

"Then no."

"As you wish."

Someone cleared their throat and I looked up. It was Alex with a dishtowel.

"Miss Sarah says quit making a mess," he said a little sheepishly. I took the towel and looked past Alex to see Sarah behind the counter wink at me.

I grinned at Alex and accepted the towel before he hurried back to his post.

Leo watched me in silence for a moment as I clumsily cleaned up my spill.

You don't act like you like your job very much," Leo observed.

"Because I don't," I said.

"Then why do you keep doing it?"

"It's what I do," I said defensively without raising my voice.

Leo didn't respond, he just watched my face.

I felt my brow furrow, "It's what I am."

"'I am what I am?'"

"That covers it."

"You're Bill Freaking Kemper," Leo poked a cold finger at my chest and cool air swirled around me. Nobody else in the shop seemed to notice the arctic breeze. "That's all. You are you. Everything else is just noise."

I let out a slow breath, "Spoken like a true spiritual guide."

Leo frowned.

"Vague and unhelpful," I explained.

"I am what I am."

I chuckled despite myself.

"If only you could see things through my incorporeal eyes," Leo said, "the 'vague and unhelpful' things that I say to you would make so much sense to you."

"But I can't."

"No," Leo agreed, "you can't. And I'm sorry for that."

"I'll take your word for it, then."

My cellphone beeped. I groaned and opened the old flip phone. A text message from Regis:

Report?

I punched in Coffee Break and hit send. Leo raised an eyebrow as the phone beeped again.

Report. Impatient bastard.

I worked my jaw back and forth, debating on a selection of colorful responses. Heroically, I refrained.

I heaved an unnecessarily heavy breath and raised my eyebrows at Leo.

The spirit nodded, "Yeah. I think I found the loci. North of here."

"Wanna come?"

"I don't think so," Leo said. "But be careful. This vampire is unusual."

"How?"

He shrugged, "Those things you've been fighting, they're hers. But they're not vampires."

"Coulda fooled me."

"Come on Bill. You know what I mean. They're just thralls. Mindless drones. She's throwing them at you like grenades."

"They were a bit easy to put down," I admitted, "considering there were five of them."

"Five? Jeez, you're a machine. Do you know what kind of energy and strength it takes for a vampire to make thralls? Five would put a vampire into a coma for weeks. I'm telling you; this is not your routine bloodsucker."

"Don't matter," I said.

"Just be careful. I don't want to see what your soul looks like if it's all shredded up but something you underestimated."

"Real comforting."

"My purpose isn't comfort," Leo said, "it is wisdom."

"And tracking," I added.

"Guidance," he corrected. "I can guide you to that for which you seek."

"Guide?"

"Fine, I can point you in the right direction without actually accompanying you there."

I punched in a new message on my cell: *5 thrall retired. Primary by end of day.*

I dug a map out and unfolded it on the unstable table, careful not to lay it in the wet spot from the spilled coffee. Leonard studied the lines for a moment as if struggling to remember what they were.

"There," he said pointing at a spot along the freeway.

"You sure?"

"Sure as death."

"Says the ghost who didn't die."

Leo soundlessly tapped at the location on the paper.

"Shit on a stick," I said too loudly and took another bite of toast.

The little lady huffed audibly.

"I know right?"

Sarah looked up from her duties behind the counter, "Stop scaring the customers."

"Sorry," I grumbled.

"You got this," Leo said enthusiastically. "You'll be fine."

"Thanks, Coach."

"I can see more than just your soul, Bill. I can see what's happening in many places all at once. You got this."

"What's happening??"

"Doubt and regret," he said with an exaggerated mysterious flair.

"Those are just words."

"These words are yours. Do with them what you will."

"You're a really frustrating guide."

"I don't pick the songs," he said. "I just play them."

I laughed quietly.

"Fine," I said after my smile faded. "There's dirty work to do."

Leonard touched two fingers to his forehead in a tip of the hat gesture before fading away with a brief wisp of cold air. I finished the rest of my toast in one bite, took another deep swig of the hot coffee, and dropped a twenty on the table as I stood up. Without looking back, I exited before Sarah could protest.

I had dirty work to do, and my cleaning supplies were at home.

Chapter Three

My house is in a quiet neighborhood, far enough south of the 44 to feel like a suburb but still close enough to make you lock the doors and listen for bumps in the night. If you drive down my street, you'll see rows of nicely kept red brick apartments and narrow, multi-level houses with small yards and one tree each for curb appeal. Huddled in among them is a small, single-story house, plucked from 1948 and dropped right in the middle of the lower to middle-class neighborhood. That's my house.

The street was empty, most everyone was off to work or school already. Those that weren't were probably sleeping in or watching their morning talk shows and courtroom dramas. It was a quiet neighborhood, inhabited by mostly ordinary people. Not the kind of place you'd expect to find a seasoned monster hunter.

I parked my 1984 Monte Carlo SS in the street in front of my house. The old car wasn't quite old enough to be a classic, but far from new. It was a relic, like me. It was also big and reliable, like me. That beast had taken a beating over the years and had all the scars to prove it. The black paint was scratched all to hell—a side effect of being the personal chariot to a Hunter. There were dents and dings surrounded by generous patches of rust. Bullet holes peppered the driver's side, which I cleverly concealed those tacky fake bullet hole stickers. More than a few bloodstains had ruined the driver seat upholstery, hidden under cheap seat covers. The dash was sun-bleached and cracked. The stereo speakers crackled if you turned up the volume loud enough to hear the music. The windows didn't roll down anymore. The seatbelts didn't always unlock when you wanted. The speedometer didn't work. But the engine... that bit of engineering that was still badass. It was loud and intimidating and powerful.

My car was beaten, worn out, and not great to look at, but it was built like a freaking tank with the heart of a stallion. So yeah, it was like me.

I didn't bother locking the car, because the locks didn't work, and zipped up my jacket against the chilled air. The last bits of winter had finally melted away, but spring hadn't sprung yet. The air was damp but not bitter, which was fine by me. I like the cold weather; it gives me an excuse to wear a jacket or coat so I can keep my tattoos covered up. I get enough weird looks as it is, my are numerous and strange. Most of my ink had been done by a rune-maker from Norway who also taught me some incantations to go along with them. Many of them were a mixture of ink and strange herbs that equated to permanent magic potions inlaid under my skin. Since rune magic requires a truckload of faith, conviction, and concentration, I rarely used them. Those things are not easy to come by in a fight. I had more guts than faith.

I was nearly to the front door when a familiar short bark from behind stopped me cold. I turned around slowly, one hand outstretched, palm down. There, at the bottom of the rough concrete steps stood a large dog that looked like a cross between a German Shepherd and a yak. She was mostly brown with patches of black on her face almost in the pattern common to German Shepherds, but the hair was much longer and shaggier. God knows what mixed breed she was. I don't think there is a name for it. Besides the unusual fur, she had mismatched eyes; one was light brown and the other a brilliant grey. She barked again, a low-pitched, short ruff that would send lesser men running. Or men who hadn't already met and discovered this dog was not violent.

"Lady," I said and sat down on the bottom step, "it's been a while." Lady was the name I gave her.

She was a stray and God knows if she ever had an owner or family.

She approached slowly to sniff my outstretched hand and

sneezed.

"Sorry," I couldn't imagine what kind of stench I must be putting out to an animal with a super sense of smell. Vampire blood has a particular odor even I can detect. To a dog, it must be horrid.

After a moment, Lady pressed her muzzle into my hand, ignoring the dried filth. I scratched her chin and moved up to scratch both of her ears. She groaned in approval and let me continue for a full minute.

"Hungry?" I asked as I stood up. Her ears perked up. She followed me up the steps and sat when I stopped at the door to disarm the locks. Yes, disarm. The three deadbolts didn't look like anything out of the ordinary, but the neighbors didn't need to know what these locks were really for. The enchantments built into them could only be disarmed by the matched and counter-charmed keys. I was no wizard, so magic isn't my strong suit. Every magic thing I owned—including Mr. Machete and the Holy Handgun—was made by someone else. The best of them was by a friend in KC who had a talent for enchanted weaponry. It's a niche market and he's the king of it.

The door looked like it belonged on any in any normal neighborhood, but it was lined with expertly concealed strips of rowan, blood ash, copper, and iron. The edges were inscribed with old-school runes that mostly focused on preventing demons and hellspawn from getting in. The magic would do a fair job at slowing down vampires too, or so I was told.

Most mortal homes have a natural threshold power that hinders magical malice, but few people don't know about it. It's one of the mysterious rules of the universe that just works. I've been told family love is very strong magic. Without getting all cheesy about it, love is strong protection against evil. So yeah, homes have threshold magic. Homes. Not houses. There's a difference. My house was the latter and required extra security measures. The dangerous thing about this kind of magic was—unlike my rune tattoos—it didn't matter what you believed. They worked regardless of what anyone believed. Like a match and gasoline. Put them together and things get hot no matter how much you try to believe they won't.

I disarmed the locks and pushed the door open before asking the dog, "Wanna come in?"

She tilted her head curiously at me as if she understood the question but didn't know why I'd asked. Always the same reaction. No matter how hard I coaxed or cajoled, she never followed me into the house. She was no house dog and certainly wasn't my dog. Lady indicated she'd be fine waiting out here.

I didn't have dog food since I didn't technically have a dog. I kept meaning to buy some just in case, but sometimes Lady went weeks without stopping by. I just never knew when she'd show, so I never really thought about keeping extra food around. It's probably for the best that I never had pets. I'd be a poor caretaker.

I had some old bologna in the fridge, and that was pretty much it. I didn't cook much and often ate out on the fly; cheap lunch meat would have to do. I opened the package and sniffed it. It didn't smell bad, but I don't know that I could say what bad bologna smelled like. I put it on a plate and brought it back out to the front porch. Lady sniffed at the meat as I placed it before her but didn't dig in right away.

"Sorry," I said. "It's all I got."

The dog's eyes met mine and she tilted her head again. I shrugged apologetically. After a moment, she dug into the food and ate enthusiastically. I watched her as she snarfed down the cheap meat. She was well-fed and obviously didn't need my meager offerings. I think she was eating more for my sake than her own. And had to wonder, though, where did a stray dog this size find enough food to stay fed?

She ate quickly, and as she swallowed the last bite, her ears perked up. She looked suddenly toward the end of the block and barked a quiet huff.

"What's wrong?" I asked. As if she'd answer.

She barked again, louder, then got up and bolted, bounding in huge strides. In fewer steps than a horse would've taken, she ran across the street, disappearing between the houses. As quickly as she had appeared, Lady disappeared again, for who knows how long.

The moment she was out of sight, a large blacked-out SUV whipped around the corner and screeched to a stop inches from my Monte Carlo's rear bumper.

I growled.

The driver didn't bother shutting off the engine. She didn't even get out. When the passenger door opened, I caught brief a glimpse of her. A small-framed woman with a ponytail, dressed in black, pointedly not looking in my direction. It's the opposite of staring and people do it all the time. She looked pissed but that's all I could tell before she disappeared behind the man in the passenger seat as he leaned forward to open the door.

The stout man in plain black fatigues stepped out of the SUV and slammed the door with enough force to rock the vehicle. Though there were no identifying patches or tags on the uniform, I knew he was a member of the Council's Security Detail. I'd know this jerk in or out of any uniform. Colonel Samuel York.

He was as tall as me but not as meaty. That's not saying he wouldn't be a formidable opponent in a real fight. He could have been a stunt double for Dwayne "the Rock" Johnson, except he had no charisma and much darker skin than the actor. He strode up to my steps with the arrogant confidence of someone who believed he could kick anyone's ass and welcomed the opportunity to prove it.

He wasn't visibly armed at present, but I'd seen him packing everything from Glocks to RPGs, depending on the situation. Even if he didn't have any weapons on display, I knew a guy like York was never not packing.

The Council had a well-equipment and decently trained security force, but it took more than guns and GI Joe wannabes to impress me. As far as I was concerned, the Detail was just a bunch of high-paid mercenaries who were good at keeping secrets and weren't afraid of the boogeyman. A little like me, but not as cool or tough.

The Detail was made up of a mix of ex-military vets, martial arts experts, and retired SWAT types. I'd bet a stack of dollars that York was ex-marine. He had that bearing. Jarhead all the way.

As its commander, York was the face of the Security Detail. And it's head asshole.

He stopped one step inside my personal bubble and tried to stare me down. He was one of the few people in the world who could look at me eye to eye without a step ladder.

I didn't give him the satisfaction of a reaction. A wise man once said the best battle is the battle not fought. Something like that. Sometimes, I decide to not let people make me fight them.

"You look like shit, Kemper," he finally said. His voice was precise as his posture, his words sharply pronounced as his jawline.

"Homesick?"

His jaw worked back and forth. "I have no doubt you like the smell but maybe you should try killing your targets instead of dancing with them Maybe you wouldn't get so messy."

I said, "Can I practice with you?"

"Be my guest," he said, "I'm always ready to dance Kemper."

"When the music is right," I said calmly.

"When the music is right," he agreed. "In the meantime, shouldn't you be doing your job?"

"Shouldn't you be at the library with your thumb up your ass?"

York's nostrils flared as he breathed in deeply and held his breath in for a few seconds.

"The Archives are in fine hands," he said without moving his jaw, his teeth clamped together. "I have many... duties that are no concern of yours."

"Mall cop? Crossing guard?" I asked.

"My job," he said. "My business." With precise movements, he pulled a scrap of neatly folded paper from his pocket and held it up between us. "Intel on your target."

"How'd you get intelligence?" I asked, "It is written in crayon?"

"With regards from the Archivist," he said ignoring my childish jabs.

"Dean sent this?" I took the paper looking at it without unfolding it.

"Mr. Forrester, yes," York said.

"Tell him thanks."

"Tell him yourself, I'm not your personal courier."

"You're the mailman then?"

"I'm nobody's errand boy Kemper."

"Dean coulda sent me this without you." I waved the small note in front of his nose.

"Master Regis requested that I check up on you; he's still waiting on your update," York said with obvious disdain. I knew him long enough to know he was a practical man. He preferred a straight-up fight. Fists and guns. He didn't like dealing with wizards and magic and whatnot; those things were for freaks. Freaks like me.

Honestly, I didn't much like it either.

Master Regis was one of the senior members of the Council, the second most senior on the continent. He was also a douchebag. The Council and Detail seemed to like the type.

"Job ain't done yet, and I need a shower," I said turning to go back inside.

"The wizard didn't send me here because he wanted to wait until you're ready to behave like a grown-up."

I stopped and turned back to York with a smirk, "So, you are his personal courier?"

"I'm nobody's anything."

"No?" I waved the little piece of paper at him again.

A vein stood out on York's forehead. Coming here was a menial task, well beneath the head of security for St. Louis. I knew it and he knew it. Either Regis was punishing York, or he was using the man to make a loud point with me. Hard to say which.

"He'll get his update," I said.

York let out a slow breath through his nostrils, "I don't care what you do Kemper. I do care that your insubordinate behavior translates into me being sent here to exchange pleasantries with you."

"This is 'pleasantries?' You need some practice."

"This is as pleasant as I get," he crossed his arms, which made his biceps look a lot bigger. The man was a stack of muscles.

"You must be big fun on a date," I didn't bother trying to flex. My muscles weren't for show.

"We aren't on a date," he said, he uncrossed his arms and squared his shoulders, "Just do your job, Rat Catcher, so I can do mine." He turned on his heels and marched back to his vehicle.

"Whatever you say, Sammy," I said as I turned away and stomped up to my steps.

"Call Master Regis."

I didn't reply or look back.

I heard the SUV door open, "And Mr. Forrester says there's no more information on your target, so quit asking and just finish the job." The door slammed loudly before the large vehicle sped away.

I unfolded the piece of paper York had given me and read the words written neatly in Dean's pristine handwriting: MEHIRA FIODNIAGH.

"That's a mouthful."

My house was small and cheap. The décor and furniture were leftovers from the previous occupants, the original owners. They were the poster people for retired middle-class Americans from half a century ago. Random pictures of fruit, mildly interesting scenery, and old architecture hung on the walls. Subdued earth-tone curtains, maybe brightly colored a few decades ago, covered the windows. Actual lace doilies rested on the end tables. The old recliner was undoubtedly older than me, but easily the most comfortable item in the house. A strip of duct tape, in stark contrast to the faded brown upholstery, covered up a tear on the left armrest. An old floor lamp cast dim yellow light on dark wood floors and an old rug, so faded I wasn't sure what color or pattern it was supposed to be. I had never taken the time to develop any style of my own. Plain, maybe? If that was a style.

A large bookcase occupied one whole wall in the living room, which I had filled with a respectable collection of reference material, stuff decent people would consider fantasy at best. There were old books covering folklore, mythology, superstitions, and the occult from several cultures around the world and throughout history. These were mythical histories which modern and rational people might scoff at. A few were wildly inaccurate and speculative; I'd learned the hard way which were which. Some were dangerously accurate. The bookshelf's top row was dedicated entirely to books I'd collected for my own consumption. Douglas Adams, Frank Herbert, Raymond Chandler. Generally, I avoided horror, fantasy, and thrillers. My life was already of a mix of those.

I took my time in my Spartan bedroom changing into what had come to be my fighting uniform: a pair of denim jeans, a sturdy cotton shirt, and a heavy leather jacket. This jacket had taken a beating and it wouldn't hold up much longer. This was my seventh, or eighth. I had lost track. I had more in the closet to replace it.

I laced up my ass-kicking boots slowly. Like my jacket, they were rugged and well-built, more for demolition than combat. In my line of work, sometimes combat is demolition. I retied the knots twice before admitting to myself that I was stalling.

"Hell," I said, getting up. No use putting off the inevitable.

The house sat on a dark and damp cellar, the kind you only went down to when you needed to use the worn-out washer and dryer or to kick the noisy old furnace. A stack of old cardboard boxes lined one wall, random crap that I never bothered going through or getting rid of. A few hand tools, older than me, hung on hooks. A wooden shelf full of more cardboard boxes and unlabeled totes covered most of another wall. I grabbed a corner and yanked sharply. The entire shelf popped loose with a click and swung away on hidden hinges to reveal a heavy metal door. The door was the single most advanced piece of technology in my house, or beneath it. A keypad in the center lit up when I stepped closer. I punched in a code and held my thumb over a print scanner. There was a beep followed by a heavy metallic *thunk*. I pulled the door open with a grunt and stepped inside the vault.

As far as Hunters' armories go, mine was modest. Over the years, I'd pared down my gear to just what I needed. A selection of guns, mostly revolvers and shotguns, covered one wall. Few of them had rune-work on them like the Holy Handgun. Not all weapons needed to have magical properties to be useful to a Hunter. A workbench for maintaining my equipment and reloading ammunition took up much of the space along one wall. Above it, on hangers, were displayed a selection of bladed weapons: a pair of tarnished tomahawks, a WWII era samurai sword, a Roman gladius, and a variety of knives. In the wall opposite the door, a hefty, yet small safe had been built into the wall. I punched in another code and opened it. Bundles of money and rolls of coins filled the safe. Eight million, five hundred twenty-two thousand, three hundred sixty-three dollars, and forty-nine cents.

I'd been saving for a long time. Longer than most Hunters lived. Hell, most Hunters didn't bother saving. They tended to live the way they fought. Loud and hard. I guess we always believed in that old song lyric: "It's better to burn out than to fade away." We spent our money stupidly and freely because as a Hunter, you're living on borrowed time.

I thought that way back in the early days, but then a funny thing started to happen. I kept not getting killed. I survived one ridiculous encounter after another, living to see another day, and all the booze and women and fast cars and stupid flashy clothes started to lose their appeal. They became background noise. What matters after you stop caring about that stuff?

I had decided retirement, that's what mattered. Or the prospect of it. Eight million dollars would go a long way on an obscure tropical island where you didn't have do to anything but drink weird coconut drinks and tell made-up stories to the island girls who wear hula skirts. That's a thing, right?

I lived like a miser, fueled by fantasies of warm days and cool evenings. I imagined myself in a lounge chair under a palm tree umbrella, in nothing but swim trunks. Tanning in the sun, scars and all. I imagined those scars and tattoos fading with time as they changed slowly but steadily into a dark tan. And like the lonely sting of a Hunter's life, those scars would fade into a vague memory. It's a nice dream.

I stood there staring at my accumulated pile of cash and contemplated a happy future. But only for a minute. With practiced resolve, I closed the safe and locked it. I took two deep breaths and shook my head to clear away all stray thoughts. Back to work.

First, I reloaded the Holy Handgun with the last of my vampire's curse bullets. I left Mr. Machete hanging on its hook and took down a large bowie knife instead. It had been hand-forged by my enchanted weapons guy. The carbon steel blade had a higher than usual amount of silver forged into it along the sharpened edge. Silver is not ideal in a knife, as it tarnishes easily and doesn't hold an edge well. What it does do, though, is kill werewolves and wendigos with considerable efficiency. It also works wonders on vampires, in combination with the magic runes inscribed along the length of the blade. It was heavy and gaudy, but also dangerous and effective.

I turned to leave the weapons vault and stopped. My eyes were drawn back to the machete hanging on its hook.

"Why not," I said and grabbed Mr. Machete. The weapon had never failed me. It was a good tool, plain and simple. With that, I was as armed as I needed to be.

Time to go be a badass.

Again.

Chapter Four

The "loci," as Leo had called it, was in Old North St. Louis. It was a perfect place for vampires to disappear and feed. Condemned buildings littered the neighborhood, some worse than others, mixed in with houses and businesses all out of place next to each other. Trendy bars and renovated townhomes shared the streets with shuttered storefronts and derelict brick apartment buildings. Kids, who you'd probably say were up to no good, loitered near graffitied buildings and empty lots. Police patrolled the area with heavy-handed efficiency, ensuring that crime remained behind crumbling walls.

The sun hung low in the west as I pulled up in front of the place Leo had pointed out on the map. I had an hour or so of daylight remaining. Black soot along the roofline and windows of the 5-story apartment building and windows, though somewhat washed out by recent rain, indicated a fire had gutted the building some time ago. Some of the windows were boarded over, some wide open and empty. Some sections of the exterior walls had fallen away into piles of red brick and old drywall. Abandoned and hazardous apartments seemed to hang in mid-air; floors sagged, ceilings rotted, weather-worn materials clung to the crumbling framework of an unloved home.

I didn't bother locking the doors when I got out of my car. Locked doors wouldn't stop anyone anyways. Besides, I'd rather have random crap taken from my beat-up car than drive home with smashed-out windows.

The chain and plywood fence had been forced open so many times that it was more landmark than barrier. I found an opening so big I that could squeeze my bulky form through with little effort no effort and cautiously approached the structure. Poorly secured plastic-covered apartment windows on the ground-level, but most had been shredded by time and weather serving no real purpose other than creepy ambiance. I peeked inside without getting too close. Random trash—mostly empty bottles and scraps of moldy fabric littered the floors. In one room, an old mattress lay in the corner with a handful of ragged clothes and a long burned-out cooking fire in the middle of the floor. Buildings like this were havens for the city's homeless, but the homeless wouldn't last long if a vampire had taken up residence. If a vampire had moved in it would not be in any of the above-ground apartments. There was no security while it slept and, more importantly, no shelter from the sun. That meant my target had to be in one of the basement apartments.

"This sucks," I mumbled as I studied the basement windows. All but one of them had been covered with thick plywood and secured with heavy lag screws. Great place for a lair.

Near the corner, where a pile of bricks had covered most of the opening, a single window remained uncovered. I squatted next to it and built a mental map of the interior. The room inside was empty aside from a thin layer of water standing on rotten carpet. I dug a small glow stick from a jacket pocket and cracked it to activate the chemicals within. After a few seconds of shaking, it glowed dimly. I tossed it inside and watched for movement. After waiting long enough to believe there wasn't an ambush waiting for me, I climbed through the window and dropped down into the room behind it.

I suppressed an urge to hold my breath as my boots squished onto the submerged carpet. I breathed in through my nostrils and forced myself to accept the assault to my senses. Aside from the unmistakable stench of mold and mildew, another heavier odor hung heavy in the air like damp, rotten cigarette smoke. Old death. I would have bet I'd find the rotting remains of rats and mice if I bothered to look. Probably stray dogs or cats as well. The homeless weren't too proud to eat those things. Hunger is hunger, meat is meat. A desperate vampire would eat about anything too, if desperate enough. But they preferred human blood. I was willing to bet this building hadn't been abandoned, it had been harvested.

I edged across the room to an old wooden door. Beyond it, if I had guessed right, would be the hallway shared by all the apartments. Importantly, there would be no windows, no outside light. I popped another glowstick and hung it from a string around my neck. I readied Mr. Machete in my right hand before pulling the door open with my left. It squeaked ominously the whole way; it might as well have been a doorbell. It didn't matter. Vampires have amped up senses. They'd have heard me clearly as I entered the building, but I felt the need to proceed quietly anyways.

The hall was as dark as I had expected, though not as damp as the room I had just left. Nearby, a doorway stood open, its door propped carelessly against the wall. At the far end of the hall, where a stairwell should have been, a pile of debris blocked the way, apparently from when the floors above had collapsed. I had to pass the open doorway to get to the closed ones, where my prey had probably taken refuge. I stopped and let my eyes adjust to the darkness which was pushed back slightly by the dim green light hanging from my neck. I stepped to the opening and looked inside. Two large shapes lay motionless against the far wall. Human-sized lumps.

This room was the source of the rotting smell. The large shapes were the remains of people. Food for the vampires. But there were only two. Vampires tended to pile up corpses in a common area, like an impromptu mass grave. Regis had told me that some vampires did this to convert a common room or building into a mausoleum. It made sense. Tombs were increasingly hard to find in the new world. Modern cultures didn't treat their dead like their ancestors did. If such things mattered to vampires, finding suitable places for refuge would be increasingly difficult.

Still. Only two corpses. That meant the vampires weren't feeding here. Or Leo was wrong, and this wasn't the loci. I didn't believe the latter. Leo was especially good at locating concentrations of magic, known as loci. Even the faintest traces of magic leave a distinct signature. An especially sensitive tracker, like Leo, could tell what kind of magic it was, how old the trace was, and what had made it.

His guidance was often cryptic but never wrong. I knew my target was here.

The next door was shut, but scratches on the wood indicated it was used frequently and carelessly. I placed my hand on it and leaned in close to listen. There was quiet activity inside. Though muffled through the door, I made out a faint rustle of movement, wood creaking under pressure and barely audible grunting. The soft groaning that people make when they finally get to eat something after having gone hungry for too long.

I took a deep breath, braced myself for horror, and kicked the door, literally off its hinges.

The occupants were slow to react, giving me more time than I deserved to take in the scene. A large wooden slab filled up the center of the cramped room. It was a broken tabletop, propped up from the damp floor on stacked cinderblocks. Three figures crowded the surface, hunched greedily over a fourth. The first three were pale and thin, like the five thralls I'd already put down earlier. They flinched at my entrance but remained focused on their victim, slurping loudly at the blood flowing from her arms.

"Motherfuckers," I growled through gritted teeth. I'd seen bastards like these while feeding before and it never got easier to witness. It seemed like a violation in every way.

But why hadn't they reacted to my sudden badass entrance?

Then I realized what I was actually seeing. The female laying across the tabletop wasn't a victim. She was another vampire. They were feeding on another vampire's blood. I have seen a lot, but I had never witnessed this. I'd heard rumors of it.

There was a sick sense of desperation to this sight. The males' hair was greasy and stained with blood and gore. Their clothes—what tattered rags remained—were filthy with the fluids rejected by their body when they became undead. They reeked of death and human waste.

In stark contrast to the three males, the fourth figure appeared as human and healthy as any woman. Healthier even. Inviting... tempting. For a moment, I was stunned by the perverse beauty of the female form, spread upon the table in open invitation, allowing itself to be taken by three ravenous abominations, back arched in exaggerated ecstasy. The creature wore a flowing dress of dark silk, cast green by faint light from the glowstick I wore. Long, raven black hair covered much of its face, but I could see its full lips parted, whispering gentle words of encouragement and forgiveness.

For a moment I stood transfixed, the female's head rolled slowly toward me and its eyelids parted to reveal brilliant green eyes that pierced the darkness.

"Oh shit!" I whispered. This was her... it. This was my target. The "mother." The males were her thralls. More thralls.

Green eyes stared ahead without seeing me, like a heroin addict slipping into the brief euphoria between ecstasy and death. Then, suddenly, they focused and met mine, widening.

"No!" the creature shrieked. The three males spasmed and turned suddenly to face me. They hesitated only a moment then rushed recklessly.

Game on!

I sidestepped the initial rush and spun a sweeping arc with my machete hand. The blade cut into the closest thrall's throat, almost taking its head clean off. It dropped away from me clutching at its ruined throat. I bowled through the other two and lunged for the makeshift table and its occupant. The Mother hadn't moved, it was slow from having let the others feed on its blood. It attempted to roll away from me, but I grabbed a handful of silky hair to keep it on the table. The creature screamed in agony as I plunged Mr. Machete into its back. The blade tore all the way through, and the tip emerged below the creature's breasts. I couldn't help but winced at the Mother's ear-piercing cry of pain as it lurched away from me. It rolled from the table, yanking Mr. Machete from my grip, leaving a chunk of luscious black hair in my other hand.

The two remaining males jumped on top of me, clawing and biting. My jacket offered limited protection against any real damage, but human-shaped mouths can bite hard; it hurts like a bitch. I rolled over, pinning one of them beneath my large body. I punched the other in the mouth several times, cutting my knuckles on its jagged teeth. The creature underneath me bit hard on my shoulder. The leather jacket prevented its teeth from cutting my flesh, but it still hurt like hell. I roared and grabbed the one on top by the lapel of its disgusting shirt and rolled, throwing it into the nearest wall. I let my momentum carry me off the table and on the damp floor with a squish. I sprang quickly to my feet, yanked the Holy Handgun from its holster, and fired three times at the vampire on the table. The first shot missed and blew out a chunk of wood. The next two shots hit the torso and stomach. Flashes of white light and smoke erupted from the open wounds and the creature died violently in loud thrashing spasms while clutching uselessly at the wounds. The other vampire leapt onto my back, clawing from behind at my face with its filthy hands, and I caught flashes of gore encrusted fingernails and the stench of dead flesh. I grabbed one arm, pinning the vampire in place, and dropped backwards, landing on top of the nasty thing with a satisfying crunch of the vampire's ribs. Without wasting time to move, I pointed the revolver over my shoulder and fired point-blank into the creature's face. The blast left my ear ringing.

I looked up in time to see the Mother pull Mr. Machete free of her body and throw it at me. I dodged the sloppy throw, but it bought the creature a moment to bolt through the open doorway. I scrambled to my feet to follow. Before I reached the door, something slammed into me and we crashed through the wall and out into the hallway.

Chapter Five

I landed in a heap of flesh and drywall and wood. A searing pain lanced through my body and I cried out. I prodded around with my fingers and found a jagged hunk of wood protruding from my side, below the ribs.

The thing that had tackled me let out a nasty, raspy snarl. Damn! It was the first vampire, the one I thought I had decapitated. Sloppy work. I let out a snarl of my own and shoved the creature away from me. It tumbled several feet before gaining its footing and spun back toward me. I still had the Holy Handgun in my hand, so I pointed and shot. The nasty bastard was already moving, and the bullet struck its leg, crackling and sparkling. I didn't have time to fire again. before It jumped on me and attacked with its ragged fingernails and broken teeth. In the struggle to keep the damn creature from biting me, I couldn't get the barrel positioned to shoot so I bludgeoned it with the heavy gun several blows. I rolled to the side and screamed in shock as the floor shoved the chunk of wood harder into my side and I dropped the gun.

Despite the pain, I still had to fight. I shoved a thumb into the vampire's mouth and pulled at its cheek, twisting its head. With my other hand, I yanked the wood from my side in a flash of pain and shoved the oversized splinter into the creature's eye. It fell off me screaming again, clawing at the wood. I pawed for my gun and found it. I didn't need to aim. One shot to the face. The vampire's skull nearly exploded in a flash of holy light, smoke, blood, and bone.

That left only me.

A lone figure stood motionless at the far end of the hall, leaning against the last closed door. The Mother watched me intently, its breasts rising and falling slowly with each deep breath.

Vampires don't breathe, I told myself.

My chest heaved in heavy, labored breaths as I struggled slowly back to my feet. I pressed my left hand against my side to try and slow the flow of blood, as I leaned against the wall steadying myself, watching the Mother. A deep scratch over my left brow bled freely, blood welled up around my swollen eye. A fresh wound below my left elbow trailed blood down my arm and plopped onto the wet floor. The Mother shivered visibly.

"Want some?" I asked with a raw voice.

The Holy Handgun hung heavy like a boat anchor in my right hand. Partly from fatigue, partly from the Proportional Mass runes on the barrel. It got heavier with continued use. I raised the gun and pointed it unsteadily at the figure. My aim wavered, but only because I was tired. That's what I told myself. I squeezed the trigger. The six-shot cylinder rotated as the hammer rolled back into the cocked position and snapped forward. Click. The dark figure flinched.

"Shit!" I barked.

The figure straightened slowly and stood more erect.

"Six," It whispered defiantly.

I sighed. Why couldn't anything ever be easy?

The Mother opened the door and disappeared into the room.

"Dammit."

I rushed after it and stopped in the open doorway. The creature flung itself at a boarded-up window over and over, but the window held firm. It clawed at the plywood, trying to pull it away, but the wood stayed in place. Even fledgling vampires are stronger than humans. This one, the Mother, was reportedly hundreds of years old. It should have busted through the window like paper. But it had let the other three feed on too much of its blood on this night and now it was weak.

Hesitantly I stepped into the room with slow, deliberate steps, still holding the nasty wound on my side, the empty revolver still heavy in my other hand. My boot squished on the soggy, rotten carpet. Squish, squish. I stopped half a dozen paces from the oldest vampire I had ever seen in person. My heart thundered within my chest, sending dull shockwaves of pain throughout my battered and tired body. My gun hand trembled.

I had never stood this close to my prey before. I had been closer, countless times, in a violent embrace of life and death. But never like this. Never just stood. Never looked. Never thought about what was about to happen.

I shoved the Holy Handgun into its worn leather holster, feeling the weight settle on my hip. I pulled the large bowie knife from its sheath and held it low by my side.

The Mother stopped clawing at the wooden barrier and sniffed the air. It moaned softly and faced me.

My god was she beautiful. No, not she, it. "It," I whispered under my breathe.

It was a vision of beauty and grace. Eyes like emeralds pierced the darkness, glowing with brilliant passion. Dark brows furrowed in frustration, full, blood-red lips pressed together, appearing to hold back curses bottled within. Beneath the form-fitting silk dress that trailed to the floor, breasts heaved in rhythm with its shallow breathing. Even in its weakened state and even painted in its own blood, the Mother radiated raw sex appeal. Its narrow waist rolled into rounded hips and enticing legs fit for a dancer or gymnast. How easily such a creature could tempt a mortal man. Vampires were known for their ability to hypnotize victims into submission, but this was different somehow. This creature was stunningly beautiful. Like a forbidden lover.

The creature spoke.

"You come with silver and iron," it said, "which do you offer me?"

Her voice... its voice was elegant and betrayed an old-world accent I couldn't place. It practically oozed sexuality and nobility, but also fatigue. Oddly humanlike fatigue.

I shrugged, "Both for you."

"You know so little," pity flashed across the stunning creature's face.

"I know enough, Mehira Fiodniagh," I said between labored breaths. I probably butchered the pronunciation.

The light in the creature's eye flared slightly, "You have no idea what the meaning behind that name holds, do you, Lover?"

Lover? That was out of the blue. What the hell?

"We ain't lovers, Mehira," I said.

"You have no power over me," Mehira said, glaring with fiery eyes. "You have no claim with that name. No right to speak it."

"Stop me," I said.

Mehira growled soft and low. Not the sound of a preternatural creature, but that of a tired and frustrated woman. Her lips parted to reveal clenched teeth. No fangs, not chipped and jagged like the other vampires I had killed today. Just simple white teeth, almost perfect. Almost human.

"You have taken everything I had left in this accursed world. You cannot have my name."

"This ain't personal. I don't want your name."

"Personal? Do not dare to tell me this is just business," Mehira spat out the last word as if it were rotten. She... it pulled its blood-covered hand away from the jagged wound on its chest and held it out toward me as if presenting evidence.

"This blood—the blood of my entire family line—is on YOUR hands."

"On your hands too," I said tiredly, too tired even to appreciate the stupid pun.

"YOU did this," Mehira said, her voice wavered. Her lips quivered. She thrust her hand toward me urging me to look. Her fingers trembled, the blood dripped from them and disappeared into the wet carpet. Her eyes shone... no glistened. Tears welled up in her eyes. Its eyes. It.

This was no woman; this was a creature. It, not she. There was no humanity in a vampire. Only evil, only impulse. Drink, murder, propagate. I had to keep telling myself that. But this Mehira was unlike any vampire I had seen. There was something otherworldly about her... it. Something deeper than "vampire." Something beyond a curse. I did not know what.

I said without conviction, "I don't pass judgment."

"So, you say."

"You ain't a victim or an innocent."

Anger flashed in her eyes, behind the tears, "Nor are you!" Mehira took a step toward me on wavering legs. She fell to her knees, one hand pressed against the wet floor.

"Especially not me," I said and took a step closer too. Mehira cringed away from me, her eyes widened, fixed on the knife in my hand.

I frowned. Fear? I had never seen fear on the faces of the creatures I had put down. Anger, yes. Malice. Hatred. Yes. Sometimes lust at the intoxicating scent of blood. Sometimes ecstasy in the rush following a feeding frenzy. But mostly malice. Unchecked and unfiltered. Never fear.

But I had never spoken more than a few words to a vampire. I had never been so close to one for this long without actively trying to kill it.

What was I waiting for?

"Especially not me," I said again, quieter.

"Oh? What do I hear?" Mehira said, voice soft, almost a whisper. "You know what you are? You know then that you are the worst of us. You are an executioner."

"Hunter," I corrected.

"Killer. Murderer," Mehira's voice grew stronger as her anger rose, and her eyes glowed more fiercely. Its eyes. Not hers. Its.

"So, you say," I countered

"I am what your God made me," Mehira said.

"No god did this to you."

"I am a monster because I am a monster," Mehira's voice quaked. The arm supporting her shook as if bearing a great burden. "As are you!"

"I am what I am," I said. Monsters come in many forms.

I am what I am. Leo's words echoed in my head.

"What are you waiting for Iron Wielder?" Mehira asked harshly. Why did the iron matter?

"You've already destroyed me," Mehira said. "You've already taken everything from me. I have no more children and no more sisters. I will take no more lovers. There will be no more singing and no more dancing. Never again."

What the hell was she talking about? It. What was it talking about?

"Act now," the beautiful creature said, "destroy this body too. That and my name is all that is left of me. The unfaithful are mine no more. Mehira Fiodniagh is no more." She spoke the name with a deep accent, one I still couldn't place.

Still on her knees, Mehira raised her head and met my eyes defiantly. She tried to straighten the silky dress and smooth out the wrinkles, but blood and moisture had caused the fabric to cling enticingly to her body.

I tightened my grip on the knife handle and tilted the tip toward Mehira but made no other move. This time, Mehira did not cower. This was the Mehira I had expected to confront. Strong, defiant, fearless. No. No, this wasn't defiance or fearlessness. It was resignation. Resignation in the face of fear.

"Do it!" She said sharply; her voice cutting. A tear rolled down her cheek. She lowered her head again and her shoulders shook. Its shoulders. It. Damn it.

Her long black hair fell to one side, revealing pale skin and a bare, slender neck with the visible lumps of each vertebra. Almost human. A simple thrust through her spine. Silver and iron through bone and blood. Just like that. The line ended. Whatever line it was. Then what? The next job. The next target. The next monster. Until there were no more, another line broken by the great and prolific Bill F. Kemper. Just like that.

"Just like that," I muttered. Mehira's shoulders stiffened.

"Make my ending swift if there is any mercy left in you," she said.

I did not move. The blade hung heavy in my hand.

"Do tarry," Mehira said softly. "Is it not enough to exterminate me and all the memory I have? Do you seek to punish me first? Am I to suffer needlessly as my flame is snuffed out? Have you not punished me enough, Slayer?"

"Punished?" I asked. "As if you don't deserve it. After all you have done..."

"All I have done? Deserve?" Mehira's eyes locked with mine again, "You've taken everything from me. You've killed my entire bloodline. You've murdered all my children."

"Those weren't children, and they weren't your family. They were mindless beasts. Guard dogs. Weren't even animals after what you did to them."

Mehira let out a slow, sad breath, "You know nothing, except that there is no truth in your words Monster Killer. Not all babes are born of the womb. We shared the same blood, my children and I."

"It ain't all yours to take or give."

"Nor yours," Mehira said.

"No... it ain't."

Mehira said, "What I have taken, I cannot return. That is my curse. What is yours?"

I lowered the blade and looked into Mehira's fading green eyes. The light was nearly gone. The last light of the last of her kind.

"My curse... the same as yours."

"No," Mehira said. "That is your job, not your curse."

"My job is killing monsters," I said quietly.

"Your job is to be a monster... to be the monster wizards and magic makers dare not be. Be the monster, Bill Kemper. Destroy me. Erase my name. Kill my memory. End my misery. Do your job."

I breathed in and out. God, I was tired. So tired. My body hurt... my soul hurt. All the lives I had taken had weight. Heavier and heavier... they all sat on my shoulders. And never had one of them begged me to do it, to finish them. To kill them. Never had a monster looked me in the eye and asked me to end the misery I had brought upon them. Until now.

My side hurt. Blood still trickled through my fingers. The same color as the blood on Mehira's hand, from the wound I had caused.

"Fuck my job," I said. I opened my fingers and let the knife fall to the floor with a dull thump. I had no idea how much weight I had been holding. So much more than what was contained in the steel of the blade.

"What is this?" Mehira said.

I squatted down to meet its... no, her eyes. There was no hatred or malice in her eyes or the tears she shed. There was only sadness and fear and confusion.

"What is this?" she demanded more fiercely. "End this now! I demand it. I will not cower like an animal, waiting for your killing blow. I will not abide even more endless days waiting for your final stroke."

"That," I said pointing at the knife on the ground, "is my final stroke. I'm done."

I pulled the Holy Handgun from its holster, "It's over." I dropped the gun on the ground next to the knife with a heavy *thunk*. Heavy as my heart.

Mehira flinched at the sound, "Over? After you have done this to me?"

"Yeah," I said. "Too late to matter, I guess, but I'm done. I quit."

I walked out of the room while Mehira sobbed angrily behind me. I wanted to say I was sorry, but apologies wouldn't change anything.

Chapter Six

It was late, but the Blue Sky was open. It always was. I don't know how they stayed in business, running 24/7, but they managed.

I didn't even bother going home to change or clean up. I didn't plan on going in. I wanted to sit and look at the familiar setting, at my usual table near the window, at the modern-rustic décor, and the dimly lit even ambiance. I wanted to look at normal.

I shut off the engine and then I just sat there and breathed for a while and bled on my seat covers. After a few minutes, I dug my first aid kit out of the glove compartment: a few chunks of gauze, a bottle of rubbing alcohol, and a bottle of holy water. Most of my injuries were superficial. I'd had worse. As bad as it was, the ugly wound caused by the chunk of wood was more inconvenient than dangerous, aside from the risk of infection and the very real need for stitches. I dumped a splash of alcohol on the wound and clenched my teeth hard enough to bite through steel plates as the solution did its work. The pain subsided, and I pressed a piece of gauze in place and held it until it soaked up enough blood to stick which didn't take long. I'd need to change it soon. It was gonna need stitches.

To keep my mind off that wound, I splashed some holy water on the others. Holy water is something like peroxide on vampire bites, but more painful. I pounded my fist on the dash while the water fizzed and burned. The aftermath of my fights was always worse than the fight. This time it would probably be even more so.

I took in a long, hard breath and held it a few seconds before letting it out slowly. It did it again.

My whole body ached. Sharp lances of pain shot up my side violently with each breath I took. My knuckles were raw and felt like I'd been using them to grind glass. My elbow felt like salt rubbed into an open wound. My face throbbed. I heard that pain is a reminder that you're still alive. So, I was alive. That was something.

But I couldn't do anything like this. Not in this pain, not tonight.

"*Smerte Forsinket*," I mumbled. It was a power phrase, borrowed from an old Norse spellbook. I translated poorly as "pain deferred." It was linked by incantation to a rune tattoo on my arm.

"*Smerte Forsinket*." My body throbbed and ached. My arms hurt. My side hurt. My heart hurt. But I told myself pain can't beat me. It can't break me.

"*Smerte Forsinket*." I am strong. The rune tattoo on my hand began to glow and pulse with each of my heartbeats.

"*Smerte Forsinket*." I am not my body. I am not my pain.

"*Smerte Forsinket*." Pain is temporary.

"*Smerte Forsinket*." With this power phrase, I can borrow from tomorrow, where there is no pain yet.

I don't know if it worked or not. In time, I focused more on the chant and the rune than the pain I was overcoming. Maybe that's how these things work. I never was much of a magic user. Even though the weapons like Mr. Machete and the Holy Handguns were enchanted, I rarely called upon the magic imbued within them. Brute force was my forte. With a few exceptions, magic requires belief. I wasn't sure what I believed anymore.

"*Smerte Forsinket*."

The spot on the back of my neck tingled and Leo slowly appeared in my passenger seat.

He frowned.

"That's dangerous," he said. "Pain is there for a reason."

"I know," I closed my eyes for a few seconds. "I'm tired. I just can't deal with this right now."

"Your body looks like hell."

"Yeah? How about my soul?"

"One mirrors the other," he said, "but it looks better than it has in a long time, even with the cloud of pain you're trying to dispel."

"You can see that?"

"Yeah," Leo said. "Everyone can."

"Everyone who?"

"Doesn't matter," he said. "Your soul is stronger than you think. And your choices make it stronger."

"You heard the news?"

"Yes," Leo said. "News like that gets around quickly. A lot of folk in the Otherside don't know what to make of it. You put a fly in a lot of soups."

"Hmm," I grunted. "I didn't think anyone in the Otherside would think anything about me except to be glad I'm out of business."

"Not all your targets were from the Otherside."

I knew this.

"Look, Bill, you're going to regret this decision for a long time... but you'll always be glad you did it. Does that make sense?"

"Actually, yes. It does."

"Good," Leo said. "I'm not always sure. If it helps, you've got some good vibes flowing around you right now."

"Well... that's something."

"It is."

"There's gonna be hell to pay, isn't there?"

"You know it. Sorry to say so, but not all the vibes are good ones. I think you know who you've pissed off."

"Yup."

"The Council doesn't see your soul, Bill. They have a hard time seeing past the end of their nose. They don't understand what they don't understand."

"That sounds about right."

"There's something else," Leo said. "It's like... like a bad feeling."

"You get feelings?"

"It's the best analogy for what I'm experiencing," Leo said.

"Something else is happening to shake up the currents in the Otherside."

"That sounds... ominous."

"It feels ominous."

"Well, maybe I picked the right time to get out of the game."

"Maybe," Leo allowed, but didn't sound convincing.

I had always told myself the best time to get out is when you're still alive. It would have been better to have not been in the game at all, but it was too late for that. Retirement was always an idea for tomorrow.

"Bill," Leo said, "You've done a lot of good."

"I guess."

"Few things are black and white. A lot of people are alive today who wouldn't be if not for you."

"A lot of flames are forever snuffed out because of me."

Leo didn't reply.

"Do people really change?" I wondered out loud.

Leo nodded, "You people are like a bag of paint. You never know what you're gonna see when you dump it out."

I laughed, and it made my side hurt again.

"God, I just want some relief."

"And this place gives you that?"

Inside the Blue Sky, a lone barista stood behind the counter, leaning over a laptop. Sarah.

"What is it about her?" Leo asked. What do you see? What is the draw?"

"Moth to a flame," I said.

"You're no moth Bill Kemper," Leo said solemnly.

"No, I'm not," I admitted, and shrugged, "She's like a daisy in a briar patch."

Leo studied her for a moment and nodded, "I like that. Daisy in a briar patch. I'll be pondering that for some time. But don't put her on a pedestal. That's not fair."

"I know. I'm so tired, Leo." I wasn't talking about sleep.

"I know," Leo said, "be strong. Your spirit has never looked better."

"Thanks," I opened the driver's side door.

"You're going in looking like that?"

The bell dinged as I entered the Blue Sky. Sarah looked up from her laptop and her eyes widened. I guess I looked as rough as I felt.

"Mr. Kemper!" she rushed from behind the counter and ushered me to one of the tables, "Oh my God you're hurt!"

"Yes. Wait, no... no, I'm fine," I said unconvincingly. "I'm fine."

"No, you're not, I'll call 911."

"No!" I said too harshly, and added more calmly, "No, I'm fine. Really."

Smerte Forsinket. I thought fiercely.

"You're not fine. You're bleeding. You need to go to the hospital."

She didn't know the half of it. My jacket covered the worst of my injuries. All she could see was my hands and my face.

"I'll go," I lied, "later. Just... just not yet. I have a doctor."

"Doctor? You need an ambulance."

"I'll go when I'm done here," I assured her.

"What are you even doing here?"

"Really, I'll be ok," I held a hand up wearily, "I've been through worse. I just want some coffee."

"Coffee? Are you insane? You look really bad. You're hurt"

"Hurt? Yes. That's accurate. But I'll be ok."

"Dios mio," Sarah slipped into her native tongue, "¿Qué pasó?" Then she shook her head.

"I gotta do something," she said. "Let me do something." She spun and hurried into the back room of the shop, ignoring my feeble protest. She came back quickly with a first aid kit, one of those in a metal box with a fat red cross on it. She sat across from me and opened the lid to reveal an organized array of generic treatment options. She dumped out the contents and rummaged for something useful. I watched in bemusement for a moment.

"There," I touched a small packet. Alcohol swabs, or whatever they put in these kits nowadays. Sarah snatched up the packet and tore it open. She dug out the little one-inch square patch of cloth and stopped.

"Where to start?" I asked.

Sarah nodded, "Yeah, I—wait, are those bite marks?"

"Some of them, yes."

She shook her head wearily dabbing gingerly at one of the deeper scratches on my forehead. It stung like a bitch.

"Ouch," I added quietly.

"I'm sorry! I'm so sorry," Sarah's voice pitched. "I've never done this."

"It's ok," I pushed her hand away, "I'll do it." I took the swab from her trembling fingers and scrubbed too harshly at one of the cuts.

"You'll make it worse," Sarah said.

"Impossible," I continued.

Sarah opened another packet and squeezed out some goo, some kind of antibiotic.

"Bandage?" I asked.

"What? Oh!" She deftly tore into a packaged roll of gauze without losing the paste on her finger. "Here." She smeared the goo on the gauze and wrapped it around my hand several times, cautiously covering the deep scratches.

"Good as new," I said.

"Hardly," Sarah said, "It's a poor start. What next?"

"Really, Sarah, I just want some coffee."

She ignored me and tore open some adhesive bandages and

applied a small dab of antibiotic to each of them.

"You look terrible," she said quietly as she applied the last bandage.

"I know."

"Sorry," she said, that was rude.

I smiled to show it I wasn't offended.

She scrunched her nose, "And you stink. Dios mio! What have you been doing, wrestling rats in the sewer?"

"Something like that."

"I'm worried Bill. I don't like this. Whatever your job is, it's not good for you."

I nodded slowly, "You're right about that."

"But you can't tell me? Or won't?"

"Both," I admitted. "Look, I didn't come in here to scare you. I just... I needed... I want some coffee. Really. That's all."

"Coffee? You come in here looking and smelling like you lost a fight with the Swamp Thing, and I'm supposed to believe the one thing that will help you is a cup of coffee?"

"Sounds overly dramatic when you say it like that."

"Yeah? Does it?"

"Sorry."

Sarah shook her head, "Ok... Fine." She stood up headed for the counter. Bill Kemper special?"

"Yes. No!"

"Can't be both."

I pointed at the chalkboard sign, "I wanna try something new. Gimme one of those pumpkin spice lattes."

"You're kidding."

"No. That's it. That's what I want. Why not? I'm trying new things today." My cellphone beeped, and I ignored it.

"That's scary coming from you."

"You have no idea."

A minute later, Sarah set a Blue-Sky mug near my folded hands, "What happened to you, Bill?"

I wrapped my hands around the mug and enjoyed the warmth for a moment. The cellphone beeped again.

"I quit my job tonight."

Sarah's eyebrows went up, "Must have been a hell of an exit interview."

I took in a deep breath and inhaled the aroma from the coffee, "It was a hell of a job." My phone beeped again.

"Are you going to answer that?"

"No."

"Mr. Kemper? Bill?" Sarah put her hand on my arm. "Are you ok? I mean for real?"

"I'm good," I said and pointed at the bandage on my elbow. "See? Good as new."

"You know what I mean."

"I know. It's been a big day for me and a hard one."

"Big day? You mean aside from sustaining medical trauma, swimming in swamp water, and quitting your job?"

"Mostly that," I said. "Quitting my job. It was a big deal."

"I can see that. Do you regret it?"

"Not yet," I said and took a sip of coffee then scowled, "God, that's awful."

Sarah giggled. Nothing else mattered.

Chapter Seven

Sarah was right, I needed to go to the hospital. But I couldn't go looking like I had just fought a handful of vampires in the basement of an abandoned building. So I went back home to change first.

The day before, I would have gone to the tiny clinic over on Southwest Avenue next to Bogue's Cigar Shop. Not tonight, though. That place was Council sponsored; it would probably not be a great idea to show my face in "business" circles for a while.

I got halfway to the steps and felt eyes on me from somewhere. It was a rough neighborhood according to some people, but I was a rough guy. I didn't usually worry about the neighbors, but it wasn't people that I felt. It was Lady. She stood half a block away, her ears perked up, her tail low, watching me.

"Hey girl," I said softly, "how ya' doing tonight?"

The dog looked toward my house and huffed once.

Nothing looked out of the ordinary to me. The lights were on, which wasn't anything unusual, I wasn't good about shutting them off when I left.

"What's wrong?" I turned back toward Lady, but she was gone.

I soon wished I'd have gone with her.

The front door locks were intact, but as soon as I stepped inside, I knew someone unwelcome was in my house. Dammit.

I marched in, ready for a fight. An old man sat in my recliner with a thin, gnarled cane lying across his lap. A young woman trying poorly to not look like an assassin stood a few steps behind the chair.

"Son of a bitch," I grumbled. The old man smiled amicably. The assassin didn't move a muscle. I ignored them both and went into the kitchen to get my last beer. I opened it on the edge of the countertop, and then went back into the living room to face the intruders. I'd expected a visit from Council people. Regis or York, or both. Not Master Winters, the High Councilor himself.

"I expected you home sooner, William," the man said with mock sternness, although I suspected he wasn't mocking. Winters had a round head which was bald with a few stray white hairs and brown spots all over his pale scalp. He wore a pair of wireframe glasses with circular lenses that reflected light no matter which way he was looking. The effect was that you could never see his eyes. His earlobes were too long as if gravity had won a lifelong tug of war. His neck was thin but skin hung loosely beneath his chin indicating he might have once had a strong jaw and muscular neckline. He wore a brown herringbone tweed suit with a brown bowtie. The High Councilor looked in every way very old.

The woman by contrast was a picture of youth and energy... and hostility. She had dark red hair, pulled back into a tight braid that was currently draped over her shoulder. Her eyes were brown, accented by dark eyeliner and dark red lipstick. She reminded me of someone I'd seen recently but I couldn't put my finger on it. She was young, late teens maybe early twenties with an athlete's body, made obvious by the form-fitting clothes she wore. She was dressed in black from neck to toe. A black jacket of stretchy fabric zipped all the way up to her throat, with those sleeves that have a thumb hole in them, black yoga leggings that women wear these days whether they work out or not, and a pair of black knee-high biker boots laced tightly. Forget the leather catsuits and high-heeled boots you see in the movies. Those are impractical—sexy as hell, but impractical. This girl was dressed for a workout—a deadly workout probably—with no loose fabric to catch on anything while still allowing for a full range of motion. Practical.

She stood with her feet shoulder-width apart, her arms folded across her chest in a false show of casualness. But I wasn't buying it.

"It's Bill, and you're in my chair," I said to the old man while keeping my eyes fixed on the woman, "and my house."

"You are late," The man waggled a bony finger at me.

"It's my house, and I come and go on my own schedule." The young woman uncrossed her arms and let her hands hang down by her side. She closed her fists loosely. Expecting a fight, huh?

The old man clicked his tongue, "You didn't report in. Master Regis was quite agitated. I'm worried about you, William."

"Worried?" I took a long pull on my beer.

"Concerned," he said. "This sort of behavior is not like you."

I shrugged, "Well, things change."

"No!" Winters slapped his knee. In an instant, the room felt colder and smaller.

"No," he said again, his voice as cold as the room. "Things do not change. Not on matters such as ours."

I leaned casually against a narrow console hall table to show how relaxed I could pretend to be. It creaked under my weight and I silently hoped it wouldn't fall apart, thus ruining the illusion. I took another long pull on my beer. The yoga chick was watching me now with laser focus. She was not only expecting trouble, I think she was planning on it.

"Not in the mood, Winters."

The girl took a small step forward, "It's Master Winters, show some respect." Her voice trembled with passion.

Ah, the misguided energy of youth and hatred.

It clicked in my head, I had seen that hostility before, and I realized why I recognized her. She was York's driver. That would explain her sour disposition. I'd be miserable too. But she was directing it at me. I resisted the impulse to roll my eyes. God, I didn't have the energy for someone like her tonight.

The old man held up his hand, "Restrain yourself, Miss Red."

"Misread?" I chuckled. "Really? That's her name?"

She didn't rise to the bait, at least not all the way. Instead, she crossed her arms again and scowled.

"Please, don't be rude, Mr. Kemper. Her name is Lucille Red,

Lucy, if you must know. Pay her no attention," the old man said.

"I should pay no attention to the trespassers in my living room?"

Winters folded his hands across his lap, "It seems we have some Council business to discuss, you and I."

"No, we don't."

"In fact, we do. You have an open contract. You neglected to finish a Council sanctioned job."

"I retired. You missed it."

Winters' eyebrows arched from behind his glasses, "Oh really? Just like that?"

"Just like that," I leaned back in an exaggerated show of relaxation and pretended I didn't notice the wood groaning under the increased strain. "I figured I'd save everyone from all the paperwork."

"Oh, William," the old man shook his head slowly.

"Bill." I stood up.

Winters leaned forward, folding his hands across the cane, "One does not just simply retire from your profession."

"Sure one does. It was easy."

"There is too much at stake here. After everything we have invested in you."

"Invested? I call it a paycheck."

"Oh, the money is inconsequential," the man waved his hand dismissively. "It's all the other investments. The resources afforded you are of incalculable value."

I said nothing.

"Intelligence. Education. Experience. I could go on."

"Go ahead. Go on," I said, "because you didn't give me any of that."

"One cannot put a dollar value on the investments we have committed to your success. Nothing as specific as... eight million dollars."

A chill ran up my spine.

I didn't like the look on his face. The cat that ate the canary came to my mind.

The side of Lucy's red lips curled in a satisfied smirk, and her eyes flicked briefly toward my cellar door. I felt the blood rush into my face and a wave of heat washing over my body. With an angry grunt, I slammed my beer down on the abused console and it crumbled under the impact. Ignoring that, I marched to the basement, almost yanking the door off the hinges. Everything in the basement appeared to be as I had left it. I jerked the shelving unit aside, dumping some boxes on the floor in my haste. The instant I touched the vault door, I felt a tingle throughout my entire body. The lingering effects of magic. What magic, I couldn't be sure. I unlocked the vault door and flung it open but didn't enter. No point. It was bare-assed empty. They didn't even leave the hangers on the walls. The smaller safe was wide open as well and bone stock empty. They had cleaned me out.

I stomped up the stairs with enough force to disrupt the foundations of the neighbor's houses. Lucy Red had moved closer to Winters in my absence and now stood with one hand on the backrest behind his head and the other hidden behind her back. She stiffened visibly when I burst out of the cellar. I snatched up the half-drunk beer bottle from the rubble and threw it into the living room. Lucille swiped at it in midair, sending it smashing against the TV. It wouldn't have come close to hitting Winters anyways. I was pissed, not stupid.

"Put it back," I said through gritted teeth. "Every bit of it."

The old man shrugged, "I cannot."

"Try. Really. Hard," I stepped towards him. In a fluid motion, Red's hidden hand whipped from behind her back to reveal a small pistol and stopped with the barrel pointed dead center between my eyes. Her brows furrowed in angry determination. I looked past the barrel locking eyes with her. Winters sighed irritably, still seated comfortably in my recliner.

"Go ahead," I said. The pistol remained steady for several seconds, Lucy's finger on the trigger. I waited. She held several more seconds before the end of the gun dipped, almost imperceptibly. It was enough for me to know she was no assassin. Not yet at least. Lucy hadn't got her hands dirty. She was just another member of the Detail who hadn't seen any real action. Lucille Red wasn't the real threat here. I directed my attention back to Winters.

"Don't bring your porch dog if you're not going to let it bite," I said staring hard into the shiny circles concealing Winters' eyes.

"I bite," she said sharply and moved her other hand to steady the pistol in the guise of a combat grip.

"All I hear is yapping and that's just annoying."

She lowered the gun until it was pointed at my crotch.

"She's dead weight," I said pointedly ignoring her. Some people can't handle that. "Useless."

"Try me!" she snapped, too loudly.

Master Winters raised his hand, "Calm yourself, Miss... Lucille. Put that thing away."

The pistol wavered in her hand for a moment then she slowly lowered it until it wasn't pointing at any of my favorite parts anymore and put it away behind her back.

Winters tilted his head toward the girl for a moment, his eyebrows screwed down, disappearing behind the shiny little glasses. He pursed his lips as if pondering a decision. A faint smile formed on his lips and he nodded.

"I have an idea," he said suddenly.

"Me too, you can put my money back," I said.

"No, not that," Winters said waving his hand. "This will benefit everyone. As I said, the Council has invested considerable resources into your development, we cannot let you just walk away..."

"I'm not asking for your permission," I said, my voice deadly calm. Red's hand went behind her back again and stayed there.

"I think we can reach an agreement that will be beneficial on many facets. The Council would like to reframe the conditions of your services." He raised his withered old man hand in a grand gesture toward Red. "I propose that to train your replacement."

"What?" Red and I said in unison.

Winters laughed.

Chapter Eight

"Not a chance," I said shaking my head, "No way."

Red spun on Winters, "That's insane!" She gestured toward me with horror on her face and her mouth open to spew a predictable barrage of protests. The old man held up a withered hand before she could unleash them.

"Do not say anything regrettable, Miss Red."

"The guy is a brute!" her voice cracked.

"Train your lapdog yourself if that's what you want, I don't care," turning my back on the old man, "I'm retired and I'm not training anyone." I wanted to storm out. But it was my damned house. Where was I going to go?

"Of course you will, William," Winters said, "You are honor-bound to the Council and it appears that you are also quite suddenly penniless."

I balled up my fists as I turned back to face him, "We're not done discussing that yet."

"Indeed, we are not. Train Miss Red, and the fair portion of your savings..."

"No, you'll return all my money," I said, "and I'll refrain from pummeling you with what's left of your yappy lap dog's arms and legs."

"Try it!" Red stepped out from behind the chair. Feet planted wide, fists curled loosely. God, she wanted a fight, more so than York usually did. I could never bait him this easy.

Winters sighed, "This is counter-productive."

For once, I ignored him.

"Ever been hit by a sledgehammer?" I balled up my meaty fist. I wouldn't punch a girl, but she'd didn't need to know that. "What do you weigh, little girl, ninety pounds soaking wet?" It was a gross exaggeration of course, but I'm prone to hyperbole when I'm trying to piss people off. And I'm pretty good at pissing people off, it's proven to be a useful skill set.

Lucy's hand went for her gun again. In a quick whip of motion, Master Winters moved his little cane from his lap and tapped it firmly on the floor. A rumble shook my walls and the windows rattled as if a volcano had erupted beneath my ancient oak floors. The girl flinched. I scowled deep and profoundly.

"Do not draw that weapon again in my presence," Winters said, his voice deeper, with more authority.

Red took in a long breath through her nose, and nodded, "Yes, Master Winters."

Even though his eyes were still hidden behind those silly little spectacles I could feel Winters' gaze fall back on me.

"Be civil. This is a negotiation, is it not?"

"No, it isn't," I said.

"Of course, it is," Winters said, his patience nearly spent. "The Nine-Fold Council is an organization of reason and wisdom, even if you are not."

"Reason? I gave you the better part of my life," I said. "That's not unreasonable."

"Most Hunters give all of their lives," Winters said.

"Well, I ain't them."

"Precisely," Winters tapped his cane again, this time without the thunder. "That is why you are the best man to train your replacement."

"No," I said and crossed my arms.

"Allow me to state a simple fact for you, Mister Kemper. You will not see your savings again unless I arrange it," Winters said. "No amount of violence will compel me otherwise."

"Worth a try," I mumbled. The thin red line that Lucille's mouth had become, twitched.

"William," Winters said, "Do not make an enemy of a friend."

"You did that, not me."

"Please, do not go to war with the Council," Winters returned his cane to his lap and leaned back in the chair, "No doubt, the resulting spectacle would be memorable, but also quite devastating."

I clenched my teeth hard enough to make my jaw hurt. I could handle Red, no problem. But Winters... he wasn't just a wizard. He was the High Councilor and the most senior member. I didn't need another demonstration of his power to know he'd be no easy fight. I couldn't take on one wizard, let alone an entire council of them.

"I earned my retirement once already," I said injecting some calm into my voice, "You're double-crossing me."

"Unfortunately, yes, we are," Winters said with a shrug. "You must acknowledge that your unplanned departure creates a considerable vacuum."

"Sucks to be you," I said, deadpan.

"Sometimes it does, in fact," Winter acknowledged, "But that is not pertinent. Fill the vacuum your debt is paid."

"This was never my debt."

"It was always your debt," the old man said, "you are simply the first to live long enough for the debt to come due. This is not an overly complex task that I am asking of you, William."

"Bill," I said. "It's no small thing either. Besides, look at her, she's too fragile."

"Try me." If Lucy's eyes were fire, there'd be a hole burned through my head, right between the eyes. I smirked. Her size was an obvious issue against me, she had to know that. I'm practically Mighty Joe Young compared to her. No amount of posturing could change that. She couldn't hide it. But she wanted a shot at me. She wanted to kill her doubt or die trying. It was written in her eyes.

"I don't need him," Red said turning to Winters.

"I disagree, Lucille. You have good training, some of the best, from what I am told. Yet, much of that training comes from men who have not stood face to face against a creature of evil in decades... perhaps longer. Some of them never. You have theoretical skills, now you much learn the practical application."

Her cheeks flushed. I'm not sure if it was anger or embarrassment. Both maybe?

"Experience comes with experience," she said as if repeating a rote.

"I will not debate this with you," Winters said to Lucy, then me, "Or with you. This is the offer placed before you. Train Lucille to take your place. When that has been completed, you will find all your... things as you remember them."

"My nest egg as well."

"Everything," he said.

I took several controlled breaths, "What exactly do you consider 'completed?' It takes years to become a real Hunter. I ain't in this for that kind of long haul."

"A test. Let us consider it a final exam for Lucille."

I didn't like the sound of that and said so.

"I am confident it is not anything beyond the scale of your capabilities," Winters' voice bordering on condescending, "if not outside your realm of comfort."

I pressed my lips together to keep the string of profanities in my head from pouring out and counted to ten. Winters had me by the shorthairs and we both knew it, but he was dragging this out.

Winters paused as if choosing from an array of options. "We will consider our debt complete when your new protégé delivers a prescribed judgment."

"What judgment? A new one?"

He nodded, "We have launched an investigation into a new disturbance. It seems that someone has successfully facilitated an incursion."

"That happens all the time," I said. "You have people for that."

"In point of fact, we do... or did. Two Agents were dispatched, and we have lost communication with both of them. We suspect they are dead."

That's not good. Incursion Agents are among the best magic users the Council has in circulation. They ain't wizards, but they're dangerous if you get on their wrong side.

"The incursion succeeded and wasn't reversed?" I asked, my arms still crossed. I wasn't open to any of this.

"It would seem so."

"What came through?"

"The diviners believe Dudael may be involved."

My shoulders slumped, "Shit."

"Who is that?" Red demanded.

"Are you kidding me?" I said to Winters, "She doesn't know this shit?"

Winters said, "The education of Hunters is not my arena of concern."

"No? Then what is your area of concern, extortion?"

"Let us not fall back into that unproductive line of discourse."

"Who is this Dood...whatever guy?" Lucy asked again.

Winters sighed, "Dudael is not a person. It is a territory within the realms of the Orbis Alius."

I watched her translate the Latin in her head, "The Otherworld?"

"The Otherside, and don't sugarcoat it," I said. "Dudael isn't just a territory, it's the ass crack of the Otherside. The underworld's underworld."

Winters bowed his head in modest deference.

"The underworld... so what, it's like Hell?" Lucy asked rolling her eyes.

I said, "It's hell's very own Alcatraz."

Lucy cocked her head, "Seriously?"

"Believe what you want, Puppy Chow," I said. Lucy's eyes hardened, and her mouth pressed into a thin line again. "It doesn't pay to be a skeptic in this line of work."

"Whatever caveman."

"Where did you get this thing?" I asked Winters while jerking a thumb at the spiteful little redhead.

"Please try to avoid being any more antagonistic than necessary, William," Winters said.

"No promises," I said.

"Mr. Kemper will teach you all you need to know," the old man stood up and pointed his cane at me. "You may begin first thing tomorrow."

"I'm ready to start now," Lucy said. "I'm not waiting any longer than I have to."

"Don't be brash," Winters said, "Mr. Kemper looks like he needs a hospital and some rest. Tomorrow is soon enough."

"I don't need any rest, I drank some fancy coffee earlier, I'm good," I said. "Let's get this over with."

Winters shrugged, "You are the Hunter."

"Was the Hunter," I said. "This is just a rerun." God, I didn't want to do this.

"As you say," Winters said.

"Where was the incursion?" I asked, hating myself for it. Just like old times. Times I had already made up my mind to be done with.

"Not far from here as luck would have it," Winters said, "St. Charles, in a quaint residential area near the university."

"Luck?" I grunted. "Nothing lucky about Dudael. And don't try to tell me it's a coincidence that members of the Council were in town when it happened?"

"Doubtless," Winters said, "and the circumstances are... unusual."

"Yeah?" I raised an eyebrow, Spock style.

"Signs point to St. Charles being the origin point, not Dudael."

Lucy wrinkled her nose, "Meaning?"

"Someone was trying to facilitate an incursion," Winters explained.

Things have a way of getting worse right after you decided they're as bad as they can get. "Meaning... it's a jailbreak" I rubbed my temples. "Someone from this side reached into Dudael."

Winters nodded solemnly, "Such an event is highly complex. It should not have been possible for a mortal being."

"Then some average Joe pulled off an impossible crossover."

"That would appear to be the case, but we have not determined the method."

"He had help," I stated.

"That is our conclusion."

"Why me?"

Winters shrugged, "We must seize upon the opportunities as they present themselves. Circumstances have aligned in your favor. This is your chance to redeem yourself with the Council."

"Retire myself," I corrected. "What came through?"

Winters hesitated, "We are not certain."

I don't know is something unheard of from the mouths of the Nine-Fold Council. Not that there are things they don't know, but they won't outright say so. They have many alternative ways to say it. We are not certain meant that Winters didn't know and was uncomfortable admitting it or that he was lying. Either option was probable, and I was unlikely to get a straight admission of either.

"That doesn't help," I said.

"I am aware."

"I need better leads."

"You are the Hunter, not I."

"Was the Hunter," I said, growing irritated at having to keep saying so, "I need something to go on here."

Winters reached inside his jacket and removed a small piece of parchment paper, "The address. I have nothing else of value to offer you."

"We both know that's not true," I said.

"This is the task," he said. "The incursion must be undone."

"And the judgment?"

"Retire the intruder. Bring justice to the incursor."

"So little red know-nothing pops a cap and job's done?" I asked. That got Lucy's attention and her eyes snapped to Winters.

"Crudely put, but yes."

"Fine," I said at last. "When this is over, it's over. Period."

"Agreed."

"And you'll get Regis off my back about the previous... gig?"

"Master Regis shall be assuaged," Winters said slowly. "He has other concerns to occupy his attention."

"Ok," I said and with a force of will added, "Deal." No need to shake hands. A verbal agreement with a wizard is more ironclad than any contract.

"Very well," Winters said happily, "Be a good student, Lucille and listen to this man, he knows many useful kinds of violence." He tapped his cane again and the room vibrated. In an instant, my vision blurred to the point of blindness; then it cleared up and Winters was gone, leaving me alone in my house with an angry red-headed assassin I'd done my best to piss off.

I held onto the silence as long as it took for me to remember how much my side hurt, "Can you stitch up an open wound?"

Chapter Nine

Lucille Red did not have a gentle touch, nor a friendly bedside manner. I much preferred Sarah. She stitched the gash in my side without any care for aesthetics or the level of the pain inflicted on me, or maybe encouraged by it. It would leave a hell of a scar... yet another in my extensive collection. I took it in my usual manly, stoic style, saying nothing and reminding myself that pain is the proof that I'm still alive. Damn, but I'd like a different reminder.

After finishing with the stitches, Lucy re-doused the wound with liberal amounts of alcohol and slapped on the bandage, using more tape and pressure than was strictly necessary.

"Are you this friendly all the time or just when you're really trying?"

Lucy kept her mouth shut as she applied the last strip of tape with a sharp jab and walked out of the kitchen.

"Let's get this over with," she called from the living room, near the front door.

I ignored her and instead washed the excess blood from my hands then cleaned up the mess she'd left on my counter. After that, I went to my bedroom to find some clothes that weren't caked in vampire gore or my own blood. This was my second set of clothes ruined on the same day. I hadn't done laundry in a few days, but I had a lot of changes of clothes, a lesson I learned early in my prolific career. I groaned as I stripped out of the jeans and sat down on the edge of my bed in my underwear. God, how nice would it be to lay back and sleep for a few days? Screw the beach. Just give me a pillow and the back of my eyelids.

"What are we waiting for?" Lucy appeared at my door then quickly averted her eyes when she saw me sitting there, mostly naked. I could only imagine what it looked like to her. To anyone who didn't know better, I was just a large freak with years of ruin painted on my body. The tattoos and scar visible when I'm fully dressed don't hold a candle to what Lucy was getting a glimpse. I couldn't say how many scars I had at this point. Most of them were nasty looking but superficial. A few of them, though, should have been fatal. The lion's share of the tattoos that covered my body were wards against curses that couldn't be extracted or healing runes for injuries that might never have healed otherwise. They were stylistic gibberish to the unenlightened. Hell, I didn't even know what most of them actually meant, just why they were there. For example, there was a jagged star-shaped scar on my chest, above my heart, encircled with a Sumerian spell inked in extra fine detail. All I knew was I should have died from that injury but the Inker and the Healer had proven they were worth their weight in gold.

"Take it all in Red," I said. "It's just three hundred pounds of unrefined manhood."

"You look like a circus freak," Lucy sneered.

"You have no idea."

"Put some clothes on before I get sick."

"Are you always a bitch?"

"Are you always a giant ass?" Lucy spat.

"Not always," I spat back.

"Then back off!"

"Why? Because you're with the Nine-Fold Council Security Detail? I should show you some respect for that?"

Lady showed me her teeth.

"You're nobody," I said. "You're a wannabe without a merit badge. You're just York's driver."

Lucy's fists clenched. I wondered which part stung the worst. I could almost feel heat radiating from her. After a moment she relaxed. A little.

"Who knows, maybe I'll punch your ticket someday," she said casually. "I'd have gotten where I want to be without your help eventually. I don't need you."

"Oh really?"

"You're a has-been, Kemper. You're the nobody. If not for Master Winters' mercy, you'd already be dead. And what do you do? You spit on his generosity. You disrespect him openly, like a monkey flinging shit. What do I have to learn from you? Petty name-calling and insubordination? Quitting? Running away?"

"Disrespect huh?" I chewed on the world for a moment. "What do you call breaking into my house and stealing my money?"

"I call it justice."

"Justice," I whispered. I'd used that word a million times in my head. It was the cornerstone of my world. It was the cornerstone of any Hunter's world.

Time to start training.

I sprang from the bed and in three fast steps, I covered half the distance between us in a second. Her eyes widened and she stumbled away from me.

"The fuck do you know about justice?" I said, thunder rising in my voice.

Lucy's eyes darted from my face to the front door and back to me.

"You ever decapitate a bloodsucker?" I slashed my hand sideways before her face and she flinched. I took another step.

"You ever kill a litter of cubs fresh out of a dire wolf's womb?" I made a wringing motion with both hands. She cringed.

"You ever hang a man by the neck and watch him lose control of his bowels while he dies? Hanging because that's the Council judgment for trying to make forbidden a contract with a demon." I stomped one more step.

Lucy said nothing and took another step away from me. Her heels met the wall behind her, and she stopped. I towered over her and she had to crane her neck to meet my eyes.

"I've killed more monsters than you ever knew existed," I said through my teeth and held up both hands, "There's more blood on these hands than you'll ever have pumping through your entire body. All in the name of the Nine-Fold Council's justice."

I curled the fingers of my right hand into a large fist, "I'm the Fist of Justice," shaking the fist dangerously close to Lucy's face until finally, she went for the pistol behind her back. She was fast, but I was ready for it. I slapped her wrist hard as the gun came up and the weapon tumbled down the hall. She jerked a knee up, obviously trying to catch me in the groin, but that was an old trick. I shifted my hip and took the blow without injury. At the same time, she lashed out with her other hand and raked her nails down one side of my face. It stung like a bitch and white-hot pain shot through my face. I grabbed her wrist and slammed it against the wall then grabbed her throat with my free hand. Her eyes widened and she thrashed. But I'm a big bastard. I had too much mass over her. She pawed uselessly at my arm with her free hand.

I let her struggle for a few seconds then I quickly stepped back and shoved her down the hall away from me. She tucked into a roll and came up with her gun in her hands, aimed at me. The girl was good. The gun trembled for a moment then settled, dead calm. To her credit, and mine, she didn't shoot.

There I stood an oversized gorilla of a man, half-naked facing down a scared girl with a gun. Hating myself for it. I felt like a giant bully, and I was.

"What the fuck?" Lucy spat at me. The gun did not waver.

"You got a nasty temper," I said and dabbed at the tender scratches on my face. "It'll get us both killed."

She held the pistol rock solid, her finger tight on the trigger, enough pressure to take up the slack. The slightest movement and I'd eat lead and copper for my last meal.

"First lesson," I said. "Know your limits."

"Fuck you," Lucy said.

"God, you are so pissed off, it's ridiculously easy to bait you into a fight you can't win," I said tiredly, "I can snap you in half without trying." I stared her down, my eyes—eyes which had peered into the bowels of hell more times than I could count—boring into hers. Her eyes, which had nothing but hatred for me and the whole damned world.

"Get your shit together," I said then went back into my bedroom to finish getting dressed, hoping I didn't take a bullet in the back. When she didn't shoot me, I let out a breath.

As I finished lacing my boots, Lucy reappeared in the doorway. No gun in hand.

"I resent you," she said factually.

"No shit," I said.

"I don't need you."

"So you said."

"I earned my place with the Security Detail. I worked my ass off to get there," her voice rising with each word she spoke, "I was days away from my first solo assignment, then I came here tonight with Master Winters to confront you, to... back him up. And he changed everything around and handed me over to you." She screwed up her face like the word reminded her of lemons. "You. The man who walked away from a termination. You turned your back on a sacred duty. And now I have to pretend you have something left in your bloated black heart to teach me."

"Take it or leave it, Sister," I said. "I want my life back and I gotta go through you to get it."

"I have nothing until we finish this job," she said reluctantly but with thorns in her voice. "I'm stuck with you until this is over."

I nodded, "On that point, we agree."

We stared each other down for a moment. I finally broke the silence.

"Truce. We have to work together, for now. We finish this and we go our separate ways?"

Lucy said nothing for a minute, and I wondered if she would tell me to go to hell out of spite and whip out that damned gun again.

"True," she finally said.

I held out a hand. Reluctantly, she shook it and I nodded. Despite her hand being dwarfed by my meat hooks, she had a firm grip.

"But," Lucy added, "if you touch me again without my permission, I'll kill you."

"Fair enough," I said. "You may regret it, but deal." Lucy held my gaze for some time but eventually pulled away and withdrew her hand.

"Ok. If you're done comparing dick sizes, let's get to work."

Lucy scowled. She was pretty good at that.

"We need to go check out this place in St. Charles," I pulled on my leather jacket, one that hadn't been covered in blood yet. I was as ready for action as I was going to be. I'd rather have Mr. Machete or the Holy Handgun, but that wasn't an option so I headed for the door, determined to make do with what I could get.

"You think you can find something there the Council couldn't?" she didn't even try to hide her skepticism.

I stopped and looked at her, "No, Smartass, but the Council didn't even try."

"Oh really? How do you know that?"

"Two Agents down? Suspected dead, not confirmed? And no intel? Nothing but an address and rumors. No, the Council isn't going in there."

"You think it's dangerous?"

"Of course it's fucking dangerous," I pounded my chest, "That's why they call me for this shit. Whatever comes from Dudael brings a shit-ton of trouble with it. That's more trouble than I can handle with my bare hands, and guess what, my armory is empty. What do you think of that?"

Lucy had the good sense not to say anything.

I closed my eyes and counted to ten again. When I opened them, Lucy was still standing there waiting for me to add something useful, "I know a guy that can get us some useful artillery, but he's not a quick option. We're gonna have to wing it for now. Got any cash?"

Lucy raised an eyebrow.

"Were you planning on getting by with your good looks and charm?"

Lucy didn't respond.

"Lesson number two," I said. "Don't trust anyone, especially not Master Winters." I stepped to a wall and punched, smashing a hole through the drywall. Lucy flinched but kept her composure. I reached into the cavity and pulled out a small plastic bag. From it, I dumped out a handful of money rolls onto my bed.

The look of shock on Lucy's face filled me with guilty pleasure.

"You got wheels?" I asked.

"I came here with Master Winters."

"Figures," I said. "Alright, we'll take mine. Car's out front, I'll be there in a minute. I gotta take care of something." Lucy looked as if she was going to refuse but eventually shook her head and left me alone.

Once the door slammed behind her, I rubbed the faint tattoo behind my head until it itched. Leo materialized in my recliner and mimicked an exaggerated shiver.

"Was there a ghost in this chair or what?" he said and got up.

"Yeah, he just don't know it," I said.

Leo strolled over to the hallway and looked at the wreckage of my side table, "Earthquake?"

"Something like that," I said.

Leo gave me the "ok" sign, "Never a dull moment with you, man."

"I wish that wasn't true. Look something came up, I need your help."

"Came up? So soon?" he came back into the living room.

"Bad luck travels fast," I said.

Leo opened his arms as if inviting me for a hug, "Are you in need of comfort? I am a bastion of peace and solace."

"Something a bit more useful," I said and sat in my chair, the one Winters had been sitting in. Oddly, it did feel cold.

"What can I do for you, my wayward friend? I live to serve," Leo said. "Or rather, I don't live but I serve."

"You said something is freaking everyone out in the Otherside."

"I said weirding," Leo corrected, "but yes."

"I got news."

"Yeah? What is it? Because saying things are weird is leaning towards an understatement."

"An incursion," I said.

Leo shook his head, "That's not news. We get those all the time."

All the time? I didn't know that. But that was beside the point. I shook the thought away.

"An incursion linked to Dudael," I said.

Leo's eyes went wide, "Who would do that?"

"Dunno," I said uneasily. "Nobody up to any good."

"That's an understatement man."

"This stinks, bad... Can you dig around for me?"

"Incursions create shock waves that vibrate through all the realms. Bridging into Dudael would take a big incursion. And that would leave some big shock waves."

"Hard to go unnoticed."

"More like impossible," Leo said. "I mean... I don't even know how it would have been done."

"It shouldn't be possible," I ran my hands through my almost nonexistent hair, "Not for a human... right?"

"I would bet against it. But I'm just enlightened, not omniscient."

"If I'm wrong, and it ain't Dudael, then it's just another demon that got out of its cage, and I'll have to put it back. But if I'm right..."

"If you're right," Leo nodded, "Then we'll get to see the literal meaning of 'all hell breaks loose.' Unchecked, it could get strong enough to move between your world and the Otherside at will."

"That's not optimal," I said unnecessarily.

Leo came closer and I felt the air around me swirling a little, like someone had turned on a fan.

"To say the lease," he said. "Upsetting the balance to that extent... it disrupts everything."

"I know."

"No!" Leo flailed his arms around, "I mean everything!"

"I guess," I raised my hands in a totally inadequate calming gesture, "that's why I need to stop it quick."

"The sooner the better."

"That's why I called you," I got up from the chair and realized the air was flowing toward Leo. He was super upset and probably expending a lot of energy to keep his shit together. He looked at me dead still for a moment, then shook his head and the moving air stilled.

"Ok man," he said at last.

"I'm gonna go check out the reported location, but I' bet whatever happened is long gone."

"Reasonable bet."

"Can you track the shockwaves?"

"Tricky," Leo said, "and dangerous, even for a spirit. And scary. I don't like it."

"Me either."

"But life is an adventure. Non-life doubly so. I'll do what I can."

"Appreciate it."

"Are you already back out of retirement?"

"No," I said. "Just wrapping up a pension disagreement."

Leo bend over the now broken TV and ran a nonexistent finger along the cracks, "Who won?"

"Still unresolved."

"Can't wait to see how that turns out," Leo said standing upright and straightening his robe.

I shrugged.

"Alright then," Leo said, "let's get cracking... but be careful." He looked toward my front door, "Whoever is waiting for you outside the house has some dark clouds hanging around them."

I nodded, "I noticed. Thanks, Leo." Leo waved and faded away a lot like a cloud in the wind.

When I stepped out the front door, I found Lucy standing beside my car with her hands planted on her hips, shaking her head slowly. Against my better judgment, I tossed her the keys.

"Let's go, pipsqueak you're driving."

"I'm not even getting in that thing," she said.

"I don't see York's SUV around here," I said, "or is he coming to pick you up later?"

"Fuck you."

"Later," I said and pulled open my passenger door. "Just get in. I'm dead on my feet. I shouldn't drive."

Reluctantly, she complied.

I eased into the passenger seat, for the first time since I had bought the car and felt a little vulnerable. I was the driver. In all things.

This was not my normal.

"And swing by a drive-thru," I said as I leaned back. I'm starving."

She leaned down to look at me through the open window, "You're going to eat? At a time like this?"

"Damn right. This body takes a lot of fuel."

"I can only imagine," Lucy said as she slid behind the wheel with a look on her face like she had scooped up a turd. After scooting the seat way forward—I kept it as far back as it would go—she pushed the key into the ignition.

She couldn't hide a smile when the engine thundered to life. After unnecessarily revving the engine, she yanked the gear shifter out of park and stomped on the gas. She left rubber on the road as we tore away from the curb, engine roaring loud enough to wake the dead as we sped down the street.

Chapter Ten

Fortunately, traffic in St. Louis is not heavy at 3 a.m. and we didn't see any police. I could have gotten to St. Charles in about forty-five minutes. With Lucy driving, we made it in thirty, even with a quick stop for a double cheeseburger and extra-large fries.

The address on Winters' fancy little piece of paper took us west of Lindenwood University and into a quiet neighborhood built in a mazework of streets that didn't seem to follow any residential planning logic. The streets curved and turned back on themselves, dumping you back on one of the main roads or into dead ends. The place we were looking for was at the end of a somewhat secluded cul-de-sac with only three houses. It was a simple off-white ranch-style house with a one-car garage, squeezed in between a split-level eyesore with a lime green paint and two-story brick house. The brick house had a giant white SUV in the driveway with those white stickers in the window that said the owner had four kids, represented by little stick figures. Two hybrid cars sat in front of the lime green house. A nondescript black sedan sat in the driveway of "our" house. Lucy and I exchanged wary looks. Since the Feds weren't likely to be part of this, the vehicle probably belonged to our missing Incursion Agents. I wasn't hopeful that they were inside waiting for us. Pessimism has been one of my top tenets of longevity.

The left and right houses were dark and quiet as we rolled into the center house's driveway. I noted that Lucy didn't give the keys back after she shut off the engine. That old car was much more fun to drive than you might expect, and probably more than someone like Lucy would freely admit.

We took a minute to search the car for useful weapons, which I would have done sooner if I hadn't been so out of my groove. I was used to bringing my tools with me, not having to improvise on the fly.

We found a multi-tool with a knife blade in the glove compartment and tire iron in the trunk.

"I have this," Lucy showed me her gun.

"I've seen it, Quickdraw, but people live around here. How bout we skip the gunfire for now"

"Your funeral," she put away the gun and snatched the tire iron, "then I get this."

The multi-tool was ridiculously tiny in my hands, even with the knife unfolded. But it was better than nothing. Right?

The lights were on, but no one answered when I hit the doorbell. Lucy pounded on the door with the tire iron. Still no answer... and who wouldn't answer for the likes of us.

I tried the doorknob. Locked. I raised a foot to kick it open, but Lucy held up a finger.

"Do you have to go straight to barbarian?" she mumbled then nudged a conspicuous plastic rock next to the sidewalk with her toe. She had a sharp eye, I had to give her that. I picked it up and found a key inside it.

The smug look on her face disappeared when I opened the door.

It was a vision of horror inside.

Lucy puked. I had a cast-iron stomach, but I wasn't so tough that I didn't wretch a little.

There was blood everywhere. Literally. The walls, the floor, the ceiling. Chunks of flesh and bone and God-knows-what else clung in horrid clumps, drooping from the curtains and hanging from a ceiling fan like hellish kudzu. The thick coppery smell of blood hung heavy in the air and mixed with the distant odor of burnt hair and the unmistakable rotten-egg stench of sulfur. The carpet squished under our shoes as we stepped inside. I gave Lucy some space and approached the middle of the living room.

At the center of the room, there was no blood. No carpet either. Just a large perfect circle, six or seven feet across. The edges were charred as if they'd been burned but the exposed subfloor beneath was clean and clear, except for where a few glops of blood and gore dripped from the ceiling. I'd seen incursion sites before. This was not like any of them. This was something way worse.

Lucy spit out the last of whatever she'd eaten for lunch then collected herself and shot me a nasty "don't say a word" glare.

The room had either been unoccupied or cleared out before the ritual. I assumed the latter. There was no furniture, no wall decoration, nothing except blackout curtains. Near the edge of the circle across from me, a thicker lump stood out amongst the rest of the carnage. It was larger than the other random hunks of stuff and more solid. Less lumpy. I skirt the edge of the circle and squatted down to inspect it more closely, prodding it with the end of the small knife. It was a shoe. Or the remains of one. A dark leather shoe. Next to it, there was another shape, just the sole of the matching shoe. Holy shit.

Lucy stood me and pointed with the tire iron at another set of rubber soles a few feet away.

"What the fuck happened here?" Lucy asked, her voice muffled because he had her forearm across her mouth and nose.

As I breathed in uneasily through my nostrils, I slipped the end of the tiny blade under the shoe and tipped it over gently. There was clean, tan carpet beneath. Well, not clean, but not blood-soaked. Something had been painted in red on thin pile carpeting with intricate strokes. The lines blended into the blood, but the part covered by the shoe had been preserved. It was a partial set of runes. I flipped the other shoe over to reveal more and the edge of a sweeping set of arcing slashes that indicated a symbol.

"This is a summoning circle," I said waving at the circle and runes in front of us.

"What does that mean?"

"How the hell are you supposed to be a Hunter?" I said. "You don't know shit."

"Now isn't the time Mr. Miyagi," Lucy spat. "Just answer the question."

"Circles are a big part of magic. Dunno why, just is. You wanna cast a protection spell, you use circles. You wanna do séance, you use circles. Some jackass wants to summon a demon, he uses circles."

"Ok, I get it," Lucy said through her arm. "Circles are a big magic deal. And you use them for incursions?"

"Dunno. They always originate on the Otherside."

"Until now. And the runes?"

"Basically, written spells with magic binding. Specific runes for specific things. Like a prescription... or instructions."

"Or a like a computer program for magic?"

"Like that." I stood up and tried to picture these runes following the circle all the way around.

"What do these symbols say?"

"Dunno," I said, "I'm not a rune expert."

"You're covered in freaking runes."

"Are you a dermatologist?" I looked down at her standing next to me. She looked up at me with obvious suspicion.

"What the hell is that supposed to mean?"

"You're covered in skin, does that make you a skin expert?"

"That's the stupidest analogy I've ever heard."

"Stick around," I said, "I full of these gems."

"I'd rather not," she stepped away from me, trying to step in the footprints she already made. The *squish squish* was no less disgusting.

"The point is, I know about runes, not what makes them work. Not by a long shot."

"Well, what do you know?"

"A lot," I squatted back down and pointed at the marking with the knife, "You see how small the runes are? They were less than half an inch tall.

Lucy nodded without really looking.

"Either our particular idiot is very wordy, or this spell is complex."

Lucy's head swiveled to look at the runes, "That's not a good sign, is it?"

"No it ain't."

"What is that?" She pointed at the edge of the sweeping symbol. It was larger than the runes and didn't have the same flowing strokes.

"It's a sigil. Part of one."

"Sigil? Like a demon logo?"

"Pretty much," I said. "If you know a thing's sigil, you got some magic influence over it. If you have a sigil and summoning circle" I paused and tried to picture what the rest of the sigil looked like. There was enough to identify, but it just wouldn't come to me, like it was tickling the back of my mind.

Lucy took her arm from her face long enough to snap her fingers at me. God, she was impatient.

I grunted and stood up, "You have a sigil and summoning circle, you got a heap of trouble."

"Yeah, no shit. The blood is a subtle clue."

I waved at the room at large, "If this really was an incursion to Dudael, the power that came from there might have been too much for anyone not being protected by the circle."

"Anyone," Lucy said, "as in two Agents who showed up in time to witness the fireworks?"

"Looks that way," I said and stood back up. "I don't know why the carnage is so contained though."

Lucy's eyes went wide, "Contained? Are you kidding?"

"No," I said. "I mean it's localized. Just this room and nothing outside. This much destructive force, there should be a path of destruction leading away from the house."

"Maybe it's still here," Lucy said and hefted her impromptu

weapon in one hand, still covering half her face with the other.

"Maybe," I allowed. "let's hope not."

"Why not? Let's kill it and be done."

"With that?" I motioned at the crooked hunk of steel in her hand, and waved the little multi-tool knife, "or this?"

Lucy looked at her tire iron as if noticing it for the first time.

"I have a gun," she offered.

"It's useless in this case."

"Useless? Really?"

"What part of this ain't you getting, Red? This is a shit storm. That," I pointed at her tire iron, "is a piece of wet toilet paper."

"You're a freaking drama queen," Lucy barked. "Grow a pair and let's get this done."

I tapped the side of my head, "Get this through your thick skull, your twelve bullets from that little pistol will do jack shit to the thing that caused this hellscape."

Lucy pulled her arm away from her face and took a breath, as if it were an act of defiance, "Well... here we are. What do you suggest?"

"We do what we gotta do," I said, "but don't kid yourself. This ain't gonna be easy."

"If it was easy, we wouldn't be here, would we, you big ass?"

One. Two. Three. Four. I stopped counting. It wasn't helping.

"Let's just check out the rest of the house," I said. "Maybe we'll find something useful."

"You're the boss," Lucy said, not convincingly.

"Try not to track blood on the clean floors."

Lucy scowled and picked up her foot. Blood dripped from it. She looked at me incredulously.

"I'm kidding," I said leading the way into the kitchen.

"You're not funny," Lucy said, and she meant it.

Of course, we tracked blood into the kitchen. And all over the house. But it didn't matter at this point. There was nothing. It was just a vacant house. Not a stick of furniture, not a stray penny on the floor. Nothing. Whoever had done this probably didn't live here. Hell, they probably didn't even own the property.

"Let's get out of here," I said.

"On that, I agree," Lucy led the way and opened the front door for me in mock chivalry.

I wasn't paying much attention when I ducked out the door, something slammed into my chest and I went down.

Chapter Eleven

My first thought was that someone had shot me. A solid strike to my chest like a hammer, followed by deep throbbing pain.

My next thought as I tried to suck in a breath was that Lucy had already double-crossed me, but she was still behind me in the house, and it wasn't a shot to the back. As I dropped to my knees, I caught a glimpse of hot pink slippers and a set of toenails in need of attention. I rolled to my side and saw Lucy emerge from the house, snapping the door shut behind her. She swung her iron with blinding speed followed by the hollow bonk metal of metal on bone. Judging by the angle of her swing, I figured Lucy was going for the attacker's knee. An aluminum baseball bat landed on the sidewalk next to my head. Lucy's other hand lanced out followed by a grunt. The person wearing the pink slippers stumbled backward and landed on his ass right beside me.

"Get up," Lucy barked at me.

I did, slowly, while wheezing to get my breath back. A man in colorful boxers, a red robe too small for him, and of course the gaudy pink slippers sat a few feet away holding his nose. Lucy held her tire iron at arm's length pointing it at him as if she were wielding Excalibur.

"You get up too," Lucy ordered.

He stood up with a great show of favoring one of his legs. The front door at the brick house opened and a woman in an oversized flannel robe appeared on the stoop with a phone to her ear.

"Don't do anything stupid," Lucy said, snarling, "or I'll shoot you in the other knee." Oh good, she remembered to get her gun out. She stood there dual-wielding her tire iron and the small Glock.

God my chest hurt, but nothing was broken. The dude probably didn't expect me to be as tall as I was. He had probably intended to hit me in the head.

"Son of a bitch," I said coughing.

"You broke my nose," the man said.

"No, I didn't," Lucy said, "you're not even bleeding."

He pulled his hand away. She was right. No blood.

"You broke my knee," he complained.

"Not quite, but I will if you keep bitching," Lucy said.

"Who are you?" I asked harshly.

"D- Dan," the man stuttered and closed the robe over his bare chest, but it was too small and just looked silly. "Don't hurt me."

"Hurt you? You hit me with a freaking baseball bat, you little prick," I said as I stooped to pick up my multi-tool and his bat.

"Oh God," he stumbled back a few steps.

The woman at the brick house pulled the phone away from her ear, "What's happening Daniel? Are you ok?"

"Tell her your fine," I grumbled.

"I- I'm fine, A- Angela," he said. "Everything's fine." He held his free hand out toward me placatingly, "Please don't hurt me...my family."

Lucy rolled her eyes, "God, you'd be dead already if that's what I was here for. Why did you attack him?" She swung the tire iron at me in a haphazard gesture, almost cracking me upside the head. I flinched away and gave her a hard look. She ignored me.

"My wife...We saw your car... nobody lives here."

"Yeah," I said, "so?"

"All the weird noises last night," Dan said. "Vehicles coming and going. My wife...we had enough."

"Who are they?" Angela called, still holding the phone. "What are they doing over there?"

"Tell her to shut up," Lucy said. Took the words right out of my mouth.

"I'll explain in a minute," Dan said. "Everything's fine." He smiled a horrible fake smile at Lucy and me.

"What noises?" I asked.

"Sounded like a horror movie in there," he pointed at the house, "or a porno. All the screaming and thunder and flashing lights."

I raised my eyebrows. So did Lucy.

"I knocked on the door," Dan said with the mounting excitement of someone reliving a confrontation, "but no one answered. Just loud noise. Way too loud. Had to be a slasher movie, right?"

"Yeah," I said. "Had to be."

"What else?" Lucy jabbed the tire iron at Dan, and he jumped.

"Nothing. Nothing else," he wrapped his arms across his chest. "I went home and eventually the noise stopped. We finally got back to sleep—I have a job you know; I have to get up early—then you two pulled in with that loud car."

"So?" I said. My chest hurt every time I talked. I felt less and less generous with each word.

"So... My wife...I had enough of all the noises and comings and goings," Dan said a little snidely. "The Hummer was gone from earlier and now you're here with this piece of—" He pointed at my car.

"Easy," I warned.

"This boat," Dan said. "My...I had my wife call the police and I came over to scare you off."

"Scare?" I choked out the word.

"What Hummer?" Lucy demanded.

"Big yellow thing," Dan said. "Drug dealers I bet."

"Or porn stars," I offered.

"Exactly," Dan said excitedly.

"God," Lucy said, "you're just an idiot, aren't you?"

"Well... no," Dan said, visibly hurt.

"Go home Dan," I said sternly, "and stay there."

"Go!" Lucy barked. Dan flinched and limped his way back to his house. His wife watched us for a moment and waved her phone at us before going back inside and slamming the door.

"We better hit the road," I said.

"I'll drive," Lucy said. We got in and she gunned the engine, making a lot more noise than necessary in getting out of the driveway and cul-de-sac.

"We are we going?" she asked as we passed the college.

"Archives," I said.

"Really?" Lucy sounded like I'd asked her to clean up after my dog.

"Yes really."

Chapter Twelve

Lucy didn't say anything until we had crossed the Missouri River and headed south again. She didn't drive as fast or as recklessly as she had before. In fact, I felt like she was going slower than was necessary, even if there wasn't any traffic.

I decided to try and break the ice by pointing out the obvious.

"You don't seem happy to be going to the Archives."

Lucy didn't take her eyes from the road or loosen her angry stranglehold on my steering wheel, "You're an amazing detective. Your talent is wasted on make-believe creatures."

I bit my tongue for the count of three, "Look, I—"

Lucy cut me off, "I'm not a nut you need to crack. Let's just get there and get what we need so we can finish this stupid thing."

"Fine, then step on it, granny," I said. "You're driving like you're headed to the orthodontist."

Lucy stepped on it.

The St. Louis Archives—the central hub for the United States—is in the Kosciusko neighborhood, south of downtown along the riverfront. The area is primarily industrial: manufacturing, distribution, bulk storage, stuff like that. There were a few trendy restaurants in renovated factories along the western edges, but the district was mostly made up of run-down empty lots, extraneous brick buildings, and a few newer buildings. The Archives is in—or rather under, an old electrical parts distributor's building, converted into a successful precious metals distributor, which is a good cover for the frequent appearance of the Council's armed Security Detail.

Aside from a blacked-out cargo van, the parking lot was empty, not a big surprise since we showed up well before normal business hours. The doors were locked but a receptionist buzzed us in and greeted us cheerfully as we entered the lobby.

She stood behind a marble-topped counter, flanked by a particularly out-of-date computer and a large push-button telephone. The overly polite lady with her hair pulled back in a painfully tight-looking bun smiled robotically as we approached the front counter. One hand disappeared under her desk while the other remained to hover above her keyboard.

"I'm sorry, Sir, we do not open to the public until 9 a.m.," she said cheerfully. "If you do not care to wait, I can make an appointment for you." Sir. She knew who I was just fine. I'd been here before and God knows I'm not forgettable. She was doing her job, as she always did.

In my friendliest voice, I said, "I'd like to book a viewing of white gold fixtures, three days from tomorrow afternoon."

"We can accommodate that," the receptionist motioned toward the open hallway. She watched us with alert yet friendly eyes as we made our way to the hall. I often wondered what she had hidden below the countertop if I wasn't friendly.

The short hallway branched off into various offices and meeting rooms. At the far end of the hall, a set of double doors led into the warehouse area. On either side of the hall were several locked doors. I hadn't ever really explored the building, but I knew there was a full barracks on sight somewhere housing the Council Security Detail. My first visit here included an overly detailed explanation of how I would be treated if I strayed outside acceptable protocols. The treatment would include a lot of gunfire and could escalate from there. I look like trouble, and trouble tends to follow me around, so people aren't always wrong when they assume my presence means trouble. Incidentally, my first visit was also my first time meeting York. We became fast friends after that day. Obviously.

At a door marked "Janitorial Storage," I grabbed the doorknob and squeezed. A hidden needle poked my hand, eliciting a word of profanity from me. Lucy snorted at my discomfort.

Something scanned my blood and confirmed I was who I appeared to be and there was an audible click followed by a grinding sound. After a few seconds, the door popped opened to reveal a narrow stairway descending into the depths. Aside from a single handrail of pipe and small LED lights overhead, the stairwell was empty and featureless. We descended 71 steps and found ourselves in a small foyer with a large double door of dark brown wood, ornately carved with runes and wards; few nasties could get through those barriers uninvited if they ever got this far.

The solitary guard in black fatigues, stood in front of the door, arm resting on the shotgun slung across his chest. We stopped in front of him to let him check each of us in turn with a hand-held retinal scanner. I bent down to make it easier for him.

"Late night, Kemper?" he asked as the device hummed away.

I tried to ignore the red beams dancing in my eyes, "They always are, Mac. How are the kids?"

"Numerous and noisy," he replied. After a moment the device beeped and flashed a green light.

Lucy had nothing to say. She stood there while he scanned her and pretended not to know him. Less cause to have to act nice that way, I guess.

"Good to go," he said.

"Thanks," I said patting him on the shoulder, "stay frosty."

"Always," he saluted with one finger to the brow.

The Archives' doors opened without a sound and we entered.

The next room was not technically the Archives, it was the waiting room, and it was as far as I had ever been. It was more like a reading room. A lobby so to speak.

It was a softly lit room, decked out with ancient chandeliers and old rugs covering hardwood floors. Shelves loaded with various harmless books and small sculptures lined most of the walls. Several antique chairs and small reading tables were scattered about the room, each with its own antique reading lamp. At the far end of the room, an elaborate wood counter stood before another set of ornate wooden doors. A thin man with finely trimmed dark hair and stylish prescription glasses regarded us as we entered and frowned. He stood up and straightened his well-tailored suit and tie before approaching us quickly as if to prevent us from venturing too far into his sanctuary.

"What are you doing here?" he asked abruptly.

"Hello, Dean," I said, somewhat taken aback. He was never what I would call friendly, but never outright rude to me. "I'm fine. How are you?"

Archivist Dean Waldo Forrester waved his hands at me in a shooing gesture, "You may dispense with the pleasantries, Mr. Kemper. You have no business here."

He glanced at Lucy with distaste before continuing at me. "I prefer to avoid disruptions in my Archives." Disruptions. Is that what I was? I always thought I was very polite and unobtrusive Archivist couldn't technically refuse to aid a sponsored associate of the Nine-Fold Council, but nobody said they had to be nice about it.

Dean Forrester was the only one I dealt with at the Archives. He was a funny man, in a Woody Allen sort of way but he was good at his job. While still being slightly patronizing and impatient, he managed to dig up obscure and useful information whenever I asked for it. I always suspected his speediness was fueled by his desire to quicken my departure from his holy sanctuary.

I'm not one to dig into the logistics of magic repositories and service providers, so I never had a clear picture of how the central Archives hub for the U.S. could operate with only one staff member. Only one that I ever saw at least. I asked Forrester about it once. By way of explanation, he told me I was ignorant and uninformed. True, but hurtful.

Dean never seemed to be happy to have me in *his* Archives, but he usually tolerated me with grace. Something was ruffling his feathers this morning.

"Disruptions?" I said holding my hands out, which probably didn't help, cuts and scrapes and all. "How am I a disruption?"

"Everything you touch becomes a disruption. Please leave."

He had a point.

"It's part of the job," I said. "It's you who helps me keep it from being too much trouble to handle."

"The job?" the Archivist adjusted his tie unnecessarily. "I thought you had separated from the job?"

"News travels fast, don't it?"

"It does," the Archivist said, "that is my job. Of late, I have been dreadfully busy keeping up with the aftermath of your not insignificant actions. I spent more time recording and reviewing accounts of your exploits than on any of my other duties."

I couldn't be that interesting.

"Really?" I asked.

"Of course, really," he said.

I nodded appreciatively, "Well, I'm trying to get out of the business. Things should slow down for you after that."

"Things do not work that way," the man said.

"So, I keep hearing," I said and jerked a thumb at Lucy, "she's my replacement. Maybe she won't cause you as much trouble."

Dean looked Lucy up and down, a formality I decided, because he clearly recognized her and had been pointedly ignoring her presence. He wrinkled his nose and gave her a mild frown of disapproval.

Dean said to me. "Not everyone is suited for your line of work."

Lucy crossed her arms.

"Nobody is. But that's how the ball bounces. Look, Dean," I said, "I need some information. Then we'll be out of your hair."

"What information do you require?"

"We just came from an incursion site and I need to know what came through."

He swallowed, "There have been no reported incursion attempts tonight."

"Really? Master Winters set me on this one... and two agents were lost in the attempt."

Dean loosened his tie then readjusted it, "Are you certain of this. No such event or dispatches have been logged."

"Pretty sure," I said.

Lucy spoke for the first time since we entered the building, "Are you accusing the Master Wizard of lying?"

"Of course not," the Archivist said a little too defensively. "What makes you think you've uncovered an incursion attempt."

I described the scene in ugly detail. By the time I finished, Dean looked a little green. He removed a handkerchief from his breast pocket and dabbed his forehead.

"That is not an incursion," he said. "You must be mistaken."

"It's an incursion," I said clearly, "just not like any you've ever seen."

"I have never seen an incursion, Mr. Kemper. I have only seen photographic records and have only read descriptions. This does not match any of the documented instances"

"This was a different kind of incursion," I said.

Dean frowned, "There aren't kinds of incursions."

"I've been let to believe that this was an incursion," I said, "into the Otherside, to Dudael."

"No," he said immediately. "That is impossible."

"Yet it appears to have happened," I said.

"What evidence do you have to support this preposterous

claim?"

"Not much," I admitted, "just Master Winters' speculation and a very grizzly scene."

I grabbed a piece of stationery at the nearest table and scrawled the partial bit of the sigil I'd identified on the bloody carpeting.

Dean barely glanced at my artwork and answered too quickly, "It's incomplete. Useless."

"Look again," I said with patience of a kindergarten teacher.

He sighed dramatically and took the paper from me. He held it at arm's length and studied it for a moment.

"A sigil perhaps?" he said while holding the paper out for me. "There is not enough to identify."

"I think there is," I didn't take the paper from him, "run it through the database. I'll bet it matches one of the Dudael inmates."

Dean didn't take his eyes from the paper, "It is best not to delve into Dudael, either directly or through research. Sigils can be very dangerous."

"I agree," I said. "But somebody delved. I have to un-delve it."

"That is among the silliest things you have ever said to me," Dean said without a hint of amusement.

I shrugged and didn't bother with a comeback. Witty banter was wasted on this guy.

He folded the piece of paper in two, "Wait here. Do not touch anything." Without further instruction he hurried through the large wood doors in the back.

"They have an amazing computer network," I said into the hard silence that followed, "Everything's on a computer now."

"I'm not an idiot," Lucy said her lips moving but her teeth still clenched together.

"No," I said. "Just mean."

Lucy closed her lips again and dropped into the nearest chair.

"You've met him before," I said. It wasn't a question.

Lucy didn't deny it.

"Does he hate you or do you hate him?"

"It's mutual," Lucy said.

"Why?"

Lucy propped her feet up on the table and crossed them

"Don't be a jerk," I said. The atmosphere in the Archives was too stuffy for my taste, but it still deserved at least a modicum of respect.

"Bite me."

I shoved her feet off the table, and she shot to her feet, "I told you I'd kill you if you ever touched me again."

"Yes you did," I said. "Get on with it or dial back your shitty attitude about five clicks."

Lucy breathed in and out several controlled breaths. I wondered if she was trying my patented count to ten technique. At length, she let out a long breath. After what felt like an eternity, she relaxed and casually adjusted her braided ponytail.

"Throw gasoline on the fire all you want.," she said as she walked slowly around the room. She pulled a book at random from the shelf and thumbed through the pages.

"You gonna throw that at me or shit on it?" I asked.

Lucy shrugged and put it back on the shelf in the exact spot from which she had removed it, "I hate this place."

"You hate everything."

"We're wasting our time here."

"Yeah we are," I said, "and you being pissed at everyone you encounter doesn't speed things up."

"Easier to kill what I hate."

"You gonna kill all these books? And Dean Forrester?"

Lucy didn't answer.

"That was a rhetorical question," I said, "but I'd still like to hear you say 'no' to it."

"I'll kill what I'm told to kill," she said. "I just want to get on with it."

"Yeah?" I asked I crossed my arms and leaned against sturdy bookcase. "Tell me smart guy, what are we killing?"

"A demon," she replied, "from hell."

"Oh? A couple hours ago, you didn't even know what Dudael was. Or believe Hell was real."

"You said it yourself, something from hell's max security prison." She ran her fingers along the spine of another book but left it undisturbed.

"Except Dudael isn't for demons. It's for angels."

Lucy her head snapped around to me, "What?"

"Fallen angels," I said. "They're not demons, they're... different."

"Lucy mulled it over for a few seconds, "Whatever. Demons, fallen angels. Same thing in my book. We still have to kill it to finish this."

I leaned forward and whispered, "Where do we find it?"

"Up your ass for all I know. That's your problem," Lucy said. "Get me there and I'll finish it."

"No, it's your problem now. You're a Hunter, I'm a hostage," I pointed at her with one big meaty finger.

"Bitching about that won't get you anything," Lucy pointed back with a slim finger. "Find me this demon or angel or fairy princess so I can kill it and be done with you."

I spread my arms, "That's why we're here you hard-headed know it all."

"I thought you just kill things," Lucy said and swept the room with an arm, "I didn't know you were a nerd too hanging out in stuffy libraries with condescending schoolmarms."

"You just don't get it do you?" I sat down in a fancy chair and it creaked under my weight.

"What? What don't I get?"

"Ok... pop quiz. How do you kill a man quietly while keeping him from making enough noise to draw attention?"

Lucy didn't even think about it, "Knife through the rib cage into a lung, or knife straight into the throat through the larynx."

"Nice," I said. "How do you kill a Lycan?"

"Lycan?" Lucy screwed up her nose. "Like a werewolf? Silver bullets."

"Nope," I said. "Lycans aren't werewolves and silver bullets are for curses not lycanthropes."

"Fine, you tell me smart guy."

"You sever the spine or cut off the head." I made a chopping motion. "The Hunter's Goodbye." Lucy rolled her eyes.

"A good Hunter uses his brain sometimes, too," I said. "Monsters aren't people."

Lucy turned her back on me again and pretended to study a book, "Sometimes they are."

I had to give her that.

The rear door opened, and Dean rushed into the room, his brows furrowed with concern.

"You were right, Mr. Kemper," he said, looking like he'd eaten a whole lemon. "I wish it were not so."

"Me too."

"I was able to identify the sigil," he said reluctantly, "it belongs to Rezruel."

The hairs on my arm stood up.

"Shit," I said. I would have liked to never heard that name again.

"Is that bad," Lucy said.

"It is not good," Dean said.

"It's bad," I corrected.

"Now please go," Dean said. "Please."

"Why are you so nervous?" I asked holding my hands up as if fending off and emotional attack.

"You make me nervous," he said.

"I have that effect on people," I admitted. "Have it your way. Let's go Red."

When we got back to the car, I told Lucy to take the driver's seat again. Lucy didn't say anything until she had started the engine.

"What now Professor?"

"We're dangerously outclassed," I said. "Rezruel is big trouble. We need some real firepower on our side."

"Yeah? Where do we get that?"

"I know a guy," I said. "It's bit of drive."

"Define 'a bit.'"

"He's in Kansas City."

Lucy frowned, "Yeah, that is a bit of a drive. Is it really necessary?"

"You got any enchanted weaponry hidden away in those tight pants?"

Lucy did not reply.

"Didn't think so."

"What about your place," Lucy said thoughtfully, "maybe Winters put your stuff back. Maybe it's all there."

"No," I said. "That's not his style. He said he wouldn't return my things until we're done, he meant it."

"He said that he'd return everything he took," Lucy said. "Maybe he missed something."

"Not likely," I said, "he's one clever little bastard."

Lucy grunted in an unfriendly way. She clearly didn't like me bad-mouthing Winters.

I handed Lucy a wad of cash, "For gas."

"You can pump your own gas," she said, but didn't hand back the money.

"I'll be asleep," I pushed the seat back as low as it would go, "Wake me up when get to KC, I need some sleep." I was out like a baby before we got the interstate.

Chapter Thirteen

I was sleeping like a baby, dreaming about defending bikini-clad girls on a beach from invading zombie sharks, when I felt the world drop out from under me. I jerked awake to discover we were air-born. After a brief moment of flight, the car slammed onto all four wheels then bounced and crunched to a grinding stop.

"Goddammit!" Lucy roared. We'd landed on an unpaved farm road running parallel to I-70. The car's hood had a huge hole in it and steam poured out of the radiator. Lucy struggled with her seat belt catch, trying to get unbuckled while I struggled to understand what the hell happened.

"What the hell happened?"

Still punching at her seat belt release, Lucy pointed up toward the highway. It was still dark, early morning probably, but I could make out the shape of a cargo van stopped on the shoulder of the road with a side door open. There was a flash of light and a thundering boom and my car lurched as something with a lot of mass slammed into the side.

"Out, out, out!" I yelled and kicked the passenger door open.

"I'm trying!" Lucy yelled back.

"Cut it!" I tossed her the multi-tool.

The car jumped again, and the windshield and driver's side window blew out. Lucy sliced the seat belt and followed me out the passenger side door.

I stayed low, pressed up against the car, using it for cover, for all the good it would do. Lucy settled next to me for a second or two and then she was gone

She rounded the rear of the car, drawing her gun, and began firing rapidly toward the van. I reached for the tire iron in the back but there was another crack of thunder and the car jumped again. Another new hole appeared in the body of the car, inches from my head. Holy shit, somebody had a canon up there! Screw the tire iron, I needed a tank. I peeked around the back of the car to look for Lucy.

Her gun barked several more times before she started running up the steep roadside embankment.

"Stupid!" I spat and ran after her. Another boom and my car leapt just as I passed the trunk. One of the rear wheels exploded in a ruin of steel and rubber.

Lucy was fast. She reached the van several steps ahead of me and fired blindly into the open cargo door until her gun ran empty. She holstered her pistol and crouched to lunge into the van just as someone leapt from inside. As Lucy and her new opponent tumbled away, the shooter, still in the van, opened fire again, at me. Chunks of ground flew up, pelting my legs and ass. I stumbled forward, regained my footing, and kept going. Behind the van, Lucy rolled on the ground, grappling with a female dressed like a high school cheerleader. She probably was a high school cheerleader once.

I closed in on the van as quickly as I could. A passing car on the highway zipped past and I caught the brief glint of something shiny and metallic reflected by the headlights. A gun, I assumed correctly. It fired again. I was close enough to see where it was pointed and dove to the ground before the shot went off. I felt a shockwave of energy pass over my head and heard the gratifying curses made by someone who'd missed a can't-miss shot.

That was six shots. If the gun was a semi-automatic pistol, I was screwed. I decided to take a chance that it was a revolver and they'd have to reload.

I charged the van and reached in to grab a handful of anything available. I yanked hard and a figure came out into the night. I caught a flash of empty light in his eyes before he collided with me and started to fight back. I got up quickly, dragging him with me, and slammed him into the side of the van leaving a sizeable dent. I twisted, spun, and slammed him into the van again. Another car whipped by and I saw what I was fighting. A kid, couldn't have been older than sixteen or so. He was young but muscular; he was probably an athlete once. His clothes were normal for a teenager, t-shirt, jeans, stylish name-brand jacket... lots of dried blood. Grey skin, wild eyes, hungry teeth. Damn.

He clawed at me, reached up to grab at my face while I slammed him against the van a few more times. I had at least twice as much mass as this kid and he was still hanging in there, not even stunned by the body slams. Another figure appeared at the van's side opening. I spun around and threw the kid against the door without letting go. The door swung into whoever was trying to come out.

I heard a scream behind me so I dragged the kid to the rear of the van to check on Lucy's progress. She and the cheerleader had parted for a second. The female charged at Lucy, who quickly dodged right and countered with a reverse kick sending the girl tumbling down the slope. Lucy immediately followed after at full speed. She had moves, I had to give her that.

I punched the kid several times in the face, saying "Sorry, Buddy" with each blow. The van door opened again; the gun swung toward me. Without thinking, I shoved the undead kid toward the weapon as it barked and dove behind the van, stopping myself before rolling into traffic. I heard a grunt of pain from the kid and a cry of frustration from the van. Buddy fell to the ground with a new hole in his chest. He was still moving, barely. That one would be tough to survive, even for a vampire. It would take a lot of blood to recover from that wound, but crazier things had happened.

I yanked on the rear van door, but it was locked. Nothing was ever easy. Fine. I went the long way around, hugging the side of the van as to not get clipped by the passing traffic which didn't seem to be bothered by our spectacle. I had a small advantage in the fact that the van had no windows on the cargo section; but if the driver was looking at the side mirror, they'd see me coming. I took my chances.

The driver wasn't looking. I pulled the door open and grabbed a surprised looking young man in the driver's seat. Human. He hadn't been turned. My guess is he'd been paid or kidnapped to drive the van and maybe didn't even know what he was getting into. I didn't get the chance to ask him.

I was dragging him out of the vehicle when a gun barked from inside the back of the van. It was a hasty shot and from a bad angle. The bullet tore long ways and crosswise through the driver's body leaving a ruin of blood and gore. I released him and fell back as the shockwave ripped past me, giving me a little extra shove. What the hell was that shooter using? A six-shot howitzer?

I fell away hard and landed too far from the van, finding myself in the middle of the highway.

I looked up to see a semi-truck bearing down on me too fast for me to dodge. I was screwed.

Like a deer in headlights, I froze. Most truck drivers know to drive straight through a deer in the road. It was safer for everyone that way. Fortunately for me, the driver recognized the difference between me and a deer. He veered too quickly and the wrong way, smashing into the back of the van with a sickening crunch of metal and squealing of rubber. The trailer fish-tailed and slid straight at me. I ducked and rolled forward, through the space beneath the trailer. One of the brake lines whipped me across the back but didn't do any damage I couldn't swallow. The van, a ruined mess, launched forward and tumbled down the slope. The truck followed and rolled over sideways.

"Holy shit," I wheezed.

Then I remembered Lucy. She hadn't been in the path of destruction. I headed down the slope to help her out and found her grappling again with her new friend. Lucy threw several sharp jabs at the girl's face, ruining her nose and splitting her lower lip in two, but doing no serious harm otherwise. She pushed the cheerleader away and delivered a roundhouse kick to Nightmare Girl's stomach, who staggered back several steps from the force of the blow then lunged back unfazed.

I ran as fast as I could down the hill without losing my balance and falling. I lowered a shoulder and rammed her square in the chest. She flew several feet and tumbled like a ragdoll but got back up quickly and charged me. Lucy stepped in front of her. They collided and fell back into me. Using their momentum and me, I steered us all crashing into the back of my car.

I grabbed a handful of the girl's hair and yanked back and yelled to Lucy, "Throat!"

Lucy reacted instantly. She punched with her knuckles just right, crushing the girl's larynx. Then she lashed out with her other hand, holding the multi-tool. The slash cut a wide path through the girl's exposed throat. The cheerleader made a sickening, gurgling sound and blood bubbled out the new wound.

She flailed, throwing feet at Lucy, fingernails at me.

I hauled back on her head.

"More!" I bellowed. Lucy struck again. And again. Opening the cut deeper with each swing. On her fourth blow, the blade hit bone and the knife jumped from her hand.

Ok, the hard way. I stuck my free hand into the open wound and dug inside, pushing past her esophagus and muscle until I got a grip on the vertebrae. I wrapped my fingers tight and yanked while Lucy froze in wide-eyed horror. I tugged and dug while the undead cheerleader struggled feebly against my monstrous grip. Finally, I got the hold I was looking for and yanked, one way with my right hand wrapped around her vertebrae, the other way with my left still holding a thick lock of her hair. I was rewarded with a sickening snap that still gives me nightmares. The girl went limp and I let go. She fell to the ground. Her throat was a horrid ruin and her head at an impossible angle to her body.

I looked at Lucy and she flinched—actually flinched—and took a step away from me. Yeah, I know. I'm a monster too.

Up on the roadside, several cars had finally stopped to investigate the wreck and the overturned truck, and I heard voices calling down.

"Time to go," I said. I was a walking catalog of incriminating evidence and everyone would be better off if they didn't have to meet me.

My car was done for. Ruined. We were gonna have to find a new ride.

A handful of people were already running down the slope to check for passengers in my car. "Come on," I barked at Lucy and didn't wait for her to follow.

I ran along the slope past the overturned semi-truck and the crumpled heap of the van. I didn't see any movement inside either vehicle and I didn't hang around to check. I got past the wreckage, angled up the slope to keep it between me and the approaching people. Once clear of all the carnage, I scrambled up to the roadside while scanning for an opportunity. Up ahead a black sedan had stopped, hazards lights on. The driver had was running to check on the accident. He didn't notice the bloody nightmare or angry redhead sneaking up the slope. I closed in cautiously, taking time to make sure there wasn't anyone still in the vehicle then squeezed into the driver's seat and waited for a count of three before putting the car in gear. The passenger door opened and Lucy climbed in without looking at me. Good. I stomped on the accelerator and sped away as fast as the car would go.

Chapter Fourteen

I drove as fast as the car would go for thirty minutes, figuring it would be a least that long before the owner realized his car was missing. I was also pretty sure all the law enforcement in the area would be converging on the evidence-laden wreckage for a while. That bought us enough time to get us to the next town where we could catch our breath. I stopped at a gas station and swapped license plates with another black car while Lucy went inside to get me something to eat.

I had left behind a scene of carnage. When the police figured out the owner of the shot-up Monte Carlo was nowhere to be found, that owner would jump to Person of Interest Number One. Lucky for me, Leonard E. Faunt didn't exactly exist but had an interesting enough personal history to keep authorities searching for a while. They wouldn't trace the vehicle back to me.

Lucy meekly offered to drive when she came back but didn't act disappointed when I turned her down. I was wide awake anyways. No sleep for the wicked. I slammed a little fruit-flavored energy drink and ate two convenience store sandwiches in a few bites before we hit the road again.

After a few miles, I couldn't take the silence anymore. I needed to get out of my own head, it was a dark place right now.

"How old are you?" I asked Lucy.

"None of your business."

I counted to three, "How did you get onto the Detail?"

She didn't answer.

"Ever been in a real fight before?"

"Why do you care? Does that make us war buddies now?"

Fine. This is how it's gonna go. Again.

"No," I said, "Not even close. I care because you blew through twelve bullets in ten seconds then lost the only knife we had."

"Fuck you."

"No, fuck you," I barked. "Why do I have to keep telling you the same shit? Fighting humans isn't fighting monsters. You obviously have no idea how to kill a vampire."

Her eyes widened.

"Yeah, Trigger," I said. "That was a vampire. You didn't know that did you? You don't know shit. You're so intent on staying pissed off at me that you actually believe you know better than me."

"How do you know they were vampires?"

"First clue would be the beating you gave that psycho cheerleader that didn't do a bit of damage. Second clue would be the dead eyes, dead skin, ungodly speed, unnatural strength, and the dried blood on her fucking face."

Lucy didn't say anything.

"I told you, if you're gonna kill monsters, you need to know what monster you're fighting so you can learn how to kill them."

She glared at me, "I know how to kill a vampire."

"Oh yeah? That's a relief. So you were just playing around. What were you waiting for? Someone to carve you a wooden stake?"

"That doesn't work."

"It doesn't?"

"That's a myth," she said, "Isn't it?"

"You're the expert."

Lucy crossed her arms and sighed, "I'm not an expert. It's what I heard."

"You hear that the same place you learned how to kill a Lycan?"

"I didn't show up at your shithole house expecting to become a big bad monster hunter," Lucy said. "You know that."

"Yeah, Winters changed that for you. So you need to know some shit. Like wooden stakes do work. Sometimes."

"That's helpful."

"It doesn't work on all types of vampires and there's only a few types of wood that will work."

"There are different kinds of vampires?"

"Yes, but a stake through the heart, is always useful; it's gonna hurt like hell and buy you some time."

"We didn't have any stakes."

"No. We also didn't have any bullets left."

"But bullets wouldn't have done any good either, smartass."

"Did you see me trying to rip out that girl's spine?"

Lucy shuddered.

"Imagine how effective several bullets into the base of the skull at point-blank range would have been," I took one of my hands, caked in dried blood, from the steering wheel to show Lucy, "and how much less messy."

"Fine, point taken," Lucy admitted.

That was progress.

"What would you have done?" Lucy asked. Her face looked like she was sucking on lemons but at least she was asking.

"I would have charged the van," I raised a finger before she could gloat or protest. "While firing a couple shots to keep their heads down then get in close so I can see what I'm shooting at. After that, bullets and brawn."

"You got the brawn down."

"My go-to is apeshit mode. Since they ambushed us, they wouldn't be expecting a quick counterattack."

"That's what I thought I was doing," Lucy said stiffly.

I nodded, "But you used up your primary weapon before you knew who or what you were shooting at. In my line—in your new line of work, you can't ever assume your enemy is a human. You gotta expect something other."

She glared at me for a moment, probably coming up with a hurtful insult, but ended up just saying, "Got it."

"Look," I said. "You're a badass, you can fight as good as anyone on the Detail. But there's a limit. You don't have the mass I do; it's a simple fact. You have agility and the advantage of speed. That's what you're built for. But you need to accept your weakness."

"What's your weakness?" Lucy snapped. Her automatic response seemed to always challenge good advice.

"Finesse," I said. "I don't have it."

I caught a brief grin in the darkness, but she quickly recovered and put her angry frown back on.

"Ok," she said, "You said we need to know our enemies. Those were vampires. Fine. Dealt with and done. Then tell me, Wise Guy, what came through that house? What does that kind of shit?"

I sighed, "Something really bad."

"Yeah, I guessed that much. When Dean said Rezruel, you didn't look happy at all. You talked about fallen angels and apparently that's different than demons."

"How do you feel about the end of the world?"

"I think it's great, everyone should try it," Lucy said. "What the hell kind of stupid question is that?"

Although I had seen a mere fragment of the sigil at St. Charles, I could see the whole thing in my mind. I saw it now, plain as day, painted in blood on the carpet. Yeah, it was blood. No doubt about it. I didn't want to admit it. I just didn't want it to be true. I sucked in a deep breath and held it there for a few seconds

"Spill it, Kemper," Lucy said.

"The Fallen brought forbidden knowledge to humans before God imprisoned them."

"More religious bullshit," Lucy mumbled.

I didn't let her derail me, "Some of them taught magic and celestial wisdom. Some taught war, some taught deception. The problem was they weren't benign and they weren't friends to humanity. They were jealous and spiteful. They made their own followers, Sons of the Fallen. In many ways, they were demons, but mostly just bastardizations of humans."

"Twisted people," Lucy said. "Whatever."

"Perversions," I jabbed a finger at her for emphasis, "perverted reflections of their creators. Rezruel was one of those perversions. A blood fiend."

"That sounds ominous."

"It is. He gets his strength from blood and blood energy."

"So, it's a vampire?"

"No. Not even close," I said. "I mean it when I say Rezruel will eat everything in his path. There will be a bow wave of death in front of him."

"You sound worried," Lucy said with a sneer in her voice.

"I am, cause I'm not stupid," I said, "and you should be worried too. This ain't a stake in the heart or a bullet in the head kind of monster. This is a rising from the heart of hell type of monster. If he broke out of God's penitentiary, we'll need some high-powered help."

"So you said. Your friend in KC?"

I nodded, "Blessed weapons. Holy water. Maybe even a Seal of Solomon. You don't kill these things."

"Wait, what? Really?"

"Yeah really," I said. "They're not technically alive. They're spirits. You banish them back to Dudael."

"You can't kill it?"

"No, not these things. You retire it and hope you do a good enough job that it can't come back for another couple millennia."

"I assume you retired this thing before?"

"Yup."

"How long ago?"

"Ten... no, twelve years," I said. "I was the last one to fight it. I nearly died in the fight," I tilted my head and tapped at the corner of a tattoo peeking up from beneath my shirt collar, "That's when I got this."

"Yes, I saw your tats, bro," Lucy said pointedly unimpressed.

"This tat saved my life," I said. "Rezruel almost killed me in that fight. Literally. Broke my rib cage, shattered my sternum, crushed my pulmonary artery, lacerated my left ventricle. Punctured my right lung and cracked my clavicle."

"Jesus!"

"Yeah," I said.

"How are you not dead, Kemper?"

"A lot of reconstructive surgery," I said, "and organ donors. Several. Also, some deep magic healing."

"And the tattoo is what, a reminder to keep your head down?"

"Binding spells," I said. "They kept the magic in place while it did its work rebuilding and strengthening my heart. I should probably be dead."

"You're some kind of... something."

"That I am," I said.

Chapter Fifteen

Lucy napped fitfully for the rest of the trip to KC, which was fine with me because I didn't feel like talking anymore. My retirement sucked so far. It was as violent and terrifying as when I was still working.

I stopped at a truck stop to clean up and buy some clothes without blood on them. Truck stops are a good one-stop shop for people with low expectations and broad standards. Naturally, Lucy didn't have any trouble finding something to fit. Some black yoga pants, a T-Shirt with a stupid joke about tornadoes on it, and a red flannel shirt. She wasn't happy with it but at least it fit her. I had to settle for a pair of extra baggy truck-stop jeans and a pair of rainbow suspenders to hold them up, a one-size-too-small T-shirt and a baby blue hoodie with a running horse screen-printed across the back. I felt ridiculous. I looked ridiculous.

We ditched the stolen car in the thick woods near Arrowhead Stadium and Lucy called up an Uber to pick us up. I didn't even know that was a thing you could do. Lucy said it was called living in the present and that there were a lot of things I didn't know I could do with my cellphone. She also said I was a dinosaur as well as an ape. Maybe she had a point. I asked her if she'd seen my cellphone and if she had she wouldn't be so surprised at what my phone couldn't do. Her response was "Di-No-Saur."

The driver took us to the West Bottoms, known to the locals as the Bottoms. It was an old warehouse district on the waterfront where the Kansas and Missouri Rivers meet. While a few industrial outfits still operated in the area, it has become mostly commercial. More accurately, it was *trendy commercial*. The area was especially popular in October when a few of the warehouses get converted into huge, haunted houses. Folks stand in line for hours to pay good money to have someone scare the hell out of them for entertainment.

People do crazy shit. Then again, I used to get paid to scare the hell out of myself. I guess we all do some crazy shit.

Not much had been left vacant in the Bottoms. Most of the old brick and mortar buildings had been renovated into microbreweries, themed restaurants, antique shops, and art studios. You know, places where a grumpy, scarred up, ape of a man dressed like a low-budget rodeo clown would stick out like a sore thumb. Lucy on the other hand blended right in. She was spitting image of the suburbanite health nut youngsters who wandered the streets of places like the Bottoms. Yoga pants and all.

The sky was grey when we got out of the car; it would be raining before the day was out. The few people who were out and about wandered in small groups, chatting and window shopping. Some of them wore oversized sweaters that are supposed to look vintage and expensive jeans that already have holes in them or leggings that look great for workouts but have probably never seen the inside of a gym. Nobody looked like they were ready for the coming storm. God, what a metaphor.

My buddy leased a small office in the back corner of one of the shops. The Arts and Oddities Boutique shared an old brick warehouse with a trendy home goods shop and a bistro. The Boutique was like a Bed, Bath and Beyond for the mystical and occult. The Addams Family or the Munsters would probably shop there if they were in town. The shop was packed with everything from harmless soaps with macabre names to actual magical relics with real sigils and workable runes on them, some of which could do real damage in the wrong hands. There were human skulls both authentic looking and not, stuffed ravens, spell books, both real and fantastical, ghastly medical instruments like bone saws and trepanning drills, a jar full of glass eyes, a rat skeleton, and some really weird stuff. I had met the shop owners on previous visits and had yet to figure out if they were serious practitioners of the arts or curious enthusiasts. Probably a little bit of both.

We had to pass through the shop to get to my buddy's office which naturally made me nervous. I felt it was a matter of time before I bumped into the wrong thing and unleashed a horde of flying monkeys or, even worse, had to buy it. Lucy surveyed the selection casually as we passed through, way too casually. She was on edge and I wasn't sure if it was me or the shop. Maybe it was just her nature. The shopkeepers were busy with customers when we passed through and didn't bother us, but there's no way they didn't notice my passing. You can't *not* see me when there are fragile finery and glass shelves in the vicinity.

Once we got through the shop and to the storage area in the back, I stopped and made sure I had Lucy's undivided attention.

She looked at me the only way she knew how. With a scowl.

"This guy is my friend," I said, "A good friend. Don't be your rude-ass self with him."

Lucy rolled her eyes, "I don't have any reason to hate him... yet."

"I'm serious," I said, "he's good people and he's part of the good fight. Don't burn this bridge."

"How would I do that?"

"By being weird about his name for one thing."

"What's his name?"

"Lazarus Grey."

"Really?"

"Yeah. Really. And try not to stare."

Lucy scowled, "Stare at what?"

The office door swung open and my friend stepped out to greet us.

He was about six-foot-tall, maybe a little less, average build with brown hair and one brown eye. I didn't know what color the other was because it was hidden behind an eyepatch made of hammered iron. Like me, Lazarus preferred subdued colors and simple clothes;

the eyepatch was attention-grabbing all on its own. Also, like me, he sported a lot of tattoos, almost all of them of runic influence. Many were purely ornamental though. He was much more stylish than me that way, and not nearly as battered.

"I thought I heard your voice buddy!"

I could hide a smile as I embraced him, "Great to see you Laz!"

"God, you look like hell," he said and he stepped back to look at me. "Did you wrestle mob of broken glass monsters or something?"

"Or something," I said. "How you been?"

He shrugged, "I get by. And who is the pretty lumberjack cosplayer?"

"Funny," Lucy didn't smile, but was at least cordial enough to offer a hand, "Lucille Red."

Lazarus shook hands, "Firm handshake. Are you a used car salesman?"

Lucy allowed herself a wry smile.

"She's an... associate," I said.

"Oh?" Lazarus said, "You're here on business then?"

" 'Fraid so."

"Figures, I should know better than to think you'd just stop by for a friendly visit. You never just come by for my warm company and witty conversation."

"Not this time," I said.

"Not ever," Laz said. "Oh well, step into my parlor."

"Said the spider to the fly," Lucy mumbled as we followed Lazarus into the office space.

The room was small and cramped. Overloaded shelves lined one wall, full of more oddities. Old leather-bound books with strange titles and symbols, half-burned candles, intricately carved wooden boxes, and jars of questionable content. Cardboard boxes and plastic totes lined another wall. A large dry erase board covered with runes and calculations blocked a large window. Lazarus's desk was an ancient oak specimen with a good hundred years or more of character including ink stains, gouges, coffee rings, and a pair of bullet holes. Unlike the rest of the office, it was pretty tidy, with only a couple of notepads, a pearl-handled dagger, and a metal rod on it. He cleared some old newspapers and an old leather satchel from two ancient wooden chairs and motioned for us to sit.

"Coffee?" he pointed at the coffee maker on the shelf, which didn't look to have been used in weeks.

"No," I said, "I still have good taste."

"Anything for you, Miss Red? Wait, is that your name?"

"Lucy will do," she said through clenched teeth.

He held up his hands defensively, "Ok, ok. I didn't mean to offend, it caught me off guard."

"I would think a man with a metal eyepatch wouldn't be so easily caught off guard by a name," Lucy said dryly.

"Touché," Lazarus said.

"Manners," I reminded Lucy.

"He started it," she said.

"It's ok," Lazarus waved me off, "I wouldn't go out in public like this if I couldn't handle people looking and talking." He tapped the eyepatch with a fingernail. I flashed an unfriendly look at Lucy, but she ignored me.

"Sorry anyways," I said. "How's business?"

"Slow," he said. "Council work has tapered off lately. They're getting paranoid. Private gigs are paying the rent at least."

"Yeah? A lot of private sector folk in the market for rune-fortified weaponry?"

"More like ritual candles and protective trinkets,"

"Really?"

"Oh yea, you wouldn't believe it," he said. "There's a good trade in hobby practitioners and superstitious urbanites. Nothing powerful really. Chime candles, bolines, totem pouches. That kind of stuff."

I tried to imagine Barbara Billingsly carving runes in a ritual candle with a white-handled knife, "Isn't that like giving a kid a loaded gun?"

"More like giving a monkey spoon," Lazarus said, "I'm not selling anything dangerous to anyone who doesn't know what they're doing. Nothing they couldn't figure out on their own."

"I guess you know what you're doing."

"Damned right I do," Lazarus said seriously.

Lucy rolled her eyes.

"So, what's up with the angry chick?" Lazarus said to me. "You never ran with a younger much more attractive sidekick before."

"The chick isn't a sidekick, and she has a name," Lucy said.

"I know," Lazarus said, "but I can't say it with a straight face."

Lucy sat up a little straighter in her chair, a little like a cobra eying a mongoose.

"She's not a sidekick," I said calmly, "She's an apprentice of sorts."

"Oh?" Lazarus raised an eyebrow, "sharing the wisdom of your many, many, many years of violent and misguided experience with the violent and misguided youth?"

"He's quitting," Lucy said plainly. "He's a quitter, and I have to clean up after him."

Lazarus looked at me for confirmation. I nodded.

"I see," Lazarus said. "And I suppose you expect me to equip her?"

"No," I said.

"Is there a problem with equipping me?" Lucy leaned forward; fists clenched.

Lazarus leaned forward smiling, then began to roll the small iron rod back and forth between his hands, "Yes there is a problem with that."

"Why?" Lucy demanded.

"Because I don't know you."

"So what? I don't know you either"

He laughed and looked at me, "Where did you find this girl?"

"She... found me," I said.

Lucy placed her hands on the table, dangerously close to Laz's, "What is your issue with me, Cyclops?"

Shit.

"My issue," Lazarus said, "is I don't give loaded guns to moody children."

Lucy bolted to her feet, but Lazarus was as quick as her, if not quicker. He held his little metal rod in hand, pointed at Lucy. It was dark, like iron with bands of gold at either end. Lazarus had acquired it shortly before the last time I had seen him. He was still learning about its unique properties when I left him.

Lucy assumed a combat-ready stance, ready to defend herself, ready to attack, "What is that? A magic wand? Try it Dumbledor, see what happens."

Lazarus lowered his hands and chuckled for a second, "That's good. You got a sharp tongue and a fast one."

"Say the wrong thing and I'll cut yours out," Lucy said.

I groaned. She just didn't know when to stop.

Lazarus smiled warmly, looking readier to accept a hug than an attack. I knew better. I wasn't sure if Lucy was smart enough to know better. He raised the rod slowly to his lips with a smirk and whispered something very quietly. Then he casually tossed the small rod to Lucy. Surprised, Lucy snatched the rod out of the air and fell over backward with it, and crashed to the floor.

She lay on the ground with the rod on her chest, struggling to breathe unable to move the rod, as if it weighed several hundred pounds. Lazarus walked around the desk and leaned over her watching her struggle for a few seconds. Then he whispered something as he reached for the rod and removed it as if it were light as a feather. He returned to his chair, twirling the rod between his fingers like a drummer who just pulled off a killer solo. and sat down. Lucy caught her breath after a moment then hopped to her feet, seething. I held out an arm—without touching her—before she committed to a drawn out fight. I'd seen what Laz can do. She'd only scratched the surface.

"What the hell is that thing?" Lucy demanded.

Lazarus said, "I'm not going to tell you its name, because it's sensitive and it likes me. But what matters to you it can have the mass and size that I ask it to."

"That's not possible."

Lazarus place the rod gently on the desktop and shrugged, "If you say so."

Lucy unclenched her fists, but not her jaw, "Do that again. Try to do that again."

"Lucy," I said. "Enough. We don't need the hostility."

"Fuck you," she said. "I don't have to take this."

"Yes, you do," I said. "We do."

I swear she clenched her jaw even tighter.

"Laz," I said, "Please, I need some new tools. You know me."

"Really? More tools? What about all the stuff you already have?"

"Well," I said, "some of it was stolen."

"Stolen?" Laz narrowed his eye, "from you?"

"By the High Councilor himself."

Lucy huffed, "He didn't steal anything from you, you big idiot."

"I ain't having this talk again," I said.

Lazarus nodded appreciatively, "Well, that old wizard is crafty. No denying that."

"Crafty?" I scoffed. "He's a clever bastard."

"Wise," Lucy corrected, "wiser than you'll ever be."

"Not the point," I said.

Lazarus rolled the rod idly back and forth between his hands,

"You said some of it was stolen. What happened to the rest?"

"I um... I may have discarded some of them in an act of petty defiance when I resigned."

"Resigned? For real, you actually quit? You're serious?" Lazarus shook his head in disbelief.

"I was serious at the time," I said.

"So... what do you want from me? A flashy sword to hang over your fireplace as a memento?"

"Do you have one?" Lucy asked.

Lazarus ignored her.

"Not exactly," I said. "I had to take this one last... assignment... and it's a big one."

"Big one huh? How big?"

I didn't want to say.

"I don't want to say."

"How big?" he asked again.

Lucy snapped her fingers at me, "Spit it out, Kemper. We need to get this ball rolling."

"Looks like it's Rezruel."

"Holy shit!"

"Yeah."

"That shouldn't be possible."

"I know. But things are bad right now. We need some of your special touch."

"Whatever that means," Lucy mumbled.

"How old are you?" Lazarus asked.

"Why does everyone keep asking me that?"

"Because you look like a sixteen-year-old cheerleader with a chip on her shoulder," Lazarus said, "but I bet you're not sixteen or a cheerleader..."

"Fuck you."

"And Fuck you. I'm not going to give a handgun to a minor."

"Handgun?" Lucy blinked, "You have guns?"

"Of course, I have guns," he said. He held up his arms in mock bodybuilder style, "Two of 'em right here."

Lucy did not laugh.

"Yeah, I got guns. I wouldn't be much of a weapon master if I didn't," Laz said.

"I'm twenty-one," Lucy said. "Is that good enough for you?"

"Suits me just fine," Lazarus said, "but the law doesn't run on your say so. How much time do I have to work with here Bill?"

I shrugged, "Don't really know. Not much I expect. If Rezruel is loose, the end of the world will be knocking on our door pretty damn fast."

"Obviously that's not enough time for custom tuned enchantments," he said. "Tell me you at least have the Holy Handgun?"

Lucy raised her eyebrows, "Holy Handgun?"

I waited for a beat or two, "That was one of the carelessly discarded items."

"Wow," Lazarus said, and his shoulders slumped visibly. "That hurts my feelings. That was one of my crowning achievements."

"It was," I agreed.

Lazarus looked at Lucy, "Smith & Wesson 629 Classic, .44 Magnum. Hand-etched runes. Custom enchantments. My own invention, the Proportional Mass runes spell was inlaid into the barrel, every bullet packs a punch like a freight train. When loaded with Vampire's Curse bullets bound to the Vampire's Bain runes on the gun... man, it was a vampire killing son of a bitch... and tuned to Bill's inner chi. God, it's a... was a work of art."

"What the fuck Kemper?" Lucy spun on me, "you threw that away?"

"It was an act of passion," I said feebly.

Lazarus slumped into his seat. "You don't make things easy for me."

"That's not my way," I said.

"Ain't that the truth," Lazarus screwed up his mouth for a second and frowned, "I'm gonna have to get creative. I have some things in my workshop that will probably work. Of course, they won't be tuned to you and not for retiring Rezruel. You'll have to make do."

"That's the only kind of making I know," I said.

Lazarus sighed, "Ok. I'll see what I can do. You two can wait here if you want or at the coffee shop next door."

"We'll need some wheels too," I said.

"Damn, Bill. Ok. North from here a couple blocks, there's a custom motorcycle shop on the corner. There's a fenced-in lot to the left, looks like a junkyard. Guy sells used cars."

"We're on a budget," I said.

"Figured. He's closed anyway. I'll meet you there in an hour and set you up with a ride. Dude's a friend, we'll work it out."

"Okay," I shook Lazarus' hand again, "thanks Laz. I really do appreciate this. You always come through."

"Don't keep me on that pedestal," he said. "I'll just fall off."

"You're snoring," Lucy barked.

I jerked awake, and saved myself from falling out of the chair, "Sorry. I'm tired. And hungry."

"You're always tired and hungry."

"I'm a big man."

"No shit," Lucy said and got up from her chair, "but I wouldn't eat anything in this place," Lucy said.

"Me either," I said and got up too, "There's a little shop next door."

"Bistro, Lucy said, "I saw it."

"Yeah. That."

"Fine, let's make it quick though. Hopefully, one-eye will be back soon."

"Be respectful."

"I am," Lucy said defensively. "What's his deal anyway?"

"He's single," I said leading the way out of the office.

"That's not what I mean smartass. The eye patch, what's up with that?"

"Ask him," I said as I stopped to idly inspect a stack of Necronomicon replicas, "His eye was... damaged while trying to stop an incursion."

"He's an agent?"

"No," I said. "Wizards and Hunters worked incursions back then, about twenty years ago. Agents are a product of your generation."

"He can't be more than thirty," Lucy said.

"Thirty-one," I said, leaving the horror prop books behind.

"So, he was like what, eleven and fighting incursions?"

"His dad was."

"A Hunter?"

"A wizard."

"Bullshit."

"Believe what you want," I stopped and turned to her. "Laz ain't a wizard but he's got a gift for magic things."

"Like that stick thing?"

"Yes, like that stick thing."

"This place creeps me out."

"Get used to it. This is kid stuff."

"I don't like it."

I shrugged, "Some people do."

"Let's get out of here," she said, "I feel like a sitting duck in this place. Like a sitting duck on a powder keg."

I said the way to deeper into the storage area, where I assumed a back door would be.

We were about ten feet from the rear exit when one of the Boutique's employees caught up to us. He was a young man—a little older than Lucy, maybe—dressed in several alternating layers of black and white, with loud circular red glasses, dark green hair that almost covered his eyes and blue lips. More black and silver jewelry than I could count and a tattoo on his neck that said "Not A Step" in stenciled lettering.

"Mister," he said quietly, "You need to go out through the front."

"Why?" Lucy demanded.

I flashed her an irritated look, "Why?" I asked less demandingly.

The young man looked around as if checking to see if anyone was listening, "Someone just came in looking for you two... specifically looking for you... a 'big beast of a man with a delicious young red-headed girl.'"

"Delicious?" I repeated.

"Who was it," Lucy asked, "cops?"

"Sound like cops to you?" I looked down my nose at Lucy.

"You maybe," she said.

"Definitely not," the green-haired kid said, "it wasn't cops. Just a woman. She was all bundled up with a way oversized hoodie pulled tight around her face. She looked pretty sketchy, if you know what I mean."

"Sketchy?" Lucy huffed, "In this place?"

"I know what you mean," I said to the kid. "What'd you tell her?"

"That you two bolted out the back," he said.

"Bless your heart," I said.

"And she bought it?" Lucy asked.

The kid nodded, "Seems like. You're Bill, right? Bill Kemper."

"That's what I tell people."

He shook my hand, "Laz talks about you. So cool to meet you in person. I feel like I'm meeting, I don't know, a character out of a book, like the Witcher or something"

"Shrek?" Lucy offered.

"Uh, thanks," I said. To the guy, not Lucy.

"I'm Arlen," he said, "just Arlen."

"Well thanks, Just Arlen," I said.

"We better get moving," Lucy said. "I'm getting antsy."

I nodded, "Thanks again, Arlen. I owe you one."

"Glad to help," Arlen led us back through the store. Lucy scanned everyone as we passed, coiled like a snake ready to strike. I gave her a little space, deciding it was best not to crowd her in this condition.

Nobody attacked us and we made it through the shop without breaking any relics or releasing any ancient curses.

"Thanks again Arlen," I shook his hand.

Before he could say anything, Lucy yanked the door open, "Come on, Colossus." She walked out the door ahead of me and turned north. I shrugged at Arlen and followed on her heels.

If we were being watched or followed there wasn't much we could do about it. We might at least see them coming since we were out in the open. Or maybe we'd just make easier targets. Sometimes optimism ain't my strong suit.

The wind had picked up a little and a light rain had started to fall while we were in the shop, just enough to wet the sidewalks and streets. Shoppers rushed into stores and climbed back into their vehicles. Lucy and I took our time. Wet was the least of our concerns at the moment.

We didn't even get a block away before shit got real again.

A grey Dodge Charger with all the lights and markings of a Missouri State Trooper screeched around the corner at the end of the block, lights flashing but no siren blaring. It fish-tailed then caught traction and made a beeline for Lucy and me. There's little else like the fight or flight reflex that wrestles for control in your body when two tons of heavy metal is racing straight at you. The driver gunned the engine and the patrol car jumped the curb.

Chapter Sixteen

There was no cover, except for a small sapling planted in a gap in the sidewalk. I waited for the vehicle to get too close to alter course and dove to the right, while Lucy dove left. I slammed into the brick wall with an angry grunt as the car thundered past me and sheared off the tree at the base. The cruiser skidded to a stop then the reverse lights came on.

"Shit!" I barked and jumped back across the sidewalk toward the road, and barely avoided becoming a smear on the side of the building as the rear quarter of the Charger crunched and scraped along the bricks. I tumbled gracelessly to a stop next to Lucy, who had already regained her feet. The car's wheels spun, and tires squealed again. The vehicle screeched back onto the street, but we were too close to it now, and we had the advantage of maneuverability. As it passed dangerously close, I caught sight of the driver and another figure in the back seat.

What the hell!?

The driver was the kid from the ambush on the interstate. The hooded figure in the back was a blur of black and green.

The vehicle skidded sideways to a stop. The dark figure didn't even bother to roll down a window. Glass exploded outward with a deafening thunder.

The shockwave passed between me and Lucy with a shower of red dust exploding out from where the bullet struck the brick building, leaving a crater as big as a car tire.

"Son of a bitch!" Lucy roared, taking the words right out of my mouth. I saw actual rage in her eyes before she charged the vehicle. Would have been a good plan if we had weapons. I followed anyway, and the gun thundered again, chewing a pothole in the road. Lucy made it to the car first and reached into the broken window. Suddenly her body slammed up against the door like someone was trying to pull her in. I caught an unmistakable flash of silver—a gun barrel—as it swept past Lucy's face and aimed at me.

I jumped forward and slammed the barrel upwards as it discharged again. The roar left my ears ringing and stars flashing in my vision. The shooter yanked the gun back out of my grasp. I rammed a shoulder into Lucy, knocking her free of the vehicle and we both fell to the wet street as the gun barked again. A familiar voice spit out a string of curses and the patrol car door swung open. The gun appeared first, followed by the hand that held it. A graceful hand with black fingernails and baby-smooth pale skin. With the Holy Handgun, pointed at my face, she began to step out of the vehicle. Her green dress became wet in the falling rain and stuck to her legs. The hood draped over her head, hiding all but her eyes. Those brilliant green eyes.

Mehira.

There's something about me that makes people want to gloat before killing me. Kinda hurts my feelings, but it had saved my life a time or two. Not this time, though. Mehira didn't say anything. Her lips drew back into an angry—no, hateful—sneer and she pulled the trigger.

As luck would have it, Lucy is an angry bitch, too. She kicked the open cruiser door as Mehira fired, slamming it against her extended arm, rewarding the effort with a satisfying crunch. The gun's discharge nearly shook my brain out of its cage, but the bullet exploded into the pavement, peppering my face with chunks of asphalt. I got up fast and rushed for the open door. Mehira pulled the trigger as I jumped in. Click!

"Six shots, Bitch!" I spat. I threw a fist at her but didn't have a good angle. The blow didn't land. Mehira swung the pistol and smacked me against the side of my head. She swung again, hitting my ear. Getting hit in the ear with a steel frame revolver hurts like hell, I don't care how tough you are. Searing pain flashed through my whole head. I pushed further into the vehicle and grabbed a handful of her hair. The driver twisted to help Mehira. He pawed at my hands and tried to bite me. Little shit! I heard the driver-side door open, followed by a flurry of fists and red hair.

Mehira grunted in frustration and hit me with the gun again on the back of my head repeatedly. My vision flashed white. With my free hand, I tried to wrench the gun from her fingers, but she was stronger than she looked. In the struggle, she worked a foot up and planted it against my chest then began to punch me with her empty hand. After about twelve million blows to the head, my grip on Mehira's surprisingly silky hair loosened a little. She extended her leg, sending me flying back out of the car. I landed on the wet road, flat on my back. Mehira tried to reload the gun with one hand, but she wasn't as practiced as I was.

Lucy screamed, and Mehira looked over her shoulder then back at me with a look of satisfaction.

It was short lived.

There came another rumble, from down the street, the deep rumble of a muscle car that grabs you down in your gut. A black early 70s model Camaro raced toward us. It closed the distance in just a couple of seconds and hit the trooper car head-on. Panic flashed in Mehira's eyes before the airbags deployed and the car leapt backward about twenty feet. The blow threw Lucy from the car, leaving her laying on the ground across from me. The Camaro survived the collision and the engine rumbled on, even though the front bumper and hood had crumpled. They don't make cars like that anymore.

"Get in!" Lazarus yelled from the driver's seat.

I ran to Lucy, who was cradling her hand against her chest. She got up before I could help her and climbed into the backseat of the car. I jammed myself into the passenger seat. Lazarus gunned the engine and we roared away from the scene.

Chapter Seventeen

The 1975 Chevy Camaro, like many cars of the era, was built like a tank. Mostly steel and rubber. The car had survived the head-on collision with relatively little damage to the body and none to the 350 cubic inch V-8 engine. Under normal circumstances, just listening to it rumble as Laz spirited us away would be enough to ease my nerves, however, Lucy's continuous flurry of profanity from the cramped back seat and the pressure inside my skull ruined the mood.

I didn't have the energy to turn around, "Are you okay?"

"No, I'm not okay," Lucy's voice too loud and an octave higher than normal, "that fucker bit me. It bit me! Oh, shit, it bit me." She clutched her hand desperately to her chest

Lucy held up her left hand, trembling. It wasn't the bloody mess I expected based on how freaked out she sounded. There was a set of bite marks on the meaty part of her hand, it probably wouldn't even leave a scar. It was bleeding some but nothing to be alarmed about. No flesh or meat missing.

Her eyes were wide, and her lips were trembling.

"It's not that bad," I said, "look at this." I pointed in the general direction of my bleeding head.

"Not that bad?" Lucy wailed. "That bloodsucking, vampire, son of a bitch bit me!"

"Hell, yeah it did," I said.

Lazarus laughed.

"Fuck you!" Lucy yelled.

Lazarus elbowed me, "She thinks she's going to turn into a vampire."

"Oh!" I said, "Wait, really?"

Lucy hugged her hand against her chest again, "Aren't I?"

"Not from that," I shook my head, and quickly regretted it. I still felt like all my marbles were loose.

Lazarus chuckled, "It doesn't work that way."

"It doesn't?" her voice softened a little. "Are you sure?"

I said, "We're sure. That bite is just a bite."

"Here," Lazarus flipped open his armrest console and dug out a small plastic bottle with a cross drawn on it in black marker. "Rinse it off with this."

"It's for infection," I took the bottle and opened it for Lucy. She snatched it from me and dumped it all on her hand. She let out another, more subdued, string of profanity as the holy water reacted with trace amounts of vampire saliva. The wound fizzed, and Lucy clamped her other hand tightly over it, gritting her teeth and squeezing her eyes shut.

I settled back into the seat, "You saved our asses, man. Thanks"

"Arlen texted me," Lazarus explained, "said someone came in looking for you guys and you bolted. He was worried there would be trouble."

I said, "He was right about that."

"They were the same ones from the highway," Lucy said. "Two of them at least."

"What highway?" he asked.

I sighed, "We were ambushed last night on the way here. I thought we took care of them."

"We didn't," Lucy said needlessly.

"Clearly."

"Do you know them?" Lazarus asked.

"Yeah. I know one of them. The woman... she's a vampire."

"A vampire? You know it's the middle of the day, right?" Lazarus said.

"It's cloudy," I offered.

"You know that's not how it works."

"She's highly motivated," Lucy said. "Like she hates his guts."

Lazarus said, "Why is that?"

"I might have wiped out her entire species and stopped right before killing her too."

"No," Lucy's voice cracked.

"Yes," I said.

Lucy kicked the back of my seat. "She's the job you quit on? Her?"

"Yeah," I said, "apparently she hates me now."

"Well, she can get in line!" Lucy spat.

"Jesus, Bill," Lazarus said.

"I know," I said.

"She had a gun," Lucy said. "Do vampires use guns?"

I didn't want to talk about it, "I don't want to talk about it."

"She had a gun?" Laz asked, "Really? That's unorthodox... for a vampire."

"A canon," Lucy said. "That gun was a monster. I never saw a pistol with that kind of power."

Lazarus looked at me and raised an eyebrow.

I nodded solemnly.

"What?" Lucy demanded.

"Are you freaking kidding me?" Lazarus punched his steering wheel.

"What?" Lucy demanded again.

"She has the Holy Handgun," I said quietly.

"What is wrong with you?" Lucy roared.

"Holy shit, Bill," Lazarus said. Lucy kicked my seat again, harder.

"I know," I kind of thought she'd be grateful for my sudden change of heart. Instead, she somehow managed to track me down and was trying to kill me with my own enchanted weapon. Seems I had left her with a much different impression than intended.

"She doesn't have any of the vampire's curse bullets," I said. "There weren't any left."

"Proportional Mass runes still work with regular bullets,"

Lazarus said.

"I noticed," I said.

"Fortunately, she isn't a very good shot," Lucy said.

"A 44-magnum kicks like a mule," I said. "Proportional Mass bumps that up a lot with each shot, and she's probably never used a gun before."

"Hatred is a strong motivator," Lucy said.

"Bill seems to attract motivated people."

"I noticed," Lucy said.

I rubbed my temples and wasn't sure if it helped or made it worse. The pain was consistent at this point.

"You need to get that back," Lazarus said. "I can't have something like that gun in the hands of a supernatural. That shit is bad for business."

"I will."

"Why don't you try to sweet talk her," Lucy said. "You're great at that."

"Shut up," I said. "One crisis at a time."

"Ok," Lucy said. "Which one is your favorite?"

"Rezruel," I said. "That one matters most."

"So? What's our move, oh wise and learned Hunter?"

"I have someone working on that."

"Who?" Lucy and Lazars asked in unison. Lucy frowned at him.

"Did you manage to get anything we can use?"

"I always come through," Lazarus said.

After several minutes, we pulled off in an abandoned alleyway. Lazarus popped the trunk and a few plastic cases. He looked around furtively before opening the first. In it was a blue-handled framing hammer and a handful of large nails.

"Um," I said.

"Peace," Lazarus said, "be still." He removed the hammer and handed it to me. It was a common Estwing, 25 ounce "Big Blue" framing hammer, one of the most common and recognizable hammers in the world. This one however had a few notable alterations. Several runes had been inlaid with silver and copper along the main shaft above the handle and along the head of the hammer. I recognized one of them, "Proportional Mass". My favorite. Additionally, a crucifix had been engraved in relief on the face of the hammer so if I hit something, it would leave an impression. Literally.

"Ok," I said. "I'll have to get in close, but it'll do."

"That's the price we pay," Lazarus took the hammer back and placed it back in the case. "And that's your forte anyway, up close and personal. Of course, I didn't have time to tune it to your soul—but you know how enchanted weapons work—it'll still do some damage."

I nodded, "And the nails?"

"A little extra help," he picked one up and showed it to me. They were about six inches long, hand-forged nails with a rune engraved on the head.

"Reactive rune?"

"Got in one guess," he said. "Smack that with the Proportional Mass on the hammer and you'll get some serious force."

"That's a good start."

Lucy was not impressed, "I'm not impressed."

"Be patient my angry new friend and open your mind," Lazarus said as he closed the box with the hammer and nails before opening the next one.

The Glock is one of the most common handguns in the world, easily recognizable and highly customizable. This one had the works.

Lucy reached for it then stopped.

"May I?" she asked with genuine respect.

"Go for it," Laz said. Lucy picked up the gun and racked the slide to make sure it was empty before examining it.

"This is a forty-five!" she said with genuine excitement.

"Yes, it is," he said, "Glock 21, chambered for 45 ACP. Its name is Holy Glockamolie."

Lucy's eyes snapped to Lazarus, "That's the stupidest thing I've ever heard."

"You're young," Lazarus said, "you'll hear stupider things."

"I'm not calling it that," she said.

"That's its name," Lazarus shrugged, "Standard magazine capacity is thirteen rounds. There's three loaded mags in the case there."

Lucy turned the weapon over, admiring the craftsmanship. Intricate engraving covered most of the surface on the metal slide. Runes—or specifically runic spells—were inlaid in copper, iron, and silver.

"I don't see Proportional Mass," I said.

Lazarus shook his head, "No. Steel frame revolvers are about the only gun that can handle that much power. Steel frame revolvers, like the Holy Handgun."

Lucy shook her head, "Shameful Kemper."

I swallowed a retort. They were right.

Laz listed some of the features as Lucy admired the weapon, "Trijicon night sights, ported barrel, enhanced trigger, beveled mag well for faster reloads."

"I'm going to swoon," Lucy said.

"It doesn't have Proportional Mass, but there are a few other tried and true goodies. Vampire's Curse, although I don't have any Vampire's Bane bullets right now. There's Holy Invocation. And Iron Heartbeat. Courageous Monkey. Happy Eagle."

Lucy giggled, actually giggled, "Are you making those up? They sound like B-movie Kung Fu moves."

"They're real," Laz said and tapped a booklet in the pelican case.

"Read the instructions. They matter."

Lucy rolled her eyes.

"I'm serious," Lazarus said. "Don't fool around with enchanted weapons if you don't know what you're doing."

"I know how to handle a gun."

"Magic gun," Lazarus said, "It's not the same thing, and take care of it. It's a loaner."

"Loaner?" Lucy protested.

"Yes," he said. "That gun is a prototype and while it's an unlicensed magical firearm, it's still a firearm. There are kinds of red tape tied to the sale of something like this that'll make your toes curl."

"Fine, Ok," she said. "I'll take care of it... as if it were my firstborn child."

I chuckled. I actually believed she meant it.

While Lucy continued to admire the pistol, I opened another one of the cases to reveal a sawed-off shotgun and a few boxes of extra shells.,

"Yeah. Wouldn't want to break any laws."

Lazarus pointed at it, "That would be a felony, except it doesn't exist."

I picked it up, "Ten gauge. Really?"

"Yup."

"No rune work?"

"No, that's just for home defense," Lazarus said. "But these slugs have toxic amounts of iron and silver in them. One box of slugs, one box of double-ought buckshot. Use them wisely; that's all there is, and you'll have a hard time finding more ten-gauge shells."

"No kidding," I said. "You're not one for mainstream, are you?"

"You want mainstream, go to the mall."

"What's that?" Lucy pointed at a bundle, wrapped in a large purple beach towel.

Lazarus unrolled the towel to reveal a pair of swords. One had a long tapering blade and an elaborate brass guard that could cover the entire hand., A genuine basket-hilt claymore. The other sword had a gently curved blade with a D-shaped brass bar covering the grip. It looked like an old standard-issue cavalry saber.

At that moment, the clouds broke briefly, and light shone on them just right, revealing runes on the steel of both swords, or rather in the steel. They were etched instead of engraved.

"Are those magic swords?" Lucy asked.

Lazarus nodded.

"Honest to goodness enchanted swords?" her voice slightly hushed.

"Killicutty," Lazarus pointed at the claymore then at the saber, "Heir Chop-A-Lot."

"You named the swords too," Lucy said.

"They have names. Killicutty and Heir Chop-A-Lot."

"I'm not calling them that."

"That's your choice."

"You had these just sitting around?" I asked.

Lazarus shrugged, "Couple of clients backed out awhile back. It's the best I can do on short notice."

"We'll make do," I said.

"The only kind of making you know."

"Can we keep the car?" Lucy asked.

"Not on your life."

"But it's all beat to hell," she said lamely.

"You're all beat to hell too," Laz said. "You'll mend. So will my car."

"We still need a vehicle," Lucy protested, "something Brutus here can fit in."

"He hasn't forgot," I said placatingly.

"Your ride is back at the Bottoms," Laz covered the swords then put the Holy Glockamolie back in its case.

"That's problematic," I said.

"Yeah, that describes most of the situations that you bring to me," Lazarus said. "The neighborhood is probably crawling with cops by now. But that's where the car is. Unless you wanna go steal one."

Lucy shook her head, "That wouldn't be ideal."

"Nothing ever is," I said. "Any other ideas?"

"Uber?" Lazarus offered.

"Funny," Lucy said, deadpanned.

Chapter Eighteen

Laz called Arlen at the shop to see how things were unfolding. He said a single KCPD cruiser car was patrolling the neighborhood but that was about it. Someone had reported gunshots but there weren't any witnesses. Cops found the beat-up Highway Patrol Vehicle, but no one had seen the driver. The trooper who belonged to it had reported it stolen from a vehicle accident earlier in the morning.

By the time we got back to the neighborhood, a tow truck had already come and hauled away the wrecked vehicle. Fifteen minutes later, Lucy and I were back on the road in a nondescript grey Crown Victoria. It's a good vehicle to disappear in. Paint it yellow, it's every taxi you ever saw. Paint it black and white, it's every cop car you ever saw. They're reliable and roomy and don't really draw much attention. I had given Laz a roll of Benjamins—most of the cash I had left—which was more than enough for the weaponry and the Crown Vic, but I felt bad about his car getting banged up for our sake. So there was some extra for that. Maybe he could get some spinning rims for something.

Lucy wanted to hurry up and get back to St. Louis before I had any other bright ideas. We could be out of KC in less than an hour if we didn't screw around; hopefully, we could do so without drawing any more attention. Lucy volunteered to drive again. I think she liked the control.

It was midafternoon and raining like a bastard by the time we hit the interstate. I was hungry, my head was pounding, my chest was sore, and my side was bleeding again where Lucy's stitch job had been pulled loose. I looked like hell and felt like hell's underbelly.

I found myself thinking about that Pumpkin Spice coffee and Sarah sitting across from me laughing at my reaction. I thought about the last vampire I'd killed, almost decapitating her with my bare hands, and what kind of reaction Sarah would have if she could have seen what kind of monster I really was. I thought about Leo's question when we sat in the car outside the Blue Sky just last night. God, it felt like days ago. But it was just last night.

"What is it about her?" he had asked. I didn't really know then. I still didn't. It wasn't puppy love, and it wasn't teenage infatuation. It was more like a pull. Like a moth to a flame, as I had said. And why did I miss her so much right now? It had only been hours, really. I'd gone days without stepping foot in the Blue Sky in the past. If I'd had my way, I would already be on my way to retirement on a semi-secluded beach somewhere where I'd never see Sarah or Alex or anyone at the Blue Sky again.

What was different now? People don't just change overnight. Do they? I'd been gradually thinking more and more about quitting the Hunt. The better I got at killing monsters, the more I found myself thinking about not doing it anymore. By the time I was the best at it I had grown to hate it and didn't even realize it. Now, I hated it even more now. Maybe it was anger for having to do the job that made me so effective. Maybe I didn't hate the monsters, I just hated that what I did was necessary.

The very person to whom I thought I was showing mercy was trying to kill me now. She hated me, maybe as much as I hated myself. And when would it end? After I find and retire Rezruel again? If I find Rezruel. Mehira wouldn't just go away after that. Would she? I'd have to kill her too in the end or let her finish me. God, that pissed me off. Bill Kemper, monster killer. Forever. Bill Kemper, a monster forever.

Maybe that's what appealed to me about Sarah. She didn't look at me like a monster, like the monster I was, like the monster people's imaginations told them I was. She didn't know. Better yet, she made me forget I was a monster. Strange, I would have thought someone like her would make me even more aware of what kind of man I was. Like a thundering dragon next to a daisy. But she didn't. She let me feel normal. Even if it was only for the time it took me to drink a cup of coffee and eat a piece of toast.

Lucy's voice yanked me out of my thoughts, "What's wrong with you? Are you getting loopy?"

"What are you talking about?"

"You're smiling like a dope," she said unkindly.

"Thinking about daisies and coffee," I mumbled.

"You got a concussion?"

I shrugged, "Probably. I get hit in the head a lot."

"You're not going to pass out, are you? I can't carry you anywhere."

"I'll survive. Believe it or not, I've been through worse."

"If you say so," Lucy looked at me skeptically.

"I fell into the Grand Canyon once," I looked out the side window at the cityscape zipping by but only saw red desert stone, "Broke a lot of bones, and punctured a lung."

"Fell into the Grand Canyon?"

I nodded, and my head protested, "Technically I jumped. I had hold of a vampire at the time."

Lucy raised an eyebrow, "You're kidding."

"Morning was coming," I said, "and I was already beat up pretty bad. I had to keep him from escaping. So, I grabbed him up in a bear hug and just tumbled over a cliff."

"Bullshit."

"Dropped about twenty feet or so then hit the slope and tumbled down for god knows how far, hitting every damned rock on the way. I was still holding the bastard when the sun came up and fried the vampire to ash. Leaving me all alone, bleeding and broken."

Lucy shook her head, "How do you survive shit like that?"

"Dunno," I said. "Sometimes you just decide you're not gonna die."

"It doesn't work that way," Lucy said.

"No?"

"You're just lucky."

I rubbed at the many bumps and cuts on my head, "Don't feel lucky."

"You're still alive," Lucy said. "That's something."

"It's something," I admitted. "But if you don't make up your mind that you're gonna survive, you won't."

"Easy as that?"

"Nothing is easy. But everything you do is a result of your mindset."

"Mind over matter?"

"No, mind over mind."

"That's stupid."

"God, why do you have to buck every damned thing I say?"

"Because you're full of shit," Lucy said softly and shook her head.

"I'm trying to teach you something useful."

"I don't need life lessons, Dr. Phil," Lucy fixed her eyes on the road. She wasn't gonna look at me.

One. Two. Three. Four...

I sighed. I didn't want to fight. I was sick of fighting. I just wanted some rest and some peace. But there I was. Stuck in a car with two-thirds of the people responsible for my current situation. I didn't want to be here. Screw her for being pissed at me. This was as much her fault as mine. She was the one that came into my home and took my stuff. She was the one that had been hung around my neck like a boat anchor. She was the one running headlong into fights without a clue, making me nurse her along. She was the pissed-off girl, scared of her situation, trying her best to come out alive against overwhelming odds. She was way in over her head and didn't even know how deep the waters really were.

Shit.

She needed me and she hated me for it. As much I hated that I had to work with her. Probably more.

"Lucy," I tried not to sound patronizing, "I'm not trying to be your friend or your father or your life coach."

I saw her jaw move back and forth but she didn't speak or take her eyes from the road. She was doing her best to swallow her venom. That was something.

"Most Hunters don't survive for very long," I said. I was trying to sound reassuring without coddling. Hell, I'm not sure I even knew how to coddle. "You can scoff, but it really is like mind over matter, in a way."

"K," was all she said. It was a tiny concession. It was enough for now; she was listening.

"Look, I've seen people with a little flesh wound just lay down and die. I've seen people with a hole in their head walk away to fight another day. If you decide you're gonna die, you'll die. You give up, it's over. Your brain listens to you more than you think."

"I don't lay down," Lucy said tersely. "I don't give up."

I nodded, "Good. Don't. Ever."

"I just have to be confident, and I'll live forever?"

"You have to be a stubborn son of a bitch. Tougher than life. Life's a tougher bitch than death."

"Son of a bitch? Not just a bitch?" Lucy asked with a wry smile.

"You're halfway there," I said.

Lucy caught herself smiling and tried to wipe it off.

Just then, when I thought I might have made some useful progress with Lucy, the tattoo below the base of my skull started to itch. A lot. I rubbed it quickly and Leo appeared in the back seat. Cold air swirled around in the car as he became visible. He reached toward me as he appeared, but he suddenly seemed to remember he couldn't touch me. Instead, he wrapped his hands around each other and wrung them nervously. No, not nervously. Frantically.

"Dude!" he said, his voice higher pitched than normal. "I'm so glad I found you."

"I'm here," I said soothingly.

Lucy looked at me with irritation in her eyes, "I know you are. What's wrong with you?"

"Dude," Leo said again. "I got lost man... oh man. I was lost. Do you know what that's like? In the Otherside? Being a lost soul?"

I raised my hands in what I hope was a calming gesture, "It's OK Leo. You're here. You're not lost. I'm right here."

"Who's Leo," Lucy asked. "Who are you talking to?"

"Don't tell her," Leo's eyes darted back and forth from Lucy to me. "Don't tell her who I am. She's got a dark cloud around her. Don't tell anyone. Oh jeez, man."

"I'll explain later," I told Lucy. Yeah, that would satisfy her curiosity. Then to Leo, "What's wrong? I've never seen you like this."

Lucy tried to follow my eyes and screwed up her eyebrows, "Are you talking to the car? Did you name the car Leo?"

"Just chill," I barked. "Please."

The anger in Lucy's eyes returned, "Fine." Her knuckles became white under the tremendous pressure of her grip on the steering wheel.

"It's something from Dudael all right," Leo said. "It's probably Rezruel. I can't be sure. He had help."

"What kind of help?"

"Sorcerer."

"A sorcerer? Are you sure?"

Lucy looked at me again, "What the hell are you talking about?"

"Later," I said. "Leo are you sure?"

"Yes," he said, "And he's using some dark dark magic. Blood magic."

"That's sorcery all right," I said.

"But this has some weird mojo."

"Sorcerers and blood magic are a big noisy combination," I said.

"The Council can't *not* know about this."

That got Lucy's attention. She turned her eyes and looked at me long and hard. Too long.

"Road," I barked.

She corrected her steering and kept us on the road.

Leo took a deep, unnecessary breath, "Trust me on this, this sorcerer is performing some dark magic and he knows his shit."

"What happened?"

"I went to the site of the incursion," Leo said. "Let me tell you, it looks bad when you see without the veil. It looks like something tore into the Otherside like Alien bursting out of a chest."

"I saw it, too," I said, "on this side. The place is painted in blood and guts."

"I know," Leo said. "It's the same in the Otherside too. The spirits of the victims are chowder."

I scowled, "Incursions don't work that way."

I was starting to sound like Dean, not acknowledging things I didn't want to be true

Leo shook his head, "But this one originated in the mortal world. Completely unaided, completely un-bridged. Someone reached into Dudael and pulled Rezruel out."

"I was afraid you'd say something like that," I said.

"You're not surprised."

"No," I said.

"Well... it happened. No denying it."

"That's not good."

Lucy's voice had more irritation in it each time she spoke, "What's not good? What the fuck is going on?"

"In a minute Lucy," I said. "Leo, how is this possible?"

"Sorcerer," he said.

"You said that."

"Sorcerers work in conjunction with the Yokai," Leo said. That was an old word that wracked my brain. Yokai. One of the names for demons and bad spirits. Something from Chinese legend. I'd have to dig into that later.

"Sorcerers steal energy from life," Leo continued. "Steal, not borrow. I think your bad guy figured out how to sap life energy from the mortal world and the Otherside at the same time."

"That sounds like some dark dark shit," I said.

"Bingo," Leo said. "The spiritual ruin leftover at the location by the incursion event will never heal. It'll be years before anyone on the Otherside can go near there and not be affected. It almost killed me."

"Killed you?" I said. "You're already dead."

Lucy's head swiveled toward me again with a look of pure confusion in her eyes.

"I'm not dead. And besides, there's dead and then there's dead," Leo said. "This, whatever this is, it can destroy a spirit. Rezruel learned a new trick in this incursion. He's not just after blood. He's after life."

"That's not good," I said.

"What's not good?" Lucy again.

"No, it's not," Leo said.

"How do you know all this?" I asked.

"Everything's dead at that spot in the Otherside," Leo said and visibly shuddered.

"What else?"

"Nothing. Nothing but dark clouds, man. Don't forget that."

"I won't, thanks. Can you find a safe place to recuperate?"

"I think so," Leo said and faded away. The air seems to stir for a second then stilled.

Lucy shivered after Leo was gone. Could she feel his presence?

"What was all that?" She demanded.

"Just drive," I said, "I need to think."

"Like hell, I'm gonna 'just drive'. You're either losing your mind or you're having a séance. I want to know which kind of whacko I'm stuck in a car with."

"The big, confused kind," I said.

"What the hell is going on? Who were you talking to?"

This whole thing sucked from the start. From the moment I found Winters and Red in my house, I was being set up. Even before that. They cleaned me out before I got home from fighting Mehira. They—Winters and Lucy and whoever else—were planning something even before I threw down my gun that night. They were already planning to strong-arm me. Why? Something was adding up wrong and I couldn't put my finger on it. It was like doing math in the dark with no calculator. And Leo's warning about dark clouds. He didn't come out and say she was evil or in league with something evil. In fact, he didn't even say if she knew it. Dark clouds were there. Was she being influenced? Was she under threat neither of us knew about?

"You're worrying me," Lucy said. "Have your brain injuries finally kicked in?"

I didn't answer. I wasn't trying to be a jerk. I just didn't know what to say. I couldn't "out" Leo to her when he asked me not to. It was important to him for some reason. He was worried about more than just a demon at large and a wizard gone bad.

"I can't tell you everything," I decided half-truths were gonna have to suffice, "I have a... source in the Otherside. Something I can't really explain. It's been doing some scouting for me, trying to track down Rezruel."

"You said a lot of weird things to your 'source,'" Lucy said. "Blood magic, sorcery. Dark magic."

"I did," I admitted. "There's a lot going on here that I don't like."

"I don't like any of it," Lucy said.

"Rezruel is not the worst option of all the things in Dudael someone could mess around with," I said, "not even in the top one hundred. But he's still a whole lot of bad. There's a lot of evil spirits in Yokikai and Diyu and even at large here in the mortal world."

"Yokikai? Diyu?"

Jeez. More basic shit she didn't know anything about. Why the hell didn't she know any of this?

"Yokikai is the shadow world and Diyu is the name for the nations of Hell."

"Nations?"

"There's a lot to the Otherside, including Hell and Hell's a complex place."

"Ok," Lucy worked her jaw as if chewing on the idea like a bad taste, "so Hell's big and bad."

"That's not the point," I shook my head. "The point is, there are a lot of bad mothers at large in the Otherside and this world. You don't gotta go break an inmate out of Hell's prison to start trouble. There's plenty of nasty shit that ain't already locked up."

"Oh," Lucy said quietly.

"Yeah," I said. "This is overkill in a crazy big way. You don't unleash end-of-the-world types of spirits into the mortal world unless you intend some end of the world shit."

Lucy licked her lips nervously, "So... someone wants to start the apocalypse?"

"Dunno," I said. "Wants to or doesn't know that's what'll happen."

"Neither is a good scenario," Lucy said.

"No," I agreed.

"It feels like we still don't really know what is going on here."

"You got that right," I said. "And our Archivist wasn't very helpful." Then a new thought came to me.

"You're grinning again," Lucy said.

"Yeah? Well, Dean isn't the only Council Archivist in the phonebook."

"Huh?"

"St. Louis isn't the only town with an Archives."

"There's one in Kansas City too, isn't there?"

"There is," I said. "Turn around."

"Great," Lucy said and took the nearest exit, "more stuffy librarians."

Chapter Nineteen

The Kansas City Archives is downtown, hidden in a high-rise on the edge of the Power and Light District. There wasn't a need for a clever false front, you couldn't find it or get to it unless you already knew how. Go through the lobby, ignore reception, and take the second elevator to floor 5R. If you can figure out how to get to 5R, you're welcome at the Archives. I'd never been there but as a good Hunter, I knew the protocols for all but three of the Archives in North America.

The elevators opened to an extravagant foyer with too many plants and too many seats with too many pillows on them. There was no one to greet us but the doors had a retinal scanner. Lucy and I both got the greenlight and passed through the heavy doors into the reading room. It was very similar to the one in St. Louis but smaller. Lots of little tables and shelves. Dimly lit. Old rugs. But the colors weren't as muted. The reds were sharper and brighter. The wood was still polished and crisp. It felt like entering the library of a fairytale castle.

I was a mess, still battered and bloody, and felt conspicuously out of place in this room like I didn't belong there. I probably belonged in a trauma ward. But there I was. There we were. Lucy wasn't very happy to be there either.

The resident Archivists—a man and a woman—greeted us cheerfully as the door closed behind us.

The man had blonde hair, slicked straight back on top and shaved to the skin on the sides. A thick mustache with curled ends that twitched when he smiled and bushy eyebrows arched liberally to accentuate his expressions. He wore a red sweater vest with a plain white button-up beneath and a thin necktie along with tight jeans rolled up above his ankles. Both ears were crowded with rows of earrings of various size and material. The woman had nearly the same hairstyle, except her hair was dark brown and curlier. S didn't have the mustache or bushy eyebrows either. Her sweater vest was a blue argyle pattern, and her jeans weren't rolled up but ended at the top of a pair of canvas sneakers. Her bright silver finger rings and ear and brow piercings were a perfect contrast to her dark skin and deep brown eyes.

I was staring and told myself to stop.

"I'm sorry. I was expecting someone..."

"Stuffier," Lucy finished.

"Older," I said. "And stuffier."

"It happens all the time," the man said as he shook my hand vigorously, "Miles Granning. Welcome, welcome. We don't get visitors often. Especially new ones. You've never been here before. Not since I've been here."

"Er," I said intelligently.

"Leslie Jannek," the woman said and shook hands with Lucy then me.

"Bill Kemper," I said and jerked a thumb at Lucy. "Lucille Red."

"Bill Kemper!" Miles' eyes brightened, and hands froze mid-shake, "Are you kidding me. Oh my gosh! You're Bill Kemper? The Bill Kemper?"

"The one and only," Lucy said. "In all his oversized glory."

"I've been following your career for some time," Miles said and shook my hands again, both of them, "You're very famous."

"That's not always a good thing," I said.

"You're a legend," Miles said. "Oh my gosh, I can't even believe you're here. I have so many questions. Can I see your biding runes? Did you know you're the longest living Hunter of the modern age?"

"I heard that."

"Really?" Lucy asked and looked at me as if I'd been keeping a secret from her.

Leslie held a hand up before Miles could launch into another barrage of accolades, "There's some increased scuttlebutt about you lately." Her voice, less enthusiastic than Miles' but still very warm.

"Figures. What's the latest?" I asked.

Leslie handed me a wet rag, which I hadn't noticed her carrying, "You have an open contact, and yet you're already working on another. Double-dip much?"

"Not exactly," I said and dabbed the rag at the side of my head.

"Apparently, we have some gaps in our information," Leslie said motioning at me in general. I assumed she was referring to the obvious signs of recent combat.

"Apparently," I said off-handedly.

Lucy snatched the rag from my hand and started scrubbing dried blood from her hands, "You don't know the half of it."

Miles clapped his hands once, "I can't wait! So rare to get the story straight from the star. So rare. Everything's always second-hand. Dispatches and calls and letters and little hints in the ephemera. Can wait to hear you tell it all!"

"Don't mind him," Leslie said in a not unfriendly tone, "he's very enthusiastic about this job."

"Aren't we all?" Lucy said in a not enthusiastic tone. "Your only news on Big Bill is that he's double-dipping assignments?"

"It's a little more detailed than that," Leslie said, "but that's it in a nutshell."

"Nothing about him retiring," Lucy asked.

"Retiring?" Miles laughed. "Oh my gosh. Could you imagine? Could imagine the chaos? The panic? No. I can't imagine it. It's unimaginable."

If they didn't know that news, it wasn't in the database yet. If it wasn't in the database, Dean didn't enter it. That wasn't good.

Leslie shook her head, "You retiring would be like yanking a knife out of a sucking wound. I wouldn't want..." She stopped and studied my face then Lucy's. Lucy gave her a single nod.

"Wait, you're serious?" Leslie's voice cracked. "You're retiring?"

"Retired," I said.

"I don't believe it!" Miles said. "You're really getting out of the game? There's no way! I don't believe it!"

"It ain't a fun game," I grumbled, then added, "You guys really didn't know?"

"Forrester already knew," Lucy said, "and that was only a couple hours after it happened."

Miles and Leslie exchanged dubious glances.

"That's irregular," Leslie said.

"Irregular?" Miles's voice pitched, "It's unspeakable. Accurate history is our bread and butter. It's why we're here. Incomplete records are a blemish. A big ugly zit on our reputation."

"Maybe he was too busy," Lucy offered, "he appears to be alone there."

Again, Miles and Leslie exchanged uneasy looks.

"Alone?" Miles said. "Really?"

"Are you sure about that?" Leslie asked.

"Pretty sure," I said. "Dean's the only one I ever see there."

Miles frowned, "What about the Senior Archivist, Marten?"

"Never met him," I said. "Is he some kind of assistant?"

Miles' eyes bulged, "Assistant? Are you kidding? Ronald Marten, the Senior Archivist, the head of all the Archives. He *is* the Archivist."

I shrugged. "He ain't there. Or he's avoiding me."

Leslie sat down in the nearest chair as if she'd been dealt a serious blow, "If that's true, something really odd is going on."

I said, "Odd follows me like a shadow. That's why we're here. Dean wasn't much help."

"Unbelievable," Miles said very softly as he lowered his head. I'm not sure which unbelievable thing was bothering him the most.

Leslie stared down at the floor for a moment then shook her

head as if clearing away a fog, "Ok." She stood up, "We're here to help. We'll sort this all out in time. What do you need?"

"What doesn't he need?" Lucy said.

"Ever heard of Rezruel?" I asked.

"Doesn't ring a bell," Leslie said and tugged at one of her ears, "demon?"

I shook my head, "One of the One Hundred in Dudael"

"Ah," Miles nodded enthusiastically, "old school bad guys. Of course. Naturally, we don't know them by name, but definitely by reputation. That is pretty heavy subject matter. Why the sudden interest in Dudael? In the One Hundred? Is that your new assignment?"

Lucy crossed her arms and arched an eyebrow. This was, I realized, her standard "don't expect any help from me" expression. It was an improvement over her "I hate you" expression.

"There's been an incursion," I said. "Rezruel's the prime target."

"From Dudael?" Leslie frowned. "That's highly unlikely."

"Like, really not likely," Miles agreed. "Dudael's like a supermax. Locked down. No phone calls."

"A lot of unlikely things keep happening to me. But there's an added one in this case."

"What connection?" Leslie asked.

"Me."

"I knew it!" Miles said and slapped his leg.

"I retired Rezruel about twelve years ago." I confirmed what Miles had guessed.

"You retired Rezruel," Miles asked, "to Dudael. Ok. Ok. I remember this. That's an old story. I have to go look up the details, but I think I remember now."

"Bill," Leslie said tilting her head as if I were speaking nonsense and she didn't want it getting in her ear, "if you sent Rezruel back to Dudael, in your lifetime, there's no way he could have made an incursion already. Not for a least a few hundred years. Six hundred eighty-eight years. It's not a matter of will. It's a matter of how the universe works. You know this."

"I do know this," I sat in an oversized chair near Leslie's, careful not to rest any of my bloody parts on the fabric, "but I don't think it was a regular incursion."

"What other kind is there?" she asked.

"I think it happened the other way."

"The other way?" Miles asked.

"Oh for god's sake, Kemper," Lucy said. "You're wearing a hole in the grass from all the beating around the bush. He thinks it was a jailbreak."

"Jailbreak? You mean like an extraction?" Miles said. "Really? A reverse incursion?" He turned to Leslie, "Is that even possible? Can someone do that? Can someone reach into Dudael?"

She raised her hands in surrender, "I don't know. I wouldn't think so. Besides, who would want to do that? Why would someone want to?"

I shrugged. I'd been asking the same questions.

"I have a source that suggests a sorcerer is involved," I said. "Blood magic or something."

Leslie sucked air through her teeth, "Yeah, that might make a difference."

"That opens a lot of possibilities, but more questions too. It might be possible," Miles said. "You can't practice sorcery without the Council getting wind of it. It draws too much attention. Especially what you're talking about. Not on the scale you're suggesting. Not in the States. The Council is too paranoid about that kind of thing."

Lucy shifted uncomfortably. She did that every time somebody talked about the Council. She was loyal beyond reason.

Leslie tugged absent-mindedly on a large earring dangling from her lobe, "They're paranoid for a reason. Sorcery isn't just forbidden magic. It's bad magic. It's the kind of magic a mortal can get wrapped up in... and they won't get out."

"I know," I said. I didn't know much, but I knew sorcery was unconditionally banned by the Nine-Fold Council.

"I see some possible threads here," Leslie stood up, "but we'll need to do a little research."

"Yes. Maybe more than a little," Miles nodded eagerly, "Come back in two hours. That should be long enough, I think. Probably."

"I'm not really dressed for dining out," I said. My ridiculous truck stop clothes had not been improved by the bloodstains. "Can't we wait here?"

"We have changes of clothes," Leslie offered, "something that might fit you. And a shower. How about that?"

"Sounds like heaven," Lucy said.

"Ditto," I added.

"Freshen up, then see how you feel," Leslie said. "You're only two blocks from Power and Light. Go have a drink and something to eat. Enjoy yourself. Try to relax. You both could probably use it."

"I am pretty hungry," I admitted.

Lucy heaved a sigh.

"But I don't think she knows how to enjoy herself," I said.

"I hate you," Lucy said.

Chapter Twenty

A hot shower and a fresh set of clothes was just what I needed. Even Lucy seemed a little less hostile after a good scrubbing. We each got a pair of jeans, a plain T-shirt, and a jacket, nothing fancy but they fit almost perfectly as if the Archivist had our exact measurements. Which makes sense, I guess. The Archives record everything, I guess they have my inseam in the database as well.

Lucy reluctantly agreed to go with me to get something to eat and try to chill out for a while, but only if she could bring the Holy Glockamolie. As if I would try and stop her. She managed to conceal it beneath her jacket so it wouldn't be too conspicuous. Not as conspicuous as a sawed-off shotgun or a 3-foot long sword, for example. I left those in the car.

The Power and Light District takes up a city block of stacked bars, restaurants, and shops surrounding a covered courtyard with seating in the open area. At the south end of the courtyard, a small stage offers a venue for live music.

The place wasn't very busy; apparently, weeknights weren't hopping. We stopped at the bar closest to the main entrance and picked a table on the patio. I sat facing the main entrance, with my back to the stage across halfway across the pavilion. I took in the scene, scanning for trouble, while Lucy sat brooding in her standard fashion. We were separated from the courtyard by a narrow metal rail that was supposed to look like wrought iron. On the stage, a band rattled out jazzy, acoustic covers of popular songs. A handful of people stood nearby listening to the music, chatting loudly, and drinking. I watched as a pack of college-aged boys roamed aimlessly, ducking in and out of bars, leaving only moments later with drinks in hand. They chattered noisily, egging each other on to drink faster. Nothing seemed out of the ordinary. But nothing ever does right before all hell breaks loose.

Since I had my back to the bar, I didn't notice the waitress until she came right up to the table.

"Hi, I'm Jesse."

I jerked and my knee hit the underside of the table, almost toppling it over onto Lucy. Lucy caught the condiments tray before it landed on her lap and put it back at the center of the table while giving me a dirty look. Damn. I'm too on edge. I'm always ready for trouble, but I wasn't in the mindset for quick, friendly service. God, I'm a cynic. A jumpy cynic.

The waitress, Jesse, stood about 4'10" and had long coppery hair, worked into dreadlocks interlaced with a few streaks of black. Her tanned skin was reminiscent of a Caribbean sun. She had a wide mouth with thick lips that curled into a faint smirk at the corners. A small handful of dark freckles spotted her upper cheeks and small, upturned nose, drawing the eyes to them, then to her eyes. They were light grey, so light that they almost looked silver, and were lined in thin rings of black makeup. A single silver stud adorned the side of her nose and thick earrings hung from her ears, like curled harpoons.

"Oh!" Jesse said and laughed, "Sorry, I didn't mean to scare you there." Jesse had an Irish accent, and her voice went up and down in an almost singsong manner.

I tried to smile at her without scaring her, "Sorry. I'm a little jumpy."

"I'm a shifty one," Jesse said conspiratorially, "but I'll try not to sneak up on you anymore."

"Yeah, be careful, he's a regular scaredy-cat," Lucy said.

"Been a long day," I mumbled and dropped my eyes.

Jesse leaned closer, "Maybe a drink'll take the edge off."

"Water," Lucy said still scanning the pavilion, not bothering to look at Jesse.

"Be nice," I warned

"This is nice. Fine," Lucy waved a hand, "Beer."

Jesse smiled, "You're gonna have to narrow it down for me. You have a preference?"

"No," Lucy finally looked at the waitress.

"Jesus, Lucy," I said.

Lucy sighed, "Something light. I don't care."

"And you?" Jesse asked, turning her attention back to me.

"Something strong," I thought for a moment. "Jack and Coke and make it strong enough to knock out a horse." From the corner of my eye, I took note of Lucy's obvious look of disapproval.

"Are you expecting a party to break out," Jesse winked, "or trying to start one?"

"Trying to forget about the last one," I said.

Jesse nodded, "I'll fix you up right. There's the menu," she gestured at a couple of laminated pages being held up between some condiment bottles that were supposed to look like tiny kegs, "I'll be back with your drinks in a jiff."

Lucy scowled, "You really think a stiff drink is what you need right now?"

I shrugged, "One drink ain't gonna shut down this body."

Lucy scoffed, "Just don't lose your edge. I can't afford to watch your back if you're drunk the next time a fight breaks out."

"I don't get drunk," I said.

"Well don't start tonight."

A couple of teenage girls, hanging on to each other like newlyweds, strolled past us. When they caught sight of us, they did a double-take and whispered excitedly to each other as they continued to a bar a couple of doors down. Lucy shook her head in disgust.

I missed the Blue Sky. The people there were used to my brand of freak. I was scaring a whole new class of people now.

"God," Lucy said, "what are they staring at? Haven't they seen a girl without makeup before? Not every woman has to be all dolled up and frilly to go out in public."

Really? She thought they were staring at her. Why? What did she have to be self-conscious about? She was a very attractive young woman. Admittedly, she looked like a pixie across from me, but that was on me not her. Even wearing a hostile frown and no-name clothing, she was a standard for beauty. Hell, she could be on a poster for a high-end fitness center. I was the poster child for the dangers of steroids and auto accidents.

"I think they're staring at me," I said gently. She met my eyes and her frown softened.

"Oh," she said. "Yeah." Wow. She'd forgotten I was a monster for a minute there.

Jesse brought our drinks and asked if we wanted anything to eat. Lucy refused with a quick shake of her head.

"What's the biggest thing on the menu?" I asked.

Jesse's eyes widened, "Eating for two, are you?"

"Ha!" I laughed involuntarily. "I eat enough for two... or three."

"Well, Hungry Man," she pointed at the menu, "that one. The Supreme Burrito. That would feed your friend here for a week."

Lucy rolled her eyes.

"I'll take it."

"Be back in a bit. Enjoy the drink."

Lucy drank half her beer in a single draw.

"Damn Lucy," I said. "You're worried about me drinking too much?"

"Don't worry," she said, "I'm a pro."

"Hell yes, you are!" The young man was part of the pack of bar-hopping male hormones. They had stopped just outside the completely useless fence that separated our table from the rest of the pavilion. He and his friends were wannabe frat stereotypes in trendy modern college fashion and hedonistic hair styling products and a couple of backward ballcaps.

"Let me buy you a shot," another young man said.

"Fuck off," Lucy snapped at him. The group laughed as one.

"Only with you," another said.

"Move on," I said and met the kid's eyes, my voice dangerously calm.

A few smiles faded. Nobody tried to meet my gaze, and nobody had a smart comment for me. Instead, they quickly shuffled off to find another bar, but not without looking back at Lucy as they went.

"I hate that," Lucy mumbled into her beer.

"Me too," I said.

"Whatever," she said, "don't act like you care about my feelings."

"Ain't always about your feelings," I said.

"What's it about then," Lucy asked, "oh Wise and Compassionate One?"

"Jesus Lucy," I said with a sigh. "It's about treating people like human beings."

Lucy met my eyes, "People are human, that's the problem with everyone."

"True," I conceded.

"Besides," Lucy let a faint smile cross her lips, "You're big enough to be human enough for the both of us."

I grinned, "Maybe."

Lucy drank from her beer again, a smaller sip this time, "So what happens next, Mr. Human?"

"Dunno," I said. I really didn't know. Usually, Regis pointed me like a loaded gun at a target and pulled the trigger. This time, I had to figure out what the target was and then find it myself.

"You know," Lucy said, "you look like an angry gorilla when you're thinking?"

"That's why I don't do it very much." Rewarding me what would almost pass as a genuine smile from Lucy.

I finally raised my glass and tasted the drink Jesse had given me. Boldly, I took a large gulp and swallowed the fire that lingered afterward. Holy cow, that woman made one strong drink.

"You know," I said, "you talk like a scorned ex-wife?"

"That's because I'm an angry bitch," Red said.

I snorted out a laugh, "Your words not mine."

"You were thinking it," she said matter-of-factly.

"I guess," I admitted with a shrug and took a smaller sip of my drink, "You know, I'd like to see what you'd be like without that mask."

"It's not a mask," she said seriously.

"There ain't a soft and warm Lucy inside there somewhere?"

"No. I killed her off a long time ago," Lucy said. "She did nothing but get in the way."

"In the way of what?"

"Being taken seriously. I'm not a vet or an ex-cop or a martial arts instructor. I don't have years of experience or a gargantuan physic to speak for me. Or a dick."

"But You got balls, sister," I raised my glass to her, "I've seen that much."

"I'll take that as a compliment," Lucy said and sipped her beer, "but you know what I mean."

"I do," I admitted. "But being a big brute don't make life easier. You don't make a lot of friends when you look like a comic book henchman."

"I'm not looking for friends," Lucy said. "I'm looking to be taken seriously. Try doing that in this business with tits."

"I get it," I motioned back and forth between us, "but people like us need friends."

"Why? They're overrated. I'm not into networking."

"You need people you can trust," I said.

"I don't trust anyone," she said.

"You trust Winters."

"Master Winters isn't my friend," she said plainly. No scorn, no humor. Just a fact.

"Maybe not. Just don't kid yourself. Being a badass ain't enough."

"What are you saying. We all need love and hugs and all that crap?"

"Grounding," I said.

"What the hell is that supposed to mean?"

"When you're a Hunter," I looked into Lucy's eyes and held her gaze, "you're a killer. Every time you make a kill a piece of you fades away. You start to become something else."

"What?" I could clearly hear her skepticism.

I emptied my drink and set the empty glass down gently. "A shadow of a person."

"You're no shadow." Lucy shrugged off the idea.

"No, I'm not," I said. "I'm a giant murderous bastard."

Jesse, who was approaching our table, stopped several feet short and smiled uneasily.

"Don't mind him," Lucy said. "He's a drama queen."

"Sorry," I said feebly feeling like a giant murderous idiot.

"Just checking to see if you need another drink," she recovered quickly.

"Another beer. Half." Lucy said.

I shook my head, "I turn into a drama queen if I drink too much. How about coffee? You got coffee?"

"We do but isn't anything fancy."

"I'll take it," I said.

"Cream, sugar?"

"Black."

"Like his murderous heart," Lucy offered. Jesse winked at Lucy and left.

Lucy lowered her voice, "Jesus Bill. Dial it down. What makes you think you're a murderous bastard?"

"Do you have any idea how many kills I have?"

"No."

"Me either," I said. "I lost count. Literally."

"So?" Lucy said. "You're a monster hunter. That's your job. It's what you do."

"Yeah," I said, "it is what I do. And it's a shitty way to make a living."

"It's a shitty world."

"I'm tired of killing, Lucy. I'm good at it and I've been doing it a long time. And it grinds away at your soul."

"Monsters, Bill. You kill monsters," she put extra emphasis on the word. "They kill people. They steal babies and eat souls and destroy lives. Right?"

"So do I," I said plainly, staring across the courtyard.

Lucy had her glass halfway to her lips and stopped, "You're kidding me. Right?"

I didn't say anything.

"You honestly think you're one of them? You really think you're a monster like... like that vampire bitch?"

Jesse came back with my coffee and food, so I kept my trap shut. Lucy didn't break eye contact with me while Jesse placed our drinks on the table and a large plate on my table.

"Your giant burrito," Jesse said, rolling the R's.

It looked like heaven. Big enough to wear as a shoe, steaming, coated in cheese and guac. I couldn't wait to dig in.

"God," Lucy said, "I'll puke if you shove that whole thing in your mouth."

"Careful there," Jesse warned, "it's very hot. Give it a minute."

"Will do," I said, already salivating.

"Can I get you anything else?"

I shook my head. Lucy though had a look in her eyes I didn't trust and a smirk.

"Yes," Lucy said. "Jesse, right? Are you Irish?"

"I am," she said happily, "Cork."

"Jesse from Cork, are you married?" Lucy asked.

She snorted, "Oh god no."

"Boyfriend?"

Jesse's eyes darted toward me briefly, "Um... not technically, no."

Damnit. I breathed in slowly. What was she doing?

Lucy pointed a finger at me, "Would you date this guy?"

My heart stopped. Shit.

"I... uh..." Jesse tilted her head and avoided eye contact with me.

"Lucy," I said sternly. "Stop."

"No, it's alright!" Jesse said a little too quickly, "I don't date much."

"Let me rephrase," Lucy held up a hand as if heading off an argument, "What would you do if this man asked you out on a date? Hypothetically?"

"Hypothetically," Jesse repeated the word, a bit of a challenge with her Irish accent, shrugging half-heartedly, "I don't know..."

"Come on, Jesse, rip off the Band-Aid," Lucy said harshly and motioned toward me as if maybe Jesse didn't know who she was talking about.

"Well... he kind of reminds me of my dad," Jesse said, "you know, like a nice chap. I'm into a more adventurous type. Like biker guys or drummers."

Lucy choked on her beer.

"I'm sorry," Jesse said to me. "I'm sure you're a bang-up guy."

"Oh, I'm a real hoot," I said, trying to keep the amusement out of my voice.

"It's ok, Bill," Lucy patted my arm while barely withholding a laugh, "some girls just look right past all the scars and tattoos."

"I'll check back with you in a bit," Jesse backed away mouthing sorry at me as she did.

"Thanks," I said taking in the wonderfully strong smell of my nothing-special black coffee and the piping hot burrito. "That helped a lot."

Lucy pointed toward the bar, at Jesse who kept looking over at us, "That crazy-looking Irish girl didn't look at you like you were an ogre."

"I'm no Robert Redford."

"Nobody is," Lucy said harshly. "Quit acting like you're Drax the Destroyer. You're closer to Dave Bautista."

"They're the same guy," I said lamely.

"You know what I mean stupid," Lucy said. "Quit pretending you're some hideous monster."

"You don't know me," I said. "You don't know what I've done."

"Yeah, I remember," she said. "Killed puppies and hanged men and ripped out the throats of vampires. Did you enjoy it?"

I frowned, "Fuck no."

"Then quit feeling sorry for yourself. When you start to enjoy all that, that's when you've got something to really worry about."

I thoughtfully took Lucy Red in for a moment. She was too young to have seen the things I had. She was too pretty to have been shunned for her looks. She was too green to have the wisdom of experience. But she knew something about reality.

I slowly nodded, "You know, for an angry red-headed pain in my ass, you're not so stupid."

"That is the worst compliment I've ever heard," she said, "and I work for a bunch of misogynistic wizards and their testosterone-fueled bodyguards."

I tipped my head in a mock bow and raised my coffee cup at her.

She took a long pull from her beer then pointed her empty mug at me, "I still hate you."

"I wouldn't know what to believe if you didn't."

"Now," she said conspiratorially, "when that fine little Irish lassie comes back, I want you to ask her how she came to be here in the middle of nowhere and then ask her out on a real date. I want to see what happens."

"Not a chance," I said. "Unless you go pick up on one of those frat boys." Pointing at the pack of idiots standing near the stage and still talking way too loudly and drinking way too fast.

Lucy shook her head, "Negative. I refuse to be friendly until this job is done."

I held up my coffee mug and touched glasses with Lucy's beer, "Here's to the job."

"May you live to regret it," she said and drank again.

"You're starting to sound like a Hunter," I said.

"That's depressing," she mumbled. "How did you get into hunting monsters?"

"Get into?"

"You know what I mean. Why this job?"

"This ain't just some job you find in the classifieds. It's a life. It ain't something you choose."

"Ok, so what then, it's destiny? Or you stumbled into it?"

"Sorta."

"God, it's like pulling teeth getting anything but lectures out of you."

I took in a long slow breath. I lowered my eyes and focused on the coffee mug in front of me. "When I was seventeen... I lost my family to a demon."

"Jesus, Bill."

"I survived," I paused and tried to keep from remembering that night, but sometimes you just can't hold back the flood. "I survived and then I killed those responsible." I hadn't spoken about it to another human being in years. Over a decade. I'm not sure how I felt about it. I couldn't tell the whole story. I didn't want to. I didn't want to dig up those details. But just saying as much as I did... It was kind of like tugging on a splinter.

"I had no idea. Shit," Lucy whispered.

"Few do," I said. I turned the coffee cup around in my hand a couple of times. "Regis brought me into this life. He saw the fire in me. He called it 'potential.'"

"And the rest is history."

I nodded once.

"That's why you have a problem with me being a Hunter, isn't it?"

"Every Hunter I have ever known has a story like mine. Every one of them," I tapped the table with each word. "They're out for vengeance and retribution. They live hard and angry. And in the end, most of them die hard and angry."

"Then along comes me."

"Then along comes you," I picked up the coffee cup and sipped from it. Jesse was right. Nothing fancy. Just black coffee. But that's what I liked. I enjoyed it for a second, and then I looked Lucy in the eyes, "I got nothing against you. But you didn't choose this. Hell, you don't even want this."

She opened her mouth to protest but I stopped her, "Winters pushed you into it. You don't do that. You don't just turn someone into a Hunter. They are one already," I pumped my fist against my chest, "in here."

"Master Winters knows what he's doing," Lucy said without conviction. "I trust him."

"Good," I said. "Go with that."

"Don't ruin this moment," Lucy snapped. She took a breath and seemed to calm herself. Why don't you trust him?"

"I don't trust the Council."

"The whole Council?"

"Pretty much," I frowned, trying to come up with specific examples, "Well, Regis is a douche."

"Well, no shit," Lucy said. "And with a guy like York in his pocket, who wouldn't be?"

"The Council is all secrets and superstition."

"They're freaking wizards!" Lucy threw her hands up. "What do you expect?"

"Wisdom."

"That's a tall order, Bill. In any world."

I chuckled, "True."

The musicians on stage finished their set and announced they were gonna take a break. Thankfully, they didn't put on any musak to fill the silence. The causal background noise of people shopping idly and talking a little too much about nothing at all was as much music to me as any song. It was the soundtrack of regular people, doing regular people things. I liked it. It reminded me that there were people who didn't know vampires lurk in the shadows. That werewolves hunt in the woods near cities. That demons from dark places seek willing hosts and unwilling victims. That goblins really do come for babies in the night and trolls really do hide under some bridges. I wished I was one of them. Happy. Ignorant. But I wasn't. I never would be because I could never un-know all those things. I couldn't un-remember everything I'd seen and done. And if Lucy stayed in this, she'd become like me.

I had to talk her out of it somehow.

But first, something to eat. I'd been ignoring that burrito since Jesse brought it, trying to keep myself from digging in and scorching the roof of my mouth. Or worse, making Lucy puke by shoving the whole thing into my mouth.

Lucy watched me with casual disinterest as I cut it open with a fork. Steam spill out along with bean and beef and more cheese. Oh god, this was gonna be good.

I had a heaping forkful up to my open maw when a squelching sound cut through the awkward silence. Lucy slammed her glass down on the table and the last of her beer sloshed out. She was staring wide-eyed over my shoulder toward the stage. I turned around to see what she was looking at. Someone new had taken the stage. He wore a long black trench coat bedazzled with chains and metal studs and spray-painted summoning runes. Oh shit. Those were real runes. His hair was jet black, obviously a cheap dye job, spiked haphazardly in all directions. Heavy makeup made his skin paler than natural, almost white, and his eyes and lips blacker. As weird as he was, I'm pretty sure he wasn't what had gotten Lucy's attention. It was the two creatures next to him.

They looked like baboons if baboons had chattering shark teeth and red leathery skin instead of fur and two uneven rows of horns running from the sides of their heads down their back. They only came up to spikey dude's waste, but they were bulging with muscle and quivering with unspent anticipation.

Lucy jumped to her feet, "What the hell are those?" Holy Glockamolie was already in her hand.

"Lesser Imps," I said dropping my fork and getting to my feet. "I think we're done relaxing."

Spike pulled the mic close to his mouth and roared in a deep guttural voice, "Mood music!" The speakers thundered to life with the chaotic crash of death metal cranked up so loud, the speakers crackled and distorted. The imps howled and charged straight for us.

Chapter Twenty-One

Lucy leapt over the iron rail but thankfully didn't start shooting yet. She'd be just as much danger shooting into the chaos that followed. Spectators screamed. People scattered in all directions, literally. Some away from the danger, some toward. People do stupid stuff when they panic.

The beasts plunged through the people, shouldering them out of the way heading straight for Lucy and me. One of the boys who had harassed Lucy earlier went sprawling to the ground with a terrible gash on one leg. An unlucky older woman took a wayward horn to her stomach. I gritted my teeth and swallowed a flood of profanity. I didn't bother climbing over the rail, I shoved against it and pushed it over in a heap.

I didn't bring any weapons so I was gonna have to improvise. As usual. I grabbed part of the iron rail and yanked out one of the spindles. This would be almost useless, but it would have to do.

The imps split up. One sped toward Lucy. The other leapt at me. I caught it as it landed on me and shoved the iron bar sideways into its mouth. We fell back together and crashed into the table, spilling beer, coffee, and scalding burrito innards all over us.

The imp crunched down on the iron bar, not biting through the iron but mangling it with its rows of triangle-shaped teeth. The metal bent in the middle and the imp surged forward. I let its momentum work against it while directing its head to the left and drove it hard into the concrete floor. It shuddered and thrashed wildly. I grabbed the ends of the iron bar and twisted, wrapping it around the beast's lower jaw.

Somewhere nearby, gunshots thundered, accompanied by Lucy's brand of rapid-fire profanity between the shots.

The imp's horns dug into my arms as I wrapped it in a bear hug. I squeezed anyways, taking in the pain, and fighting to keep my hold of the imp as it struggled to get free of my grip. It twisted, and the horns dug deeper into my left arm. I felt the deep and profound pain of the horn digging against my ulna. I let out a primal roar and rolled to the side. Keeping my left arm wrapped tight, I worked my right hand free and pushed against the imp's muzzle, forcing it into an impossible angle, hoping to break its neck.

Imps are technically spiritual beings, usually originating in the nations of Hell. But when summoned, they take up a physical form with enough imbued strength they can manifest into a dangerous creature like this one. That meant it not only got summoned but it also got empowered. The upside is the body can be killed. If you don't get killed first.

I kept pushing at the imp's head until it would go back no further. One of its clawed hands found purchase on my free arm and dug in. My arm buckled, then about a million serrated teeth bit into my shoulder. Fortunately, the iron bar was still in place and kept the bastard from biting clean through. I bellowed in pain anyways, because it hurt, and anger because I was pissed. I ripped my other arm free of the hug and shoved a thumb into one of its eyes.

I don't care how wild, ferocious, or otherworldly you are, if someone tries to dig out one of your eyes, you get distracted. My eye gouge maneuver did just that. It jerked its head away from me. I retrieved my thumb and then punched at the eye. The impact cracked my knuckles and rocked the little demon's head. I punched again. And again. Each blow shook through the imp causing it to shutter against me. Finally, the imp shook its head and opened its maw to chomp again. The iron bar fell out and I knew I was screwed.

Suddenly there was the sound of glass shattering and the imp convulsed as something hot and chunky fell across my chest. I looked up. Jesse stood there above us with the remains of a thick plate in her hand. I took advantage of the moment and shoved both thumbs into each of its eyes and wrapped my fingers around a horn for leverage. It shook and thrashed, but I wasn't letting go this time. Jesse stumbled several steps back and I saw her eyes look past me. I heard Lucy bark something and Jesse squatted, covering her head. Holy Glockamolie barked twice. The imp yelped. Two large holes appeared in its head, and it went limp.

There were a few people running around screaming and unable to decide where to go. One of the frat boys had stopped to help the old lady who'd been gored. Good on him. Jesse remained crouched and covered. Lucy stood before me; her gun still pointed in my direction. The sleeve on one arm was gone and blood flowed freely from a long, jagged wound. Another wound bled, visible from behind a rip at her midriff. The other imp lay dead behind her with several bullet holes in it.

The music continued to blare over the damaged speakers, but the stage was empty. Spike was gone.

Jesse uncovered her head and stood up slowly from her crouch. She was still holding the hunk of plate in one hand. The warm chunky stuff all over my chest was my dinner. The remains of an exploded an uneaten burrito.

"Are you okay?" I asked her.

She trembled, "Wh-what?"

"Are you hurt?" I asked.

"I don't think so," Jesse said. "No. I'm fine. You... you're hurt."

"You saved my ass," I said.

"I... I came back..."

"Yes you did," I said proudly. "Thank you for that."

"I was going to," Jesse extended a hand. She was holding a piece of paper.

"What's this?" I took it from her gently.

"It's my number," her voice lilted.

"Ha!" Lucy pointed at me and had an actual smile on her face.

I got to my feet as gracefully as I could, which wasn't much, and surveyed the mess I'd made, chunks of meat, beans, and rice now littered the floor and my shirt along with blood and melted cheese.

"Damn, that burrito looked good." I mumbled ruefully as I carefully folded the small slip of paper and stuffed it into my pocket.

Flashing red lights caught my eyes and sirens blared from near the main entrance.

"Come on Wreck It Ralph," Lucy said, "I'm not in the mood to talk to cops tonight."

"Me either," I said. "Sorry again, Jesse. Take care." I pressed a handful of bills into her hand while Lucy tugged at my arm.

We got back to the Archives without further incident, which was an accomplishment since people seem to have a way of finding me even when I'm sure I'm not being followed.

Once we got into the waiting room, I tried not to bleed on anything that looked expensive, but I couldn't tell the difference. It all looked expensive to me. Not that I really had much control over what kind of bleeding I did. I felt like a walking bite wound. The hole in my arm throbbed with intensity and the bite on my shoulder stung like a son of a bitch; imp bites have a lot of nasty germs in them. The holy water wash was going to sting like a mother.

Lucy had fared a little better than me. The cuts on her arm and belly were nasty but not fatal, maybe not even infectious. They might even heal without a scar. She'd used her remaining shirt sleeve to stop the bleeding and chastised me for not doing the same. I grunted at her irritably and dripped blood on the carpet. I didn't have enough sleeves to stop all my bleeding.

Miles rushed in with a handful of gauze and directed me to a large chair. Without being asked, he went to work tending my wounds while Leslie went to work on Lucy.

"I have sneaking suspicion that neither of you really knows how to relax," Leslie said.

"You're a mess," Miles surveyed my damaged body, "you've been through the wringer, haven't you! I'm don't even sure where to begin."

I held up my mangled arm. "Here."

"Yes," Miles said and went to work, "yes of course. Good idea."

Thankfully, neither Miles nor Leslie talked while they worked their magic. And I literally mean worked their magic. Miles applied an ointment, laced with holy water and something that smelled like cinnamon and eggs. I'd seen—or smelled—it before. Our healers called it barleywink and it worked wonders when applied by the right hands. Miles worked the ointment around and into my wounds while softly chanting an ancient, yet familiar Tibetan prayer. I'd heard that one quite a few times throughout my illustrious career.

Archivists fulfilled many roles, including paramedic and field surgeon. Barleywink and obscure healing prayers were standard fare among the services they provided. They didn't have natural magic abilities like wizards, but they sure could use the heck out of magic. Dean Forrester had done some work on me once a few years back. He hated every second of it and made sure I knew it, but he did a bang-up job.

Miles repeated the chant two more times then fell silent so he could concentrate on closing the wounds with tight, precise stitches. He had some impressive skill and a much more pleasant bedside manner than Lucy. Despite the healing salve and the prayers, the whole process still hurt like the blazes, and I did my best to take it all in my typical stoic fashion.

Lucy, on the other hand, hissed frequently and cursed like an angry longshoreman while Leslie worked her own magic.

After he finished, Miles nodded as if he just finished painting a masterpiece then announced he was going to go make some herbal tea. Leslie double-checked all my bandages and adjusted the fit, giving Lucy a moment or two to collect herself. By the time Lucy finished settling down, and Leslie finished her inspection, Miles returned pushing a cart loaded with a tea service, a plate full of cookies, and another change of clothes for Lucy and me.

Miles served us bitter-tasting tea and spiced cookies and I tried my best to bring them up to speed on what had just happened at Power and Light. I managed to eat all the cookies in the process, except for the two Lucy managed to snatch away.

Miles and Leslie listened, intently as I recounted the attack and our hasty departure. Lucy peppered in a few details here and there but didn't really have much to add. Neither of us included or personal conversation or our interaction with Jesse. I didn't see it was relevant, even though I knew Miles would say otherwise.

Miles slapped his leg when I finished, "You are something else. Really. It's fascinating how you work!"

"Yeah, it was a real gas," Lucy said.

Leslie placed a hand on Miles' shoulder as if to settle him down, "We don't mean to underplay the trauma. But these stories are our primary purpose."

"I checked the feeds while I was in the back preparing your tea," Miles said. "The incident is being reported by police as a 'freak attack by wild dogs.'"

"Wild dogs?" Lucy said waved her hands toward the exit. "Did they even look at the carcasses we left behind?"

"They're imps," I said.

"Yeah, I know."

"When you destroy an imp's body, it disintegrates," Leslie explained. "Sometimes very rapidly."

Lucy dropped her hands, "Really?"

Miles nodded eagerly, "Oh yes, they're projections into our plane of existence. Their forms are ephemeral. Their projection deteriorates when inflicted with enough physical trauma."

"Well, they're pretty vicious projections," Lucy said.

"Oh yes," Miles said, "they would be. Naturally. I mean, they are projections of spiritual beings from the nations—"

"Nations of Hell," Lucy finished for him with an irritated sigh. "Yeah, I heard. Still... dogs?"

"I flexed my arm and wiggled my fingers. The pain was finally starting to fade to something tolerable.

"Don't matter," I said absent-mindedly, as I tested the range of motion at the elbow. "They'd still call it a dog attack even if they were there to see the whole thing.".

"Don't be stupid," Lucy snorted.

"It's true," I said. "People can't deal with things they can't explain rationally. They go with the least insane explanation."

"Wild dogs," Miles said. "That's what the witnesses reported. They really didn't know how else to explain it. Oh, they did mention a young woman with a gun shooting at the dogs."

"Did they mention a few well-placed headshots?" Lucy asked smugly.

"Unfortunately, not. No report of that," Miles admitted. "But I'd love to hear more if you'd like to elaborate."

Lucy ignored the request and crossed her arms, "They weren't so tough with a few bullets in them."

"Bullets from a magic gun," I said.

"Wait, what?" Lucy frowned.

"Bullets from a magic gun," I repeated. "The Holy Glockamolie."

"You mean those silly sounding runes your buddy went on about?"

"Holy Invocation," I said. "Runespells."

"Oh!" Leslie said excitedly, "You've been to see Lazarus Grey!"

I nodded, "Earlier today."

"That's definitely going into the database," Miles said. "What else did you acquire from him? Have you secured his services for your current assignment?"

"Are the cops looking for us?" Lucy asked before I had to blow off Miles' questions.

Miles shook his head, "Not specifically you, no. They are currently looking for two persons of interest. A handsome professional wrestler and an attractive redhead co-ed."

"Co-ed?" Lucy moaned.

"Still, that's a pretty vague description," I said.

"Not vague enough," Lucy smirked then added with a terrible attempt at an Irish accent. "Big tall handsome wrestler. That's wall Jesse from Cork."

"Who's Jesse," Miles and Leslie asked in unison.

"Our waitress at the bar," Lucy said. "Bill got her digits."

I flashed Lucy a deadly look.

Miles clapped, "That's going on the record too! This just keeps getting better. You're a wealth of interesting developments."

"That's very nice," Leslie said and patted me on the back, "Good for you."

"Thanks," I said without a smile.

"For all the good it'll do him," Lucy said. "He'll just throw it away. He's such a monk."

"You don't know that," I said too defensively. "Besides, it ain't relevant."

"Everything's relevant," Miles stated, too enthusiastically. "Everything. You have no idea!"

"I don't know about relevant," Leslie said, "but it's not our job to discriminate what's worthy or not."

"Speaking of jobs," Lucy said, "what did you find out about ours? This whole mess happened so we could give you nerds some time to google some useful information for us."

"Your job is proving to be an interesting can of worms," Leslie said, "and troubling."

"Tell me about it," I said. I leaned back in the chair and stretched. It was the first chair I'd sat in for days that didn't seem to mind my tremendous weight on it.

"Turns out," Leslie continued, "that it is theoretically possible to perform an extraction, even from Dudael."

"Not only is it possible," Miles jumped in, "it's revolutionary. If it actually happened, it's a world-changing accomplishment. Completely unprecedented."

Lucy said, "Explain."

Miles nodded eagerly, "It can't be done by a mortal. Mortals don't have the innate magical ability. Even practicing sorcerers. They simply can't tap into the depths of power necessary. It can only be done by a wizard."

I said, "Like Winters?"

"Master Winters didn't do it," Lucy glared at me.

"She's probably right," Leslie said, "because the phenomena also requires the practice of sorcery."

I said, "Winters isn't a sorcerer."

"Correct," Leslie agreed.

Lucy snarled through gritted teeth, "Winters didn't do this."

"But a sorcerer did?" I sat back upright again and leaned my elbows on my knees.

"No," Miles said.

"Are you doing this on purpose?" Lucy asked.

"Ok, let me explain," Miles said excitedly, "Incursions require a great deal of life energy, tapped into from both sides of the veil. The life energy is the conduit... the link between the two planes in an incursion. Mortal participants have been able to link up with influencers on the Otherside, mostly through Otherside magic. But an unbridged incursion—"

"Jailbreak," Leslie interjected.

"Yes, a jailbreak," Miles said, "is considerably more difficult.

Especially a reverse incursion, extended into a realm like Yokikai which is surrounded by and operates by dark magic. The link originates here in the mortal world and serves as an anchor," he extended a finger on his right hand and curled it like a hook, "while the user attempts to find the target and pull them out." He hooked a finger on his left hand and tugged. "It has to be rooted in dark magic," he wiggled his left finger, "and fueled by light magic, or life magic," wiggling his right finger.

"Naturally," Leslie added, "this is all super sketchy."

"So, a wizard, doing sorcery?" I asked.

Miles wiggled the fingers on both hands as if that was the answer.

"It sounds ridiculous," Lucy added.

"It does, doesn't it?" Miles said and put away his fingers, "but that's the kind of the point. It's completely unorthodox, by the standards we have come to accept.". You see, the entire concept requires a very specific concentration of life magic and death magic." He popped up the two fingers again but wiggled the right one more vigorously. "More life than death in this case believe it or not. Only a wizard can tap into those levels of life power then he'd—"

"Or she," Leslie added.

"Of course. Or she, yes," Miles nodded, "would then have to draw from life magic, using death magic." He wiggled both sets of fingers again, tapping them together, "Specifically blood magic, in this case. It's a dangerous combination and difficult and very... messy."

"We've seen the messy," Lucy said.

I tried not to think of it.

A new look of concern formed on Leslie's brow at the mention of the mess. She paced back and forth for a moment then stopped and turned to me, "I'm very troubled that none of what you have described has been entered into the database yet. It's just wrong."

"We're operating knee deep in all kinds of wrong," Lucy said.

"Who can do this kind of magic?" I asked.

"Who knows?" Miles said. "It violates so many tenets of the wizard's code. It's punishable by death according to the Nine-Fold Council's laws. No recognized wizard should be able to exercise black magic without drawing the attention of the entire magic-using world."

"Yet they did," I said.

"Apparently," Leslie furrowed her brows.

I ran my hands throw my stubbly hair, "This is growing more turns than a pretzel."

"No legitimate operating wizard could pull this off," Miles said.

"So... we're looking for an undocumented wizard performing forbidden blood magic, using skills developed under the cover of an unrealistic amount of secrecy," Lucy said.

Leslie shrugged.

Lucy growled, "So we just need to find an underground contraband black magic practitioner?"

"That's not our highest priority," I said.

"It's not?"

"Don't forget what they pulled out of Dudael."

"Right, how could I forget?" Lucy said, "Rez-whatever. What do you have on him, it?"

"Rezruel," Miles said in a very sinister tone. "If it was somehow incursed, it will have to be retired by a very specific means."

"What specific means?" Lucy said.

"We don't know," Leslie admitted, "that information is gone."

"Gone how?" I asked.

"We can't find it," Miles said casting a troubled look at Leslie, "There are sections of the files that have been removed from the Archives database. Much of the data concerning Rezruel specifically has become unretrievable. We had a hard enough time just confirming his existence."

"He exists," I stated flatly.

"This a problem," Lucy said.

"It is," Leslie agreed. "For more reasons than you understand. To hide or remove information in the Archives is tedious by design and can only be done by a master archivist."

Lucy clenched a fist and opened it, "And Forrester is one of those, isn't he?"

"He is," Leslie nodded, "I know Mr. Forrester. This is not like him at all. He is the consummate professional."

"Stuffy professional," Lucy corrected.

"True," Leslie admitted, "but a professional. He takes his job very seriously."

"As do we all," Miles piped in.

"Of course," Leslie conceded. "We tried to check in on him while you two were gone, but the link between our Archives is not functioning right now."

"What link?" I asked.

"The link," Leslie said.

As always, there were things I didn't understand, but I didn't want to get off on another tangent.

"So, Dean is screening his calls?" Lucy asked.

"It's a little more complicated than that," Leslie said. "But he isn't responsive to our inquiries."

"Will you check in on him for us?" Miles asked.

"Oh, you can count on that," I said.

"Please, be gentle," Leslie added. "He may be a victim in this terrible situation. I have a feeling none of this is what it seems."

"It rarely is," I said.

By the time we got cleaned up and ready to go again, it was pouring rain. Lucy's led foot had us several miles down the road before either of us had anything to say. I was leaning my cheek against the window, enjoying the cold glass against my skin. I let the fresh memories of a simple cup of coffee and the pleasant cadence of an Irish accent wash around in my head as I started to doze. Then Lucy spoiled it.

"What's your connection with Rezruel?"

"Huh?" I pulled my face from the window. "Connection?"

"You and Rezruel?" Lucy said. "Obviously he's trouble. And obviously you have history. What's the connection? Are you like soul sisters or something?"

I shook my head, "No. Ain't no connection. I fought him. That's it. It was a bad fight, but it was just a fight."

"Then you have history."

"I retired him," I said. "That's all."

"Well, maybe it isn't personal to you, but it is to somebody."

"Looks that way."

"Why? Because of a grudge?"

I watched the wipers swish back and forth as I tried to think of a better explanation. But I couldn't come up with one.

"I don't know," I finally said. "I guess."

"So, some asshole wizard or sorcerer or whatever is willing to unleash Armageddon on the world because you pissed in their cereal?"

"I've pissed in a lot of cereal, Sister," I said.

"Yeah, well, somebody had enough," Lucy kept her eyes fixed on the road, but her hands had a white-knuckle grip on the steering wheel.

She was right of course. Somebody was making this personal in an epic way.

I heaved a sigh, "I don't know what to say."

"That vampire bitch seemed to hate you a whole bunch," Lucy offered.

"You noticed that?"

"Yeah, I'm real observant. I got a real vendetta vibe from her."

"She is laying it on pretty thick, but I don't think she wants to end the world."

"Why not?" Lucy finally looked at me, her face softer than I expected. "You said so yourself that you pretty much ended her world already. Maybe she wants to return the favor."

"True," I said then after a second I shook the thought away, "but no. She's not a wizard. She couldn't be the one doing this."

"If you say so," Lucy shrugged unconvincingly, "Then somebody else hates you more than her. If that's possible."

"Seems like," I said. "As much as I hate it, it doesn't change the mission. Our first priority is getting rid of Rezruel. Then whoever invited him. 'Why' comes after."

"Alright, then what's our next move? We've got some shiny new weapons. We know what our target is. Let's go finish this."

"Just like that?"

"Just like that," Lucy nodded once as if the decision had been finally made.

"Ain't that simple, Red," I said tiredly.

"Nothing ever is if you don't let it be," she threw a hand up in frustration. "Just like getting that Irish girl's number. Just do it. It'll work out or it won't."

I looked at her sideways, "You don't strike me as the carpe diem type."

"I'm the 'quit wasting my time' type. Put me in front of that thing and I'll put a bullet between its eyes, or its belly button or whatever it takes, and can be done with this mess."

"If they're doing this to get at me, they'll find us whether we're ready or not. That's something I don't like about this mess. Hell. There's a lot I don't like."

"So?"

"So. We've been on this job for less than twenty-four hours and we keep bumping into trouble where we ain't looking for it. Where it shouldn't be. And none of it has been Rezruel. All of it stinks of a setup, and that's pissing me off."

"Join the club," Lucy said, her knuckles white again.

"I don't like being the target," I mumbled.

"Who does?" Lucy snapped, "I don't like being forced into a job I don't want. I had better things to do than to join your crusade."

"That wasn't my choice," I said.

"Fuck you, Kemper," she snapped. "You made all kinds of choices, and they affect everyone. Everything you do sends out a tidal wave of bullshit. You don't just quit on the Council. Nobody does that."

"What do you know about it?"

"It's not government work," Lucy said, "and you weren't in some monster hunter's union. You told me yourself. You were all-in. You signed up for this shitty life. Deal with it."

"You don't know what a shitty life is," I spat back.

"Fuck you," she said again. "You don't have the monopoly on pain and suffering, you giant ass."

"No? Then tell me. How hard was your life? How hard is it being a—"

I didn't get the chance to finish, because a bolt of lightning exploded in the road right in front of our car.

Chapter Twenty-Two

The flash was blinding. Lucy screamed. I screamed. The lightning missed the car, but I felt the tremendous tingle of a jillion volts of electricity snapping through the air a few feet in front of us. The car died and Lucy tugged hard on the steering wheel to avoid the new pothole in the road. We hit the edge of it and bounced.

Cars zipped by, honking horns, as we rolled to a stop on the shoulder about a dozen yards or so past the pothole.

I looked behind us and spotted something shaped like a person standing near the spot where the lightning struck.

"Start the car," I said very calmly. Lucy turned the key in the ignition and the car protested.

The person-shaped thing was a little shorter than an average person and hunching forward as if the weight of two shoulders and a head was too much for it to bear. The pouring rain soaked into its ragged clothes and ran down onto the road in streaks of brown.

"Start the car," I said again more urgently.

"I'm trying!" The car whined and whirred and chugged a little. It wanted to start but not without a little bit of drama first.

The figure reached into his muddy coat and pulled out something bright and pulsating that looked a lot like a ball of lightning. Fingers of electricity lanced out from the small bundle, crackling against the road and the figure's arms and head.

Our car's engine rumbled to life. I reached across and stomped on Lucy's foot on the accelerator and yanked on the steering wheel hard just as the figure threw the ball at us. The car screeched into a tight right-hand turn, and the ass end whipped around. The crackling ball of electricity flew past the car and exploded into a burst of light and thunder against the pavement several yards away. We spun around until we were facing him. I let off the gas and Lucy quit cursing.

A passing minivan stopped, as a passenger rolled down the window to yell at the figure standing in the road. The figure smiled, and it was not a friendly looking smile and not one you wanted pointing at you. He pulled another ball of lightning from his coat and slammed it against the side of the van. The orb exploded with a blinding flash and the van literally jumped in the air then landed on its side in the next lane of traffic. Cars skidded to a halt, careening sideways. One slid into the van's rear end. Another veered off the road to avoid running over the nasty figure. He watched the wreckage with obvious amusement.

"Fuck this!" Lucy roared and hit the accelerator. The back end fishtailed on the wet road then caught traction and the car sped toward the figure. He saw the oncoming Crown Vic and his smile disappeared. He raised his hands in defense as the car struck him head-on. His greenish skin and long, pointy nose lit up in the headlights before the collision sent him flying back over the nearest stopped car.

"What the hell is that?" Lucy screamed.

The icky green guy didn't stay down for long. He sprang up quickly and climbed to the roof of a stopped car.

"Reverse," I barked. Lucy yanked the shift lever into reverse and hit the gas. The car's tires squealed, and the car shot backward. Lightning exploded on the highway, just missing the front of the car. Lucy roared in anger and frustration, then threw the car in drive again. She swerved sharply and we slammed into a vehicle, it bounced into the next and the dirty green man tumbled from the roof. Without waiting to see what Lucy would do next, I kicked the passenger door open and jumped out into the rain.

I ran forward the jump and slip across \the crumpled hood of a hybrid electric car and landed on my feet. The ugly little green dude was still on the ground. Up close he wasn't as small as I'd thought. He had long, thick arms and legs and wicked long fingers ending in nasty brown fingernails. He popped up quickly and faced me looking up at me with that nasty, jagged toothed grin. He was five feet tall, at best. He was bald with knobby, wart-covered skin that had the consistency of a dead fish. Up close, he kind of smelled like a dead fish too. Rain dripped from his pointy nose and his long pointy ears.

"You gotta be kidding?" I groaned. A freaking goblin. Today of all days?

"Ahhhh, Hunter! So nice to meet you!" his voice was horrid, like his throat was crammed with mud and water. He sneered at me for a moment then his left hand lashed up and punched me square in the nose. It was a reached, but still a solid shot. I stumbled back and fell on my ass.

Over the sound of rain pelting the roof of the car behind me and the honking horns from people who had no idea what was going on, I heard the distinct growl of Lucy's voice. She flew over the hood of the car, feet first. She planted a two-foot stomp kick square in the goblin's chest. The nasty little bastard flew backwards, rolled twice then quickly sprung back to his feet. Lucy closed in and met him with a flurry of punches and kicks. Several of them. The goblin staggered back. Lucy's right foot flashed out and delivered a swift kick to his leg, above the knee, that would have broken a normal person's leg or seriously dislocated their kneecap. It didn't do either. It must have hurt though because the goblin roared angrily and toppled over sideways.

I used the karate demonstration as an opportunity to get back to my feet. As goblin reached into his coat again, I kicked him in the ribs, hard. I don't care what realm you're from. That hurts. The blow sent him sprawling several feet away. He slid to a stop up against the side of an SUV.

"Who are you?" I demanded.

The goblin cackled. It was a nasty sound, as nasty as the bastard looked and smelled. He rolled over to face us and his eyes flashed down to his hands. He was holding one of his damned lightning balls.

"Shit!" I jumped toward the nearest car as the lightning ball exploded. Although I didn't take a direct hit, the shockwave propelled me on over the vehicle and I landed flat on my back on the wet pavement. Lucy landed next to me with a familiar grunt, but she tumbled past me a little more gracefully.

I rolled to my side and tried to get my breath back. Lucy didn't wait for me. She rushed back to where he had been then stopped.

"What the hell?" she said.

I forced myself to get up and staggered to where she stood.

"Hell," I said. The goblin was gone, leaving behind a smudge of mud. It was too much to hope that he was dead. My luck didn't work out that way. He'd be back, that was for sure, and he'd be back at the worst time. That was my luck too.

Some people were getting out of their vehicles, now that there was no way they could be helpful. A few had their phones to their ears.

"We better keep moving," I said to Lucy and headed for the car. She beat me to it and slid into the passenger seat. I guess I was driving.

Chapter Twenty-Three

"Are you gonna tell me what the hell that was?" Lucy said as we zipped away at a responsible speed.

"A goblin."

"Don't fuck with me today," Lucy said.

"I'm not."

"So, goblins are real, now? As if vampires and demons and wizards aren't enough."

"That's just the tip of the iceberg Red," I said. "There's a lot of weird out there."

"Goblins?" she shook her hand and ran her hands through her soaking wet hair, "So, they're just hiding on highways, waiting for the right moment to throw lightning at passing cars?"

"The lightning thing is new," I said. "I don't know why they do what they do. We don't see them very often. They don't belong here."

"You think?"

"They come from the Otherside smartass."

"You mean like, the fairy world?"

"I mean like the Otherside," I said, "home of the Fae, among other things. Don't call them fairies. They don't like it.

"Well, I wouldn't want to upset them," Lucy said.

"You really don't," I mumbled.

"Have you seen that creep before?"

"No. Don't know him," I racked my brain to remember the last time I'd dealt with a goblin before. It had been years, and not in the Midwest. It was in Washington state maybe.

"How do you know it's goblin then?"

"I've seen goblin before. They're more common on the coasts for some reason."

"What else is real? Werewolves, you already told me that. Trolls? Chupacabra?" Lucy counted them off on her fingers, "bigfoot?"

"Allegedly. Don't know anyone who fought one."

"The boogeyman?"

"Boogeymen," I said seriously. "Nasty bastards. Feed on fear. Hard to find, hard to catch."

"How do you kill them?"

"Dunno," I admitted. "Not my field."

"Dragons?"

"Haven't seen any."

"Gremlins?"

"They're all real, okay?" I tilted my head back and looked up at the ceiling of the car for a moment, then I put my eyes back on the road, "Everything you ever heard is probably real. The world is full of nightmares."

"Ok," Lucy crossed her arms and snorted, "Jeez. Excuse me for not being at ease with all this shit, you jackass. It's all a little hard to digest."

"Well, chew it up and swallow it because it ain't going away," I waved my hands in a wild gesture, "And once you get sucked in, you can't pretend it ain't real."

"Got it," Lucy sucked in a long breath. "You win. Hunters suck. Monster hunting sucks."

I started to count to ten then stopped myself. "It kinda pisses me off that I have to hold your hand through all this.

"Fuck you," Lucy she jabbed a finger at me. "Nobody told you to hold my hand and I sure as hell didn't ask you to. You know I didn't sign up for this. You know Master Winters sprung that shit on both of us. And fuck you again because not all the scary bullshit in this world comes from some fairy tale magic land."

She was right about that last part. There are wives and children all over the world who live in fear, in their own homes, terrified of the people they should run to for comfort. People disappear every day and unspeakable things are done to them and there's nothing supernatural or paranormal about it. Some people are monsters of the highest degree and they're as mortal as any other human. The world is a shitty place. I had chosen to fight the supernatural monsters because, strangely, they made more sense.

People, good or bad, could be in any one of the cars we sped by on the highway. I had no way of knowing. That's why monster hunting had been a simple business for me. Somebody else was always there to tell me what the monsters were, and I did something about it. I didn't pass judgment. I was carrying out simple justice. That distinction used to bring me some small degree of comfort.

Right up until I faced Mehira. How did she make me question that? She was unquestionably a monster. A murderer. An old one, from the old world. Why didn't I put her down like every other beast I'd slain before her? Why couldn't I?

Because, somehow, I started to think of Mehira as her and not it. Something changed in that moment. She became a woman. Albeit a vicious and dangerous woman. I couldn't execute her any more than I could Lucy or York or Dean.

I let the tension hang in the car for a few miles. Lucy and I had both earned it. We were two angry people stuck in a shitty situation. That was all.

Eventually, I tried to cut through the tension, "What did you sign up for?"

"You really don't know?"

"You hinted about being a Council assassin," I said, "but that ain't you. I know that much. You're a badass but I just don't get how you can be hooked up with the Council and not know any of the basic shit that we're dealing with here."

"I've lived a sheltered life," she said plainly.

"With a bunch of misogynistic wizards," I said. "You told me. But that don't tell me anything."

"I've told you more about myself already than I ever planned to.

I'm a mysterious bitch. Leave it there."

"Is there a switch that you flip?"

"No. It just resets all on its own."

We stopped for gas once. Lucy pumped fuel and I stayed in the car. I felt like there was a spotlight on me everywhere I went. The evidence to support this sensation was growing by the hour. I couldn't go anywhere without some bit of trouble finding me. I didn't like being back on the interstate either. The goblin attack came just a day after Mehira ambushed on the same highway, though over a hundred miles apart. Law enforcement would have to take notice, maybe even set up checkpoints or random stops. I didn't need that. Not on top of everything else.

By the time we crossed the Missouri again, it had quit raining. The roads were busy with early morning commuters, going about their charmed, ignorant lives. I got off the interstate and headed for downtown, snaking through all the side streets without an actual plan or destination in mind.

"Where are we going?" Lucy finally asked.

"Dunno yet," I said.

"I thought we decided to go to the Archives."

"We did," I said, "that's why we ain't going there yet."

"What are you implying?" Lucy narrowed her eyes at me.

"That we're being followed or tracked, and I don't like it," I kept my voice neutral, "I don't feel like leading them straight to the Archives."

"Makes sense," Lucy's tone softened a little. "Then what are you thinking then?"

"I'm thinking I'm tired, beat up, hungry, confused, and pissed off," I poked my finger at the windshield without looking at Lucy. "I keep getting sucker-punched from outta nowhere and I'm fed up with it. I wanna start a fight and I wanna do it on my own terms."

Lucy actually smiled, "I can relate to that."

"Thought you might."

"What's the plan?"

I didn't have one. I'd been winging it. Then I had an idea.

"Let's go somewhere with some fighting room and see which asshole shows first."

"You're speaking my language Slugger," Lucy shifted in her seat eagerly as if preparing for an exciting ride.

I headed for the riverfront then turned north. Just past McKinley, there were a few abandoned lots among the industrial storage depots and manufacturing plants. I found a secluded lot west of the garbage transfer station where grass pushed up through the cracks in the concrete and scraggly trees around the edges offered a little concealment. It wasn't completely hidden from passersby, but it should allow us to make some noise without attracting too much attention too quickly. I parked in the middle of the lot. It would do. We were surrounded on three sides by trees with an opening on one side where we busted through a rusty-chain link gate to drive in. The fourth side was a concrete wall, separating us from fertilizer storage lots on the east.

Lucy paced like a lion in a cage behind me as I popped the trunk contemplated the selection of weapons. The boxes of shotgun shells had been busted open from all the action earlier and the ammo was scattered all around. The shotgun was wedged up in the corner. The box with the hammer and nails was tangled up in the beach towels. But the large claymore and the saber sat exactly where we left them. Each of Laz's creations was unique and came with their own quirks. I didn't know what Killicutty's quirks were. I really didn't have time to find out either.

Lucy didn't seem to care. She stepped around me and took up Heir Chop-A-Lot without hesitation. She was in a killing mood.

Then she reached back in and snatched the shotgun.

"Here," Lucy shoved it into my hands. "It's loaded."

I nodded and didn't say anything while I checked it. I believed her, but I checked anyway. The quick road to getting yourself killed is taking other people's word for things you ought not to have. I took one of the big nails out of the plastic case and slid it into my belt like a dagger.

"Just take the damn sword," Lucy barked.

"Fine," I said. I picked up the sword, expecting a heavy steel burden. It was lighter than I expected, balanced mostly toward the hilt. It practically begged me to swing it. This was a blade that wanted to do some chopping.

"Alright Conan," Lucy said. "What now?"

"We wait," I said. "It's not long until sunrise. If Mehira's gonna attack, she'll do it before sunrise."

"You sure? The time of day doesn't seem to matter to her."

I shrugged, "I'm not sure of anything at this point."

"What if it's one of the other nightmares we've been dealing with?"

"Won't matter much. I don't think sunlight matters to them."

"What if it's both?"

"Then we're in for a real adventure."

Lucy spat on the ground, "Well, Irish Jesse would just swoon if she knew about the adventures she's missing out on."

"I'd just as soon miss it myself."

"Yeah. I know." She didn't sound sympathetic. The opposite, in fact.

She started pacing again, "How long do we wait?"

"Until something happens."

Lucy shook her head and pressed her lips together.

"Believe it or not," I said, "this isn't my usual way of doing things."

"Yeah, I know," she stopped pacing and swung the sword back and forth a few times then held it up and looked down the length of the blade. "You're a heat-seeking missile, or whatever." She swung the sword again.

"My monsters weren't hard to find. It was never the other way around. They didn't hunt me."

"Sucks to be you."

"Don't forget, you're in this too, Sister."

"Oh, I haven't. It fuels my boundless rage."

I laughed despite the situation. Lucy knew who she was. Or at least she knew who she was going to let people see. I envied that. A little. I also knew how exhausting it was to keep up appearances.

The sound of tires squealing broke the quiet morning. Lucy shot me a questioning look and set her jaw. She adjusted her grip on the sword. Too tight. White knuckled.

Moments later, a red minivan bounced through the open gate and skidded a stop in the grass across from us.

Lucy switched Heir Chop-A-Lot to her left hand and pulled out Holy Glockamolie.

The driver revved the van's 4-cylinder engine, making it sound more like someone who couldn't figure out how to get out of park than someone trying to make intimidating pre-vehicular assault sounds.

"You're creepy girlfriend?" Lucy tightly.

I didn't bother to answer. Instead, I walked sideways several steps, putting distance between me and our loaner car. I wasn't ready to trash another car just yet. We still needed it. Lucy stayed by my side but didn't take her eyes from the minivan.

I walked until I was clear of the concrete and standing on wet, un-mowed grass and plunged the tip of the sword into the ground, leaving the hilt within reach. Lucy planted her feet, right foot a little forward and adjusted her grip on the pistol. Opening and closing her fingers several times.

The driver-side door opened, and High School Buddy stepped out, holding a shotgun, one eerily like the kind found in police cruisers. Ignoring us, he walked around to the passenger side of the van and slid the side door open.

Without flourish or fanfare, Mehira emerged.

She wasn't wearing the dark hoodie anymore. Now she wore a long billowy dress of dark green fabric that touched the ground and hid her feet. She told tall and still for a moment, her chin raised, her shoulders squared. Defiant. Strong. Then, she walked to the front of the van in long graceful steps, her fierce green eyes fixed on me. With one hand covered in fine black leather gloves, she reached up and pushed some of her raven black hair back behind her ears. Her other gloved hand hung to her side, fingers wrapped around the solid wood grip of the Holy Handgun.

"Ok," I said through gritted teeth, "let's do this."

Then Lucy said, "What the hell is that?"

A pinpoint of light appeared in the air halfway between us and Mehira. It was painful to look at directly, like a welding arc. The light flickered rapidly and some of the wet grass caught on fire. I stumbled back a few steps from a shockwave of hot air. The light faded and at the center of the burning grass stood a mass of familiar shapes.

"Shit," I said.

"Fuck me," Lucy added.

Half a dozen baboon-like imps seethed as a group as if waiting for a command to attack.

Turns out, that's exactly what they were waiting for.

"Go get 'em boys!" The command came from a familiar yet distorted voice. The spikey haired demon punk bellowed from the tree line where'd he gone unnoticed.

Half of the imps charged toward Lucy and me. The rest turned and headed for Mehira and Buddy. All four of us opened fire at the same time.

Chapter Twenty-Four

"Bullet dug up chunks of ground and imp flesh. Mehira used up her six shots in the time it took me to fire off both of my shotgun's barrels. Lucy rattled off several shots. Two imps went down. But more came.

I hurled the empty shotgun, tomahawk style, at the closest one and struck it between the eyes. The imp faltered a step or two but kept coming. I snatched up Killicutty in a two-handed grip and swung down just as the imp leapt at me. The creature slid to a stop just inches from my toes with a split open skull. But there were still more coming.

I heard Lucy's murderous roar of profanity and frustration followed by another barrage of gunfire. Damn, but she knew how to spend ammo. Another imp leapt at me and I had time to get the sword's blade between it and me before we both went to the ground. The edge of the blade bit into its torso but it wasn't a fatal wound. I wriggled the sword up against the imp's throat, but I couldn't get any leverage. The imp chomped and snapped at me with its jagged teeth and tore at my arms with wild claws. The little bastard was going to undo everything Leslie and Miles had done to fix us up.

Something clamped onto my left boot. I kicked with my free foot, but I couldn't see what I was kicking at. The other imp had me pinned down and I couldn't get Killicutty into a better position without letting it chomp on my face. Then I remembered I still had another weapon.

I worked a hand free and dug around at my belt. There! I grabbed the large nail and yanked it free.

I prayed, "Benefictum!" and shoved the nail into the imp's eye. It bellowed and thrashed. I hammered the nail again with the palm of my hand and repeated the word. The imp wailed and flopped to the side. I shoved it away so I could get at the one trying to chow down on my leg. The creature saw an opportunity as soon as I presented it. It released its grip on my leg and lunged for my face. I dropped the sword and grabbed its jaws with both hands, one on the upper and the other on the bottom. Teeth cut into my thumbs. It shook its head side to side, but I held on tight, gritting through the searing new pain in my hands. Claws grabbed at my chest and shredded my shirt and some of the skin beneath it. I pushed it to one side hoping to get my weight advantage into play, but it was at least as heavy as me and fueled by ugly magic.

OK, this wasn't working for me. I straightened both legs flat on the ground the launched one knee up and between the imp's legs. Imps don't have genitals, but it was a good bet that it was still a tender area. I wasn't gentle about it either. It was a hard kick. The imp flipped forward and over top of me. It chomped at my face as it flew over, missing my nose by less than an inch. It landed on its back, with arms and legs sprawled out awkwardly for a second.

I kicked up with my other knee letting the momentum carry me into a reverse somersault and curled both legs. I landed hard on the imp's torso with both knees and was rewarded with a series of cracks. I didn't know if it was ribs or a demonic exoskeleton, but cracking meant something breaking or something painful or both. I punched with both fists into the imp's throat. It made a choking sound and heaved its body, bucking me off to the side.

I rolled once and found Killicutty laying there waiting to be used. Oh, hey there pal! I wrapped my blood and imp-juice-soaked hands around the hilt and swung. The blade dug into the imp's shoulder as it turned on me. The front arm went limp, and it tumbled sideways. I yanked the sword back then stabbed. The tip tore into the imp's throat and the rest of the blade followed, buried all the way to the basket hilt handle. The imp made another, longer choking sound then collapsed. Ok. Who's next?

Lucy was still on her feet, facing down two more imps. She

flicked Heir Chop-A-Lot back and forth, the gleaming blade missing the two imps' noses by a hair but close enough to keep them at bay. They took turns lunging at her. But she was fast. One lunged, and she dodged to one side while jabbing at the other with her sword. Then the other lunged and she dodged. It was a deadly standoff that wouldn't last for long.

One imp jumped, and Lucy caught sight of me moving toward her, so she met it with an upward thrust and plunged Heir Chop-A-Lot into its chest. The other imp took the opening and leapt. I took the opportunity to cleave its head off midair with a mighty chop. The headless body tumbled to the ground and rolled into Lucy's legs, causing her to fall. The sword fell from her grip and landed out of reach. Another imp leapt... right over her and at me. Shit! I took one step back and raised my arms to block the impact. The blade flashed in front of my face and cut through the beast's lower jaw. It yelped and fell beside me.

"Sanctu Spitu," I said, a plunged Killicutty down, through its head pinning the imp to the ground. The magic phrase would keep the blade lodged in place until I released it.

Lucy got to her feet glowering and picked up Heir Chop-A-Lot. She took a step toward me and picked up the Holy Glockamolie from the grass and raised the gun. I spun around and there stood Mehira. Less than ten yards away. Several imps lay dead around her, her hands covered in blood and gore. High School Buddy stood behind her, still holding the shotgun, but the stock was broken and covered in imp goo.

God, I was tired.

I mumbled, "Sanctu Ritu," and felt a soft buzz of power dissipate from the sword. I pulled Killicutty free of the now dead imp and the ground and turned the blade toward Mehira.

She whispered softly. I thought she said, "at last," but her voice was drowned out by a deafening crack of thunder and a bolt of lightning. I felt a jolt of electricity, like someone had hit me with a taser, but much worse, and fell on my back. After a second, my vision cleared. And there stood the hideous goblin with his hideous grin and a horrid stench. Another ball of crackling energy bounced eagerly in his hands.

"You've got to be kidding," Lucy whined.

"What is this?" Mehira demanded.

The goblin looked at her with genuine surprise.

"You!" Its voice sounded like mud and worms, somehow. "What a surprise!" It cackled and hefted the lightning ball, at the same time Mehira raised the Holy Handgun and pulled the trigger. I knew the gun was empty. She'd shot all six rounds early in the fight. But the goblin didn't know. The gun clicked and the goblin flinched. I shifted my grip and threw Killicutty like a spear. The blade stuck into the goblin's side and hissed like cold water on a hot skillet. The goblin's eyes went wide, and it screamed. The ball of lightning sputtered and disappeared as the goblin danced around trying to remove the sword from its side without touching the iron. Mehira watched in confused shock. High School Buddy looked from me to Mehira, the implication clear. Why wasn't she attacking me now that I was unarmed? Good question.

I rushed toward the goblin, meaning to take hold of Killicutty, but he was moving around too much and too quickly. There were several gunshots from behind me. The goblin staggered as several wounds blossomed on his chest.

"Out of the way dammit!" Lucy yelled. I dropped to the ground, and she fired another shot. But the goblin was quick. He jumped at Lucy and smacked the gun from her hand. Then he finally shook the sizzling sword loose from his side. The claymore fell to the ground with about a foot of charred gore encrusted on the blade. The creature held its side, panting heavily, looking angrily at each of us in turn. With a growl of frustration, he grabbed another ball of lightning from his coat in a quick motion and threw it down at his own feet.

And again, with a flash, he was gone.

Mehira watched the empty spot where the goblin had stood with confusion on her face. The pistol hung down at her side, obscenely large in her feminine hand. She looked as tired as I felt.

"Why?" she demanded.

"Why what?" I asked, exhaustion thick in my voice.

"You refused to kill me at my weakest moment," she said pointed at me accusingly, "Again and again. I attack you and I provoke you, yet you still fail to kill me. And here, now... You have the audacity to save my life! As if I could owe you any more contempt than I already do. What manner of cruel beast are you?"

High School Buddy racked the slide on his shotgun but Mehira raised a hand, and he lowered the barrel.

"Why won't you kill me?"

"I'll do it," Lucy said.

"Shut up," I whispered.

"Then fucking do it already," Lucy snapped. "This is the reason we're in this mess."

"Shut up," I said again, harder.

Mehira quickly closed the distance between us. Her green eye glowed intensely as she grabbed me by the lapels of my jacket. She like a garden.

"What kind of man are you?" Mehira asked, her voice trembling. "Twice! Twice you have robbed me of my death. My life is not yours to play with like a toy."

Buddy ran up behind Mehira and tugged at her sleeve, pointing urgently toward the east.

Mehira didn't acknowledge him. Instead, she locked eyes with me.

"What are you?" She asked.

I didn't answer. I didn't know how to answer that.

Buddy continued to tug and point urgently. I pulled my eyes away from Mehira's and looked eastward. A soft glow had spread across the horizon and the night's stars had begun to fade.

"Shall we sit together and watch the sunrise," Mehira asked enticingly. "Will you embrace me as a lover and bask in the reflection of the golden sun in my loving eyes?"

I frowned, "We are not lovers."

"No," Mehira agreed, "and you will not treat me as an enemy either."

"No."

"Then, what are we?"

"We," I said slowly, "ain't anything."

"On that, we agree," Mehira said.

"Bill," Lucy's voice was quiet, but hard, "don't fuck this up again."

"She's not the job," I said, more to me than to Lucy.

Mehira narrowed her eyes at me. His face was close enough to mine that I could see Lucy reflected in her eyes standing impatiently behind me. She raised the saber. "No!" I spun and slapped the blade savagely aside, and it fell from Lucy's hand. She turned on me, seething. Fist clenched.

"Not today," I said.

"When?" Lucy demanded.

"When it's your job," I said tiredly. "But ain't today." Two car doors slammed, and an engine fired up. I turned away from Lucy's hate-filled eyes to watch the minivan lurch into motion and speed out of the lot just as the sun broke over the horizon.

"You're an idiot," Lucy turned her back on me and picked up her sword. "You're a giant, stupid, idiot and you're going to get both of us killed because of your big stupid sense of honor." She stalked back to the car.

"It ain't honor," I said.

She didn't reply. Instead, she climbed into the passenger seat, weapons still in hand, and slammed the door. She had nothing left to say.

"It's not honor," I repeated more quietly. If it wasn't honor, what was it? I shook my head.

I didn't have an answer for that.

Chapter Twenty-Five

There couldn't be any doubt anymore that we were being tracked, but I had no idea how. Mehira, Demon Punk, and the muddy goblin kept showing up at just the right place, ready for a fight. All this added up to someone tracking me and feeding my location to all these players. And that wasn't the weird part. Mehira was out driving cars, shooting guns, and going about in the daytime. It didn't make sense. This was not vampiric behavior. Nothing was what it should be. What was the common factor?

My money was on Dean Masters the Antsy Archivist. He was acting a little too fishy for my liking. Too nervous. Granted, I'm an intimidating presence, but he'd never been like this before. Something was foul. He had withheld information from the record, which was practically a capital crime among the Archivists. And he was doctoring or removing information, again, a huge no-no. If all this wasn't his doing, he was still involved. Of that I was certain.

Lucy didn't argue when I told her we were heading back to see Dean Forrester. She didn't have much to say to me anyways. She was pissed that I had let Mehira go, and I can't say I blamed her. I really couldn't explain why I did it. Again. Nothing made any sense.

The secretary wasn't at the front desk when we entered the building. That was the first red flag. The second was the distinct smell of gunpowder and blood hanging thick in the air.

Lucy rounded the counter first, Holy Glockamolie leading the way, then stopped cold. A dozen or so men and women in Security Detail uniforms lay dead in the hallway. It had been a massacre. Spent brass, broken firearms, and mangled littered the floor. Bullet holes and blood peppered the walls. I couldn't figure out what they had been fighting, but it was a big fight. There was no sign of the enemy, whoever or whatever they were. The dead had gone down fighting. They had been beaten and slashed and mauled. It wasn't a man that did this.

Lucy squatted down next to one of the dead, "I knew him. Spencer."

"Friend?"

"He was a dick," she said quietly, "but we trained together some. He was unstoppable with a shotgun." The man's fingers still held tightly to the pistol grip of a combat shotgun as if someone might try to steal it from his corpse. Apparently, unstoppable wasn't enough.

I squatted next to Lucy and touched the blood on the floor. It was tacky and dark. This had happened at least an hour ago. It would have been just around the time we were preparing for our own fight. At the empty lot.

"Imps?" Lucy asked.

I shook my head slowly, "Don't think so. Something bigger. Worse." Lucy looked down the hallway. I knew what she was thinking. Are they still here?

"Come on," I said and stood up. I pried Spenser's shotgun as gently as I could from his hand and checked the magazine tube. It was full. He didn't even get off a shot. I shouldered the weapon and moved forward with Lucy by my side, her gun at combat-ready, finger on the trigger. Mine too.

The janitorial storage door was a crumpled mess of steel and wood, as if someone had crushed it like a beer can. The back wall had been smashed open to reveal the concealed stairway. The steps descended into darkness, a few of the remaining lights flickering eerily. I descended quickly, feeling strangely exposed in the confines of the stairwell.

The lone guard at the bottom had put up a valiant fight. But again, it wasn't enough. He'd shot through a full magazine on his submachine gun and even had time to get out a fighting knife before something crushed his skull and disemboweled him. Lucy turned away. The sight of a violent death is hard to swallow and nearly impossible to ignore. Even worse, this man, unlike those upstairs, had died alone.

The security door stood wide open with no apparent signs of forced entry. It was almost as if it had simply opened to welcome a friend. Lucy and I looked at each other warily before entering. I took a deep breath, expecting more carnage. Instead, the waiting room appeared untouched. It was the same as every other time I had visited... except for Dean's lifeless body lying in the center of the room.

He looked calm, almost as if he had died in his sleep. There were no signs of struggle, no apparent wounds, no blood. His skin had a sickly gray tone to it and his cheeks were slightly sunken. If he'd been killed, it had been done by something different than what had taken out the Detail. This wasn't a violent death. It seemed.

I squatted next to him to look a little closer while Lucy stood behind me, continuously scanning around the room with the Holy Glockamolie.

"That's not normal," I said.

"What isn't?" Lucy came closer and looked over my shoulder.

"His skin tone. He hasn't been dead long enough for lividity."

"Huh?"

"Lividity," I said. "When a heart stops pumping, the blood pools at the lowest parts of the body."

"Oh... I didn't know that's what it was called."

"You learn all kinds of terrible things in this job," I said.

"He's been drained?" Lucy's voice pitched and I sensed her tense up.

I nodded.

"Then a vampire did this."

I pursed my lips and shook my head slowly, "I don't think so."

"Stop defending that vampire bitch and face the truth," Lucy said angrily.

"You see any bites?" I spat back at her.

She didn't answer.

"Check," I said.

Reluctantly, Lucy holstered her gun and squatted next to me to investigate. I knew she wouldn't find any bite marks. There wasn't any blood anywhere. If you've ever seen the victim of a vampire attack, you don't forget it. Fangs are good for pretty little punctures like you see in the movies, only if your victim just sits there and takes it nice and calmly. In my experience, they don't. Vampires who hypnotize and seduce their victims are a rarity these days. People struggle and pointy teeth tear the skin. And fangs aren't straws. They're for making the victim bleed. It's messy. Even if the vampire drains a victim, blood still gets on clothing and the ground. And not all vampires have fangs. Some are messier.

Dean Forrester clearly hadn't been drained by a vampire.

"I don't see any bites," Lucy admitted after a brief inspection.

"Didn't think so," I said.

"But check this out," she added and showed me his arm where she had pulled up his sleeve. Something had been written on his forearm in black marker.

aQ3s@7!r

"What the heck is that?" I asked, "A code?"

"Looks like a password to me," Lucy said.

"That's a password? Don't people use passwords like Pinkbunny323?"

"Not Forrester," Lucy said. "He's a stickler, right? Password rules usually dictate a mix of numbers, letters, and special characters with a minimum of one upper case letter and no less than eight digits."

She was right. Dean was a perfectionist and a rule-follower. We would have followed password standards to the letter.

"Ok," I said, "let's see what he was hiding. You know how to use a computer?"

Lucy rolled her eyes, "God, how old are you? Of course I know how to use a computer."

"Well get cracking Mr. Roboto," I said.

"Who is Mr. Roboto?"

"Just go."

Stepping behind the elaborate counter at the end of the waiting room almost felt like trespassing. Dean had always been adamant that I didn't approach the polished wood and marble. As expected, the shelves and drawers were perfectly organized, nothing out of place. A single computer rested atop an antique secretary desk that looked like it wouldn't hold the weight of one of my feet. The computer was still powered on and had a login prompt blinking on the screen. Lucy punched in the password from Dean's arm. It unlocked the computer and showed us a single icon labeled "Security Feed." Lucy looked at me dubiously and clicked the icon.

A window popped up and filled the screen. It was a video recording of the waiting room. I turned and after a quick scan spotted the security camera mounted high up in the corner of the room. I had never noticed it before.

Lucy clicked the PLAY button and we watched the replay in silence.

Just inside the corner of the screen, Dean tapped away at the very keyboard Lucy now sat at, looking nervously over his shoulder toward the main entry doors. After a few minutes, he pulled up his shirt sleeve and wrote the password on his arm with a Sharpie. He replaced the cap, put the pen in a drawer, and with a final keystroke, locked the computer. He stood up, pulled his sleeve down, straightened his jacket and tie, and walked slowly to the middle of the waiting room, dead center of the camera's view. He stood with his hands clasped behind his back, chin held high. Damn. He knew he was about to die.

The security door swung open slowly. Dean raised a hand to

cover his mouth and nose but otherwise remained composed. A figure wearing an oversized black trench coat with a hood entered the room and the video image wavered.

"Strong magic will do that to electronics sometimes," I said. Lucy nodded curtly but didn't speak.

The figure walked a few steps into the waiting room then stopped. He raised a hand a motioned with a single finger. Then another shape appeared in the doorway. It was as large as a bison standing upright on its hind legs. It loomed in the doorway but didn't move into the room until the hooded figure motioned it forward. As it stepped into the waiting room, the video image distorted. We could still make out what was happened, but this thing was putting out a lot of interference. It had red skin like the lesser imps we'd been fighting, but this was no imp. It had two pairs of horns on either side of its head and a vaguely humanlike face, except long and wider with a wide nose and a wide lipless mouth. Its four lidless eyes glowed brilliant white like a welding arc with smoke trailing from them. Each hand had seven long fingers ending in jagged black claws.

"Is that Rezruel?" Lucy asked in a hushed voice.

"Not even close," I said. "That's a minor demon."

"Minor? Are you kidding me?"

I wish I was.

The demon took position beside the door like a sentry and didn't follow as the hooded figure approached Dean. Judging from his build, it was a man, walking with a slight limp. He stopped a couple of paces from Dean and extended his hand in a friendly gesture of greeting like he wanted to shake hands.

The Archivist politely refused and took a step back, probably instinctively. The two of them talked, or rather appeared to argue. There was no sound on the video but they appeared to know each other, speaking passionately, their hands moving in grand gestures.

Dean was clearly agitated, maybe even angry. It was hard to be certain through the distortion. Dean pointed at the man and the demon repeatedly. The debate continued, and Dean became more animated and gestured repeatedly to his left. Finally, the man in black turned his head, following Forrester's gesture.

"Clever bastard," I said as the hooded man looked right at the camera.

Lucy paused the feed. There was an aura of distortion around the man so we couldn't make out his features. Still, I couldn't shake the feeling I knew him.

After a moment of study, Lucy resumed the playback.

Forrester gestured wildly and pointed to himself and at the man. The figure shook his head slowly, as if disappointed. He said something and Dean shook his head and began to back away holding his hands out as if to stave off a threat. The man in black held up a hand, palm toward the Archivist, then closed his fingers into a fist and shook it, the image distorted even more. It was hard to make out what happened next. The distortion intensified and we could only make out flashes. A whisp of a red cloud materialized around Dean. The image flickered and the cloud swirled like mist in a breeze, but only around Dean as he stood there, stiff, as if frozen in place. The hooded man raised his arms, outstretched. The minor demon began to sway from side to side. Then the man in black dropped his arms and unclenched his fist. and the flickering image settled. Dean Forrester fell to the floor like a puppet whose strings had been cut.

The hooded man looked down on Dean's lifeless body, motionless. I thought the feed had locked up, but then the figure seemed to reluctantly turn away from the corpse. He limped out of the room and the demon followed. Nothing more happened. The distortion cleared up and the playback continued. Lucy fast-forwarded. Nothing else happened in the video until Lucy and I arrived to find Dean's body and logged into the computer, about thirty minutes after his death.

"What the hell was all that?" Lucy looked at me.

"I think it was blood magic," I said. "I think that guy drained Dean."

"Blood magic?" Lucy got up and backed away from the computer as if it was the source of her concerns, "Who can do something like that?"

"Dunno," I looked back at Dean's body on the floor, "I've only ever heard rumors. Never seen it."

"And that demon just stood there and watched," Lucy said. "After all the carnage in the hall, it just stood there calmly and waited."

"It's a servant," I said.

"Like a butler?"

"Like a slave," I said as I walked back toward Dean, "that dude in black was controlling it. He summoned it and it was obeying him."

"Another incursion?"

I shook my head curtly, "No. A summoning is different." I squatted down and gently crossed Dean's arms over his chest. I suddenly felt like I owed him a level of gratitude I'd never recognized before.

I stood back up, "A summoning is temporary. Usually pretty brief."

Lucy pointed toward the main entry, "If it was brief, then it was extra violent to make up for it."

I nodded, "In most cases, people summon demons for guidance and information. I've never seen one summoned and used like this. It's dangerous."

"Clearly."

"No, I mean demons have only one master, and it ain't the summoner."

Lucy's eyes widened, "Oh... shit."

"Yeah, and they don't switch loyalties. If that thing was obeying the Phantom of the Opera, it's just a matter of time before the dude loses command of it."

"That's not good."

"No, it's not," I agreed. "It needs to be expelled before he loses it."

"This keeps getting worse."

"That's how it works around me."

"Forrester knew that guy," Lucy said after a moment of thought. "Did you notice that?"

"I did."

"Could it be that guy... the Senior Archivist?"

"Dunno," I admitted. "I wouldn't know him if I saw him. But Archivists ain't wizards."

"Or sorcerers?"

"No," I looked around the room, sure I was missing something. "No, you won't see them using much magic beyond healing arts."

"Well, it's connected, somehow," Lucy threw up her arms in frustration."

I motioned toward the counter, "Maybe you can log back into that computer, check the video feed further back."

"I tried before logging out," Lucy said. "That video feed was the only thing we could get to with that login."

"Another freaking dead end," I sighed.

"We gotta figure something out."

"Yes, we do," I said. "You need to call Winters. The Archives is unmanned and undefended."

"Ok," Lucy nodded. "Yeah. You're right. Then what?"

"We need to go back to St. Charles. I feel like we missed something at that house."

"I feel like we missed a whole bunch."

I couldn't disagree.

Chapter Twenty-Six

As a Hunter, my methodology was to find a target and tear through it like a high-yield explosive. I didn't like all this investigating and puzzle-solving. It didn't help that I didn't have all the pieces of the puzzle and I didn't know exactly what the finished picture would look like. Somebody kept shuffling up the puzzle pieces and stealing them and actively trying to kill me with them. I don't like puzzles. Never had the patience for them. Give me a hammer and nail any time. Nail meet hammer. Hit one with the other and see what sticks. I needed to find some nails to hit.

Lucy said she didn't feel like driving, so I did. Traffic in the city was as busy as you would expect late on a Thursday morning. It was business as usual for the rest of the world. People went about their daily business, blissfully unaware of how many things the big man and the angry redhead in the Crown Vic had killed in the last two days. People believed the world was a place that made sense. Good for them.

I had wanted to be done with all this. God, I was tired. God, I hated this life. But I was good at it and I'd been sucked back in too easily. As if I belonged there.

"You're thinking again," Lucy said, not taking her eyes off the road, "I can see smoke coming out of your ears."

"A lot to think about," I said absently. "Either your mind is empty, or you've put on a new poker face."

"Don't start being a dick again," Lucy said.

I said, "If you were in charge if you were the Hunter, what would you do next?"

"I don't know," Lucy said and furrowed her brows, "I don't know. I assumed this would be something like a hit. You know, here's your target, here's the last known location. Get it done."

I nodded, "Sometimes it is."

"And when it's not?"

"Follow the trail."

"What trail?"

"The bodies. Targets always have a body count. They always leave a blood trail."

"Always?"

"Every single one," I said.

Lucy didn't say anything for a minute, "So where's the trail?"

"Good question."

"That blood-soaked house," Lucy said. "There's got to be a trail. Something. Right?"

"I didn't see it."

"We missed something."

"Likely."

"So?"

"So," I said. "Like I said. We go back and look better."

"It's not something I want to look at closer."

"Me either, but I don't always get what I want."

Lucy looked sideways at me but didn't comment. I was talking about life in general, but I think she took it a little more personal.

"And if Dan the Slugger is on guard?" she asked.

"No more sucker punches," I said. "I'm tired of the blindsides. It's pissing me off."

"Now you're seeing things from my perspective," Lucy said.

As we rolled into the cul-de-sac, I noted one thing right away. No police tape or barricades anywhere. The bloodbath house remained undisturbed. This area should have been on lockdown by now and crawling with forensics and hazmat, and maybe even feds. There was no way the police could have ignored the scene inside the house.

Lucy glared, "Dan's wife didn't call the police, did she?"

I grumbled.

"I don't think I like her."

"Me either."

The giant SUV wasn't in Dan's driveway so I figured he wasn't home and wouldn't be bothering us.

"Park there," I said, pointing at the lime green house.

"Not the blood house?"

"Not yet."

"What if they're home?"

"I hope they are," I said.

They weren't. At least, no one answered the door when Lucy knocked long and loud.

"What do you think?" Lucy asked.

"Let's be nosy."

The front door had a small window that I was tall enough to look through without straining. It offered a partial view of the living room. I could make out some second-hand furniture, a few energy drinks cans on the armrests. A pizza box lay open on the coffee table with one half-eaten slice and few crusts remaining. But that was all I could see at that angle.

"Bill," Lucy whispered harshly, "over here." She was peeking through a gap in the living room picture window curtains. She stepped aside so I could hunch down and see in.

Black velvet covered most of one wall with a silver pentagram at its center. Poor reproductions of human skulls with half-burned candles on them were bunched together on a shelf made of cinderblocks and wood planks. Next to them was what was supposed to be a demon skull or something with ram horn and sharp teeth, clearly something from a Halloween supply store. Other walls sported several posters with some of those ridiculous death metal bands who plaster satanic and demonic imagery all over their album covers. There were a few knock-off demon sigils and ritualistic symbols spray-painted on open spaces with thick strokes of red so that it dribbled to look like running blood. That was the idea at least.

None of it was authentic or accurate.

"These guys are posers," I said to Lucy.

"I'll take your word for it," Lucy said, "but that's too much of a coincidence, don't you think? Right next door to the epicenter of an impossible incursion?"

"I don't like coincidences."

"Me either."

I stepped back from the window and surveyed the neighborhood. Three houses, two of them with apparently demonic connections. Quiet location. No through traffic. Good location for nefarious activities... as long as the neighbors mind their own business.

"Let's go talk to Dan," I said.

Lucy turned to look skeptically at the house, "Think he's home?"

"Someone's home," I said. "Take a look at the second story."

All the windows had Venetian blinds. One of them upstairs had a dark gap on the corner, an obvious sign that someone had lifted a slat to peek outside.

"Good," Lucy said and headed for the house. I smiled to myself. Lucy was decisive if she was anything.

I followed closely behind while keeping an eye on the upstairs window. Once we reached the yard, the gap in the blinds disappeared.

Lucy pounded on the door long and hard. No one was going to mistake us for friendly solicitors.

After a minute the door opened a crack. Dan's wife, Angela stood in the gap, barring us from entry. Not that she could have stopped me if I really wanted in; but this wasn't that kind of visit. Yet.

She was wearing a red bathrobe—the one Dan had worn the other night—and had her hair pulled back in a tight bun. She didn't look like she'd been asleep. In fact, I would guess by her makeup and hair that she was getting ready to go out. She didn't look happy to see us. In fact, she acted almost as pissed as Lucy, if that was possible. She was on full alert like she was expecting a fight. Not scared, more like on guard. Tense like a boxer waiting for the bell.

Although she was blocking the way, I could still see inside, looking over the top of her and Lucy's heads. A living room with modest but nice furnishings and a generous scattering of family pictures, mostly of kids.

"What do you want?" she demanded.

I decided to take the lead before Lucy started a war, "We want to ask about your neighbors. The boys across the street. What do you know about them?"

"They're just people," she said harshly. "They mind their own business like we do. Like you should."

"Ever seen them go into the little house there?" I asked pointing at the white house.

"No," she said with finality.

Lucy had had enough, "Look. We're just—"

"I called the police," Angela said, "they'll be here any second."

"Will they send out the same units they did the other night?" I asked.

Angela glared.

I raised my eyebrows, "Did the police find anything unusual in the house.

"They didn't go there. They just talked to Dan, to my husband."

"Interesting," I said. "You called the cops about strangers in a house they didn't belong in and they didn't even check out the house?

"Why is that, you suppose?" Lucy added.

"Ask them," the woman said and pushed the door closed. Then came the sound of the deadbolt locking. I thought for a second about busting it down. I'd kicked open better doors than this before.

"Ok," I said after some thought, "Fine. Come on, Red. Let's go."

Lucy followed me back to the car, "Why are we leaving? That bitch is clearly hiding something."

"Clearly," I agreed.

"Then why are we leaving? I was ready to beat some truth out of her."

"I saw."

"That what gives?"

"I wanna know what's up with the idiots in that house," I said pointing at the green house.

"Fine," she said, "let's go kick bust in there then."

"Not yet," I held up my hands in a slowdown gesture. "I wanna know a little more before going in."

"You flip flop more than a fish out of water," Lucy grumbled as she walked away from me.

"I wanna do a little research."

Lucy threw up her hands, "Back to the nerd factory again?"

"Not this time," I got in the car and started the engine. "I have other resources."

"Whatever," Lucy said as she buckled up. "Let's go." As we exited the cul-de-sac, we met the big white SUV that had been parked at Dan's house that other night. My first thought was that Dan had bad timing and we'd get to talk to him after all. But I didn't even get the chance to slow down. The SUV made a U-turn in the middle of the street and raced up behind us.

Lucy turned to me, "Let's fight!"

"We will," I said. "Hang on. Let's get them away from this neighborhood."

I put on a good show of trying to lose the SUV while making sure not to. I worked my way to the riverfront and took a frontage road running parallel to the water. The trees grew thicker on either side of the road and after a couple of curves, we couldn't see the SUV behind. That was all the gap I needed.

I slammed on the brakes and threw the car in reverse. I watched in the rearview mirror as I drove backward. The SUV came into sight and the driver's eyes went wide. He yanked his steering wheel sideways and skidded to a stop longways across the road. Our car hadn't even stopped moving when Lucy bailed out, gun in hand.

Chapter Twenty-Seven

Three guys poured out of the vehicle. None of them were Dan. They each wore hooded, black velvet robes, the kind a poser might buy at a costume shop if he wanted to look like he was in a satanic cult. I caught sight of jeans and name-brand tennis shoes beneath the gaudy knock-off robes. These guys had to be the kids living across from Dan and Angela. All three had symbols on their forehead in rough red markings that looked like they were branded. It wasn't Rezruel's sigil, but it was familiar.

They were also armed. One had a pistol, one of those really cheap ones that was as elegant as a brick and as heavy as one. Another had a hunting rifle with a scope on it. Not ideal for up close combat, but still dangerous in the right hands. The third had a silly jagged dagger—one of those gaudy fantasy things you can order off the internet. Completely impractical and ridiculous looking, but it still had a pointy end and was still dangerous if that pointy end when into your body.

There was no exchange of clever banter or evil threats. No posturing or sizing each other up. Pistol boy simply opened fire gangsta style. Few professionals shoot one-handed in combat, none of them do it sideways like a TV banger. This was probably Pistol Pete's first real gunfight, and he made the classic mistake. He ran through a whole magazine without hitting anything useful. At twenty yards, it's harder to hit a target with a handgun than people think. Even harder shooting offhand without aiming. Lucy, on the other hand, was a professional. She planted her feet, gripped the Holy Glockamolie in a two-handed combat grip, and squeezed off a single shot. The bullet struck center mass and the gunman fell backward.

The Rifleman took time to raise his rifle and aim. Bad choice. At twenty yards, it's nearly impossible to keep a moving target in the picture through a standard hunting scope. I was a moving target. A very large moving target, but a quick one, juking as I closed the distance.

He tried to track me with the rifle but I was getting too close; he couldn't wait anymore. He fired and missed by a mile. Lucy placed a shot into his chest and another through his left eye. He dropped like a rock. Damn that girl was efficient in the right circumstances.

Pistol boy was bleeding badly, but because of the robes, I couldn't tell where he'd been hit. s. All gunshots wounds can be fatal, regardless of placement. But some are more survivable than others and a lot of factors can push the odds one way or the other.

Knife Boy must have fancied himself the leader because he stood back and watched while the gunmen attacked and were quickly put down. He didn't seem very bothered by their condition though. He said something that was either a hip new kind of profanity or something from another language and came at me, swinging his stupid knife in wild frantic swipes. I met him halfway and extended a quick jab with my right arm, planting a fist in his chest. He flopped backward to the ground wheezing. Never underestimate the effectiveness of a human's innate need for oxygen. I kicked the knife away from his hand and squatted next to him looking hard into his eyes as he gasped for breath.

"That was as soft as I plan on hitting you," I said to him. "The next one break something. Probably your nose." Knife Boy didn't say anything. Which made sense, since he couldn't talk yet.

"Catch your breath," I said. "You got ten seconds, then you answer questions, or I start hitting." I showed him my teeth.

To my left, Lucy gasped and said something vulgar. I looked in time to see Pistol Pete tackle her and they both fell to the ground. Holy Glockamolie tumbled from her hand and landed out of reach.

She was good though. She reacted before I even stood up. In a blur of motion, she wrapped her legs around the kid's torso and locked her ankles together. He tried to grab her throat with both hands. She laced one arm between his arms and wrenched down on his wrist, keeping him from getting leverage on her throat. But she was still struggling. This kid was stronger than he looked. I punched Knife Boy in the chest again and then went to assist Lucy.

I took a step and tripped as Knife Boy grabbed my foot. What the hell? I regained my feet and turned back to face him. Miraculously, he was back on his feet already and the sigil on his forehead was glowing. That was an ominous new development.

He sprung at me, throwing fists. I stepped toward him to deliver a haymaker which he dodged. Somehow, he'd gotten really fast. He stepped back half a step to dodge my follow-up blow and pounced with an impressive uppercut. He almost had to jump to land the blow, but it was solid. My head snapped back with a flash of light. It was a harder punch than this punk should have been capable of delivering. I staggered back. Before I could catch my balance, the kid followed on with a succession of kidney punches and a swift jab at my nose. The jab came at a bad angle and I turned my head to avoid getting a broken nose. He swung again, reaching. I ducked my head and took the hit to the top of my noggin. He had a heavy hand. A couple of snaps told me he broke some fingers. Good for me.

He backpedaled quickly, shaking his hand, fingers crooked in the wrong ways. I risked a glance at Lucy. She had managed to roll pistol boy off her chest and was on top of him now, delivering a series of blows to the jaw. Then she cupped her hands and slammed them onto the sides of his ears. She was fine.

Knife Boy on the other hand was about to get a dose of angry Bill. I twisted and swung a mighty fist with the momentum of my whole body, connecting the side of his head. He staggered a few steps but didn't go down. He returned with an attempted uppercut, but I saw it coming this time and slapped his blow aside with a quick knuckle jab to the forearm. He swung again, feebly clipping my ear this time. It stung, but I can deal with stinging pain any day. I lurched forward with my foot, kicking him square in the knee. That got me an ugly cracking sound and a hideous scream from the kid. He went down crying out and grabbing at his knee. He wasn't getting up from that one. I kicked him hard in the stomach to be sure. I almost felt bad. For a second there, he looked like some normal kid trying to fight way outside his weight class. But he wasn't normal. Something was at work in these boys.

Lucy boxed Pistol Boy's ears two more times before delivering a crushing blow to his nose. It wasn't an instant kill like in the movies. Yeah, it can be deadly but usually, it has the effect of crushing all the cartilage in the nose. It's not just a broken nose, it's a ruined nose. And it doesn't always knock a person out. It hurts like the blazes and sends the "give up" signal to the brain. If you don't lose consciousness, you wish you had.

Lucy stood up panting and left him writhing in new heights of pain. She collected her pistol and trained it on him.

My head ached, and my jaw was sore, but I didn't have any bullet holes in me or any new broken bones. Neither did Lucy, as far as I could tell. We made out ok. A little rougher for the wear than made sense, but essentially ok.

"He gonna die?" I asked Lucy, pointing at Pistol Pete.

She shrugged, "He should be dead already."

"Maybe you should just shoot everyone in the head," I said pointing at the Rifleman.

"It's not like I don't try, smartass," Lucy said.

Pistol Pete groaned and his head turned toward us.

Lucy's eyebrows furrowed, "Why is his head glowing like that?"

"Good question," I said. "Ask him."

Knife Boy got his breath back and began yelling at Lucy and me in a string of colorful curses in English and at least two other languages I couldn't understand. I didn't know the words, but I knew cursing when I hear it. He was spewing foreign profanity of epic proportions. The symbol on his head pulsated.

Pistol Pete started talking too. Same weird spread of languages, but with less hate speech. His tone felt more like taunting than cursing.

Lucy leaned down and slapped him, hard, "English, Shithead!"

I grinned at him as I squatted next to her, "She doesn't get any nicer than this."

"The Lord of the Wilderness mocks you," the kid said in tired, strained English. "All has been corrupted, and all has been defiled."

Lucy slapped him again, "The fuck is that supposed to mean?"

He slipped into the strange language again, glaring at her, anger and hatred boiling up in his voice. The sigil glowed brighter and brighter as he spoke. I reached out to touch it. It was hot, crazy hot like blowtorch hot. It didn't make sense.

Lucy grabbed him by the folds in his cloak and shook him, "Where is he? Where is Rezruel?"

The kid spoke slowly, "It will be too late when you finally know the truth. The Warmaker reaches out to us all. He takes what is his. The Seducer has already touched us all. We are all his legacy. You cannot undo all that he has wrought."

"Who is the Seducer?" I asked sternly. "What is his name?"

The kid smiled a wide smile with too much glee, "He is the one who pulls back the curtain."

Lucy looked at me with arched eyebrows. I shrugged.

"Beats me," I said.

"Let's beat some sense out of him," Lucy said.

A brief flash of fear crossed the kids' eyes before changing to anger and he began to spew gibberish again. Then an engine started. The SUV engine to be specific.

Holy shit! I spun around. Knife Boy was gone. Or rather, he had gotten to the vehicle we were playing twenty ridiculous questions with Pistol Pete. Lucy drew her gun and fired several shots at the vehicle as it sped away. She growled with mounting irritation. I couldn't blame her. I was feeling it too. Rifleman's body, though dead, convulsed and twitched. The symbol on his forehead suddenly lit up brilliantly. Too brilliantly. It was like staring at the sun. Then his body burst into intense red and blue flames.

"What the fuck, Kemper?" Lucy demanded.

I didn't get to answer. Pistol Pete laughed wildly and spoke in rapid gibberish as his sigil glowed brighter and brighter. Lucy and I backpedaled several steps before he burst into flames as well. We stood awestruck and horribly creeped out as the kid screamed in agony and defiance. We were so engrossed in the display that we almost didn't notice the sound of approaching sirens.

"Time to go," I barked and ran for the car. Lucy beat me to it and hopped in the driver's seat.

Chapter Twenty-Eight

Lucy was a marble statue of calm as she drove us back toward the city, away from the flaming corpses. At least, that's what I thought at first. It took me a little while to finally notice she was driving slower than usual. She had latched onto the steering wheel with a death grip and her eyes were fixed on a point a thousand miles outside the windshield. She clenched her jaw so tightly that I could see the muscles on the side of her face straining. Her arms were stiff, her spine rigid. No movement. No emotion. No weakness.

I kicked myself mentally for not expecting it. I'd seen it before. Hell, I'd experienced it.

"Lucy," I said gently, "look at me."

She didn't acknowledge me. Instead, her fingers seemed to wrap around the steering wheel even tighter. She blinked once. A long slow blink. Her nostrils flared as she drew in and let out one breath after another.

"Lucy," I said again.

"Leave me alone," she said through tight lips.

"I can't do that."

"I'm fine," her mouth barely moved.

"You're coming down from an adrenaline dump," I said softly. "This is what—"

"This isn't a fucking sugar crash," Lucy snapped and pointed a finger at me, "and it's not adrenaline, so don't give me any of your touchy feely psychobabble bullshit."

I watched her index finger as she barked at me. It was shaking. Her whole hand shook. She realized almost instantly what I saw and returned to a stranglehold on the steering wheel.

"You're standing on the edge of a dangerous cliff, Red," I tried to keep the edge out of my voice.

"I don't care," she drained all emotion from her voice. It was almost robotic.

"You can't put this genie back in the bottle," I looked down at my own hands and flexed my fingers, remembering my first time. It was a long time ago. Long enough that I rarely thought about it. I intentionally never thought about it.

"You took a life today," I stated plainly, clinically.

She tried to shrug it off, but her shoulders were too stiff, her whole posture was on lockdown, "Not the first time. I killed those imps."

"You didn't kill them, you sent them back to hell."

"Same thing," her voice was still tense, she was trying too hard to force control into her words.

"You know it isn't."

Lucy breathed in and out through her nose, several more deep, hard breaths then finally looked at me. Her eyes met mine and I saw, neither sadness nor regret, but anger.

"Talk to me," I said.

A long moment of silence passed between us, then her eyes narrowed. Without looking away from me, she yanked the steering wheel, cutting across two lanes of traffic, and nearly crashing into a small SUV. She slammed on the brakes and skidded the Crown Vic to stop against the curb. The SUV driver honked long and loud and gave us the bird but kept on driving.

"Talk to you?" Lucy said and held out both hands for me to see. They were shaking. "Look at this. What should I say?"

"I know," I said, "I've been there."

"What do you want me to say? That if I stop for two seconds to think about what just happened, I might just freak the fuck out?"

I held my breath. This was her moment. I let her have it.

She closed her hands into white-knuckled fists, "I shot that kid. Me. I did that. Shot him right in the fucking head. And you want me to talk about it?"

"I don't want anything."

"Then get off my back."

I counted to three and held my peace. Now wasn't the time to get pissed at Lucy's stubbornness. It was her only defense.

She squeezed her eyes and shook her head once.

"I trained for this," she said keeping her eyes closed. "I was supposed to be ready for a fight like that. I was supposed to be ready to..."

"You can ever really be ready," I said levelly, as neutral as I could.

She opened her eyes and looked at me, anger flashing again, "I killed a person today."

"Yes, you did," I said and turned so I could face her straight on, "and it ain't fair."

"I did it without thinking," her lips trembled. "I pointed my gun and I squeezed the trigger and I shot him twice and he's dead."

"Your training kicked in and you did what you had to do."

She clamped her mouth shut and pressed her lips together again, as if holding back the words that might come out.

"That's the adrenaline dump. Fight or flight. It focuses you like a laser. Tunnel vision on crack, and you do what it takes to survive the moment. No guilt. No joy. No thought. Just action and reaction."

She whispered. "I didn't know it would be like this."

"Nobody does."

"Then," Lucy said, almost too softly for me to hear, she showed me her trembling hands again, "this."

"The fight is the easy part," I said. "The aftermath is the bitch."

"All I see now is that kid's face and bullet holes... bullets that I put in him." She looked away from me.

"That's right," I nodded slowly, "and it'll never go away."

Her eyes snapped back to me, "Never?"

"No," I said firmly. "Don't ever let it either. That's your humanity. Never let it die."

"What if it kills me?"

"It won't," I assured her.

Lucy let out a slow, quavering breath, "I didn't want this."

"I know," I sighed. "But you have to live with it. One of these days, you need to take it up with Winters and make him tell you why he did this to you."

Lucy furrowed her eyebrows, not in anger but frustration. "This isn't his fault." There was no conviction in her voice though. She knew it as well as I did. Winters put her onto this path.

I settled back into my seat and looked out at the street, "You're a warrior, Red. Own it, and for damn sure don't let it own you. Don't let anyone put a burden on you that you didn't earn."

She put her hands back on the steering wheel, "God... you suck at pep talks."

I had a feeling the Archives weren't safe yet, and we wouldn't be able to get any info useful intel there, not without an Archivists anyways. Winters and the Council would probably have it up and running again soon, but I didn't know how long that would take. Besides, I needed some grounding. I wanted some coffee and I wanted it from the Blue Sky. So sue me.

Lucy wanted to bring in Heir Chop-A-Lot but gave in to reason and settled for Holy Glockamolie in her concealed holster. I went in unarmed... as I always do. The Blue Sky was my sanctuary. Honestly, I'd probably tear down the gates to hell if that's what it would take to keep this place unspoiled. It was bad enough bringing Lucy Red here. She already knew where I lived and now, she knew where I breathed. If she ever decided to kill me, she'd know the two most likely places to look.

The regular crew was working today. Happy and chatty. Completely unaware of the chaos unfolding in their city. Which is how it always was.

I recognized a few customers, including the little old lady who, again, was sitting in my spot. I put on a friendly face, but I was feeling like, as Lucy had put it, an angry gorilla. The old lady ignored me as we eased into the next table over and said hello to Lucy instead. A little taken aback, Lucy returned the greeting with halting yet vaguely genuine cordiality.

I wiggled the table. The same wobbly table. Maybe I shook ask Sarah to get it fixed. Or offer to fix it. Or just quit fixating on fiddly details.

"Bill!" Sarah came from behind the counter and hugged me.

"Hiya, Doc," I said awkwardly. "How are you doing?"

"How am I doing?" she said incredulously, "Oh I'm just fine. Last time you saw me I was bleeding, and I probably needed stitches and I promised to go to the doctor even if I didn't mean it."

My face warmed over.

"Oh wait," she said, tone dropping an octave, "that was you."

"Look," I said, I'm—"

"You scared me to death," she said. "You know that? I was worried to death."

"I can—"

She held up a hand to stall my feeble apology, "Don't do that to me again. You take care of yourself."

"Yes," was all I could say.

"Who's your friend?" Sara extended a hand to a now smirking Lucy, "I'm Sarah."

"Um, nice to meet you," Lucy said, looking at me, not Sarah. "I'm Lucy. I'm his daughter."

I scowled at Lucy.

"Oh?" Sarah said looking at me, "I didn't know you had a daughter."

"I don't," I said, "Lucy's a liar. She's um, my niece."

"Yeah," Lucy said, "Uncle Bill has no sense of humor."

I rolled my eyes.

"You've never talked about family before," Sarah said.

"She was... unexpected," I said uncomfortably.

"You got that right," Lucy added.

"Fair enough," Sarah said. "Quit your job, get mauled by a tiger, show up with secret family members. You're full of little surprises."

"It's been a weird couple of days," I said meekly.

Sarah raised her eyebrows, "You don't say?"

"Look I'm sorry... Sometimes I'm kind of a jerk..."

"No, you're not. Don't be a jerk," Sarah stated. "Just be good. Ok."

I nodded.

"That's all it takes?" Lucy asked, "She says, 'don't be a jerk' and that's that?"

I shrugged helplessly.

"He's a kitten," Sarah said.

"Ha!" Lucy laughed. "Sorry. That's not the... the family's nickname for him."

"Oh really?" Sarah asked with genuine interest. "What is the family nickname for him."

"Enough," I said, "that's too many secrets for one day."

Sarah leaned closer to Lucy as if sharing a secret, "He thinks he's so mysterious."

"He thinks too much," Lucy said.

"Probably," Sarah said then asked me, "You want the usual?"

"Yes... please."

"And you?" Sarah asked Lucy.

"What's the usual?"

"Bill Kemper Special," Sarah said, "Strong black coffee and toast."

"God you're boring," Lucy said. "I can't believe people don't just fall asleep in your presence.

I looked down at the table, "I like the taste of coffee without all that crap in it."

"Black coffee with no crap for the cage fighter," Sarah said. "What can I get you?"

"Nothing for me," Lucy said.

"Suit yourself," Sarah said as she left to get my coffee and toast.

"Why are we here?" Lucy said. "So you can play good neighbor with Rosy the Barista?"

"It's Sarah and stop being so hostile."

"Hostile's all I have left today," Lucy said.

The little old lady raised her eyebrows as if Lucy had a point.

"Listen, Red," I tapped the wobbly table for emphasis as I spoke, "We've been attacked from one side of Missouri to the other by at least three different factions, each acting according to god knows how many agendas. And I put up with all of it with nothing but a couple of cat naps and thirty seconds of quiet before the next round. So, I'm feeling pretty hostile too."

"Not too hostile to stop for a cup of tea."

"Coffee," I said, "and this is the closest I've come to being relaxed since I found you standing in my living room."

"Get over yourself."

I closed my eyes and counted to ten. I wasn't going to let her drag me back into this same argument again.

"We're wasting time," Lucy said. "Seriously, why are we here? You can rest when you're dead or this is over."

"Ok," I said. "Sarah is taking some online college classes. She's always got her laptop here. I figured we could talk her into letting us use hers."

"God, Bill," Lucy said. "Libraries have computers. They're not that hard to find."

"So?"

"So, I know how to use a computer," she said. "We could have gone to the library, used one of their computers, and done it without taking a nice little side trip to Sleepy Town."

"Wow," I said. "You really know how to turn off your soul, don't you?"

"I never turn it on."

"Well. Suck it up. We're here. Make the best of it."

"Fine, Uncle Bill, but let's get on with it. This place is creepy. You playing Ward Cleaver is creepy."

Sarah returned with the Kemper Special and an additional glass of water and set it in front of Lucy, "I've met creepier guys than Bill."

"Yeah?" Lucy said. "If only you knew."

I shot some invisible daggers with my eyes, "Boundaries, Red."

Lucy sighed and said to Sarah, "Sorry... Uncle Bill is the best."

Sarah laughed.

"Sarah... I hate to do this," I had to make a conscious effort not to wring my hands, "but I need a favor."

"Need a broken bone set?"

I smiled, "No."

"Appendectomy?"

"Already taken care of," I said.

Lucy rolled her eyes, with torturous intensity, "Enough with the clever banter, man."

"Sorry, Sarah, my niece is rude and impatient."

Sarah smiled generously, "It's ok. We all have our burdens. What can I help you with?"

I opened my hands to show how empty they were, "I need to use a computer. Just for a little while. Right here. I'm sorry to ask but I don't have one and this is closer than the library."

"Holy cow," Lucy said, "you really are a martyr, aren't you?"

Sarah giggled, "He's not very good at asking for help, is he?"

"No. He's not."

"I'm sorry," I said. "I hate to ask."

"Clearly. It's not a big deal," Sarah said. "Hang on a sec." She went behind the counter and dug her laptop from a well-used bookbag.

"Here," she set it in front of me and opened it. "You know how to use it?"

"He's a dinosaur," Lucy said. "He barely knows how to use a car."

"I'm teachable," I said.

"I'll help him," Lucy said.

"What are you working on? Updating your resumé?"

"No. The idea was to quit my job and stay quit."

"Some people call that retired?" Sarah said.

"I'm not very good at it."

"He's helping me with some research," Lucy interjected impatiently. "I broke my laptop, and he insists on being helpful."

"Ok, be careful and no porn," she winked, "I have to get back to work."

Once Sarah left us, Lucy pulled the laptop in front of her and opened the browser, "Ok Mr. Wizard, what are we looking for?"

"Start with those houses in St. Charles. The addresses. And maybe if there's any supernatural history in the neighborhood."

Lucy was already tapping at the keyboard before I finished talking.

We followed a lot of trails, all of them leading to dead ends. The St. Charles area was under Spanish rule during the colonial era. Later, it became a jumping off point for the Lewis & Clark expedition. The first Catholic church in St. Louis area was built in St. Charles although the original location had been lost. The suburb has a historic downtown. A very old cemetery, a convent, and a few unsubstantiated haunted houses. Interesting trivia, but no red flags.

Next, we tried searching for Dan but we couldn't find anything useful about him or his family. Not without his last name.

The other houses were equally uninteresting. The demon

wannabe house was a rental, but we couldn't find a lead on the current tenants. This wasn't going anywhere.

"Try Rezruel."

There weren't any hits. Not that I was surprised of course. Rezruel was a minor servant of the Fallen and didn't warrant being named in any of the common texts.

"Try fallen angels," I said, "or demons or Dudael."

The little old lady scowled at me—not Lucy—and shook her head. She was getting a real show today.

"Just a sec Mister Discrete," Lucy said. She did some more internet magic. "There were all kinds of hits on fallen angels. You want religion, fringe science, esoteric history, Anime, fantasy, fan fiction, or erotica?"

"Jeez," I mumbled. "Go with historical then religion."

"There's a lot. Satan and his faction of angels weren't the only ones that rebelled against God. There are some references to a second fall. Here... they were called Watchers... Grigori."

"I didn't think of that. See if there's anything about fallen angels or Watchers or Grigori relative to St. Charles."

"Already on it, Sherlock," Lucy said. "One hit."

Lucy rotated the laptop so I could see it. It was a tacky looking website. Cheap, homemade with lots of gaudy demonic iconography and animated flames. Just like something put together by a few college-aged kids fascinated with the occult but didn't know what the hell they were doing.

"Lemme guess," I said. "Three members."

"Yup. The Church of The Servants of Azazel, Most Exalted of the Grigori."

"That's a mouthful," I said.

"It sure is," Lucy agreed.

"There is an address?"

"You know there is, and you know what it is," Lucy said.

"Well," I said. "They might have been onto something."

"But that's an Azazel fan club, not Rezruel. Are they the same thing?"

"No. Not the same. Rezruel isn't a Grigori."

"What's a Grigori?

"Watcher," I said. "They were angels sent to watch over humanity, but they go too... familiar and violated their own prime directives."

"And Azazel was one of them?"

I nodded, "One of the worst offenders."

"Did Rezruel work for him?"

"Not that I know of," I said. "But his history is spotty."

"What's this mean for us?"

"I don't know," I admitted. "Dean said the sigil we found belonged to Rezruel, not Azazel."

"Maybe he was lying," Lucy said.

"I have to admit, he was acting pretty shady last time we saw him alive," I wobbled the table gently. Everything was off kilter. Unstable. I stared at the silly looking website. These kids were tourists in the black arts. How did in the hell did they make an actual connection?

Lucy slapped a hand on the table to stop me from wiggling it, "Focus Big Guy."

"I'm not convinced Dean messed with the Archives. Whoever did do it knows something. And we need to know which one of Hell's inmates we're actually dealing with here."

The old lady frowned and shook her head.

"Yes, we do," Lucy said. "We already know what we need to know. That doesn't answer anything."

I shook my head in frustration, "I know. God this is a pain in the ass. We need to know who we're fighting so we can figure out how to fight."

"How did you beat Rezruel last time?"

"Luck," I said. "Bullet in the forehead, right through his sigil. That didn't kill him of course, but it bought me some time to hack away at his body like a lumberjack on crack until he couldn't fight back anymore. Then holy water and decapitation."

"Your Hunter's Goodbye," Lucy said with a mysterious flair.

"Yup."

The little old lady was watching me speak now, mouth agape.

"Yeah," I said to her, "crazy right?"

"Don't mind him," Lucy said, "he's a cave troll." The old lady got up and left. I resisted the urge to move over and reclaim my table.

Sarah returned from the counter, "How's it going, Uncle Bill? Find what you're looking for?"

"I never do," I said.

"Then look harder," Sarah said and looked at the awful website on her computer screen. "Are you joining a cult?"

"No, this one has closed membership," I said and closed the laptop.

"Not your style anyways," Sarah said.

"Thanks."

"Keep looking, you'll find your place," she said and picked up the computer, "Maybe you can go back to your old friends at the sewer rat wrestling club."

Lucy watched her leave, "I don't know what the hell she's talking about. But you know what... It would be nice to have the Holy Handgun right now, wouldn't it? I've been doing all the heavy work."

"Yeah," I said, "you're practically the Grim Reaper. But you have a point and Sarah gave me an idea."

"You wanna wrestle sewer rats?

"Sort of. Let's go for a ride."

Chapter Twenty-Nine

The abandoned apartment building in Old North St. Louis looked the same as I remembered it from a couple of days ago. Empty and isolated and kind of scary. Even in the daytime, it looked like a dangerous place. The minivan Mehira had been in was parked out front, near the opening in the broken fence. We took the time to check but the vehicle was empty.

Lucy followed me in silence, as we approached the window entrance. She carried the Holy Glockamolie and Sir Chop-A-Lot, in each hand, refusing to choose one over the other. I left my weapons in the car. I wasn't looking for that kind of fight this time. I hoped I wasn't being stupid again.

I stopped before entering the building and pointed at Lucy's weapons, "Go easy."

"That's asking a lot," Lucy said.

I knew she was right. This was not an easy situation to defuse, and this was not a great building for it. The last time I entered this building, I'd come in with a destructive disposition.

"I get it," I said, "just follow my lead. Don't start a fight unless I say so."

Lucy frowned.

"This is not the job," I said.

"Fine."

That was as good a commitment as I was gonna get. It would have to do.

I squeezed through the open window and stepped into the room so Lucy could join me.

The floors were still damp and squished under our feet. The hallway was empty, except for some of the rubble where I had crashed through the wall. The bloodsucker I'd killed in the hall was gone. The room where I'd seen the pile of bodies had been emptied out. All the corpses were gone. There was a faint musk of death but not the horrid stench of rot I had expected. Weirdly, this was more disturbing. It was just dead now.

The small apartment where I had first seen Mehira stood open. I had destroyed the door on my previous visit and left a big hole in the wall. It was dark inside the room, but cracks in the boarded-up window let through slivers of outside light.

Mehira sat on the makeshift table, crossed-legged with her head down and her long black hair covering her face. She hugged herself tightly and rocked slowly, as if to a song I couldn't hear. Two items lay on the table in front of her. A cellphone and my gun. The Holy Handgun.

High School Buddy crouched in the corner, watching Mehira. As we stepped into the room, his attention snapped to us and he rose to his feet clenching his fists.

"No," Mehira said quietly but sternly. Buddy bowed his head and crouched back down.

Lucy alternated between pointing her gun at Mehira and Buddy but neither seemed very threatening at the moment. That, of course, is often a trap. When known threats don't seem dangerous, bad things tend to follow. But this didn't feel like that. The atmosphere felt like sorrow.

Questions flooded my mind, but few of them would get us anything useful at the moment. I picked an easy one.

"How did you know where to ambush me on the highway?"

Mehira lifted her head. Her eyes glowed fierce green from behind the veil of hair. She sneered.

"I followed the stench of righteousness and arrogance. It led me straight to you."

"You were nearly dead when I left you here. How did you regain the strength to turn two healthy humans so fast?"

Mehira shuddered and lowered her head again, "I became the

monster you believed I was."

"The hell does that mean?" I asked.

"Somebody helped her," Lucy stated.

"The same somebody who knew exactly where you and I would be," I said to Lucy.

Lucy frowned, "What do you mean by that?"

I ignored the question, "That's not your phone, Mehira. Is it?"

Mehira didn't answer.

"Who gave it to you? Who's helping you?"

"One of your own," Mehira said softly.

I felt my blood rising, "Another Hunter?"

"Don't be a fool," Mehira said and pointed at Lucy, "One of hers. A wizard."

"I'm no wizard."

"No, but you are covered in their stench. You live among them."

I spun on Lucy, "You've been feeding our location to Winters?"

"No!" she said. "Progress updates, but that's all. No details."

I stepped toward Lucy and she backed away one step, then held her ground.

She spoke through gritted teeth, "I told you I'd kill you if you touched me again."

"I didn't forget," I said. "Either Winters double-crossed me again, or you did."

"Fuck you!" Lucy said. "I've been in the line of fire in every one of those fights too, you big dumb bastard."

"Yeah. It looks that way."

"Take it too far," Lucy said, "see what happens."

"How childish," Mehira said with disappointment in her voice. "Humans behave so childishly."

"No shit," I said and turned my back on Lucy to face Mehira again.

"What a broken thing your soul is!" Mehira said. "Here I sit, within striking distance, yet you bicker with your little fighting girl like petty siblings?"

Buddy rose again. His face was blank, emotionless. Like the others before him, he was just a guard dog. A thrall. Yet, he seemed familiar. Had I seen him before? Even before that night on the highway?

"You could barely walk when I left you here," I waved vaguely toward the hallway. "What happened after I left? Who is helping you?"

"My sins are my own."

In one quick motion, I spun, yanked the pistol from Lucy's hand and, pointed it at Buddy's head. Lucy cursed at how quickly I'd taken her gun but stayed put.

Buddy didn't move. Mehira didn't react.

"Tell me," I demanded, "or I'll put him down now. I'll end it here."

"It has already been ended," Mehira said sadly. She uncrossed her elegant legs slowly and eased off the table gracefully, leaving the Holy Handgun and the cellphone where they lay. She reached up with her graceful hand and pushed silken hair behind one ear, drawing my attention to her slender, flawless neck and the pale skin that contrasted with her dark robes and dress. For a moment, I was stunned at how beautiful she was. Such beauty couldn't also be evil, could it? I could almost forget what she had done, how many people died at her hands. Maybe they deserved it. Were they victims or targets? They weren't just food, right? She called them her children. She had been trying to build her family. She was protecting her family, providing for them.

God, she was beautiful. I watched her lips as she wetted them with her tongue. I imagined what it would be like to taste what they had tasted. I followed her voluptuous curves, the way her breast rose with each breath, and the way her hips moved when she shifted her weight slowly from one foot to the other.

Beautiful. Like a dream. Like a fantasy. Like a forbidden love—

"Bill!" Lucy barked in my ear.

I flinched and shook my head. Without even realizing it, I had walked toward Mehira, one hand halfway extended toward her.

"What the hell is wrong with you?" Lucy said. "I said shoot her! Before it's too late."

"It's already too late," Mehira said sumptuously, and her lips curled into a faint smile.

Then I saw it. The smirk on her soft red lips was only skin deep. Her lazy, inviting gaze was just that. An invitation. She was trying to draw me in, asking me. Opening a door for me, to walk into her welcoming embrace. To lower my own defense, as she had lowered hers.

I pointed Lucy's pistol at her and squeezed the trigger. The bullet zipped by Mehira's head. She didn't even blink.

"Oh, you see right through me, Lover," Mehira said.

"Put a hole in her," Lucy said, "so we can all see through her."

"Stop it," I said quietly. "I'm not your lover. I'm not falling into your web of lies."

"Lies?" Mehira said the word as if testing it out. "I have never lied to you, Killer."

"Then tell me the truth now," I said. "How did you get your strength back? You couldn't play your tricks on me last time. You're different now. Who helped you?"

"I told you," Mehira said. "One of your own magic men, a man with a heart as dark as mine."

"Who?"

"A wizard. He came to me where you left me," she pointed toward the wall, toward the room where I'd walked away from everything.

She held out a hand and Buddy came to stand beside her like a puppy waiting for attention.

"He came bearing gifts," Mehira said, speaking to me but looking at Buddy, stroking his short hair. "He was a clever man. He knew exactly what to bring."

"What did he bring you?" I already knew the answer, but I wanted to hear her say it. No, I didn't want to hear her say it. I dreaded it. But it needed to be said.

"Three healthy young humans," Mehira said somberly, still stroking Buddy's hair. "Children really. Less than eighteen years on this Earth. Triplets, if you can believe it. Bound and helpless. Like putting mice in a cage with a hungry snake. It was pathetic, really. But I was pathetic too, wasn't I?"

The glow in her eyes pulsated, slowly. I remembered the night I left her. Those eyes were so dim. Fading away. It was part of why I had spared her. I couldn't bring myself to snuff out that last bit of light. What had I done?

"You left me broken, Hunter," Mehira said, and a sad smile played across her lips. "But I was a monster, wasn't I? I was already broken. You reduced me to the terrible creature I always was, the thing faerie tales always remembered me as being. Baby Stealer. Husband Taker. Life Eater. Sister Maker." Her voice grew stronger with each word she spoke.

"So, yes, I took one of them. It didn't matter which one. They were all the same, weren't they?" she held her hand out toward me as if she were holding something precious in it, "Healthy and fit and full of life and full of fear. Fear makes you more alive than anything doesn't it? It fills you with an urge to fight, a desperate need to fight. To escape, to survive. Fear. The greatest spice. I took the one with the greatest fear in her. She was so alive, and I took all that life from her. Every. Last. Drop."

"Kill her!" Lucy yelled and whipped the tip of her sword at Mehira, "Do it now! Or I will!"

I didn't move. I still had the Glock pointed at Mehira's head. I wouldn't miss this time. But I didn't pull the trigger.

"You still won't do it, will you?" Mehira said and caressed Buddy's cheek. "Not even when you stand face to face with my sins, with the evidence of my evil looking back at you."

The boy stared at me with expressionless eyes. I couldn't meet his gaze. I just couldn't.

"I gorged myself," Mehira continued, "and then I had strength again. Strength that I had denied myself for decades. Oh, I was strong again, and it was intoxicating. So I gave the other two the gift of my strength, a gift that takes everything else from them. They became thralls, to aid me in my ugly work. Nothing more."

I felt the anger welling up inside me. This was why I had been a Hunter. Because of monsters like her. Because of the callousness with which she took lives, discarded lives, destroyed lives. She'd murdered someone's beloved children. Those she'd turned to thralls were just as murdered as the others. They were dead, they just hadn't stopped moving.

Mehira watched me defiantly. Her chest heaved as she drew in deep breaths.

"I did what I have always done," she said. "I acted the monster. I am a monster. What do you say to that?"

She was a monster. I had always known that. But so was I. Things change. I had to believe that. That was why I quit. Because nothing is black and white. Nothing is one thing or the other. There may be no redemption, but there could be repentance.

I saw it in her eyes. She took no pleasure in what she had done. Maybe once upon a time she did. But she didn't anymore. She was ashamed. And she was angry.

"Who did this to you?" I asked.

Mehira blinked and let out her breath. She hadn't expected that. "What?" she asked.

"Who did this to you Mehira? Who was the wizard?" I fought down the anger threatening to take me over and kept my voice calm and steady. I didn't come here to lose my cool. Not this time.

"A man," she said defiantly, "otherwise they are all the same to me."

"Describe him. Was he a little old man with round glasses?"

Lucy stirred next to me; clearly, she knew who I was suggesting. I held my free hand out to her with one finger extended.

"Old? Perhaps by your standard," Mehira said. "But not as you describe him. Not little or frail. He gave me no name, only gifts, and this talking device." She pointed at the cellphone next to my handgun. "He suggested I keep your awful weapons of silver and iron and use them to kill you. He suggested it would be poetic justice."

"But you didn't," I said.

"Gods, I tried. I used that awful thing again and again and you just won't die." She jammed a finger at me, "You won't die! And you won't kill me!" Anger flashed in her eyes and the green grew brilliant. Buddy clenched his fists and rocked from side to side.

Interesting, I thought. He was responding to Mehira's anger. The only emotion he seemed to have. He was angry when he died, I realized, and when Mehira turned him. He can't fight her because she made him. He can only do as she commands. His anger lingered. That's all that was left when she turned him.

Her hand wavered and she lowered it. Buddy bristled for a moment. Mehira touched his cheek again and he relaxed.

"What do you want from me?" I asked calmly.

"I want you to die!"

"Bullshit," I said. "You had your chances. You're strong enough, you failed because you wanted to. What do you want?"

"I want to die!"

Buddy shivered, and his head jerked toward Mehira with confusion on his face.

"I'll do it," Lucy said and turned her body, shifting the sword, ready to thrust.

"I want the wizard," I said, ignoring Lucy.

"It does not matter what you want," Mehira said calmly.

"It matters to me," I said. "I need to finish it."

"You didn't finish me, Monster Lover."

"We all live with the choices we make," I said.

Mehira's eyes flashed from me to Buddy then back to me, "That is true."

Lucy growled angrily, "Enough of this stupid back and forth. Kill her already or let me do it."

"I don't want to kill you, Mehira," I said, "but things are getting bad. I can't walk away from the things that are happening."

"I care not," Mehira made a show of examining her fingers.

"I'll make a deal with you."

She dropped her hands and eyes widened with a flicker of excitement, "Oh?"

"The wizard that did this," I pointed at Buddy, "is trying to unleash hell on Earth."

"You bore me, Bill."

"What he's doing could throw open the gates to Dudael."

Mehira tilted her head and repeated Dudael quietly, "I have not heard that word spoken in centuries."

"Yeah, well, it's about to become a household name."

"What do you mean by that?"

"Your wizard is trying to unleash a minion of the Fallen," I said. "You know what happens if he succeeds?"

Mehira shifted her gaze from me to Lucy.

"Yeah," Lucy said, "he's telling you the truth."

"He told me nothing of his plans," Mehira said. "He told me only that he could lead me to you. He called me later, on that device and told me how to find you. That is all. He calls me, and I go where he says I will find you. And there I find you each time and you do not die."

"Yeah, I'm really aggravating that way," I said.

"What do you wish of me? What more can you take?"

"Help me find him so I can kill him," I said.

"Me," Lucy corrected. "So, I can kill him."

Mehira reached out and touched the Holy Handgun's wood grip and ran her finger along the worn checkering, carefully avoiding the metal. She looked at me, her eyes studying mine.

"Very well," Mehira said at least. "I will deign to help you."

"Ok," I said.

"On the condition that you swear to kill me. You will put an end to my miserable existence once and for all."

"Take the deal, Bill," Lucy said.

"I spared you once, Mehira Fiodniagh."

"Does that name on your tongue tickle your lips?"

"I spared your life," I said, "I do not want to kill you."

"And I do not want to help you save your precious world of petty mortal children. But this is the bargain I offer you."

I looked away from her. I was tired of being bullied into bad choices. I just wanted out of this mess. Out of being responsible for the world. I just wanted to be done.

"Ok," I said quietly.

"You must say it," Mehira warned.

"You help me stop this apocalypse and in exchange, I kill you?"

"That is the bargain. Do you accept?"

I looked into Mehira's eyes, "I accept."

"Shall we seal it with a kiss?" she asked, her voice dropping lower.

"No."

"Then we trust each other now?" she said, with one corner of her mouth drawn into a smirk. "How wonderfully naïve of us all."

"This isn't trust," I said. "But a deal is a deal."

"Indeed," Mehira said.

I pointed at my revolver, "I'll be needing that back."

"As you wish," Mehira said. "I have no taste for it."

I leaned over the table to retrieve the Holy Handgun. She didn't move back or give me space. She smelled of wildflowers and linen. Not death, not decay, but of something beautiful. I hesitated a moment then grabbed my gun from the table.

"When will he call you again?" I asked, stepping away from Mehira several paces.

"He calls me on that device, and I go where he directs me. He acts on his according to whims. Not mine."

"Let me look at the phone," Lucy said.

"Do as you wish," Mehira said, but made no move to retrieve it. Neither did Lucy. Again, I moved uncomfortably close to Mehira to grab the phone. Her scent distracted me again and I thought of dancing in a meadow. God, how did she do that?

I handed the phone to Lucy without looking.

She did something and grumbled, "The incoming number is blocked. We can't call it. But I got this phone's number and MAC address."

"Yeah?"

"It means we might be able to tap it."

"Ok. Good," I took the phone and offered it to Mehira. She didn't take it.

"When he calls me," she said, "he will grow suspicious if I don't attack you."

"Then attack us," Lucy said, "and we can seal the deal that much faster."

"Do not be so hasty little one," Mehira said. It was the first she had addressed Lucy directly.

"Just be ready," I said. "Once we get him cornered, he's gonna want you in a hurry. Come in ready to fight."

"That is all I live for now," Mehira took the phone from my hand, brushing her fingers against my hand slowly as she did. They were cold and soft. Not clammy, not like the vampires I'd encountered before. She was something else. Without taking her eyes from me, she placed the cellphone gently on the table.

Without turning my back on Mehira, I handed Holy Glockamolie back to Lucy. She immediately pointed it at Buddy's head.

"No!" Mehira bellowed, almost painfully.

"Wait," I told Lucy.

"Why?" Lucy said. "This is a walking crime. She's using him as a pet. He's already dead. He should be put down."

"Maybe," I said, "but not yet. We have the allies we have, not the ones we choose. You have me. She has him."

"For the time being," Mehira said sadly.

Lucy flicked the tip of Heir Chop-A-Lot out at Buddy and the blade scratched his chin. He hissed but held his place.

"For now," Lucy said.

"Let's go," I said and walked out of the room without waiting to see if Lucy was going to follow me. "I need to go buy some more bullets."

Chapter Thirty

I stopped at a pawn shop and bought a couple boxes of bullets for the Holy Handgun. I wished I had more of the Vampire's Curse bullets, but that wasn't gonna happen. Besides, I was pretty sure we weren't dealing with vampires anymore. The Vampire's Curse bullets and Vampire's Bane runes wouldn't be any use. Gunpowder and lead would have to be enough. I had a feeling it wouldn't be. Nothing was working out like it was supposed to.

With the Holy Handgun back in my possession and loaded, I felt a little more prepared for trouble. I didn't feel "good" or "right," just less naked. It was little comfort though. I wasn't any closer to figuring out who was behind all this. I needed answers. I need to pull information out of someone who wasn't as good at playing coy as Mehira was. I needed someone who could be intimidated.

We were going back to St. Charles. Again.

"If Dan and his wife are home," Lucy said, "I'm beating one of them senseless."

"Some of the bits are falling into place," I said absent mindedly. The gears in my head were finally spinning freely. This wasn't just a hunt. This was a conspiracy. This was something with shadows and trapdoors and hidden rooms. Something that looks like one thing but is something else. If only I could figure out what that something else was. I was painting in a dark room.

High School Buddy was in my head now. He was familiar, like the name of a song that's right on the tip of your tongue but you just can't come up with the name. Could he have been one of the thralls I thought I'd killed the other night before sparing Mehira? It didn't seem likely. They were older, not fresh. Whatever you call it. And they were scrawny, probably homeless people from the very building Mehira occupied. No. Buddy was something else. Someone else.

The cul-de-sac was deserted. No cars in any of the driveways.

I wasn't all that surprised. I was pretty sure Angela was about to leave last time we saw her. The demon boys had her SUV. They had either stolen it, or she was sharing it with them. Or Dan was. I was beginning to think he wasn't the cowardly fool he'd pretended to be.

We parked in Dan's driveway this time. No more pretenses. Lucy pounded viciously on the door for a solid minute, but no one answered. I was sure they had flown the coop.

"Let's go check out the Church of the Idiot Demon Worshippers," I said and led the way across the street.

"If any of them are home," Lucy said, "I'm going to freak out and shoot them in the head before they get a chance to explode."

"Me too," I said. I didn't bother knocking. I kicked door, and half the door frame broke free.

I had expected the stench of death or even brimstone, but it smelled like a bunch of slackers whose idea of cleaning was spraying deodorant and air freshener to cover up the smell of sweet and old food and half-smoked, convenience store cigars. As we'd seen from outside, there were empty power drink cans everywhere, some overflowing with cigarette and cigar butts. The empty box was still where I'd seen it earlier. A cheap entertainment center with a large TV and gaming consoles sat across from the sofa. Shelves beneath it were crammed full of games and horror movies. Nearly every horror movie I ever heard of.

I walked up to the poster-covered wall, trying to decipher some of the symbols the boys had painted. Some were familiar, like the ones on their website. One of them was probably the sigil of Azazel. The central one on the wall. It was like the ones branded on those guys' foreheads. Close but not exact. My guess was they were wannabes, and the sigil was a poor reproduction

Lucy thumbed through some of the books on the shelf. None of them were authentic spellbooks but they weren't outright nonsense either. One of them was a cheap reprint of a dark magic grimoire.

There were also a handful of volumes from the Time-Life Mysteries of the Unknown series. None of them would be of any real value to a true practitioner. Lucy showed me the one she was holding. It was a manual for ritual sacrifice.

"Are these kids stupid or just inept?" she asked, dropping the book on the floor carelessly.

"I don't know. I'd bet they didn't know what they were playing with."

"Boys are idiots."

"Generally, yes," I said. Admittedly, I'd seen enough evidence to support her suspicion.

The kitchen wasn't anything unexpected. Dishes were stacked on the counter and piled in the sink. The trashcan overflowed with fast-food wrappers, old pizza boxes, and empty beer cans. They were just boys, barely out of high school with a fresh taste of personal freedom and no sense of responsibility.

Between the kitchen and the living was a narrow door leading to the basement. Lucy opened the door and recoiled. There was something dead down there. Nothing as dramatic as the house next door but still unmistakable. Lucy held her breath as she stepped onto the stairs, her pistol leading the way.

"Ok," I said as stepped off the stairs into the damp basement, "these kids are stupid."

The basement was lit by a single, dim bulb hanging in the center of the room. The walls had been painted black for ominous effect and the small crawl space window had been covered in dark towels. The room was mostly empty, except for an altar built out of stacked bricks, topped with a piece of black fabric with a summoning circle embroidered in red thread. It was too precise to have been made by the boys, I decided. They must have bought it from an occult supply shop. The crude symbols painted around the perimeter of the circle were more of their style.

So was the scattering of tiny carcasses on the cement floor around the altar. Cats, raccoons, squirrels, rats, mice, and lots of birds.

"What the actual hell?" Lucy said.

"My thoughts exactly."

"Is this real?" Lucy approached the altar, her gun trained on it as if it might come alive and attack. "I mean, could they have summoned Rezruel?"

"No," I said. "This is too sloppy. I mean, the summoning circle is real enough but it's an off-the-shelf reproduction. It's useless without specific sigils. These... they're too sloppy. You have to be precise with rituals."

"But they tried, didn't they?" Lucy said, nudging a dead bird with her boot.

"They did," I admitted. "They might have stirred something up, but they didn't summon a demon and they definitely didn't spark an incursion."

"Maybe they got the attention of the agents?" Lucy offered.

"Maybe," I said. "Dunno. This is small fries. Dangerous, but small."

"What if they were doing it at the same time the summoning mess was going on next door?"

"Two at the same time?" I wondered. "That'd be a weird coincidence."

"You don't like coincidences."

"No, I don't."

"What doesn't add up here?" Lucy asked.

"It's all funny math," I said. "But you know what comes up zeroes?"

"Huh?"

"Dan," I said. "Two demonic rituals going on right next door, and he doesn't know anything?"

Lucy gave me a skeptical look and shrugged, "People mind their own business." She wasn't buying it any more than I was.

"Did Angela seem like she was minding her own business?"

"No."

"And Dan was snooping when he caught me off guard."

"True."

"And he didn't notice anything? That's weak."

"Frail as a baby giraffe," Lucy said. "Let's go break into his house."

"Agreed."

I kicked the door in clean off its hinges, sending it flying halfway down the hall. As we stepped into the living room, I saw what Angela had been trying to hide from us. An end table had been knocked over and lamp lay broken on the floor next to it. A large plant in one corner had been knocked over too and the soil had been hastily scooped back up, but the light tan carpeting was stained. There had been a struggle here.

Otherwise, the house was lifeless. The air had an empty silence that accompanied a house no one lived in. The furniture was there. Pictures were there. A television. Rugs. All the carefully selected and placed accessories of a happy home.

It looked like a home. But wasn't a home anymore. It had the hollow silence of a house whose residents had left. The life was gone.

"Why is it so quiet?" Lucy asked.

"No appliances running. No heat or a/c."

"What's going on here?" Lucy swept the gun around as if hoping to find a target.

Everything seemed "normal," with exception of the few overturned items. The furniture. The television. The rugs. The pictures.

The pictures.

I'd gotten a glimpse of them on our previous visit, but Angela was blocking the way and I didn't get a very good look.

I took a better look. A framed picture on the mantel caught my eyes. I picked it up.

Shit.

I showed it to Lucy.

"Fuck me," she said.

Dan and Angela had four kids. They were a good-looking bunch of kids. Healthy, happy, stylish. They were a picturesque white suburban family. The youngest, a daughter who looked like she was in middle school, had braces and wore pink-framed glasses. The rest were teenagers. Two girls and a boy, and they looked remarkably similar. Triplets.

The boy had a photogenic smile. He'd have been popular in school. He had the natural look of a charismatic athlete. The type who would have been captain of the football team. His hair was cut short but precisely styled. Sharp chin. Strong jawline. Every bit the face of a dead boy who'd been trying to kill me.

It was Buddy. Mehira's only remaining thrall. This was the family her wizard had brought to her. She'd fed on one of the sisters and turned the other two into mindless servants. One of which I'd brutally killed on the side of a dark highway, in the middle of Missouri.

"This is some kind of messed up," Lucy said as she picked up another picture from the mantel.

This one had the whole family. The father had sandy blond hair, parted on the side. The mother had a perm of dark brown hair in tight curls, hiding her ears.

"This isn't Dan," Lucy said.

"No, it isn't," I said. "And that ain't Angela."

"What the hell happened here?" Lucy put the picture back and turned around to scan the room again, as if it had changed suddenly,

"That vampire bitch didn't say anything about parents. Where are the parents? Why did she leave that out?"

"I don't think she did," I said.

"What?"

"She didn't know there were more," I ran my finger across the photo.

Lucy stopped scanning and let out a sad breath, "They died trying to protect their kids."

"Probably," I said.

Lucy shivered, "This is giving me the creeps, Bill."

"Me too," I wasn't showing it but I sure as hell was feeling it.

"For real, what is going on here?"

"I really wish I knew."

"Who does this? And why? What's the end game here?"

"You're acting like I should know." I took the picture of the whole family from the mantel and removed the photo from the frame. At least one photograph of the family should go into the permanent record at the Archives. This family was part of the history now and I had a feeling these photos were all that was left of them. This and High School Buddy. But he only looked like the kid in these pictures. That kid was dead. Mehira's thrall was nothing more than an automaton at this point. But there was still one question I didn't want to ask.

Lucy asked it anyway, "Where's the fourth kid? Where's the little girl?"

I looked at Lucy but didn't answer.

"Where the fuck is the little girl, Bill?"

"I'm not sure if I want to know," I said softly, "but we have to look anyway." Neither of us moved. Lucy stared at me defiantly. Her lower lip trembled for a second and she pressed it tightly into a grimace. She nodded once.

We searched quietly, moving from room to room, trying not

to disturb anything. As if our reverence could somehow soften the reality of what had happened.

We didn't find any answers. It didn't look like the family had packed up and left. It was more like they had simply disappeared, which they essentially did. All the other rooms were undisturbed, as if frozen in time. A snapshot of a normal suburban family life, right before it was violently snuffed out. There were still name brand clothes and snack wrappers scattered about in the boy's room among his trophies and random sports posters. The other girls' shared bedroom sported a lot of pink and purple and white. Clothes were put away. Vanities were piled with makeup and jewelry. The beds were made and covered with too many pillows. The younger girl's room was painted in a rainbow theme, with fluffy unicorns and winged horses on the bed and plastic clouds hanging from the ceiling. The master bedroom had a hastily made king bed. Laundry baskets were full of clothes waiting to be put away. A treadmill with clothes hanging on the arms and a pile of shoes on the tread surface.

I half expected the family to come bursting through the front door at any moment, kids chattering, parents barking orders about hanging up jackets and putting away shoes. But that wasn't going to happen. Not for this family.

We checked the garage last, partly because I was afraid of what I might find. It wasn't as bad as I had expected. It was worse.

Bicycles hung from racks along one wall, along with a collection of yard tools and a hula hoop. On the opposite wall, half a dozen large eyebolts had been screwed into the wall studs, about four feet up from the ground. Below them, the concrete was stained in large blotches of brown. It was dried blood. This was where half of the family had died, while the other half watched.

Lucy stared at the stain. I could almost see the gears turning in her head, trying to imagine what had happened here. I wanted to tell her to stop. That it wouldn't help anything. But I knew better. I'd been there too many times.

"What kind of monsters are we after here?" Lucy whispered.

"The worst kind," I said. "People."

"God," she said quietly. That was all that needed to be said.

We stood in silence for a minute. I didn't want to see this, but I couldn't bring myself to ignore it. It needed to be remembered.

"He was here," Lucy said angrily, "wasn't he?"

I fixated on the stained concrete. The blood. Which stain belonged to which person?

"Rezruel was in this house," Lucy pointed at me, "right under our fucking noses! While we played around with our thumbs up our asses." A tear rolled down her cheek and she wiped it away angrily before turning away from me.

She was probably right. Some of this family was probably alive while we questioned Dan outside on the lawn that night. The triplets at least. The rest... I couldn't be sure. I had a bad feeling they were part of the incursion ritual. I had a bad feeling we had already seen what became of them.

Lucy's head snapped up suddenly, "Do you smell smoke?"

"Yeah," I hit the garage door button.

The white house, the incursion site, was on fire. Smoke billowed from the edges of the roof and through some of the now broken windows. Flames belched out from the large living room window and the garage. There had been no sign of activity when we arrived. That meant someone snuck in behind us to torch the place or the fire was set with a time delay. If any of those assholes had come back to burn the places, they'd have done Lucy and me too. Dan and Angela must have set it up before bolting.

Lucy elbowed me. Across the street, the demon boys' house was burning now too. The timing was too coincidental.

We ran. We made it to the car before we heard a muffled explosion from within the house behind us. Windows shattered and flames erupted from some of the windows.

Lucy didn't ask where to. She just drove.

Chapter Thirty-One

Everything was a mess, but I felt like most of the pieces were right in front of me now. I couldn't see how they fit together yet, but they were there.

The demon boys were playing with supernatural fire, trying to summon dark forces with sloppy magic. They tried an incursion and failed but it attracts the incursion agents. Meanwhile, something worse is going on next door at the blood house. The agents investigate, showing up in time to be part of the show and explode in a mass of blood and guts. The sorcerer who did it somehow gets the demon boys possessed and uses them for minions. At some point the real Dan and Angela investigate and the sorcerer takes the family prisoner, probably sacrificing the adults and the youngest child to Rezruel or Azazel. I wasn't sure which. Rezruel was unlikely enough. Azazel was impossible. Should be impossible.

Then, the sorcerer puts Mehira on my trail to slow me down while he's helping to build Rezruel's strengthen. What about the Imp Wrangler? An ally of the sorcerer? The sorcerer himself? No, it had to be a helper or an ally. The sorcerer wouldn't be chasing after Lucy and me. He wanted us off his scent. The Imp Wrangler was another player altogether.

And the goblin. How could I forget that horrible thing? It was straight from the Otherside. I didn't know there was a Way from the Otherside in this part of the country. Usually, they're in the older parts of the country, near New Orleans and the New England states. There's one in Seattle for some reason but the Hunters there keep a close eye on it. I had never heard of one in St. Louis.

There were too many variables. I couldn't do the math without knowing where the numbers belonged. That was the whole point, wasn't it? Kill me or keep me confused and far from the truth. At least I was starting to see why it wasn't making any sense.

"Alright," Lucy finally said, "I can smell something burning again. What's on your mind."

"I think we've been on a wild goose chase this whole time."

"Explain."

"Ok, we found enough of the summoning circle in the blood house to identify Rezruel's sigil. That was a hell of a convenient discovery, wasn't it? In that bloodbath, two people happened to be standing in precisely the right place to protect just enough evidence of the sigil, which happens to be a demon I have a personal history with."

"Not just convenient," Lucy admitted. "Deliberate."

"Right," I said. "It was a setup from the beginning, to get us to follow a smoke trail."

"So... not a jailbreak?"

"Don't know. An unbridged incursion is a crazy theory because it's crazy difficult. I don't think that's what happened. I'm starting to think it was a summoning, and a deal with the devil, so to speak"

"What about the Incursion Agents?"

"They gotta be working with the sorcerer."

"Come on," Lucy said. "That's not realistic... Is it?"

"Look, I appreciate your loyalty to Winters. I accept that, and honestly, I don't think he's involved. But you gotta admit, I'm a prime example that not everyone associated with the Nine-Fold Council is infallible."

"Why fake an incursion and then throw a vindictive vampire into the mix?"

"Red herring," I said.

Lucy didn't say anything. She made a show of focusing on the road, but I could see the gears turning in her head.

"It was a setup to keep you... us off balance and suspicious," she said after a minute.

"To make me distrust Winters and you," I said with a touch of bitterness, "And it was starting to work."

"Yeah," Lucy said, "I noticed."

"So, what do we have?" I asked.

A wizard or sorcerer making some dark deal with Azazel," Lucy said. I held up a finger.

"Three demon fanboys possessed in the mix," Lucy added. I raised three more fingers.

She thought for a second, "Two agents turned rogue." Two more fingers.

"A murdered family used to enlist a vampire," I said and extended another finger.

"Oh," Lucy pointed at me, "and we can't forget the disgusting goblin thrown in the mix just to fuck up everything really good."

"Yup," that was seven fingers, "And on top of all of that, we discover Dean Waldo Forrester, the most strait-laced Archivist on the planet, happened to know the evil wizard with a demon bodyguard who came in and killed him using blood magic."

I let all that hang in the air for a moment.

"Holy Shit," Lucy said. "It wasn't a wizard. It was the other Archivist."

"Who else has access to the necessary information behind all this, and who else would know that I didn't finish a contract?"

"Makes sense."

"Makes sense? It's been staring me in the face the whole time. It explains why Dean was acting so weird when we went for his help. That's probably why none of the news had been put in the database yet."

"That's a big load of red herrings. Where does that put us?" Lucy asked.

"In the fog," I said. "We can't trust anything Dean told us. And I'm sorry but if the Archives have been compromised, it's possible the Council has too."

"Maybe," Lucy said, "but I won't believe Winters is."

"He's not a liar," I admitted. "So, you're probably right, and that's troublesome too."

"Why?"

"Because that means he's been duped, too."

Lucy scowled.

"He's the one that sent us out on this messed up chase."

"We should call him," Lucy stated.

"You're right. We should."

Winters told Lucy he'd meet us at the Archives. He didn't mention the entire Security Detail would be there too.

Blacked-out SUVs had taken up residence in the parking lot. Lowkey was no longer in their profile. Well-armed men and women in black fatigues patrolled the parking lot in pairs.

An unhappy man, who I knew and disliked, flagged us down as we turned onto the property.

He leaned down to my open window, "This car is almost as big a pile of junk as your last one."

"Hello, York," I said, "you missed all the excitement earlier."

"There'll be more," he said. "Trouble follows you around this city."

"Ain't that the truth," Lucy mumbled.

"Had enough of this guy yet," York asked Lucy.

Lucy didn't look at him, "I've had enough of everybody."

"When you get tired dragging my people around playing make-believe, cut her loose, there's work for her in the Detail."

"Take it up with Winters," I said.

"Master Winters," York corrected, "and I just might."

"Is he here?" Lucy asked.

"He is," York said. "He's waiting in the limo over there. He's not happy."

"I ain't either," I said.

"Me either," Lucy added.

"That makes all of us," York said. "What manner of bullshit have you stirred up on my watch?"

"The worse kinds," Lucy answered for me.

I shrugged helplessly.

York shook his head in frustration, "I've already got security concerns up to my ass, Kemper. Whatever it is that you're cooking is getting in my stew. Clean it up so I can get back to real work."

"You're a class act, York," I said.

"Wrap this thing up," he said and stepped away from the car, "and crawl back into your hole."

"I've always liked that guy," I said to Lucy as we pulled away, "First class jackass. You know really where you stand with him."

"Everyone's a jackass, Bill," Lucy said.

We parked near Winters' limo. He climbed out slowly and waved off the driver who offered him a hand.

"We are garnering quite the public appearance," Winters said as Lucy and I emerged from our vehicle.

"Things have gone all to hell since you blackmailed me into working for you."

"That is apparent," Winters said with a sigh. "And you may be surprised to know that your task is not the only concern with which I am coping today."

"Well," I said, "my task has morphed into a massive clusterfuck."

"I don't have time for vagaries, William," he said.

"Bill," I corrected. "And I'm neck deep in vagaries."

"Why am I here? I am in the middle of something important."

"What?" I asked.

"He's talking about the Council, dummy," Lucy said. "The Council is in town."

"No shit?" I said with more than a little surprise.

Winters frowned and inclined his head toward her. Although his eyes were concealed behind his shiny little spectacles, I swear I saw a flash of warning.

"Sorry," Lucy said.

"It is not a secret," Winters said, "but please do not speak so openly of such matters."

"Why didn't you tell me," I asked.

"It's not any of your concern," Lucy said. "And it doesn't matter."

"Everything matters," I said.

"How very shrewd of you," Winters said, "You have grown into quite the holist."

"Sarcasm?" I asked.

"I would apologize, William," Winter said. "But I am weary. I do not have the energy or patience for your brand of disruptions right now."

"Sorry to break it to you," I said, "but disruptions are just the tip of your mounting problems."

"You speak more truth than you can possibly know, but simply I don't have the time for this. Nor do you. You should be out putting an end to this incursion business."

"We're trying," I said, waving my arms around. "This business is a steaming mess."

"Let's not play games. Lucille, will you get to the point if he will not?"

Lucy opened her mouth to answer but didn't get out a word because a flash of lightning exploded nearby, sending us sprawling. Winters' limo went up in flames. Gunfire erupted from all around us. The Detail was quick to react to the sudden attack.

A nasty gurgling laughter cut through the gunfire followed by another crackle of electricity growing intensity.

"Are you kidding me?" Lucy spat as she got to her feet. She was already firing before I could even find the target.

I pulled out the Holy Handgun, turning around quickly, hunting for the attacker. Attackers. Turns out there were a few of them. They were much like the goblin that had attacked us twice before, but smaller and of varying degrees of disgusting and ugly. They all looked like they had crawled out of the same mud hole as our friend had. Fortunately, they didn't seem to have balls of lightning. Instead, they hurled golf ball sized stones with deadly accuracy and speed.

"This gets worse and worse," I yelled to no one.

Chapter Thirty-Two

A stone zipped towards me, but a Detail dude wandered into the projectile's path at the wrong moment and took the blow instead. It tore into his arm and sent him tumbling past me. I dropped to a knee with the Holy Handgun at the ready. Point. Aim. Squeeze. A single shot thundered from the gun and the weapon rocked in my hand. I didn't realize how much comfort that used to give me. It was a good shot. The bullet struck the goblin and it fell over backward with a good-sized hole in its torso. I aimed another and Lucy tackled me from behind. I felt the sting of sparks as a ball of lightning exploded against the Crown Vic. Lucy let go of me before we stopped rolling and was already running. I jerked the trigger a couple of times at the source of the explosive attack. The lightning goblin laughed horridly and dodged my shots.

A man with a light machinegun stepped out from behind a van to fire on full auto at one of the goblins. The bullets tore through it but not before it zipped a handful of jagged throwing knives at him. The blades cut into the gunner's chest and neck.

"Get down!" York yelled from behind me. I obeyed and dropped to my stomach. He fired three controlled bursts. The lightning goblin jerked and stumbled but didn't go down. York spun and engaged another goblin before it could throw a stone. It went down.

I fired two shots at another. It dropped one of its knives, which shattered like glass when it hit the concrete.

The muddy goblin threw a ball of lightning, and two nearby soldiers went down with fatal electrical burns. Lucy fired a string of shots and profanity and kept moving. I took aim and hit another nearby goblin in the head. It didn't even twitch, just dropped like a sack of potatoes. There were still more than a dozen of the nasty goblins, and they had already taken out half the security detail.

I dug some bullets out of my pocket and reloaded the handgun then made myself mobile. I dove behind a van and waited as something exploded nearby. Lucy ran past me firing ahead of her. She was going somewhere with a purpose, so I followed her. Yep. She was after the muddy lightning goblin. He was moving quickly from cover to cover, hurling balls of energy and laughing sickeningly. He tossed a bundle of electricity toward York. The man dropped to a knee, evading the projectile while firing several shots. Lucy fired several shots. One struck home. The goblin roared but didn't go down. At least he didn't laugh this time.

I fired several shots in a hurry. One struck his leg and he jerked backwards like someone had yanked him with a rope. The Holy Handgun's Proportional Mass runes were building up some effect.

The goblin fell but rolled into a sitting position and tossed another lightning ball. It sailed over my head, but I heard a crackle behind me explode before I could move.

The blast tossed me like a ragdoll. I flew several feet in the air and landed flat on my back. While I struggled to catch my breath, I saw Lucy out of the corner of my eye reload her pistol and fire off several shots. I brought up the Holy Handgun and squeezed off a shot. The gun bucked and roared. The bullet missed but the shockwave knocked the goblin fall sideways. He was back on his feet quickly, though, with another electric ball in hand. I was still struggling to catch my breath but raised my gun and pulled the trigger. Click.

Shit.

The goblin smiled, showing me all his nasty teeth.

Then I heard, or rather felt, a deep rumble. It was like the deep bass coming from someone testing the limits of a large subwoofer. I felt it down in my gut. My teeth rattled and my skin tingled. The goblin paused, and his eyes widened. And there was Winters standing next to me, his cane raised above his head.

The frail-looking man stood upright, ripples of energy emanating from him like waves radiating out from a pebble dropped in a pond.

His eyes were still hidden behind his wire-framed glasses, but his brow was furrowed in intense concentration. All the gunfire stopped. The goblins stopped chucking projectiles. The lightning goblin's smile faded; his ball of electricity dissipated.

Winters slowly lowered the cane as he twisted it slightly in his grip. The deep bass sound went impossible lower and lower. My bones rattled.

Winters stood still for a moment, then thrust down, stabbing the tip into the concrete. A shockwave of visible energy erupted from the cane and swept outwards in a rapidly expanding circle. I felt it pass through me like an unbearably cold breeze, but it was otherwise harmless... to me. As it struck the goblins, they convulsed violently and then simply disappeared in a bright flash. In less than a second, they were all gone. Even the dead ones.

Winters leaned on his cane and sucked in a deep breath. Lucy rushed to his side. He waved her off irritably, but she continued to fuss over him.

"Mr. Kemper," he said, "perhaps we could go inside and chat."

York escorted us inside while the rest of the detail started the cleanup. He assured us they'd handle the police when they showed up. The Security Detail—disguised as Metal Exchange security frequently conducted drills with blanks. They'd become well-versed in lying to and misdirecting local law enforcement.

They had been busy before Lucy and I arrived. The dead had already been removed. Somehow, the blood had been cleaned up, even from the walls and a crew was already at work on the wall patching up the drywall. We made it as far as the stairwell before my curiosity got the better of me.

"Ok," I said, "what just happened and how did you do that?"

"Magic," Winters said simply.

"I guessed that much."

Winters waved a hand dismissively, "I returned those creatures from whence they came."

"Which is where?" I asked.

"Don't be obtuse," Winters stopped at the janitorial supply closet, where an armed guard stood watch. "You know where they came from."

"The goblins are coming from the Otherside? Directly?"

"Clearly," Winters said. The guard opened the door for us. The back wall hadn't been repaired yet; it was still open to the stairs.

"I didn't know there were Ways in this part of the country."

"The Ways are not what you imagine them to be. There are many paths into our world."

"Incursions are for demons," I said.

Winters raised an eyebrow.

"Aren't they?"

"Incursions apply to visitors from the Otherside crossing over without the Council's permission or knowledge."

"Does that happen a lot?"

"More than we like to admit," the old man stepped into the stairwell. York shoved past me and followed close behind. Lucy nodded for me to go ahead and followed me.

The lighting had been repaired so we could see clearly. Winters was a few steps down, descending slowly.

I called over York's shoulder, "Are all the monsters I've been hunting from the Otherside."

"No," Winters said without turning around. "Many, but not all."

At the bottom of the stairs, four more heavily armed members of the Detail stood guard in front of the large double doors. They didn't have any scanners or electrical devices. One had a simple clipboard with a list of names on it and matching photos.

Winters turned to face us as he emerged from the stairs, "Lucille, perhaps you can explain now while you have caused me to become involved in your assignment."

Lucy shifted her weight as if suddenly uncomfortable in her boots and looked at me before beginning. She summarized everything that had happened since he left us in my house together, leaving out most of my disrespectful comments about Winters. As I listened to her fill him in, I couldn't help but think how crazy it all sounded.

Winters listened to it all without interrupting, nodding occasionally. York shook his head in disbelief as Lucy relayed the gruesome details of the blood house and our fight with the imps but said nothing. The guards shared uneasy looks throughout her telling but didn't seem too shaken. They'd probably already seen the aftermath of the carnage.

Winters motioned at the guards and two of them opened the doors to let us in.

Dean's body had already been removed. Another armed guard stood inside the room, against the wall opposite the camera where she could watch the main entrance and the door to the inner Archives. Winters settled into one of the fancy chairs and rested his cane across his lap. Lucy stood by his side, a frown of concern on her face. He patted her hand and waved her off. Reluctantly, Lucy stepped away from him. York set up post behind his chair, not quite at attention. But rigid and erect.

"This is most distressing," he said at last. "I am having difficulty accepting that Mr. Marten could be involved in any of this."

York looked at me defiantly for a moment then sighed, "Marten has been missing for a few days. It is highly irregular." "Someone has been tracking us," Lucy said. "Bill assumed it was you."

I shrugged.

Winters nodded slowly, "A logical conclusion, but I have not been tracking your physical whereabouts. I am a wizard. I could have found you at any time if I had deemed it necessary."

"That's a comforting thought," I said with a scowl.

"I should hope," Winters said, "You might find comfort in knowing that I trust you. I trust your integrity. I believe you will do what you said you would do, William."

"Thanks," I said a little awkwardly, "but, someone has been tracking us. Mehira said as much. Marten seems like a likely culprit."

"Shit!" Lucy said suddenly. Winters raised his eyebrows with apparent amusement but said nothing.

"Sorry," Lucy said meekly then continued, "It's not that hard to do. We just assumed it was magic. It doesn't need to be. Cellphones can be traced. My phone can be traced."

"What?" I said.

"It's called technology, Grandpa," she poked at her forehead with a finger. "I can't believe I didn't think of it before. It's not magic, it's GPS."

"Ah," Winters said.

I dug out my flip phone, "This has a GPS?"

"Maybe not that relic," Lucy said.

I shrugged, "OK. Then yours. And anyone can... what? Hack it?"

"Not just anyone, but yeah, if you have the right info and the right access to cell towers and such, you can track a cellphone."

"Cops," York said plainly.

"Yeah," Lucy nodded, "but it usually takes a warrant."

Winters tilted his head, "I doubt your antagonist has a warrant from the police."

"Agreed," I said. "If law enforcement was tied up in this—even corrupt cops—they'd have been all over us by now."

York crossed his arms and looked down at Winters, "He's right. We haven't picked up anything pertinent to this case on the police scanners, except for a search for persons of interest concerning the incident on the interstate." He looked at me when he said, "persons of interest."

"No cops then," Lucy said.

Winters held up a finger, "However it can be assumed your suspect has considerable other resources."

"Such as the access to the Archives," I gestured grandly to the room.

"It would seem," Winters admitted with a nod.

I looked around the room, trying to guess what kind of resources they could have been using against us. Dean always got me the help I needed, but he had never really hinted at what the Archives was capable of. If I had ever known...

"Wait!" I turned on Lucy, "Can we do it the other way around? Track him the same way he was tracking us?"

Lucy shrugged, "If it works one way, it should work the other. We would need his cellphone info though."

"He was the freaking Senior Archivists, right?" I looked at Winters sideways, "we should have his cell number... right?"

"Presumably," Winters said.

"If he had one," Lucy said, "it should be in the database. Assuming he didn't remove it or hide it."

"If he did hide it, that would be a dead giveaway, right?"

York nodded thoughtfully, "I would come across as self-incriminating."

Lucy nodded, "I bet it's still there. I bet he was counting on Bill and me being dead by now and not making the connection."

I pointed toward the elaborate wood counters, "Can you get it?"

Lucy shook her head, "Unless it's in a rolodex, I doubt it. I don't have any more access to the database than you do. We need an Archivist."

"Shit," I dropped into one of the sturdier looking chairs.

Winters waggled a finger at me, "Tsk. We are not as inept as you believe us to be."

York smirked and raised his chin, without turning around, he called out to the woman standing chair, "Miss Gates, call in our temp." The guard raised a radio handset to her mouth and whispered something. A few seconds later, the door to the inner Archives swung open and a familiar figure emerged.

Leslie had changed from her argyle sweater into a maroon vest and her canvas shoes for combat boots, but her overall aesthetic remained the same. She was a historical hipster rebel fashion deviant, and she wore it well. She crossed into the waiting room and came over to shake my hand firmly and smiled warmly at Lucy. Then she leaned down to give Winters a gentle hug.

"Thank you for joining us, Leslie," Winters said.

"How could I not?" she said solemnly.

"How'd you get here so fast?" I asked incredulously.

"It's closer than you think," she stated.

"Huh?"

Winters waved a hand, "You can probe the secrets of the Archives on your own time, William."

"I haven't had 'my own time' in ages," I said.

"You've done quite a bit with whatever time you've been using," Leslie said.

"Go big or go home," I said.

York cleared his throat.

"Yes," Winters said, "let's not dally here."

Leslie motioned toward the counter, "May I?"

Winters bowed his head.

Leslie motioned for us to follow her back to the wooden counter where she powered up Dean's computer, Winters remained in his seat.

"You need a phone number?" she asked.

"Among other things," I said.

"You tore your stitches," she said as she logged in.

She was right. I was bleeding again.

"That happens a lot," I said.

"We are kind of shorthanded right now," Leslie said, "but you want medical attention first..."

"No," I said and pointed at the computer, "you do your thing there."

Lucy was beside me again, "You're gonna stain the fancy carpet."

I sighed, "Fine, York, can you get me a med kit?"

York frowned but nodded as he reached into a pouch in his belt and pulled out a field kit. He squatted down and started to dress my wound.

"I can do it," I said.

"Shut up and take the help," he said without looking at me.

"Ok," I said awkwardly, "Thanks."

"Before I get to work," Leslie said, "what have I missed?"

I gave her the quick version of what had transpired since we left KC. I didn't go into any more detail than necessary on Dean's death. Leslie and Miles had been pretty concerned about him before we left KC; Leslie was carrying herself with composure, but I could tell his death was a real blow to her. As was Marten's apparent involvement.

"We need to know," I said softly. "If we can ping his phone, we might be able to get some answers."

"That shouldn't be difficult," Leslie said thoughtfully. She typed in a few commands and frowned, "that's... odd."

"What is odd?" York asked.

"There are a lot of holes here," Leslie said, still tapping keys, "The basic personnel info is here, but the logic trails are weird."

"Elaborate please," Winters said, he had joined us without making a sound.

"Everything an Archivist does is logged," Leslie waved at her computer screen, "Every action on the Archives network is supposed to have a timestamp and tracking tag."

"Supposed to?" I prompted.

"Someone has been naughty. For instance, most of the data about Azazel has been recoded, but there's no record of who recoded it. The tag wasn't removed; it's been hidden."

"So... it's still in there?" I asked.

"I think so, but it'll be hard to find. Also, your file is way off-kilter. For instance, the termination contract for Mehira has been hidden."

"What the hell?" I said.

York shook his head, still work working on my wound. He applied several butterfly bandages.

Leslie squinted, "I don't think Mr. Forrester could have done all this. He could update information, but he couldn't remove it and he couldn't hide his own tracks. Only the Senior Archivist can do that."

"Ronald Marten," I said.

Leslie nodded.

"Maybe Dean discovered what Ronnie was doing," I offered, "and was trying to cover for him."

"Maybe," Leslie said dubiously and continued digging.

"What about their cellphones?" Lucy asked. "Did Marten have a number on record?"

"Of course," Leslie said, "their personnel files haven't been tampered with."

"Can you ping it?"

Leslie chewed on her lip for a second as she worked, "Sort of. Only when he makes a call."

"What about this?" Lucy handed her a piece of paper with Mehira's phone information on it.

"That should help," Leslie said. "I might even be able to ghost her phone."

"I have no idea what that means," I admitted, "unless you mean you're going to kill it."

York slapped a bandage over the wound and stood up, "You're a goddamned dinosaur Kemper."

I shrugged, "I am what I am."

"It kind of means I can tap into her phone," Leslie said. "We won't be able to listen in, but we'll know when she gets a call."

"It's a start," I said. "Do that."

"Already working on it," Leslie said.

I prodded at the fresh bandage. York had done a good job. I guessed he was a trained medic, maybe even had some experience.

"Thanks," I said to him.

He nodded curtly once and stepped away to take position beside Winters.

"What happens now?" Lucy asked.

Leslie shrugged, "I can't do anything until someone calls her."

I hated waiting almost as much as I hated all this smoke and mirrors stuff. Clearly, I was a man of action. Clearly, I was made for hitting things, not thinking about them. My targets were all a fuzzy mess. I didn't know what was what or who was who. Hell, I didn't even know what this guy Marten looked like.

Well, that was a simple fix.

"Hey, Leslie, do you have a picture of Marten?"

"Of course," Leslie pulled one up on the screen.

"Fuck me," Lucy said.

"You've got to be kidding," I added.

York scowled, "What is your problem?"

"You've met him?" Leslie asked.

"That's Dan," I said.

"Sonofabitch," I grumbled and ran my hand through my stubbly hair. "Marten was in the house next door to the bloodbath house, posing as a neighbor. He was right under our noses."

"I hit him with a tire iron!" Lucy said and punch one hand into the palm of the other. "I should have shot him."

"I'd have broken him in half if I knew," I said. He probably knew it too. Most likely he knew who I was and knew to be careful. When he hit me with the baseball bat, he either severely missed hitting me in the right spot or very intentionally didn't hit me where it would matter.

Lucy's jaw flexed and showed her teeth through an angry sneer, "Show me the incursion agents."

Leslie brought up their photos, side by side. "Agent Rebecca Charters and Agent James Ridgely."

"Are you freaking kidding me?" I said.

"I hate that woman," Lucy said. "And that guy."

Rebecca Charters had taken the place of Dan's rude wife. Ridgely was the punk rock imp wrangler. He didn't have the ridiculous spikey hair and clothes in the photo but that was an obvious disguise. An old trick. Make yourself look so outlandish that people don't look past the surface features. They see anarchist punk or whatever and never really look at the face or the eyes.

Winters lowered his head and leaned on his cane again. I felt sorry for him. Four representatives of the Nine-Fold Council had gone foul, apparently all in a few days' time. It had to be devastating.

He turned his little glasses toward me, "Mr. Kemper, I would like to alter the parameters of our agreement."

"Me too," I said.

Chapter Thirty-Three

York sent one of his minions for some food while we stirred around listlessly, trying to come to terms with the revelations we'd uncovered. Leslie buried herself in the computer, diving deep into her investigation rather than talk about the loss and betrayal of her beloved peers.

Winters had returned to his chair and fell into silence. I guessed he was either asleep or meditating, as he didn't move a muscle. Lucy wandered around the waiting room as if seeing it all in a new light. Like it was a different place after all we'd discovered.

York had taken the guard radio and was issuing a string of orders. He was talking in low, short sentences, so I didn't catch much. I did manage to hear "I want them taken alive" among the orders, though. Apparently, he had his own justice in mind if he got to the targets before I did.

By the time the young man returned with a couple of pizzas, I was hungry enough to eat a slice of Canadian bacon and pineapple. Lucy declined to eat but chugged a can of soda as she settled into a plush side chair. York returned the guard's radio to her and stood as parade rest next to Winters, refusing to make eye contact with anyone.

The waiting room had fallen silent, aside from the continued clickety-click of keys as Leslie continued scouring the database for holes and cover-ups.

I finished the Hawaiian pizza unaided and reached for the last can of soda when Winters raised his head suddenly and tapped his cane on the floor.

"I cannot reconcile such a betrayal," he said with rising tension in his voice. "Incursion Agents and Archive candidates undergo an extensive vetting process."

Leslie called out from her computer, "I can vouch for that."

"But they're... you're magic users?" Lucy crushed her can and set it on the nearest tabletop.

Leslie came out from behind the counter, "Magic users yes, not magic makers."

"What's the difference?"

"Wizards conjure magic," Leslie explained. "They draw magic from the universe and focus it. Witches, enchanters, healers, those people are magic users. They know how to use magic things or use spells and incantations to call upon magic."

I found it interesting that Leslie, not Winters, was explaining the concepts of magic to Lucy.

I pointed at Lucy's arm, "Leslie used magic on that." Leslie nodded, "We know a few chants and spells. But we're not wizards. We can't make magic."

I blew out a long breath, "Then Marten had help."

Lucy swatted the crushed can from the tabletop, "You mean there's still another player we don't know?"

"At least one more," I got up and picked up the can from where it had landed. "Master Winters, where are the rest of the wizards right now?"

"Some of them are at the very location which I had been engaged before your call," Winters said. I was about to press Winters on that location when Leslie's computer dinged.

She clapped a hand and rushed back to the desk, "We have a hit. Your Mehira is getting a call."

"Why does everyone call her mine?"

Leslie shook her head, "We're not getting anything from Mr. Marten's phone, though. Just a blocked caller."

"Meaning what?" I asked as I approached, looking over her shoulder, "He's out of range or something?"

"It doesn't work that way, genius," Lucy said from just behind me, "It means the call isn't coming from Marten's phone number."

"So, it isn't Marten?"

Leslie shrugged, "It isn't Marten's phone."

"Maybe it's another burner phone," Lucy offered.

"Maybe," Leslie nodded. "No way to tell really."

I looked up at the ceiling as if I might find answers there. The hammered tin tiles were lightly tarnished. The elaborate chandelier cast interlaced shadows on the tiles, some faint, some dark, some almost indistinguishable.

Lucy growled, "That bitch never said anything about more than one person calling her."

I studied the overlapping shadows. They looked different, but they were all reflections of the same thing. They were shadows of the chandelier.

We were looking at shadows. Not at what was making them.

"She said it was a wizard," I said.

Leslie turned to look at me, "Mehira told you that?"

Lucy nodded eagerly, "She did. She said she could smell it. She said she knew what a wizard smells like."

"Marten isn't a wizard," York said from the other side of the counter. "He would never have been cleared for the Archives."

"Another red herring?" Lucy asked.

"Shadows," I said idly, my mind was swimming. "Everything that's happened, everyone we've been chasing... they're all shadows."

"What are you trying to say?" Lucy asked.

"I'm saying we've been looking at shadows and making assumptions about them."

Lucy pointed at the camera, "We saw Marten in that video and what he did."

"So, we assumed he is the center of this."

"Easy assumption to make," Lucy said, "considering the content of the video."

"But he didn't have that kind of power the first time we met him."

"How can you be sure?"

"After you hit him with that tire iron, did he strike you as someone who could suck out your blood like in a cloud?"

"No," Lucy admitted. "But there is such a thing as acting. Maybe he was still weak or something, so soon after the summoning or whatever."

Leslie shook her head, "No, Bill's right. Marten couldn't have pulled off the jailbreak."

"I concur," Winters had joined us again as well. "Mr. Marten did not have innate magical aptitudes. He could not have hidden such proclivities while being vetted for the Archives."

"So that means?" Lucy said.

"It means Marten didn't start this mess," I said. "It means he's a player, not a coach. He has a sponsor."

"Such as that vampire bitch's smelly wizard," Lucy said.

"You guessed it," I said. "But it doesn't get us anywhere. There's a face in this we haven't seen yet."

Lucy glanced at Winters, "The Council is in town."

Winters grimaced but didn't say anything.

"True," I leaned my elbows on the countertop, so I wasn't towering over Winters and tried to look him in the eyes. Which didn't really work because of those little wire-rimmed glasses. "Can you help us narrow down some suspects? Are there any troublemakers on the Council?"

The old man shook his head at the question and sighed, "It is against our policies to openly discuss such matters with people outside the inner circle. However, under the circumstance, I can bend the rule. I can tell you there are indeed troublemakers on the Council. Such is the driving force behind our current gathering."

"Ok, that's vague," I said "How many?"

"Not many," Winters said, "I am one of those troublemakers."

Lucy's head turned suddenly to Winters. I blinked and stood upright.

Winters let out a feeble laugh, "I am full of surprises, even at my age."

I chewed on the questions swirling around in my head for a moment, then picked one, "Can I ask what kind of trouble you're making?"

"You may ask, but I cannot answer," the little man said tiredly. Not annoyed, just tired. I thought he was done and loaded up another question, but Winters took a breath and continued, "I can, however, divulge that your name has come up a point of contention in many of our discussions."

"I don't like that."

"Things are rarely as bad as you imagine them to be."

"They're worse," Lucy said before I could.

Winters shrugged apologetically.

"Gimme something here," I opened my empty hands, "Could one of the other troublemakers be our suspect?"

"It is very unlikely," Winters said.

"That doesn't help."

"I am aware," Winters said, "but you much understand, I have constraints by which I must abide."

"Just call her," Lucy blurted.

"What?"

Lucy held out her phone, "Call the bitch. I put her number in my phone. Call her and ask her about the call we know she just got."

Leslie smiled, "It couldn't hurt."

"It's already ringing," Lucy said.

I took the phone. After a few rings, someone answered.

"Yes?" Mehira answered extending the "s" much longer than necessary. That single word was an open invitation. Exaggerated and sensuous.

"Hello... Mehira," I said with as businesslike a tone as I could manage.

"Ah, Bill," she put extra emphasis on my name. "How wonderful of you to call! To what do I owe the pleasure of being called upon by my most hated nemesis and my most resistant lover?"

"No games," I said. "Did your wizard just call you? And did he tell you where to go?"

"He did. And he did."

"Where?"

"Oh, Bill, don't be rude. Surely you know how to coax a woman's secrets from her."

I squeezed the phone.

Lucy whispered through clenched teeth, "Don't break my phone."

"Please tell me," I said almost politely.

"You disappoint me, Lover. Be a gentleman."

I counted to three.

"Mehira Fiodniagh, beautiful and mysterious lady," I said as nicely as I could force myself to, which wasn't much, "would you be so kind as to share with me the details of your recent phone call?"

"Oh, I like that. You are a gentleman after all," Mehira said. "Very well, since we are partners now." She waited long enough to make me want to strangle the phone, then she told me.

Chapter Thirty-Four

As far as executive limos go, I guess Winters' was nice. I had never been in one before, so I had no frame of reference. Everything inside felt way too expensive for a big bastard like me to be sitting on or touching. It was roomy, which was surprising, because I take up a lot of space, and very comfortable. Opulent, seemed like an appropriate word.

We were an interesting bunch, Lucy, Winters, and me. None of us looked like we belonged in the luxury vehicle. Winters looked like a retired banker from 1927. I looked like a bouncer in a prison strip club. Lucy, like an angry mercenary ready for a paycheck.

She had secured a tactical belt and several spare magazines from some of the Detail personnel who were staying behind at the Archives. They flat out refused to give up any assault rifles or combat shotguns, and I couldn't say I blamed them. After what had gone down, I wouldn't have given up any firepower either. Lucy had also changed into a set of black fatigues and combat boots and looked every bit a paramilitary badass. The magic sword leaning against her leg seemed strangely well paired with the look rather than clashing with it.

I was a mass of stained clothes and bandages. Leslie had assured me she could find me a change of clothes if I would wait a little while, but I was pretty sure time wasn't on our side. We needed to get back to work. York had done a decent job patching up my injuries. As good as could be expected, without taking some downtime to recuperate. The guy was a dick, but he was a real pro in anything he did. I resolved to never admit to him that I had thought such things.

Not surprisingly, there weren't any 10-gauge shotgun shells at the Archives, which left me with a half dozen shells with which to make an impression. I still had more bullets for the Holy Handgun than I'd use. Between those and the large claymore, a pair of magic nails, and a holy hammer, I felt like someone who'd been equipped from a grab bag.

It wasn't going to be very a long ride to our destination, so I decided I had better press Winters a little harder for some useful information.

"Look, Master Winters, I understand Council business is super-secret and everything, but Lucy and I are running blind. We need to know what's going on."

"I hate to say it," Lucy added, "but he's right. This all seems to be connected."

Winters seemed to think about it, his shiny round glasses pointing at me for a moment. After a minute he nodded, and then tapped his cane on my knee.

"You may as well hear it now; it will come out soon enough."

He removed his glasses for a moment and cleaned the lenses with a silk cloth. I saw his eyes for the first time in the dim light of the limo's back seat. They were the baby blue, almost colorless. They were tired and weary, but also full of strength. Some people wear their lives in their eyes. You can see the culmination of all their life experiences reflected in them. Winters was one of those people. I could feel a lifetime in his eyes. More than I had expected. And a depth of experience I couldn't even understand. The strength in his eyes told of a man who'd lived lifetimes but had not grown weaker with time.

He put his glasses back on slowly, hiding his eyes once again behind the little round lenses. Had he done that for my benefit? Had he shown me his eyes so I could see a piece of him he'd never revealed to me before?

"I told you early that you have been a point of contention in our proceedings."

I breathed in and nodded.

"I have recently admitted and accepted some facts that have

caused something of a stir," he said. He was pausing too long between words. He was stalling.

"Yeah?" I prodded.

"I have been grievously mistaken on a few key issues."

Lucy's head snapped to attention, but she didn't say anything. Had she thought Winters infallible? Was this such a shock? I already knew that answer. She idolized him.

He turned his head to look out the window, "For centuries even before the inception of the Nine-Fold Council, men like me have fought blindly against what we perceived as the forces of darkness. We have been on a crusade, much like those conducted by religious zealots across the millennia. We believed ourselves to be righteous. Most still do."

I held my breath and felt my shoulders tensing up.

Winters turned from the window and looked at me, "While I know that there are indeed forces at work that are inherently and irrevocably evil, I do not believe that is true of all those whom we have deemed enemies."

He stopped speaking for a moment and let the silence speak. The gravity of what he had just said sunk in. Like a dagger in my heart.

I'd spent the last twenty years of my life being the tip of the spear for that crusade. My will, my conscience, and my drive were built upon the foundation of an ideal: my targets were evil, and I was not. For two decades, I survived on the belief that I was doing something righteous. Worthy. Noble. Necessary. Every time I had retried a target, I had done so with the firm belief that it was evil. That innocent people would die if I didn't. That I was a good man, doing the hard and dark, but right thing,

My stomach suddenly felt as if it had been filled with worms. My shoulders unbearably heavy. My heart like a cold stone taking up space in my chest.

Winters shook his head slowly, "I fear we... I have been misled in our arrogance and ignorance."

"Master Winters!" Lucy gasped.

"I fear we have done you a great injustice," Winters said softly

I pulled my eyes away from Winters and stared down at my hands. Injustice? I had been an executioner, standing on the belief that it was justice. The Fist of Justice. That's what I had told Lucy. They weren't just words spit out in anger. They had been my truth. My fuel.

I had survived countless fatal encounters fueled by the belief that I was ordained, that I was on a righteous path. I believed I could survive anything, outfight anyone, overcome any odds because I was on the side of good. Because I needed to live to fight another day. To save another innocent. To stop one more evil thing.

"I can only imagine the burden such a revelation places upon your soul." "You can imagine?" I said, too loudly.

"Easy, Bill," Lucy leaned forward, but I don't know what she planned to do in this confined space. I didn't know what I was going to do either.

The burden on my soul? He couldn't know. No one knew. Not even me. Not really. I had destroyed some horrible things. I had convinced myself that they were all horrible, that they all deserved to die. How many times had I been wrong? How many things had I killed that did not deserve it? How many times had I let myself believe in a lie, so I could carry out an execution with a clear conscience?

Only my conscience wasn't clear. I felt every one of those deaths. They piled up on my soul. They mounted, one on top of the one before, building a mountain of death and retribution on my back.

I looked at my hands. No amount of scrubbing could ever wash off the blood that was on them.

"Do you know what I've done in the name of your so-called crusade against evil?"

"Only too well," Winters said.

"Too well? What the hell is that supposed to mean?" my voice thundered within the confines of the limousine.

"From the day that Master Regis first brought you into the Fold," the old man said, "I saw a righteous fire burning inside you. I never believed it could be misused."

Lucy sat back in her seat, her gaze shifting back and forth from me to Winters.

I stared at my hands and said nothing. I couldn't speak. I only have words of rage and shame.

"The targets you were given were never my purview, but as High Councilor, I cannot deny the responsibility. Did you know that I have personally studied the reports of every assignment you have ever carried out?"

I looked at him, at this powerful wizard who now seemed like a defenseless shell of a man. And my vision blurred. Tears welled up in my eyes.

"Every single life you took, I remember. I remembered them but I decided that I must. Because I never truly believed that the universe is only black and white. That we were fools to believe that grey does not exist. Matters cannot always be as simple as good and evil."

"That exact distinction is the one thing that kept me going."

"I know."

A tear rolled down my cheek, "That was the one tiny thread of humanity that I hung on to all these years." Winters opened his mouth to speak, then closed it without saying a word.

"What am I without that?" I shouted. Lucy jumped.

I slammed my fist against my chest, "It was the only reason I thought I might still have a soul!"

"Bill," Lucy said quietly and reached a hand toward me.

I slapped it away, "Don't."

Anger flashed across her face, but she contained herself returned her hand to her lap.

"There are greater mysteries in the universe than I had allowed myself to imagine," Winters said. "We are only beginning to break the surface. Some things, we will never understand."

"That doesn't help, I said through clenched teeth.

"It is not supposed to," he said gently. "It was a simple statement of fact. And part of the reason I have begun to campaign for a change in the way the Council views incursions."

I looked down to discover my hands were wrapped around the hilt of the claymore. My knuckles white. My fingers aching.

I sighed.

My heart had been broken, and where did I go? My hands settled on a weapon.

"Mr. Marten and I have spent a considerable amount of time together studying incursion events," Winters went on. "I may have led him to the very information he has used against us."

"This isn't your fault," Lucy said quietly, almost as if she wasn't sure she believed it.

Winters smiled a wry smile, "I appreciate your loyalty, but it is unwarranted."

I pulled my hands away from the sword and flexed my fingers, "You know what you've done to me." It wasn't a question.

Winters nodded.

"You've destroyed me. You blew out the one flame that kept my soul alive."

"You are still alive, William. Your soul is intact."

"Right or wrong, you have acted according to a belief."

"A lie."

"A belief," Winters said again. "I told you, I saw a righteous fire inside you when you came to us. You came to us because of that belief. That belief that good must stand against evil. And make no mistake, there is evil. You have taken a stand against it."

"Doesn't matter," I whispered. "As I watched you, my conviction began to grow as well as my suspicion that the Council is wrong."

Lucy pressed her lips together and turned her head away.

"As my conviction in this new truth grew, I also began to see yours diminish."

"You saw that?"

"Your conviction had wavered. That much became quite clear to me. Your skill has not diminished, but your zeal has."

"No shit," I said. I wanted to punch something. I wanted to hurt someone. I shook my head. No. No, I didn't. I wanted to lash out. To deny the pain. To justify the bad I thought I had done. The trust was painfully clear. I already knew I didn't want to continue. I had already known it for some time.

"I tried to quit," I said quietly.

"I recall clearly," Winters said sadly. "It was my hope that this final task would set things straight for you. It was to be the end of such things. I had no idea it would turn so dire."

Dire. I shook my head.

"The reason I have called the Nine-Fold Council together is I am trying to convince certain members to reevaluate our stance on contact with the Otherside. The veil is becoming thinner."

"The veil?" Lucy asked.

"The boundary that keeps our world and the Otherside separate." He said "Our aversion to the Otherside is based on ancient superstitions. The Council is founded on very old traditions."

I let out a long slow breath, "And I'm willing to bet that the Council isn't very keen on letting go of those old traditions."

"That is a safe bet," Winters said.

"I have never liked the Council," I said jabbing my finger at Winters, "I have never trusted any of you. I never did any of what I did for you or Regis or the Council."

"I know."

"You turned me into a monster," I said, and my voice cracked. "You made me a monster!" My hands trembled. I suddenly felt cold and small.

"Bill," Lucy said, "you can't believe that!"

"Believe what? That I've murdered for years. Years! And all because these wizards are superstitious bastards?"

Lucy looked back and forth between me and Winters as if she had to choose one over the other.

"I know you believe you are a monster," Winters said, "but you are not."

I said nothing.

"You are a good man."

"He's right," Lucy said.

"I'm a killer."

"A defender," Winters said.

"I used to believe that."

"I cannot make you believe anything," Winters said, "but I can assure you that people are alive today because of the work you did."

"Work?"

"There are mothers kissing their children every morning because of you, William. Mothers who would still be in mourning today if you hadn't killed something evil. There are men still drawing breath only because you did what you do best. There and children who have not been orphaned because you did the difficult thing."

"Lies."

"Not lies," Winters shook his head firmly. "There have been mistakes. Far fewer than you know. Precious few. Your work, your calling has been to protect the innocent. To fight for those who could not."

"I wanted to be done with all this," I looked at Winters, trying to penetrate his glasses to see those pale blue eyes. "I tried to walk away."

"I regret my interference," Winters said.

"Me too," I said. But there was a truth we hadn't. That I was ignoring. "But it has to be done."

Lucy blinked.

"Something terrible has been called into this world," I said and flexed my fingers. "It's gonna take something terrible to stop it."

"Wait," Lucy said, "you mean..."

"Yeah," I said. "Whatever I've done, doesn't matter here. This thing is bigger than me. And it isn't grey."

"No, it's not," Lucy agreed.

"I'm the big angry bastard to stop it."

"We," Lucy said, "we're the big angry bastards to stop it."

"Then let's get back to finishing this clusterfuck.

"Right on," she said.

I looked hard at Winters, "You and I have a lot of reckoning to do when this is over."

Winters bowed his head in acknowledgment.

"But it ain't over. Until then, it's time to open up. No more secrets."

Winters opened his hands, "I will tell you what I am able to

"This meeting we're going to, is the whole Council there?"

"No," Winters said, "just a few members were invited. Much of the Council remains undecided on my proposals. I have invited those who are most adamantly opposed. These are the ones whose opinions I wish to sway."

"How do you really see this playing out?"

"If I can get them to listen to reason, we will revise our laws and revisit our philosophy. Perhaps even reach out to the Otherside."

"What's gonna happen tonight?"

"Arguing," Winters said. "Of that, I can be certain. Otherwise, I do not know."

"Whoever is behind my mess is connected to yours. They'll show up tonight."

"If they do," Lucy said, "it'll be a shit show."

"Are you ready for another fight?" I asked Winters.

Winters tilted his head and tapped his cane on the floor, "If forced, yes. But I doubt they will openly attack the Council."

"You've been wrong before," I said.

"More than once," Winters said. "But I concede your point. I will be ready, while I retain the hope that you can prevent such an occurrence."

He looked out the window, "We are here."

"Here" was Tower Grove Park. We fell into silence as the car turned into the east entrance. It's a narrow park, a little over a quarter-mile wide and a mile and a half long. Main Drive runs lengthwise through the center, with a couple of oval-shaped groves splitting the road along the way. It's not a forest, but there are a lot of scattered trees throughout, limiting visibility. Not that it matters much at one o'clock in the morning. Streetlamps cast pools of light along the street and sidewalks but most of the park was dark and lifeless at this hour. I knew of foot and bike paths, ponds and gazebos, and countless benches scattered among the numerous varieties of trees and bushes. All I could think, though, was that dangerous things were hiding out there, probably watching our arrival.

Well. There were dangerous things in the limo too.

"Ok," I said, "put your game face on, Red."

Lucy scoffed, "I never take it off." Nevertheless, she checked her weapons again and nodded absently.

The western third of the park is bisected by Center-Cross Drive. It is closest to the park's more famous amenities, such as the farmer's market, tennis courts, and the Piper Palm House wedding chapel. As we approached, I saw a handful of cars parked north of us. The big meeting was going to happen at the Ruins. The foundations of an old burned-down hotel had been restacked to create a small formation of ruins next to a pond. It became a popular backdrop for portraits and weddings and parties.

Winters told us the location had been selected due to surrounding features rather than the Ruins themselves. It was equidistant between the Circle of Flags to the southwest and the circular bandstand pavilion to the northeast.

"Circles matter in magical affairs," he said.

The limo stopped in a parking area to the east of the Ruins. The driver got out and placed his hand on Winters' door handle but didn't open it yet.

"What else is on your mind, William?" Winters asked.

"I can't cover all the angles. There's just too many variables."

"We can cover two of them," Lucy stated.

She had optimism, but that wouldn't be enough.

"This place is too open," I said motioning toward the Ruins. "Trouble can come from anywhere."

"You are here because I trust you to do what is right," Winters said. "You need not provide security. You need only to hunt."

I ground my teeth.

"This is not a termination order," Winters said. "This is a request." He took his glasses off and looked at me with his blue eyes again. There was no magic impulse behind them or trickery or guile. Only simple sincerity.

"Ok," I said and nodded stiffly.

"Good, let's get to it," Lucy said and grabbed the door handle.

"Wait. What happens if they get too close to the Council meeting?"

"No one wanders idly into the park tonight," Winters said, "nor into the meeting. If you are here, it is because you are supposed to be. The meeting itself will be... less easy to attend if you're not welcome."

"That's cryptic," I said.

Winters tilted his head in silent acknowledgment.

"Okay, Red. You ready?"

"God, yes. Let's go."

As Winters walked wearily toward the others already gathers, Lucy and I skirted quietly to the north, away from them, staying near the trees. We were looking to crash a different party. The Piper Palm House northwest of us seemed a good place to start. The oldest greenhouse west of the Mississippi, and currently one of St. Louis' top wedding venues, the Piper Palm House also has a great view of the Ruins and the pond.

"There's plenty of places to hide there," I said pointing to the brick and glass building.

Lucy nodded, "Or there." Next to the main building, there was a matching building which housed the park offices and a few maintenance buildings.

"Let's start with the obvious one first."

"Can demons go into a church?" Lucy asked motioning toward the Piper Palm House. "That's a church, right?"

"Dunno," I said. "They do weddings there but it ain't technically a church. Not sure if it's actually holy ground."

Lucy growled softly, "Can't anything ever be easy?"

"Nope," I agreed. "Come on."

We didn't get far before a low hum caught our attention. It was coming from back toward the Ruins, where the Council had gathered.

A glowing ring of brilliant white appeared on the ground, about fifteen feet across, encircling the small group of Council members. They had raised their arms and were chanting softly, words I couldn't make out clearly. Then the ring began to rise, lifted upon a shimmering wall of white, like a cylinder of pulsing gel pushing upwards from the grass. As it raised, the wall glowed more and more until it was almost too brilliant to look at directly. As the people disappeared within it, the glowing stopped. Then nothing happened.

The humming sound faded to a faint buzz.

Lucy looked at me wide-eyed. "What the hell is that?" Lucy asked.

I shrugged, "Magic?"

"Thanks," Lucy rolled her eyes, "Let's go."

We turned reluctantly from the magic show and headed warily toward the chape. I had the shotgun in one hand and the large sword in the other; Lucy left Heir Chop-A-Lot in its sheath but as always carried Holy Glockamolie at combat ready. We came upon a cast iron gate, separating the chapel from the administrative areas beyond. It was wide open, and the chain and padlock were on the ground in a few pieces.

Lucy and I gave each other the "that's not good look." Beyond the admin building was the park's greenhouse and the park director's residence further north. Lucy nudged me and pointed at the greenhouse. There was a faint, flickering glow coming from within. If I had to guess, I'd have said it looked like a small fire was burning inside. "What do you think?" she whispered.

"I think it's a little late to be roasting marshmallows," I said in a low voice.

"Yeah," Lucy nodded, "me too. Let's go tell them."

The windows were glazed or fogged over, so we couldn't see inside. We found the main entrance on the west end. The door was slightly ajar, and the smell of burnt hair wafted from within.

Lucy wrinkled her nose at the smell and clamped her mouth shut.

I took up position on one side of the door and motioned for Lucy to take the other side.

"Okay," I said quietly, "we go in hard and fast. You cover right, I'll cover left."

Lucy nodded a quick nod. She adjusted the sword on her hip and checked her pistol once again to be sure it was loaded

"On three," I held up a finger. "One..."

Lucy twisted her boot into the ground to get a good starting push.

I put another finger up, "Two..." and stepped closer to the door and hunched down.

I took a deep breath.

I raised a third finger, then I sensed movement behind me. Before I could turn, pain exploded in my head and my vision flashed white.

Chapter Thirty-Five

I crashed through the open doorway and landed on my stomach. I was a little loopy, so my reaction time was off. I rolled as quickly as I could manage onto my back, then Lucy fell on top of me before I could get up. Something kicked me hard in the ribs on my right side and then stomped on my right hand. I dropped the shotgun and my attacker snatched up the gun. The sharp pain in my fingers told me I had at least a couple of broken bones.

"If you move," a familiar voice said, "I'll blow your head off and the Lord of Darkness will bathe in your blood." Shit. Knife Boy.

The sigil brand on his forehead pulsated with a faint glow. His nose was still horridly crooked and nasty black and blue bruises radiated out from either side under his eyes. He looked like hell. He also held my sawed-off with both hands, one hand heavily bandaged and splinted. Brown shards of broken pottery on the floor suggested that was what had hit me on the head. Had he hit me with anything more solid, I might be dead already.

I didn't move. Neither did Lucy. I couldn't tell if she was unconscious or just being uncharacteristically compliant. With her on top of me, my left arm and the sword were pinned between our bodies.

"Quit wasting time, Nester," I heard someone further inside the building say. I knew that voice. It was Angela... or rather Agent Charters.

"Just kill them," she said, "be done with it."

I couldn't tell what she was doing. She was a little further inside the greenhouse and I didn't dare move my head to look. My guess was that she wasn't holding a gun, or she'd have capped Lucy and me already.

Nester raised one hand to show off the bandage, his fingers were splinted, "I paid you back for the fingers, but I still owe you a broken nose and busted knee cap. Then I'll kill you."

"Just get on with it!" Charters barked.

"Gladly!" Nester said. He pulled his booted foot back and kicked at my knee. Fortunately for me, the kid was stupid. A kick to the side of the knee hurt a lot, but it didn't do any lasting damage. If he was smart, he'd have stomped on my knee. That would have crippled even a big guy like me. Instead, I hissed in pain to give him some satisfaction. Lucy flinched. Ok, good, she wasn't out.

I spoke very softly, hopefully only she could hear me, "Lucy, I'd like permission to touch you without you killing me."

"Yes," she said equally quietly. I released my grip on Killicutty and turned my hand over, placing my palm against her chest. I sucked in a deep breath while clenching my teeth against the stabbing pain in my side. Then I gave Lucy a hard shove.

She let out a yelp of surprise as she flew up and back into Nester. His hands went up in reflex and yanked the shotgun's double triggers, firing into the air. A section of glass ceiling shattered and rained shards down on us. I threw my hands over my face as I rolled away and Lucy and Nester disappeared through the open door. I got to my feet quickly—too quickly—and stumbled for a second as my head and my brain swam in opposite directions. Pain screamed from my side. Nester's first kick might have bruised my ribs, if not breaking some.

Ex-Agent Charters was quick to the attack and came at me in a blur of sharp jabs, a front kick, and a side kick. Several of them connected, mostly to my upper body. She was too short—taller than Lucy, but still too short—to go for my head, so it was the body. And I was already hampered by the kick in the ribs. She came on hard and fast, not giving me time to counterattack. I kept my elbows in, hoping to shield my ribs some, and took most of her blows while trying to close the distance on her. The closer I could get, the less power she could put into her punches, even as well placed as they were. She was smart. She backed away as I tried to close in on her but also kept attacking me, forcing me to keep up my defenses. I kept pressing, hoping to trip her up on a stack of mulch bags behind her. But this wasn't her first rodeo. Just inches from the bags, she turned and stepped up on them then pushed on, just up high enough to throw a heavy right kick across my face. I turned my head and ducked my ear into my shoulder, taking the blow to the side of my head instead of my jaw. Then it was my turn. I planted a foot as she landed, twisted my hip, and extended my arm in a wide hook. She saw it coming and raised an arm to defend. I didn't land the blow, but she couldn't just absorb the force behind it. She staggered sideways several steps but managed to keep her footing and then did what I was trying to do. She closed in on me, jumped up and wrapped her hands around the back of my head and jerked a knee up into my right side. Before I could react to the pain, she let go, dropped, and used her falling weight to stomp down on my foot. Just as quickly she jumped and wrapped her arms around my head again and delivered another knee to my ribs. I didn't let her drop a second time.

As the pain finally hit, I gritted my teeth and bellowed like the angry gorilla I was and was rewarded with a flash of fear in her eyes. I grabbed one of her wrists with my good hand before she let go and folded my other arm across her forearm. With that, I buckled her arms and trapped them against my chest. She tried to kick again, but we were too close now and she had no leverage. I had two of the laws of violence working for me now: size matters and proximity negates skill. I slammed my head toward her face but she twisted and leaned in. Our noggins cracked against each other, but it wasn't a game ender for either of us. I had probably taken more hits to the head in my career than she had.

I staggered around a few steps, my head reeling, as I struggled with the weight of my own hulking form wanting to shut down, and Agent Charter's significantly lighter but less cooperative body.

She stomped down with her boot, catching the knee Nestor had kicked. It wasn't as damaging a blow as the previous, but the knee was pretty damned sensitive. I roared in pain and frustration. She pulled her face closer and then locked onto the side of my neck with her teeth. A surge of panic flashed through me—like it should when someone is biting you—and I wriggled my left hand free to grab a handful of her hair. I pulled hard, but her teeth were clamped into my trapezius muscle.

I released my hold on her hair and raised my arm straight up then rammed my elbow down on top of her head. She grunted hard and her teeth dug deeper into my flesh. I repeated the blow and pain shot down my arm into my fingers. Funny bone.

She wiggled one of her hands free and grabbed my right hand. The hand with at least two broken fingers on it. She squeezed.

"Yeeearrrggh!" My hold on her loosened. The agent worked a knee up and pushed against my stomach, creating a gap between us. Then she stomped on my knee again with her other foot. My grip loosened but struggled to hang on to her. She let go of my right hand and knuckle-punched my throat. It was a short jab, but effective. I released her and took a step back. She landed on her feet, took a step back, then delivered a snap kick to my liver. I tried to catch her leg, but she was too fast. She stepped back again and jumped up to add height and force to an uppercut. I lowered my head and took the blow on my left eyebrow. Pain lanced through my skull and blood immediately began to drip down from above my eye. Good hit; probably split open the brow. A cut like that bleeds a lot.

She threw another wide cross aimed at my ribs. I beat her to the blow and swung inside her arc, landing a punch directly into her armpit. It's a weird place to hit someone, but there's a lot of soft tissue there. It hurts. She staggered. I reached out and grabbed a handful of her shirt and yanked her forward, pulling her up off her feet. I met her with a fast head butt to the bridge of her nose and was rewarded with the familiar sound of crunching cartilage. That finally slowed her down some. I swung my elbow to the side of her head, and she tumbled over a cart full of potting soil. She tried to get up, but the blow had dizzied her. I stood over her then and dropped my considerable weight upon her back and pinned her face-first into the ground.

That was the first time I'd taken on an Incursion Agent, and she'd kicked my ass.

I sat there for a minute, catching my breath through waves of pain. Blood and sweat dripped from my brow and pooled in the corners of my eye. I wiped at it with throbbing and broken fingers, all aching in tune with the beating of my thundering heart. My knees felt like they were on fire. My ribs felt like knives poking me in the side. God, I hated that woman.

A few feet away, a little trail of smoke swirled up from a dark lump. It must have been the source of burnt hair. It had been a small animal, a rabbit maybe, charred black, at the center of a familiar circle drawn in blood. A summoning circle.

There was a commotion outside the entrance and Lucy and Nester crashed back into the room. Lucy fell backwards while holding onto Knife Boy's lapels. In a fluid motion, she rolled to the ground and leveraged her foot against his torso sending him flying over her head. Nester hit the pile of mulch bags and tumbled onto the ground beyond it. I got up as quickly as I could, and almost fell back down as a wave of nausea hit me. Nester was already standing with the sigil on his forehead glowed brilliantly.

Charters started to move so I kicked her in the side of the head. She dropped again.

Nester still had the shotgun, but he swung it like a club. He'd shot both shells when he blew out the ceiling.

Lucy sprung to her feet empty-handed, she'd evidently dropped her pistol in the fight. She reached for Heir Chop-A-Lot but didn't have time to draw it as Nester charged her. Lucy jumped forward and stomp-kicked with both feet square in his chest. She flopped to the ground and Nester flew backwards, into my arms. I caught him roughly and used his own momentum to throw him to the ground. I dropped to my knees at the intensified flashes of pain in my hand, ribs, and head, struggling to catch my breath.

Nester struggled to get up. Lucy stepped in and kicked him in the nose, and he dropped flat on his back.

I wheezed out my old power phrase, "*Smerte Forsinket*" but there was no belief in it. The pain was overwhelming. I couldn't concentrate on anything. I couldn't believe in anything.

Lucy drew Heir Chop-A-Lot and leveled the tip inches from Nester's face. He remained still and started mumbling strange curses.

"Tell me why I shouldn't skewer him," Lucy said.

I tried to think of a good reason, "Mercy or something."

"I'm short of that right now," Lucy said.

Charters moaned and stirred, so I wrestled the Holy Handgun from my belt and pressed the barrel against the back of her head. I had to drop to a knee so I didn't lose balance and fall on her again. She didn't stop moving until I thumbed back the revolver's hammer. That always gets their attention.

"You're bleeding everywhere," Lucy said.

"I hoped someone would notice," I wheezed between breaths. "We're wasting time here."

"Agreed," Lucy said. Without taking the tip of Heir Chop-A-Lot away from Nester's face, she reached to the utility cart and grabbed a roll of duct tape. "This will do."

Lucy applied liberal amounts of duct tape to Nester's hands and feet, then did the same for Agent Charters. Then she stuffed a gag in Nester's mouth and secured it with a couple wraps of duct tape.

"I'm tired of listening to his weird gibberish," she said when I looked at her.

"Me too," I said and sat on the stack of mulch.

Lucy then tore off a chunk of my T-shirt and pressed it against the cut on my brow then used a strip of duct tape to keep it in place. Like everything else, it would need stitches and the bandage would definitely come lose if I moved too much, but it was the best I could hope for at the moment. I chanted *"Smerte Forsinket"* under my breath, but I wasn't sure it was working. I figured I didn't have many more tomorrows to borrow from.

With a quick tug, Lucy straightened out my busted fingers before taping them to the unbroken ones. Lucy Red was no field medic, but she could make do with the best of us.

"Are you done sandbagging?" Lucy asked and handed me the shotgun.

"Yeah," I said. The chanting had helped. Enough at least that I could breathe and talk without stabbing pain. There'd be hell to pay later, Leo had warned me about that, but I had bigger problems to deal with. I tucked the Holy Handgun back into my belt as I stood up and reloaded both barrels of the sawed-off.

Lucy poked her silver blade at Agent Charters while I took in several deep breaths, testing my limits. At least my lungs seemed to be working.

"Where is the rest of your friends, Bitch?" Lucy asked.

She didn't answer of course. Instead, she turned her head away from us and spat blood on the ground.

Lucy growled in frustration and nudged her savagely with a boot, "I don't like just leaving them here."

"Me either," I said. "But we have shit to do."

"Agreed," Lucy said.

Reluctantly, we left Nester and Angela behind. I was pretty sure they weren't going anywhere, but I had stopped feeling good about taking chances a long time ago. These two had proven to be a pretty big pain in the ass, but they weren't the main attraction. They'd keep until later.

I picked up Killicutty on the way out and Lucy found the Holy Glockamolie just outside the door. We were armed and angry. As dangerous as it gets.

Lucy stopped me when we reached the iron gate.

"Okay, big guy, what are you thinking?"

"I think we were played."

"Explain."

"They were a distraction," I said and jerked a thumb toward the building we had just left.

"If they were, it was effective."

"Yup," I said, "that's what worries me. What were they distracting us from?"

"The Council," Lucy answered.

I nodded and started back toward the Ruins.

The glowing magic cylinder wall hadn't appeared to change any and there wasn't anyone around.

"It looks unguarded," Lucy said. "Doesn't it?"

"Things ain't always what they look like," I said.

"I've noticed."

"There's probably defenses, even if we can't see them."

"Well, you can bet Marten would know how to get past the defenses, right?"

"Likely," I said.

"And how to beat them."

I nodded.

"Then where is he? Where are the defenses?"

Circles. Everything is about circles.

"This is midway between two circles," I said.

"Circles matter in magical affairs," Lucy said, repeating Winters' words from earlier.

"Exactly. What were the two circles?" I pointed left then right, "the bandstand pavilion and the flag circle."

"Which one is it?"

"Both. This one makes three. Big magic I think."

"Shit," Lucy said. "Have to split up, don't we?"

"'Fraid so."

"Ok, I'll take the flags," Lucy pointed westward.

"Be careful," I said. "For real. If that minor demon is there, it won't be like the fight we just came out of."

"I got the memo," Lucy said while checking to make sure her gun was loaded.

"I ain't kidding, Red. Send up a signal or cut and run, but don't try to take them alone."

"I'm angry," Lucy said, "not suicidal. Same goes for you."

"Ok," I said, but I didn't mean it. "Back here in five minutes if you don't find anything."

"Got it," Lucy turned to go then stopped, "one more thing."

"Yeah?"

"Hulk... smash."

I let out a muffled laugh before turning away from her.

Chapter Thirty-Six

Sometimes I hate being right.

The odor of fresh blood hit me before I got close enough to see it. I saw patches of it on the sidewalk, reflected in the pale moonlight as I approached the bandstand.

The bandstand with its red roof that looks like it belongs in St. Petersburg, sits at the center of a circular sidewalk with two sidewalks forming an X like the spokes of a wheel. I could make out several symbols painted in blood on the sidewalk, highlighted by the uneven flickering illumination radiating from the distant Council circle. Faint smoke drifted from the bandstand smelling of burnt hair and flesh.

If this circle had been set up for defense, it had been defiled and repurposed into a summoning circle. A big one.

Aside from the distant hum coming from the meeting place and my own terrified breathing, all was quiet. Whatever was going to happen here already happened. Nestor and Charter's distraction had worked.

I climbed the steps onto the bandstand to be sure.

I was right. There were three bodies. Two of them were badly mangled and burned to a crisp. A third lay sprawled across the floor, a broken assault rifle next to it and a pistol a few inches out of reach of an arm that had been broken and left at a horrifying angle.

I knew this guy.

York.

I knelt next to him to check his pulse. Amazingly, he groaned, and his fingers moved.

Holy shit, he was still alive!

He slowly turned his head toward me. One eye was swollen shut. A giant slash ran up the side of his face, deep enough to show teeth through the wound. Blood pooled beneath him.

"Don't touch me," he said. His voice was barely a whisper.

"Hang in there," I said. "Hold on, I'll get help."

"No time," he wheezed. "Protect the Council."

Duty all the way. He was something else.

But he was right.

"I'll send help," I said, "as soon as I take out the trash. Hang tough."

"Just need... to catch... breath."

He was one stubborn bastard.

"Hold the line," I said as I grabbed his pistol and slid it into his good hand, "I'll be back."

"Get to work."

Lucy was already at the magic circle pacing back and forth when I got there.

"I was about to come check on you," she said. "It was a blood bath over there."

"Same over here," I said. "York put up a hell of a fight, though. Dunno if he'll live but he's still breathing."

"He's a tough prick."

"Yeah," I said. "There was also a summoning circle."

"That's not good."

"Nope. They're gonna crash the meeting."

"How do we find them before that happens? Just make a stand right here?"

"I don't think we stand a chance in the open," I said. "We need to crash the party too."

Lucy looked at the magic ring, "It's not that big. It'll be crowded."

"Maybe," I admitted, "the bad guys ain't waiting out here. We need to get in."

I stepped toward the magical barrier.

"Bill?" Lucy stepped in front of me. She had actual concern on her face. "Can we beat them? Whatever they are?"

"Dunno."

She studied my eyes as if looking for something deeper than the word I spoke, "But?"

"But that never stopped me from trying," I said. "That's all I got for you."

She nodded slowly, "I'll take it. OK, let's go get this over with."

Winters had said "invitation only." That probably meant bad things would happen to a trespasser trying to get into the meeting. The glowing wall would either let me pass, or it would not. All I could do was try.

I extended a finger, touching the shimmering surface. A tingling sensation raced up my arm then through my entire body. I held there for a moment, enduring the painless yet almost unbearable sensation. I didn't explode or melt or turn into a newt, so I took it as a positive sign. Hopefully, that meant I was not uninvited.

I gave Lucy a wink and then stepped into the boundary.

Chapter Thirty-Seven

I felt everything and nothing all at the same time.

I had nobody, yet I felt the universe moving through me. I had no voice yet I could call out to the corners of creation. I had no sight. And yet, I could see infinity as my mind raced toward insanity. My soul twisted and turned through dozens of realities, snapping from one to another before I could fully take one in. Without warning, I was in Hell, plummeting from a black sky toward a great lake of fire, the heat scorching my face and burning away my hair and clothes. The heat grew and just when I thought I would burst into flame, I shifted. I was at the bottom of a vast, forgotten sea, surrounded by bone piercing cold and oppressive pressure and heart wrenching darkness. Then I was entombed in granite at the heart of a mountain older than the earth. In a flash, I was soaring like a great eagle above a broken castle where a desperate battle raged between two armies of ancient gods. Then found myself gliding inches above rolling plains of blue-green grass. In the distance, a great golden city as vast as a mountain range radiated warmth and comfort beyond comprehension. A voice in the city sang my name with the strength of a thousand trumpets. I stretched out my hand toward it. I wanted to call out and say I was coming. But I had no voice. No body.

Then nothing. No light. No darkness. Pure oblivion.

And suddenly I was standing on solid ground. The tingling sensation stopped, and I reeled as my mind was yanked into a final reality. All other existences, which I had shifted through simultaneously, faded away until it was just me in the present. A soft breeze brushed across my cheeks and I shivered. A wave of nausea swept over me, and I fell to my knees drawing in a deep breath. I turned my head slowly and took in this new reality. Before me was a low hill, covered in brilliant white grass. I breathed in deeply again and took in the scent of roses and spearmint, although there wasn't a plant in sight. The air was thinner, like at the top of a mountain. Though the sky appeared to be a night sky full of stars, the ground seemed to glow with the brilliance of reflected sunlight.

This was not Tower Grove Park, and it was definitely not Missouri.

I pushed myself up from the ground and rose slowly, taking in deep breaths. The grass had turned red where I had put my hand down. Blood red. I was still bleeding. I was still in my body. Every ache and pain rushed back to the present. My chest, my head, my hand, my legs. Oh god. I was still alive, and my body was not ready for it.

"*Smerte Forsinket,*" I whispered the incantation but there was too much. I couldn't borrow against this. Not this time. There was nothing left to borrow. The bill was coming due.

My head spun and my stomach churned.

"Not yet," I whispered firmly. "Not yet. Let me finish." I forced my breaths in and out. In. Out. In. Out.

A shaky peace settled upon me. The pain didn't recede, but my body didn't shut down. Not yet.

The shimmering wall hummed faintly behind me. I had passed through the barrier and was somehow inside that magic ring, yet, judging by the curvature, it was several hundred yards in diameter larger on the inside than it was on the outside. I didn't know for certain where I had come.

I wasn't alone. Figures at least at tall as me, covered in hooded robes of white stood with their backs to the boundary, spaced out evenly every thirty feet or so. Each held a long white spear and tall teardrop shaped shields. None of them appeared to take notice of my presence. They faced straight ahead, toward the center of the great ring, and the top of the hill.

A large table of polished white stone stood at the apex of the hill, encircled by nine benches of chiseled stone. It had to be the meeting place of the Nine-Fold Council. But only six of the seats were occupied. I'd have to get closer to see who was gathered there, hopefully before it was too late.

The humming at my back grew higher and higher, then dropped an octave and Lucy flopped onto the ground beside me.

"Fuck me," she said between labored breaths and curled up into a fetal position.

"Just breathe," I knelt beside her but didn't dare touch her. "We're still alive, I think. I think this is some kind of pocket universe or something."

She waved me away while drawing in several breaths. I got up again, pressing my hand against my ribs and the sharp pain coming with each movement. I gave Red some space and approached one of the robed figures. His hood cast a shadow so I couldn't make out anything but vague facial features. As I drew nearer, the shadows seemed to shift, keeping the face concealed regardless of my angle of approach.

"Hey, Pal," I said as politely as a guy in my level of pain could manage.

The figure ignored me.

"Hey!" I barked and snapped my fingers at him, "Anyone else come through here? Or anything?"

The robed guard made no sign of acknowledging me.

"Dude," I said, "seriously. Trouble's coming."

Either this dude was a statue or the most focused guard ever. I entertained the idea of smacking him to see what would happen, but Lucy stepped in front of me.

"Forget it, Bill," Lucy said, waving a hand in front of the guard's face, "he's checked out."

"Well," I said, "that's just weird."

"Weird is my new normal," Lucy grumbled and turned away.

I couldn't argue with that.

"Besides, if the circus is in town, it'll be heading that way, right?" She pointed toward the hill and started walking.

"Probably," I fell into step next to her. "Keep your eyes peeled."

"No shit," Lucy grumbled. "And try not being a big distraction. Winters acted like this meeting was a big deal."

"Everything's a big deal," I said, just as I encountered even more weirdness. Although the incline was just a gentle slope, it felt like I was walking up the side of a steep mountain. Each step was like pushing against an increasing tide of gravity. Lucy mumbled quiet profanities but kept pace with me.

As we struggled toward the table, I could see and hear everyone as if I was right there next to them.

I recognized a couple of them. Master Winters was easy to pick out with his small cane and wire-rimmed glasses. Beside him sat a man with well-manicured grey hair, wearing an expensive looking grey suit. Regis.

I didn't recognize the others. Across from Winters, sat a man with swept back salt and pepper hair and a stylish green silk shirt with pressed blue slacks, a stark contrast to Winters' very old-fashioned suit and bowtie. Next to the man, sat an elderly woman with dark skin and the deep wrinkles of someone who had lived a long hard life in a harsh environment. She wore a modest suit of muted red fabric that had obviously been tailored to fit her frame. Next to her was a man who looked old enough to be Methuselah's dad, wearing an ill-fitting baby blue tracksuit.

At the head of the table sat a woman with long, straight hair, as white as falling snow that waved in a breeze that didn't seem to touch the others. She wore a loose gown that seemed like white, but when the breeze shifted the fabric, hints of color danced across the surface like a pearl. I figured her for royalty right away. She had a regal bearing, like someone haughty, not because they believed they were better but because they knew no other way to behave.

All eyes were on the man in the green shirt.

He poked the table repeatedly with an index finger, "Preposterous! Madness! Our laws have stood unchanged for centuries! Centuries! They have stood the test of time longer than the histories of most nations. Changing them at a whim is folly!"

"A whim?" Master Winters' voice carried a familiar tone of amusement. "I assure you haven't acted on whimsy since before you were born."

"Bah!" the man made a shooing motion. "Your proposal is lunacy. There are reasons we have been committed to protecting this world against incursions for as long as we have."

"Indeed, there are reasons, Master Foti," Winters said. "Those reasons are superstition and prejudice."

"Tradition," Foti countered firmly.

"Fallacy," Winters replied. "The observation of tradition on the merit of tradition is not wisdom. It is bondage."

"It evolved into tradition a very long time ago," the old man in the tracksuit said, his voice scratchy, raw, and tired, "because it worked for so long. It is proven."

"Proven?" There was no hint of amusement in Winters' voice now. "We have no proof of anything except that we can send men and women forth to kill that which we fear."

I stumbled a step and stopped. Ouch. Lucy patted my shoulder and urged me on.

"We have paid a dear price in order to secure peace and safety," the woman in red said calmly. "There has not been an invasion in over a thousand years."

"Of course you're right, Master Basnet," Foti spread out his hands as if presenting truth to those gathered. "I see no imminent danger."

"Evidence of a negative is not proof," Winters pointed a bony finger at Foti.

"Have we truly achieved safety?" Regis's voice was stern, carrying a natural authority. He met the gazes of each around the table, except the elegant woman in white, before speaking again. "Even as we sit here bickering, one of our finest Hunters is striving valiantly to counter a threat perpetrated by one of our own!"

Lucy nudged me with her elbow and whispered, "Are your ears burning?"

"No," I said, "but my head is bleeding."

Lucy let out a soft snort of a laugh.

"Posh!" the very old man said, "I thought we agreed not to talk about that without reliable evidence."

"You agreed, Master Gosse," Winters said. "We did not."

Foti slapped the table, "Then that supports my argument even more firmly, doesn't it. If you insist it is true. If an incursion agent—and I won't accept such a preposterous idea—or even more impossibly, an Archivist can be seduced... well then, the only logical recourse is to stamp out such a threat. Quickly. Decisively."

"Is it so simple?" Winters removed his spectacles and examined them for a moment before putting them back on. "Then let us start by purging all Archivists and all incursion agents."

"Madness!"

"And then each of us," Winters added.

All at the table exchanged, except the white lady, unhappy looks. Master Regis shifted uncomfortably in his seat.

Lucy elbowed me again, a little harder this time.

"What?"

"Look," she pointed toward the ring far off to our left, at the robed figures along the shimmering green wall. "Something look off to you?"

Something did look off. One of the guardians was not as still as the others. The tip of his spear swayed back and forth, just a little, as if he were holding on to it too tightly. Against the perfect stillness of his companions, he might as well have been doing the Macarena.

"Good eye," I said. "That's gotta spell trouble."

Lucy raised her eyebrows in a silent no shit.

"Come on," We change course. The quickest route would take us within a few feet of the meeting, which I was sure would be a problem. So we followed the contour of the low hill, making sure to give them some distance. Even as we moved slightly downhill from them, their voices continued to carry as if we were standing at the table.

I split my attention between the meeting and the slightly unstill guard. The Council members didn't appear to notice the change. Did they not sense it? Or did they not care?

"Our sanctity has been soiled," Master Winters said sadly.

Lucy mumbled, "That's an understatement."

I nodded in agreement.

"Traditions did not prevent this from happening," Winters continued. "I fear that they may have even contributed to such events."

"We don't know that," Regis said gruffly.

"We know more than we allow ourselves to admit," Winters countered.

Regis sighed, "We must all at least agree that troubling events have come to pass beneath our very noses. On our watch."

"Our watch?" I grumbled. "I haven't ever seen him do anything but hand out orders."

"You don't see everything that happens around here, Bill," Lucy said. I couldn't argue with that.

Regis continued, "We do know that these dark tidings bear witness to a deeper danger. They bear out evidence of collusion."

"Collusion?" Master Basnet frowned and leaned forward. "Meaning what?"

Winters shook his head slowly and dabbed at his forehead with a kerchief before answering, "Meaning, the people involved in the events I come before you to decry, have not only fallen victim to dark forces, they did so voluntarily. Intentionally."

Foti slapped the table again, "Absurd!"

"Posh!" Master Gosse rasped.

"Such an accusation," Basnet said as she clasped her hands together on the tabletop, "is very troubling. If there is evidence, it carries an immediate sentence of death."

Lucy whispered to me, "Death by hanging, right?" Obviously, she remembered our first conversation alone together.

I nodded.

"What would one gain from such foolishness?" Gosse asked.

"Power," Regis said plainly. "Those who have tasted power either fear it or hunger for more of it."

"Such power is dangerous," Gosse said needlessly.

"Either you respect such a danger," Regis continued, "or you seek to master it."

"You speak of very old stories," Foti said, "We all know the legends."

"You presume much," the elegant woman in white's voice carried across the expanse. I stopped in my tracks, astonished at her voice. The sounds of her words wafted from her like a song yet carried the weight of absolute authority. What I had mistaken for haughtiness, I realized after hearing those three words, was purity. Purity of a degree I had never witnessed.

"Forgive us, Lady Adda," Foti said meekly. "We are not accustomed to guests at our table. We do not often meet with... outsiders."

"Yet here I sit," the lady said. The hairs on my arm stood on end each time she spoke.

"I beg your indulgence," Winters said respectfully, "but I fear the recounting of legends must wait until another time"

The Lady bowed her head toward Winters, "I welcome such a time. Please continue."

I blinked my eyes as if I was trying to wake up from a dream.

"What is it with you and mysterious women?" Lucy said.

"Dunno," I said and forced myself to take a few steps toward the guardian and away from the White Lady. "I wish I knew."

"Well, get it together," Lucy said. "Our dude is getting weirder."

The robed figure tilted forward, leaning on his spear for support. His shoulders shook as if he was holding a tremendous weight I wondered if he was responding to the rising tension at the table, or if something else was affecting him. None of the other white guardians moved a muscle. Whatever was happening, was happening to just the one figure.

Foti's irritated voice caught my attention and I looked back over my shoulder as I walked.

"This discussion is pointless?" he said abusing the table once again. "Our policies are in place to protect humankind. We cannot abandon that sacred duty."

"Cannot?" Winters said. "I remember a time when the pursuit of knowledge and truth was our sacred duty. When uncovering mysteries revealed to us our own inadequacy. We were not always wizards. This Council once was young."

Gosse let out a feeble, raspy laugh, "I cannot remember being young."

Basnet sighed, "Those mysteries can contain dangers we have heretofore been unable to predict."

"What once was a curiosity of the unknown," Winters said, "has long since turned into fear of the dark."

Regis held up a placating hand, "We must be open to change. Our survival depends on it."

Basnet shook her head, "Master Regis, Master Winters... what you propose is beyond difficult to accept."

"What I propose is a return to seeking truth... and true understanding," Winters said and rose slowly from his seat. "Lady Adda, would you do us the honor—" He didn't get to finish the thought.

The struggling guardian screamed suddenly, a piercing, terrified scream. I spun back toward him in time to see a red stain appear on the front of his robes. He dropped his spear and shield and touched the red spot with a finger. Then his entire body went stiff as a clawed hand burst from his chest. The guard staggered forward, and the magic wall shimmered black as two shapes, one much larger than the other, emerged through the barrier. The larger was the minor demon we'd seen on the Archives video, and its hand was impaled through the guardian's back. The creature's entire body vibrated and twitched making it difficult to focus on or make out its details. The other figure was of course Marten, walking with a minor limp, black robes flowing around him, seeming to suck in the white of the landscape, creating a sort of vacuum of color around him.

The demon shoved the guardian with its free hand, and pulled his bloodied arm from the torso, letting the now lifeless body fall to the ground. The beast studied the blood covering his leathery flesh for a moment and licked it like a child would chocolate from its fingers. Then it turned its head to look straight at me, with those painfully bright white eyes, smoke trailing from the corners. For a moment, I could actually feel its hatred, like a blast of heat from a furnace. This thing not only hated me, it hated everything. It was a product of the Hell it had been pulled from. Pure malice crammed into a nasty shell.

"What is this!" Master Basnet's voice carried across the hillside. "Who dares intrude on this neutral ground?"

In response, Marten began chanting in a deep, guttural voice. Words I couldn't understand but could tell by the tone were trouble. He stretched his hand toward the guardian's fallen body. The corpse convulsed and the blood pooling around its body evaporated into a red mist. It swirled in the air in front of the minor demon. Marten opened his fingers and the mist split in two. Half swirled around the demon and the other around Marten. After a moment, the cloud of red closed in around them, then disappeared.

"I apologize for being tardy," Marten called out, his voice raw and distorted, his head tilted back in apparent rapture, "our invitations were murderously difficult to procure."

He breathed in deeply as if luxuriating in a breath of fresh air, then his eyes settled on me and he smiled. His eyes and his teeth shone a wet red.

"Hello trespasser," he said with a wicked smile, then he and the demon began running in opposite directions.

Chapter Thirty-Eight

Without discussion, I headed for the demon and Lucy headed for Marten. I covered the distance quicker than I expected. When I was in range, I pointed the sawed-off and pulled both triggers. The shotgun bucked in my hand and a ragged wound appeared in the beast's side where the buckshot tore into its flesh, but the blast didn't take it down. The demon lurched sideways, almost toppling into the magic wall. It stopped running and spun to face me.

It spread its arms wide in a terrifying and unappealing invitation and roared a deep chittering roar. Unnatural and unnerving. I dropped the shotgun and hefted Killicutty with both hands.

I let my momentum carry me to within arm's reach and cried out, "Sanctu Spitu!" Several of the runes on the long blade glowed a brilliant purple as I plunged the steel into the demon's chest. It roared in furious pain and backhanded me. I flew up against the shimmering wall and buzzed with weird discomfort before dropping to the ground. I rolled just in time to avoid a stomp from the demon's cloven hoof and scrambled to my feet.

The demon pulled on the sword I'd left stuck through its chest, but the blade didn't budge. Lazarus Grey's rune spells are effective if you believe in them, and I did. Sanctu Spitu worked, and the enchanted blade had effectively locked itself into the demon's body.

I risked a glance at Lucy. She hadn't fired any shots yet. Marten had changed course and was moving toward the hill and shooting at him would put the wizards at risk if she missed. He was no longer running, though, having hit the same gravity resistance Lucy and I had. An aura of black swirled around him, in stark contrast to the pure white surroundings. The Council members had gathered on the same side of the table to see what was happening, in apparent disbelief that anyone would intrude on their meeting. The rest of the white guardians remained in place as if they didn't know anything was happening.

A meaty hand grabbed my right wrist and yanked me closer. I yelped in pain as the demon wrenched my arm at an awkward angle and felt a pop in my shoulder. At the same time, the beast continued to tug uselessly at the sword in its chest with its free hand. I dropped to one knee and rotated, twisting the demon's hand at a bad angle, and pinned it beneath my armpit. I punched, as quickly as I could repeatedly with my left hand. I was of a mind to see if I could crush its skull with my bare hands. Given time, I might have succeeded. But the demon punched me once, and I swear a sledgehammer slammed into the side of my face. I flew off the creature and landed a few feet away. I sat up and blood trailed down into my eye again. Dammit. Lucy's bandage had come off.

Suddenly, the demon shivered. And it tilted its head, almost like a curious dog. Its lips drew back to reveal horrid, jagged teeth. Then it drew in a deep breath through ox-like nostrils. For a moment, the thing's entire body seemed to blur, like it was shifting left and right a thousand times a second.

Gunfire erupted, from somewhere behind me, along with sizzling sounds of electrical discharge and crackling fire, but I didn't dare take my eyes from the demon, which I just realized was a blood demon. He was getting excited at the smell of blood. And I was bleeding. That was not good.

Not good at all, but there is always room for worse.

The wall darkened next to me followed by a rising buzz sound. Then a large shape burst through the barrier and something meaty and angry crashed into me.

The lesser imps had joined the party.

I used my body weight and momentum to roll and throw the mass toward the blood demon. The demon caught the airborne imp and ripped it in half, and with a grunting laugh threw the two ragged chunks back at me.

I dove out of the way to avoid the disgusting projectiles and in the process, also by blind luck, dodged another imp emerging through the wall. It flew several feet and landed on all fours. This one ignored me and ran toward the hill. A second later, another emerged and followed the one before it. Then another. Then I stopped counting.

The blood demon, not distracted by the reinforcements, lunged and wrapped its massive arms around me in a crushing embrace. Fortunately for me, Killicutty was still firmly embedded in its torso. As the beast squeezed me into a bearhug, my own body pressed against the sword's hilt, causing the blade to shift and twist. The demon roared in pain but didn't let go. Instead, it leaned forward and licked the side of my face, and the blood that was oozing from my wound.

"Gross," I coughed and tried to twist my face away from it. At the same time, I twisted my right hand around. The minor demon hadn't paid attention to the fact that I had drawn the Holy Handgun. Even with two broken fingers, I had a good enough grip on the weapon to do some business.

"*Echuta*!" I said angrily as I shoved the barrel against the creature's side. I felt a brief tingle in the wood grip as I pulled the trigger. The gun thundered and the extra recoil almost wrenched it from my hand. The demon spasmed and dropped me while staggering back several steps. It clutched at the glowing and gaping wound in its side.

I stole a glance toward the hilltop. The wizards had formed a defensive circle and were fending off the growing numbers of imps using various forms of fire, lightning, and wind magic. And there was plenty of fending to do, as more imps kept pushing in through the barrier.

Winters' voice carried across the hillside, "Guardians! I call upon your aid!" Instantly, the white guardians along the magical perimeter leapt into action and attacked the lesser imps nearest each of them. They used their spears and shield defensively and offensively in a brilliant dance of combat, with a fluid grace of violence that was almost hypnotic to behold. But it wasn't enough to turn the tide. Imps continued to pour in through the barrier. More than the white guardians could intercept.

Some of the imps had targeted Lucy, who was defending herself valiantly, while Marten continued to push his way toward the top of the hill.

Everyone had their own problems. I'd have to deal with mine alone.

The demon swiped at me with jagged claws, raking my arm and ruining yet another jacket. I hissed at the stinging pain and lifted the Holy Handgun for another shot. The demon spun, extended an arm, and punched me square in the chest. It was like getting hit by a truck. I squeezed off a shot as I fell to the ground, but the bullet missed. I landed on my back, gasping for air. I rolled over in time to avoid another foot stomping down on my chest, but the demon grabbed me by one arm before I got out of reach and hauled me up by one hand. I shoved the end of the Holy Handgun against the demon's wrist and fired. The blast almost severed its hand from the arm. Almost.

The demon released me and howled in rage. I struggled to catch my breath; my chest still feeling like someone had parked a car there. I backed away, wheezing, and wiping blood away from my eyes. The blood demon lurched at me, reaching with both hands—one of them hanging grotesquely by strings of meat. I ducked inside its grasp and took hold of Killicutty's hilt with my free hand. I yanked on the blade savagely, but it didn't come out. I didn't want it to. I just wanted it to hurt enough to distract the demon. The demon didn't exactly move the way I wanted, but it couldn't ignore the pain of a holy sword anchored through its body. It dug its claws into my left hand, pinning my grip onto the sword and opened its maw wide, lunging down for a giant bite.

I shoved the Holy Handgun up under its chin and pulled the trigger. Its head snapped back, and gore spewed from the top of its jagged skull.

"Sanctu Ritu," I roared and yanked the sword free of the demon's body. I holstered the Holy Handgun quickly and swung the great sword two-handed. The blade cut true and severed the demon's head. I didn't wait to see what happened next. I'd already seen that show before. Besides, there was still plenty of trouble to go around.

The dark aura emanating from Marten trailed behind him like a stink cloud. It sucked in light and color, leaving a blackness so deep and dark that it was nearly impossible to focus on.

Several imps lay dead between him and Lucy. She had been trying to shoot him, to little effect. Half of the creatures were throwing themselves in front of her, sacrificing themselves to shield Marten from Lucy's gunfire. Occasionally, one split off to attack her directly and she had to deal with it more directly.

The white guardians were taking out imps as they emerged from the barrier. The rest of the creatures were focusing their attack on the wizards. The wizards—as I would expect—fought with focus and intensity. The imps never got close enough to do physical harm, but the onslaught was taking its toll. I'd seen Winters get worn out by a single powerful spell. They couldn't all keep up the standoff for much longer.

I decide the next order of business was to help Lucy with Marten. He was at the center of this mess. Stop him and end this.

Easier said than done though. The faster I tried to move uphill, the stronger the resistance became. It was hard enough without the severe pain in my knee and burning in my sides and the tightness in my chest. Also, the blood pooling in my eye and my broken fingers throbbing and the new pain in my shoulder wasn't exactly adding to my willpower.

I was a walking bag of hurt, but I was looking to share.

I didn't bother with my healing incantations as I hobbled in Marten's general direction. I figured that train had sailed. Instead, I focused on a different mantra.

"*Fietra*," I said under my breath.

Lazarus had taught me that one years ago. He repeated it over and over, whispering it into the ink spell as my tattoo guy created an elaborate sigil over my heart. It meant "fortitude."

"*Fietra*." I pushed on. The pain did not subside.

"*Fietra*." I forced one step after another. The thundering in my chest did not fade.

"*Fietra*." Gritted teeth. Clenched jaw. Heavy sword. Heavy gun. I pushed. Nothing improved... but I did not stop.

"*Fietra*!" Just keep going. Don't give up. Never stop.

As each forced step brought me closer and closer to Marten, I could make out more clearly the joyous sneer on his face. The bliss. God. He was enjoying this. The chaos. The fighting, the death, the power. He reveled in it all.

His hair and clothes rustled as if they were pummeled by an ephemeral wind. The dark aura churned behind him, too dark to define as a shape, but stretching out like a billowing cape in the wind.

I pushed on and I forced each breath in and out. I repeated my mantra over and over with each heavy step. *Fietra. Fietra. Fietra.* Despite the cool swirling air, I felt sweat trickling down my back and my face. I wiped at my forehead with my forearm. It was painted red in blood. A prickling sensation crept up past my elbow and the blood began to evaporate from my arm. It swirled into the air, carried on an unholy eddy current, flowing away from me, and toward Marten. The first wisps of red fluttered around him and he sniffed at it eagerly. Then with a flash of recognition, his eyes lit upon me and widened with sudden and intense glee.

"Finally," he said, drawing the word out like it tasted sweet to say it. "The Righteous Monster draws near." There was something of vibrato to his voice, something unnatural.

"Damn right," I said and trudged onward. *Fietra*.

"I smell your blood," he said and stopped to face me head on. "I can taste it in the air. Oh, Hunter, your pain is the sweetest spice."

"You'll get more than a taste," I said.

Marten stretched out his arms as if offering me a free view of his glory, "You have no clue, what I am, do you?"

"You're the guy dumb enough to hit me with a baseball bat."

"I'm so much more. That was me at my weakest."

"Don't matter," I said. "You're dead."

"Ohhh, that is very close to the truth," he said, the strangeness in his voice stronger.

"No, it's dead on," I said and whipped out the Holy Handgun. "*Echuta!*" I squeezed the trigger. A flash of fire erupted from the barrel. The gun rocked in my grip. And the projectile emerged... slowly. Spinning. Glowing an unnaturally bright yellow. It inched along impossibly slow. Marten smiled as the bullet approached him as slowly as a snail, then when it was within arm's reach, he raised a hand and swatted it aside. The bullet plowed the ground with all its original force and dug a deep furrow into the brilliant white grass and dirt.

Marten examined his hand as if to make sure the minor nuisance hadn't blemished his skin, "I am not one of your vampires, Monster Man, or a weak-willed meat bag you call a human. I'm not a petty elemental demon or a puppet master's imp, either. I am the voice of a god among mortals."

He wasn't an average Joe, I had to give him that.

"I am the One That Teaches Forbidden Knowledge," he said and took a step toward me. A surge of energy rushed through the air and dug into my gut like bad sushi. Suddenly, my arms felt like bags of sand, I couldn't lift my gun.

"I am the One Who Wears Your Sin," he took another step and the air rushed out of my lungs. Heat rushed over me and the sword in my hand felt like a burning thorn bush. The Holy Handgun felt like a hundred flaming bricks. I dropped both weapons.

"I am the One Who Defies the Creator, Who Leads the Rebellious, Who Waits in the Darkness Until the End of All Things." He extended an arm toward me and an unseen force picked me up and drew me into his open hand. His fingers, hard as cold steel, clamped tight at my throat, blocking my airway, enough that I had to force my breath back in.

"I am First among the Fallen," Marten's crazy voice said, and fiery light flashed within his eyes.

"Azazel," I wheezed.

"You know the naaaaaame," he drew out the word like a strange song and smiled maniacally.

"It's a stupid name," I croaked while pawing at his hand.

The smile disappeared. He squeezed my throat a little tighter, cutting off my air. Then, he drew me closer to his face, close enough that I could smell blood on his breath.

"I'm the First Deceiver and the Foremost Corrupter. Your death will be a minor memory in the long stretching shadow of my coming deeds."

I gasped for air and clawed at his hand around my throat.

"Nothing clever to say?" he gloated and relaxed his grip.

I rasped, "You're just a crazy librarian sharing headspace with a convict."

He sneered and punched me in the jaw with his other hand. He had a hell of a right cross. I saw stars for a moment and my body threatened to quit on me.

Hang in there. *Fietra.*

"You'll suffer for a thousand years," Marten said, "You'll beg for death in the end."

"You're not Ass-o-seal," I said, deliberately butchering his name. "That failed rebel is spending eternity under a mountain."

"I am the Flame of Passion and Defiance!" he bellowed and hit me again. I heard—and felt—the cartilage in my nose crunch. I don't care how tough you are, you can't ignore that. I tried to blink away the tears and the pain, but both persisted.

"You're a squirrel in the attic," I said, not sure if my words were even intelligible at this point. "You're old batteries in the junk drawer."

"Very well petulant boy. I will kill you first," Marten was no longer smiling. "Know this: After I bask in your blood, I will release my rage upon those whom you have failed so miserably." I had no more witty comebacks. I barely had any wits at all. Marten's fingers squeezed tighter like a vice closing on my neck. I pawed at him with my broken fingers and bloodied hand. It was futile, but I wasn't going down with a fight. What little fight I had left.

I couldn't take in another breath. I couldn't turn my head or even close my eyes. Nonetheless, my vision began to go dark. And just before my consciousness slipped away for good, I heard the most beautiful and equally hideous sound ever. A scream, so high and shrill that it made my ears hurt and the hair on my neck stand on end. And she appeared just behind Marten leaping high enough that it looked like she was flying. Mehira's raven hair and dark robes streamed behind her as she dropped toward us, a streak of gleaming silver in her hand. Marten half-turned and raised a hand toward her and received a stabbing blow. My once-discarded silver Bowie knife bore down on him and through his forearm.

Thank God for that evil woman's timing.

She twisted savagely with another scream and yanked the Bowie free of Marten's arm, cutting away a massive chunk of muscle. Growling in rage, frustration, and pain, he dropped me to take on the new threat.

I landed on my back and sucked in a desperate breath. My vision cleared and my head swam to catch up to the moment. My whole face hurt. Shooting pain radiated from my nose and tears rolled down my cheeks, mixing with blood and sweat.

I rolled my head to look for my young apprentice, hoping she was doing better than me. Lucy had resorted to hacking her way through the now swarming imps with Heir Chop-A-lot. She was a better shooter than a sword fighter, but she was holding up pretty well. She was still standing and still fighting and that's all that mattered for now.

I heard a shotgun blast and one of the imps near Lucy tumbled then got back up. Another blast and it stayed down. A few feet away, stood High School Buddy still toting the police shotgun. A pang of sadness and anger swept over me. I didn't even know the kid's real name. He was a nameless victim of this whole mess, but playing his mindless part in the battle for everyone's souls.

Mehira slashed and jabbed at Marten, with skill and speed. She'd clearly been in a knife fight before. Or dagger fight. Or claw fight. I don't know. She definitely knew what she was doing. Unfortunately, Marten did too, and in his possessed state, he was as fast as she was. He deflected some of her blows and took some, using his arms as shields. I watched awestruck for a moment. Mehira attacked with righteous fury and a swiftness of motion, in a mesmerizing dance of death that could be called otherworldly. Had she been at full strength when I first attacked her, I don't know that I would have survived.

The blade cut silver arcs through the air, cutting into Marten's hands and forearm. She accompanied each blow and each swipe with an impassioned grunt. Channeling her rage into her arms and by extension, the Bowie. Marten focused on the attack, stepping in and out, waving his arms to deflect blows or to reduce the effectiveness when steal struck flesh.

After a moment I realized something odd. Marten wasn't bleeding.

"What the hell?" I mumbled hoarsely as I sat up. Then something struck me in the back and teeth clamped down on my shoulder.

I cried out and tumbled forward under the heavy weight and familiar stink. An imp. It snarled and wrapped its clawed hands around my head from behind and dug into my cheeks

I got to my feet and spun around with the imp still chewing on my shoulder. A few dozen paces away, the ridiculous-looking Agent Ridgely in his Billy Idol costume and exaggerated spiked hair, had found me and was trudging doggedly in my direction. He raised his left hand and extended his fingers toward me, the right hand pointed at the hilltop and the cluster of wizards. He grumbled out a guttural chant of gibberish and the imps responded. Some surged toward the hilltop. The imp biting me trembled and tried to bite harder.

I knew I couldn't pry the imp locked onto my shoulder loose without losing a large part of myself in the process, so I did the next best thing. I reached over my head and grabbed some horns pulled down as hard as I could. The imp's mouth was forced open wider as I shoved more of my bulky shoulder deeper into its jaw. It gurgled and convulsed. It shoved at my face frantically trying to push itself free.

I locked eyes with Ridgely.

His eyes widened for a moment and I hoped fear would take him. Instead, he closed his left hand into a fist. The imp tried to chomp down on my shoulder. I felt its jaws stiffen, but the thing didn't have leverage. But I did. I pulled harder. The former Agent's steps faltered and his outstretched hand trembled. I saw his lips tighten as he forced out his chant through clenched teeth. Fear or exertion, I couldn't tell. Maybe both.

I let go with one and shoved it through a gap in the imp's mouth, reaching until found something that felt like a tongue. I grabbed it and yanked and it popped loose. The imp let go of me and fell to the ground squealing, black goo spewing from its gaping mouth.

"Nasty bastard," I said as I snatched up the Holy Handgun from the ground. Before the imp could get up, I put a bullet in its head and dropped the tongue next to its body. Ridgely shuddered then opened his fist and pointed at another imp, which immediately left its assault on the wizards and came back for me.

The imp I'd just killed took six shots. My gun was empty again.

I sucked in a deep breath. God, I needed a break. *Fietra*. I tried to ignore the ever-increasing pains in my body and the tingling sensation around my bloody wounds and my throbbing head. But trying to ignore something usually means you're going to think about it too much. Also, there was that faint red haze surrounding me. Was Marten still able to draw on my blood while concentrating on a fight with Mehira? Maybe it was a passive spell of some sort.

No time to worry about it.

I rushed Ridgely as fast as my noodly legs would carry me. I was gambling on the possibility that I could get to him before the charging imp could get to me. I yelled angrily and shouted "*Fietra!*" as I drew in on him. Realization of my looming proximity struck and he backed away, panic in his eyes.

Had he forgotten that he was once an Agent, well-trained and deadly in hand-to-hand combat? Hell, in my state, he'd be able to kick my ass even better than Charters had. What had he given up in return for the ability to control imps? Didn't matter to me now. What mattered to me was that he stepped on the bulky hilt of a large claymore on the ground behind him and stumbled. That slowed him down enough for me to close the last couple of steps.

I clubbed him on the side of his head with my heavy revolver and he fell to the ground like I'd hit his off switch. He lay there, his eyes wide open, motionless. Actually, not completely motionless. His lips were still moving and his eyes, now glowing red were still fixed on me.

The remaining imps still attacking the wizards turned and raced for me. About twenty of them.

The closest imp leapt across the last few feet. I dove for my sword, grabbing it by the hilt. I spun and thrust, impaling the beast through its open maw. I let the momentum carry it over my head then pinned it to the ground by shoving the blade through the back of its horned skull.

Another pair of imps tackled me. One bit into my already mauled shoulder, another into my ribs. I let their weight carry us all to the ground and rolled downhill. Under my weight, one of them lost its bite on my shoulder. The other one twisted its head and a horn dug into my armpit.

"Gaaahhhh!" I punched with my gun hand and the barrel poked out one of its eyes. I worked my empty hand around and found a narrow shaft of steal tucked in my belt. One of Lazarus's magic nails!

That'll work. I shoved it in the other eye. I rolled again to try and get the imp under me and grabbed for another nail. But another one jumped on me and clamped down on the back of my neck. I dropped the spike. Another latched onto my leg. Another on my gun hand and I dropped the pistol.

"Fffffffff—" I tried to force out a word of power. Claws dug into my back and my arms and side. I had nothing. No more power words. No more faith. No more tricks.

Then a fireball exploded nearby, and a sudden rush of warm wind blew across me. Then a blast of ice. And a crackle of electricity. The imps spasmed and fell away from my body.

Finally. The wizards had gone on the offensive.

Winters waved his arms in a grand gesture and a hail of ice

crystals pummeled an imp, shredding it to a pulp. Regis clenched a fist and shoved it in the air. A bolt of lightning danced along the ground then leapt onto one of the beasts and fried it. Foti clapped his hands together and a blast of cold air swept across me then picked up the nearest imp, sending it flying. The imps tried to dodge the new onslaught while still pressing their attack. Lucy tore into one with a hail of bullets. High School Buddy blasted another with his riot gun. Regis stepped close to another and beheaded another with a flash of silver. Basnet reached out her, bony fingers curled as if clutching an invisible object. She closed her fist and opened it. A ball of fire streaked out from her open palm and exploded against an imp.

It was utter chaos.

At the head of the great stone table, Lady Adda stood tall and still, watching with obvious interest but making no move to join the fight.

Oblivious of it all, Mehira and Marten continued in their deadly dance of flesh and steel. The former Archivist countered the ancient vampire's blows, slashing with his own fingernails like claws. Mehira had new gashes on her arms and rips in her robes revealing bleeding legs and torso. Her dark blood turned to mist and swirled about her, adding to the cloud of what I assumed was keeping Marten going. She roared and screamed furiously as she traded blows and cuts and slashes. And though she had caused more apparent damage on Marten than he had on her, he didn't look to be weakened at all.

I searched quickly and found the Holy Handgun before getting up. I told myself I wasn't going to lose it again. Nearby, the leather and stud adorned Ridgely continued to chant in a strange catatonic silence. The imps, though dwindling in numbers, continued to fight in a frenzied abandon. I yanked Killicutty free from where I had left it in an imp's head and raised it to finish Ridgely before he could find a way to call upon more imps. A flash of lightning struck near me, barely missing me but cooking an imp a few feet away. The energy lifted me from my feet and sent me rolling several yards.

And I slammed to the ground right next to Buddy.

His head snapped toward me and his brows furrowed in newfound rage. Right or wrong, he saw me as his enemy, from that first night on the highway. He pointed the shotgun at me and yanked the trigger. I flinched but didn't die. The gun was empty. His lips curled back, and he swung the empty weapon like a club. I batted the blow aside with my pistol and crab-crawled out of his reach. I scrambled to my feet as he stomped toward me. He swung again, but I was too tall for an effective up-close blow. I took the hit then punched him square in the nose with the sword's basket handle. That would have incapacitated most people, but he wasn't most people anymore, not even technically a person anymore.

He staggered back from the force, his face scrunched up in unchecked rage. Then he did something I hadn't expected. He dug into a pocket and fished out a shotgun shell and racked it into the shotgun.

Oh shit!

As he raised the barrel toward me, a single gunshot cracked, and his head jerked aside.

"No!" I heard myself gasp.

Lucy stood a few feet away, Holy Glockamolie in hand, pointed at Buddy. She saw me and mouthed I'm sorry then pulled the trigger two more times. Both shots were headshots. At close range. The slide on her gun locked back. The gun was empty now, but the damage was done.

I heard Mehira scream, "Noooooooooo!" She had felt Buddy's death and her focus wavered for a second. One second was all Marten needed. He swiped at her wrist and knocked the silver knife from her grasp. In a swift lunge, he stepped inside her open arm and grabbed her viciously by the throat.

And she didn't even resist. She watched as Buddy's body fell lifeless once more onto the bloodstained white grass.

Lucy punched me in the shoulder, "Get in the game!"

I looked at her. She had that angry look she always put on when she was fighting. Then it softened slightly. For just a second.

"He was already gone," Lucy said. I can't be sure, but I thought I saw tears in her eyes.

But, she was right. There was no coming back from what Mehira had made him. From what he had been put through. He existed as an angry memory of his own family's slaughter. He was a nameless victim no more. He wasn't anything anymore.

Lucy locked eyes with me, "Suck it up, Big Guy. This isn't over."

"No, it isn't," I took in a deep breath, and the pain in my lungs reminded me I was still alive. "Take care of that." I pointed at Ridgely and stomped off toward Marten.

He saw me approaching and laughed. The fire in his eyes was brilliant, terrible, and awesome, all at once.

The Holy Handgun was empty. Didn't matter. I'd already tried that, and it didn't work. Dark ichor dripped from Killicutty, but I didn't imagine I'd be effective against him with the sword. Not after seeing him fight Mehira. Didn't matter. I planned on using my bare hands this time, for as long as they still worked.

"*Fietra!*" I grunted.

Marten tilted his head as if confused by my determination. He lowered his hand, holding Mehira at his side like a ragdoll. Her eyes were fixed on Buddy's lifeless form.

I hadn't even gone a half dozen steps when Regis whirled into view and silver flashed again. In a swift downward arc, a blade cut through the air and cut off Marten's arm halfway between the wrist and elbow. The former archivist shrieked in pain and shock, staggering several paces away from Regis staring at the wizard in disbelief. Mehira flopped to the ground, unfazed. Regis planted his feet on either side of her. He sneered down at her and raised the long blade. In the flashes of light and dark, amid the chaos of the wizards' elemental spell, crashing down on the scattered hellspawn, of blasting fire and crackling lighting, I saw Regis silhouetted against the strange sky and the weapon he held aloft. I knew that blade.

"Fuck me!" It was my blade. My precious Mr. Machete!

Before I even realized what I had done, Killicutty was flying through the air toward Regis. It tumbled end over end three times before the heavy pommel struck him square in the mouth. He dropped the machete and clutched at his face with both hands as he staggered away from the immobile vampire.

I dove to the ground and snatched up the enchanted machete before either Mehira or Regis could. The word "love" flashed through my mind as I took hold of the worn walnut grip.

The battle raged on around the four of us. Mehira and Marten and Regis and me. The wizards continued to unleash elemental havoc. Imps howled and snarled and leapt and fell and fought. Ridgely had gotten up again and had Lucy in an arm lock. But only for a moment. she twisted her body and ducked and spun and flipped him back down to the ground.

Marten chanted under his breath while rocking back and forth, cradling what was left of his arm to his chest. The fire in his eyes did not fade but I guessed the pain could not be ignored regardless of his mental state.

Regis lowered his hands from his face, his eyes moving from mine to the blade in my hand as I stood upright from picking it up. Blood trickled from the new gash on his upper lip. He spit out a tooth and narrowed his eyes at me.

Mehira finally pulled her eyes from Buddy's empty body and turned them to the weapon in my hand.

"And so, we come full circle," she sighed softly, almost enticingly.

Regis held up his hands defensively, "No! You don't understand."

I swung Mr. Machete. In that instant, I saw a flash in Regis's eyes and the fear changed to something else... something worse. One hand clenched into a fist and twisted. It felt like I had hit an invisible wall of steel and the blade skittered aside. An unseen force guided my momentum and the machete slid toward Mehira. I couldn't stop it. The end plunged into her heaving chest.

Chapter Thirty-Nine

The blade crackled and sizzled as it tore into her flesh. I pulled on it, but it was not under my control, as if locked by Sanctu Spitu, which I had not invoked. Mehira slapped my hand away then shoved me away viciously and held on to the blade as if trying to keep it from moving. It burned her fingers and tears flowed from the corners of her eyes.

"Ungrateful dog!" Regis thundered. "After all I have done for you. After all I gave you."

"You didn't give me anything," I snapped back. "I paid for everything with pieces of my soul. Every nickel and dime."

"I gave you the tools to fight evil," he held up a fist. "You were our hand of justice."

"I still am," I said. "One more time."

"Insolent ape," Regis said as if disappointed. "You had such potential."

Marten started laughing.

Regis ignored him. Blood dripped from his chin and stained his impeccable shirt. Mehira grunted and wheezed and raged like a wild animal caught in a trap, the machete locked into her body. Regis watched her for a moment and flicked his wrist. The blade shifted to the right, closer to her heart. She screamed in newfound agony.

The wizard held out a hand and Killicutty flipped up into his grip. A show of power. Of power over every weapon I had. Nice trick, but something else caught my attention. The blood trickling down his face was not turning to mist like mine or Mehira's.

That was interesting.

"You're bleeding," I said.

"If you prick me..."

"Oh my God," I said softly. "You did this."

"You're no detective," Regis said dismissively. "You're not smart enough to understand."

He had to know me better than that. I was no Sherlock Holmes, but I was also no Inspector Clouseau either. He'd mentored me enough in my early days to know I had skill at ferreting out weaknesses. At finding my prey's Achilles heel. At summing up my opponent.

"You're a Hunter," he said. "Stick to what you do best."

"I do a lot of things," I said tiredly, as I searched for a weapon that would work. Stalling for an opening. "I can even name all fifty states."

"I can name all the souls in all the worlds," Regis sneered.

"You've lost your mind." The Holy Handgun was empty.

"No. I have found enlightenment. A level of clarity that you cannot begin to imagine."

"I have a good imagination," I countered. Mr. Machete was stuck in a tortured vampire's chest.

The wizard smirked.

"What do you plan to accomplish here?" I asked. He had my magic sword.

Regis tilted his head as if I'd asked an absurd question, "Accomplish? It is all accomplishing itself!" He pointed at Mehira, "I'm doing your job. I'm going to quiet all the monsters... as you have failed to do."

"I didn't fail. I quit." I still had a hammer, but I wasn't close enough to use it.

"That is failure. You didn't have the right to quit!"

I sighed, "I already had this argument with Winters. I'm not having it with you." My magic nails were scattered out of my reach.

"What do you imagine is going to happen here?" He pointed the tip of the sword at me. Electricity crackled along its length.

I said nothing.

"Do you believe a sudden flash of inspiration will empower you with the wherewithal to defeat me?"

I shrugged.

"No more clever insults in a vain attempt to anger me? No snarky jibes? Do you really suppose you are clever enough to contrive of a plan to overcome me in the short time you have left? Do you believe you have what it takes?"

"No," I said. "They do."

Regis's eyes flashed to Mehira, but too late. She shoved one of the magic nails straight into his shin bone with a ferocious and feral scream. At the same time, Lucy thrust Heir Chop-A-Lot through his chest from behind.

Regis's back arched and twisted grotesquely as he cried out. Dancing electricity exploded from the end of Killicutty, fingers of electricity dancing in all directions, lancing across the ground and across my body and those near him. Concentrated, it would have killed any one of us instantly. But it was just a release, not an attack.

I fell to the ground, convulsing as a strong magic current shot through my body. I heard Lucy and Mehira's muffled screams. Then silence. Sudden, complete, eerie silence. The electrical sensation faded, and I could breathe again. I was still bleeding. My body still hurt. I was still alive.

All the imps lay motionless around us. The white-robed guardians returned to rigid attention wherever they stood. The wizards had stopped fighting. Master Winters stood nearby with the tip of his cane plunged into Ridgely's heart. Old methods are often the most effective. The old wizard wore a tired expression on his weathered face.

Lucy lay flat on her back, gasping for air. Mehira, at last, pulled Mr. Machete from her chest with a yelp and tossed it aside... toward me. She curled into a fetal position, clutching at the gaping wound.

Regis groaned and sat as tall and arrogantly as a man with a magic sword sticking out of his chest could manage.

"It is finished, Master Regis," Winters said sadly.

"Is it?" Regis asked. "You think that killing that pawn ends anything?" He waved a hand idly at Ridgely's dead body.

"I do not know what do think," Winters replied.

Regis tested the tip of the sword with a finger, "You have no idea what is happening here, do you?"

"Not as much as I had thought," Winters admitted.

"The balance of the natural world is at stake," Regis said, jabbing a finger at Mehira, "Letting creatures like that live is a mistake."

The High Councilor removed his cane from Ridgely's chest and leaned on it, the reddened tip firm upon the white ground, "The purpose of this meeting was to examine that balance, not pass judgement."

Foti came closer to Winters, "This... this madness... this attack... on this night. It cannot be a coincidence"

"No," Winters said. "It cannot."

Gosse shuffled up next to Foti, shaking his head, "Nothing has ever moved against the Nine-Fold Council in this manner."

"None that you can recall," Winters said.

Master Basnet placed a hand on Winters' shoulder as she came up behind him, "That was a very long time ago."

"Yes," Winters agreed.

"Demons cannot cross our barrier," Foti said looking around with obvious confusion. "The pocket universe is sacred and protected."

Basnet surveyed the carnage, "Yet here they are."

"None can enter unaided," Winters said, "or uninvited."

"You're suggesting they were invited?" Foti's voice cracked. "That is madness!"

Gosse's shoulders slumped, "It is madness... yet it must be so.

They were invited and given aid."

Regis watched the exchange with a guarded expression. He should be dead or dying. But he didn't look like he was either. Why was that?

I stepped close enough to pick up Killicutty then retreated out of his reach. I had an icky feeling that even with a sword and a magic nail sticking through him, he was still dangerous. Lucy finally got to her feet and reloaded the Holy Glockamolie. She racked the slide and pressed the barrel against the back of Regis' head.

"What is this?" Foti demanded.

"This is an execution," Lucy stated without looking at him.

Winters looked at me, pleadingly, "William?"

I nodded, "It's him. All of this."

"Lies," Regis said through clenched teeth.

"Madness," Foti thundered again.

I felt a chill then a sudden warmth and was startled to see Lady Adda standing there next to me, so close.

She had remained immaculate, all in white, completely unsoiled by any of the chaos that had surrounded us. Even standing on the red-stained grass, not a single drop of blood stained the hems of her robes. She looked at each of us in turn as if we were dear friends, but she did not speak. Her eyes remained on Mehira for a moment longer than the others. Mehira stared back defiantly. The silence settled upon us like a strange, comforting blanket.

Regis couldn't take it, "I stood by your side Master Winters. I supported your fantasies."

"It would seem that way," Winters said sadly. "But all is not as it seems. Is it?"

"Look around you," Regis motioned at the dead agent. The slowly disintegrating imps and hulking form of the minor demon. At Mehira. "This is what happens when unnatural forces are allowed to move unchecked."

I pointed the tip of my magic sword at Regis, "No. This is what happens when you dip too deep into the cesspit of hell. Dudael always equals trouble."

The white lady's eyes snapped back to me.

"What do you know of Dudael?" she asked earnestly. Her voice was hauntingly beautiful. Not in a sensual way like Mehira's when she was laying it on thick. No, Lady Adda's voice was like a mother enthralled by her son's discoveries. I wanted to wrap my arms around her and hug her. Better still, I wanted her to take me in her arms and hold me and tell me everything was going to be ok. I would have believed her if she told me that.

"He knows nothing," Regis said, "he's just a—"

"Please," Adda said sternly but pleasantly, "I am speaking with this child."

Regis jerked as if he'd been slapped and fell silent.

She looked at me, her brilliant silver eyes locking onto mine. There was permission in her eyes, permission to speak.

"I'm so sorry," I said, I tried to pull my eyes from hers, but I couldn't. "I'm not strong enough."

"Pain is not weakness," she said earnestly.

I shivered, "Pain... It means I'm still alive."

"You wish it to stop?"

More than anything. I thought but didn't speak it out loud.

Instead, I said, "Just for a while. I'm so tired."

The white lady placed a hand on my shoulder, and I felt a tingle run through my entire body. All at once, every bit of pain in my body simply disappeared. My ribs, my fingers, my head, my shoulder. Nothing hurt. It was as if she had flipped the main circuit breaker for pain.

"I, uh..." I said eloquently.

She smiled at me and the sun seemed to rise on my soul.

"Speak freely," she said, "tell me what you know of Dudael."

I suddenly had no desire other than to tell Lady Adda exactly what she wanted to hear.

"I don't know much," I said lamely. "Only what I've picked up."

Lady Adda nodded in acceptance of my lame excuse.

Regis glared at me as I spoke, "It's the solitary confinement wing of Hell. All the Fallen and their followers are doing hard time there, waiting for Judgment Day."

"Religious fantasy," Foti said dismissively.

Lady Adda looked at him but didn't speak. Her hand remained lightly upon my shoulder. Foti met her gaze defiantly but averted his eyes after only a second or two.

The white lady let the silence hang long enough to feel unnatural. When she spoke again, her voice was as clear as glass yet soft as silk, "All acknowledge there is another world, the Orbis Alius as you call it in your extinct languages. And yet somehow you dismiss the idea of a darkness that resides in the far reaches of that world?"

"We deny no such thing," Foti countered. "But the Fallen? Bedtimes stories from the Bible."

"Your aversions have been repeatedly vocalized," Winters said, "but there are more things beneath the heavens than we can explain by our philosophies."

Lady Adda nodded a silent thanks and addressed me again, "What else can you share?"

"Not much," I admitted. "There are a lot of dangerous things... in my world and the other... and I've fought most of them in my lifetime."

Adda tilted her head, "Fought and killed?"

I pressed my lips together and nodded once.

"I am sorry for your pain, child," she said softly, "but, you have a strong heart... this burden will not destroy you."

What if it already has? I wondered.

My knees were weak. I felt like I could drop to the ground and cry at her feet. I felt the tears in my eyes, ready to come. I felt a great hole in my heart, like a black hole with a mass greater than the area it occupied.

"Do not despair," she said quietly, so quiet I wasn't even sure she'd said it out loud. "Be strong... your work is not done yet."

"I'm so tired," I whispered.

Adda squeezed my shoulder gently and I felt a hundred pounds lighter as if she were holding me up in a pool of water.

"I know you are," she said, "and you will rest soon... but not yet."

"No... Not yet," I agreed. There was always more work to be done. There was always one more threat. One more life at stake. One more innocent in the line of fire. One more family destroyed by evil.

"This burden is not yours," Adda said to me. "Do not keep it for yourself."

I took in a deep breath and let all the pieces come back together in my head, "Marten and Regis were working together to deceive us all. There never was an incursion." That got Lucy's attention and she looked back and forth from me to Regis. I saw her brow furrow. I saw her finger tense on the Holy Glockamolie's trigger. But she did not shoot.

"And Rezruel was never part of this," I went on.

"Are you fucking kidding me?" Lucy grumbled. "After all we went through."

I shrugged, "They set it all up to make us believe the wrong things. I was supposed to find the clues and jump on Rezruel as the prime suspect. And I fell for it."

"Rezruel?" Adda repeated the name curiously.

"One of the One Hundred," I said, "one of the trusted companions of the Watchers."

"Ah," Adda nodded slowly.

"Why Rezruel?" Winters asked weakly.

"Because Regis knew you'd drag me into this," I said, "and he knew I'd pull that thread and run off chasing my own tail." Regis watched me as I spoke, radiating hatred.

"Posh!" Gosse said looking around at the other wizards. "Why him?"

"Because of his reputation," Foti said stiffly. "He doesn't fail."

"They expected me to die in the process," I said.

Winters turned to me in shock, "What?"

I looked at Mehira, still laying on the ground, clutching her side. She glared at Regis, the way she used to look at me.

"Regis found Mehira where I left her," I sucked in a deep breath "and offered her..." I couldn't say it.

"Children," Lucy spat and jabbed the pistol into the back of Regis's head, "He fed her children."

"LIES!" Regis bellowed. He started to get up and Lucy smacked him on top of his head with the butt of her pistol. He dropped back to his knees, mumbling curses under his breath.

"It is true," Mehira wheezed. "He brought me three helpless children and placed them at my feet."

"This is madness!" Foti cried. "Can you prove any of this?"

"Of course, they can't," Regis said.

I pointed at Buddy's lifeless corpse, "That's the proof." I dug into a pocket and found the photograph I had taken from the house. I looked at it for a moment then held it up for everyone to see.

"That proves only that that creature is indeed a monster," Foti said, pointing at Mehira.

"Marten and Regis also flipped two incursion agents," I said, "who then assisted in staging the fake incursion. They murdered an entire family to cover their tracks."

Winters lowered his head and leaned on his cane. Basnet focused on Buddy's dead body as if burning his image into her memory. Gosse and Foti were dumbstruck. I could see it in their eyes. They wanted to deny it all. They wanted to call me a liar again. They wanted to believe that all wizards were infallible and incorruptible. I wanted to believe that too, but I knew better.

Lucy shoved the pistol into the back of Regis' head and twisted as if it were a knife. Probably wishing it was. "And they shared all their tricks about how to use the dark magic they'd tapped into. Like how to summon and control imps."

Foti looked at Ridgely's corpse, and his shoulders drooped. Perhaps he finally recognized the man beneath the ridiculous hairdo and the over-the-top punk rocker clothes.

"Worse yet," I added, "they all teamed up and tapped into a source of evil even worse than Rezruel."

"Enough of these lies," Regis said. Lucy grabbed the hilt of Heir Chop-A-Lot and twisted. Regis growled and squeezed his eyes closed.

"The fake incursion was more than a red herring. They were using it to hide something just as sinister."

"And what were they hiding?" Adda asked.

"A summoning circle," I said.

Lucy slapped her forehead, "Son of a bitch. It's so obvious now."

I nodded in agreement, "We stumbled on evidence that the idiots next door were trying to perform summoning rituals, stuff way out of their league. Regis found out and showed them how to do it for real."

Marten groaned softly and arched his back, nearly bending over backward to the ground. Regis's body shivered visibly, but he didn't move otherwise.

"My God," Basnet whispered. "Can this be true?"

"Madness!" Foti exclaimed. "Utter madness!"

"You keep saying that, yet everything that happened, happened," I said.

"It seems that way," Basnet said.

I watched Regis, his eyes closed, mumbling to himself. A sword thrust through his body. A gun at his head. Blood trickled from the corner of his mouth.

A wizard, fallen from grace... in pursuit of a lie.

I grunted ruefully, "They attempted to summon Azazel. But he can't be summoned."

Lucy lowered the gun from the back of Regis' head, "Wait. He can't?"

I sighed, "I should've picked up on it before. Azazel is doing hard time, with no chance for parole."

"Yet they attempted to summon him?" Gosse asked.

"Yup. He can't be freed," I said. "but they made contact somehow, like a shadow of a connection. Somehow Azazel shared some of his power and his secrets with them. That's his thing. Azazel was locked up in Dudael for sharing forbidden knowledge, among other things."

"And the demon fanboys," Lucy said, "had those damned brands on their foreheads. Azazel?"

"Yup," I nodded again. "That's why they were stronger than they had any business being. And that's how Ridgely learned to control the imps."

Lucy twisted the sword in Regis' back, "And that's why this piece of shit hasn't bled out and died yet."

All present laid eyes on Regis. His mumbling stopped, and the bleeding stopped. Strange timing.

"They learned some other nasty tricks along the way too," I said.

"Like summoning a minor demon," Lucy said.

I nodded, "And blood magic."

"Are we to believe this madness?" Foti asked.

"Indeed!" Regis said laughing softly. He opened his eyes, and they were red, glowing softly but growing intensity, "I lay proof at your feet of the dangers that surround these creatures. The dangers of mercy and compassion. I lay bare the very nature of this ancient

Mother of darkness." He pointed at Mehira without looking at her. "I threw open the door between night and day to reveal that your nightmares are well-founded." He rose slowly, ignoring Lucy's insistent tugging on the sword.

"I presented you with proof that evil is evil. With proof that humans will always fall prey to something more powerful. Proof that even hell itself can reach out into the mortal world and pluck innocent lives from beneath our naïve, protective embrace. And yet, you continue to deny the truth."

"Master Regis," Winters asked softly, "Is this all true? You were at the root of all of this?"

"This, and more than you can imagine," he laughed. He stepped toward Winters, hands extended, inviting. Lucy pulled on the sword to stop him, but he ignored her. "You need to see what I see. The folly of what you're trying to do. The folly of opening our doors to creatures that should stay in the dark places."

Winters' let out a slow breath, "You've shown me that evil exists in all hearts, not just those beyond the veil."

"Evil, yes," Regis said excitedly, "but also power! Power beyond anything I had imagined. I never knew... we never really knew."

"We knew Master Regis," Basnet said sternly, her voice trembling, "we knew all too well. It is why we have the laws that we have."

Marten's head snapped up and he spoke, his voice raw and monotone, "What you witness here is a morsel of what is possible. We've been given just a taste of that power, and yet that small taste is a power greater than you can imagine."

Regis smiled, "We have struck alliances that will ripple across the universes. Feeble mortal minds cannot comprehend the possibilities. We are but two pieces." He and Marten spread their arms out in the same grand gesture. "We are two fingers of a Fallen Angel's mighty hand, picking at the scabs of this world."

Marten rose up from the ground as if picked up by an invisible hand, "Together... we are the hand of Azazel."

A dark cloud formed around both of them, growing... dangerously similar to the one Lucy and I witnessed in the Archives footage Dean had recorded.

"Lucy," I said, "these are the targets. If you want to end the contract..."

"Nuff said," Lucy raised the Holy Glockamolie and squeezed the trigger. And aside from a loud bang, nothing happened.

Shit.

Chapter Forty

Regis spun and back-handed Lucy, sending her tumbling to the ground several feet away then turned and stretched a hand toward Winters. Marten jabbed his good arm at me, and the dark cloud expanded toward me. Winters raised his cane then stopped cold, as if frozen. Regis's outstretched hand trembled; he was overpowering Winters, but not without effort.

Basnet grabbed at Winters' arms, as if to pull him away. As soon as she touched him, she screamed and fell away, her hands smoking. Foti and Gosse each took a step back. I could almost smell their fear. Foti averted his eyes. Gosse clutched at his chest.

I didn't move. As I stood there next to Lady Adda with her hand still resting on my shoulder, I had no impulse to fight, only a strange impulse to wait and watch. Was she doing that?

The white lady's face darkened slightly. Her hand slipped from my shoulder and curled into a fist, but she didn't do anything. I saw the frustration in her eyes. She had not been affected by Marten or Regis' magic, but she was restrained from action by something else. A choice? A rule?

Regis and Marten's voices spoke in unison, creating a creepy vibrato effect, "A fallen angel and a wizard, in the same body in the world of mortal men." They laughed a single loud, obnoxious laugh, "we are unstoppable."

I came up with a few smartass things to say, but I couldn't speak. The black cloud emanating from the two of them stretched outward in all directions. Tendrils like snakes began to form from the cloud. One writhed toward me and touched my hand. I felt the stinging and prickling sensation of a thousand tiny needles; red droplets emerged and formed on my skin.

Blood magic at work again. I jerked my hand back, with Lady Adda by my side, I didn't dare step away. She seemed unaffected by it. The cloud squirmed and seemed to pulsate in rhythm with a heartbeat. It began to touch everyone else, drawing tiny droplets of blood. Winters remained frozen in place, unable to fight off the magic. Basnet cradled her hands against her chest while twisting and turning away from the probing cloud. Foti swiped at the tentacles of dark magic as if at stinging flies, but to no effect. Gosse doubled over, coughing and wheezing. The magic was working. It was drawing more blood.

And then I looked back at Regis and Marten. Wait. No, this couldn't be right. Azazel was a fallen angel, not a demon. He was a deceiver and a rebel and an inciter, but he was not a demon. Definitely not a user of blood magic.

A light flicked on in my brain.

"You're not Azazael," I said suddenly. My voice was barely a whisper as I seemed to have no strength to speak.

Regis' lip curled into an exaggerated sneer, "This ploy again boy?"

"No," I said, my voice growing stronger. "Dumb truth. Regis, you've been duped." I wasn't sure if Regis was even an individual entity anymore, but I had a feeling something of his own consciousness remained intact.

Lucy, whom I thought had been unconscious pushed herself up from the ground and stood up shakily. The blood magic cloud swirled around her like a torrent.

The tendrils of magic lashed at Foti and Gosse. The old wizard stumbled and fell. As Foti stooped to help him the smoke-like mist engulfed them both. Master Basnet struggled to get up, but the cloud throbbed closer, causing her to cover her face defensively. Winters struggled against the hold on him, but he had been weakened in the fight and seemed powerless.

Regis and Marten's voices rumbled, "I am the Teacher. I am the Leader and the First Among the Rebels Reaching into the Light from the Darkness."

"Yeah, I'm sure Azazel is," I drew my shoulders up and straightened my back in defiance of the blood magic trying to worm its way into my body, "but he's also in chains under a mountain in a back corner of hell."

I heard Adda's soft voice hum, "Interesting."

An instant of uncertainty flashed across Regis' eyes. He glanced at Marten. Marten didn't speak, he simply spread his fingers, and the blood in my entire body tingled. The dark cloud churned. The tendrils of dark magic whipped about at random, like a child throwing a tantrum.

"All this time," I said, my whole body itched and ached, "I thought those idiot neighbor kids were using a poorly rendered Azazel sigil."

The sensations intensified and I had to focus to continue. Adda watched me with concern but did not intervene.

"It wasn't Azazael's sigil," In spite of the dark magic working inside my body, I wanted to laugh. "It was a demon, a demon whose sigil is similar enough for someone who didn't know better to make the mistake. Those boys were idiots... and so are you."

The tingling in my body wavered for a second as a flash of doubt crossed both Marten's and Regis' eyes. And I recognized what was happening because it had happened to me. Doubt. Magic is fed by belief. Magic without belief is ineffective.

Lucy's head jerked up. She felt the change too.

"Clever," I heard Adda say.

"Thanks," I said, my voice wavering. My whole body throbbed. I hadn't felt pain since Adda touched me, but this magic at work against me was almost as unbearable as pain. I turned to look at the white lady. "Can you stop this?"

"I can render aid to you." She touched my arm the tingling stopped. The dark cloud continued to swirl around me like a swarm of angry bees but had stopped nipping away at my dwindling supply of blood.

"Your grasp of esoteric history is unique, if not a little weak..." she said.

"Weak?" I said, "my understanding is shakier than an earthquake."

She smiled, "But you have stumbled upon an important truth."

She addressed Regis, "Release these people, demon. They have uncovered your truth and your lies."

"Ha!" The odd voice speaking through Regis and Marten's bodies laughed. A glowing symbol appeared on their foreheads, burning brightly like an ember in the heart of a fire. It was the same symbol that had appeared on Nestor's forehead, and his friends'. It was not Azazael's sigil. It was also not Rezruel's. Of that I was certain, but whose was it? Lucy stretched her hand toward the Holy Glockamolie at her feet but didn't stoop to pick it up. Whatever hold Regis and Martin were exercising still has some effect.

"In your hubris," Adda said, "you have revealed yourself. I know what you are."

"It does not matter. I have unparalleled power. I am invited. I have the power here."

"Invited," I said as realization hit me like a ton of bricks, "not summoned?"

Marten's eyes snapped to me, "There is no difference." Even as he said it, I knew he was lying.

"An invitation is only as good as the body of the person who offered it," I said.

"Indeed," Adda said approvingly. "You know your business, child."

"I surprise even myself sometimes," I said.

Adda asked me, "Can you speak its true name?"

I shook my head, "I don't know his name."

"Silence, witch!" Regis and Marten said. "I invoke my bargain!" Thunder rumbled.

"Did I not say that I have allies?" Regis said victoriously.

A deep thunder rumbled again all around us and the ground shook. Lightning struck the ground near us and when the flash died away, there stood the muddy goblin in all its nasty glory, horrid grin, soiled clothes, and hideous smell. He removed a crackling ball of energy from his coat and smiled his ugly smile at me.

Chapter Forty-One

"Fool!" Adda cried angrily.

At the sound of Adda's voice, the creature's attention snapped to her, and his eyes widened to the point of pure terror. He dropped to his knees suddenly and lowered his head, the lightning still clutched in his hand, safely away from his face.

"Well," I said, "That's a welcome development."

"You dare intrude into this circle?" Her voice held no confusion, only authority and anger.

"I beg your forgiveness, Lady," the goblins awful voice gurgled. I had never seen actual groveling before, but this was what I imagined it would look like.

"Enough!" Adda's voice echoed across the expanse of white and red, "Your presence here is an affront, Mweg Badgerbog."

The creature cringed at the sound of its name.

"A bargain," Mweg said. "A bargain was struck."

A bargain? I wanted to ask with whom, but the authority in the white lady's voice had stunned me into silence.

Adda pointed a finger at the goblin, "A bargain with the humans or the spirits inhabiting them?"

Mweg raised his head enough to look longingly at Marten and Regis then cowed again, "I— I know not."

"Fool!" Adda's voice cut like a knife.

I looked at the lighting ball still clutched in Mweg's hand. Lightning balls! Lightning was Master Regis' trick. Mweg has learned that from the wizard somehow.

I looked to Adda longingly.

The anger in her visage didn't fade but her voice softened when she spoke to me, "Speak your mind."

"What did Regis offer you?" I asked.

Mweg glared at me, "My secrets are mine to keep stupid human."

"The human asks on my behalf," Adda thundered. "It is within my purview to mediate a bargain. Answer his question."

Regis roared in anger and the swirling cloud faded some. Lucy snatched up her gun but stayed in a crouch. Winters' cane moved a few inches. Foti cowered, hands covering his face. Gosse remained motionless. Basnet stopped flailing at the cloud. It seemed to have lost its sting.

"You will tell her nothing," Regis and Marten said, both pointing at Mweg.

"Choose cautiously how your next moments unfold," Adda warned. "You already tread upon dangerous grounds Mweg Badgerbog."

Mweg cringed And lowered his head to the white grass and rocked it back and forth.

"You will not lie in my presence," Adda continued. "Your secrets are not yours to keep. They are mine to cast into the light as I choose."

"It is as you say," Mweg said, his face still buried.

"Then raise your head," Adda commanded, "and speak."

"They promised me great power," Mweg whined as he sat upright. "A wizard's power over the storms, the power to control lightning and thunder and the winds. In exchange, I cross the veil using the magic they gave me and attack those I am directed to attack."

I laughed.

Adda tilted her head curiously, "I do not understand the humor."

"My apologies Lady," I said. "Mweg made a bad deal."

"Lies!" Marten and Regis said at the same time. The dark cloud around me swirled as if stirred by an internal wind, whipping at me but causing no harm. Ineffective against whatever protection Adda's presence gave me.

Adda looked into my eyes for a moment, as if searching for an answer, then smiled, "You are full of surprises, aren't you?"

"That's what I hear," I said.

"Explain this 'bad deal,'" Adda waved her hand toward Marten and Regis.

"Marten ain't a wizard," I said plainly.

Mweg regarded the still crackling bundle of lightning in his hand and held it up to examine it more closely. As if it mattered at this point.

"Regis," I continued, "is a wizard. He can conjure magic and power, but he cannot give it away."

"But this?" Mweg held the lightning up as evidence for all to see.

"It's a weapon," I said. "A trick. But it ain't a wizard's power. They can't share it."

"Enough!" Regis and Marten bellowed in a distorted voice, "Goblin, the power I have given you is a taste of what will become yours when your bargain is fulfilled. These humans have no true power, they are merely hosts for my presence. They bargained with you on my behalf. When all is complete, I will have the power and I will show you such gifts as you have never imagined."

"Ah," Adda said as if she finally understood a private joke, "Bill, you are a clever child."

I beamed at her compliment.

Mweg looked from Regis and Marten to Adda, back and forth, "I don't understand."

"Of course, you don't," Adda said sternly, "as I said, you're a fool. Did you not know you had struck a bargain by proxy?"

"By proxy... What? No!" Mweg he swiveled to look at Regis, "Who are you?"

"My name is my own," Regis said.=

"Your bargain was not struck in good faith," Lady Adda said. "And it is founded upon a lie."

"No," Mweg gurgled.

"I declare that your bargain with these... entities is void."

Mweg turned his gaze briefly toward Regis and Marten then lowered his face again when Adda spoke. His entire posture slumped.

"Relinquish your ill-gotten gift and depart from this circle," she said. "You will return to your hole and wait for me. I will come for you when my business here is concluded."

Mweg turned his hand over dropping the ball of electricity and watched it dissipate into the grass. With an excessive show of dejectedness, he reached into his ragged jacket and tore out a small leather pouch. He regarded it longingly then threw it on the ground.

"Traitor!" Regis and Marten bellowed in unison. Regis extended a hand toward the goblin. More lightning erupted from their hands.

"Now you interfere with my business," Adda said with a fury that even I cringed from. She raised a hand and the lightning flickered away to nothing.

To Mweg she said, "Go now before I lose my temper."

The goblin nodded once and disappeared with a pop.

"No!" Regis and Martin snapped.

Calmly, Adda said to Regis, "I said you have revealed yourself. I know your name." She whispered it in my ear. I could barely hear her but the sound of her voice and the name she spoke burned into my memory.

A name—a true name—carries more power in it than humans realize. People don't understand the deep power in knowing someone's true name, that's why they never truly listen and understand. I heard the demon's name, and with it, the thing's true nature. Like all demons, it was a deceiver. A liar. It was not capable of Truth. Truth is too noble and too righteous a concept.

A demon is not a fallen angel. There never was good in a demon. Demons are constructs of Hell. They are made in the image of their creators, or rather in the projected nature of their creators. And they are fueled by different aspects of Hell's dark magic when they come into the mortal world.

This demon was a blood demon, drawn to and empowered by the blood of innocents.

"Ha!" I laughed out loud yet again. Adda shared a smile with me.

That's why it wasn't getting any stronger drawing strength from my blood. I'm not innocent. Sure, I was a pretty good man, but I was no innocent. I was brutal and violent, and my heart was forged in my youth from anger and vengeance. Even if I grew to believe in my cause, I was not without sin.

This blood demon was greedy and jealous. It was a spawn of Azazael. It was jealous of its own creator by design, created to find a way into the word, to seek power and knowledge, to find a way to one day free its creator. To covet what its creator coveted. That's why its sigil resembled Azazael's. It was a shadow of Azazael.

"Nazufel Shigrafek," I said boldly.

Regis screamed. The cloud darkened and thickened. Lucy stumbled back several steps. Winters dropped to his knees, sucking in long, labored breaths. Basnet and Foti both covered their ears at the sounds of the scream. Gosse didn't move.

"Nazufel Shigrafek," I said again. Marten cried out. Lucy took a bold step toward Regis.

"There are no innocents here," I said. "There is no blood to nourish you here... Nazufel Shigrafek."

Marten gasped and the black cloud wavered.

"*Fietra*!" I roared and leapt forward. Killicutty cut a shining arc through Marten's remaining arm, severing it clean off. He staggered away from me screaming in rage and pain. Lucy lunged forward and took hold of Heir Chop-A-Lot's hilt, which was still plunged through Regis' body.

I yanked the blue-handled hammer from my belt and roared, "Sanctu Spitu!" The head of the hammer smashed into Marten's skull and stuck in place. He was dead before his body hit the ground.

Regis chanted in a strangely familiar language... the same I'd heard Nester and his idiot friends chanting. And I felt power radiating from him. Power I knew I wouldn't be able to overcome. The pain from all my injuries flared at once as if Adda's influence suddenly shut off. I stopped moving toward him. It was too much. It was more than I could bear.

Yet I bore it.

I was still alive. I was still on my feet.

I looked to Master Winters who was trying to collect himself. He was the most powerful wizard I have ever known and had been overcome by the magic of this false demon.

I looked to Master Foti and Basnet, both still covering their ears, strangely affected by Regis' change. I looked at Gosse, who still did not move.

I turned back and looked to the white lady Adda who stood tall and proud and angry, a hand outstretched, keeping the swirling black cloud at bay.

"This is neutral ground," I said. "Isn't it?"

Adda nodded once, "Yes."

"There are no limits in this universe," I said. "Are there?"

"Only those of faith."

Regis laughed, "Your faith is broken."

"My faith has been stretched to the limit," I said, "and beyond."

Then came a familiar and welcome scream.

"Hers hasn't," I added.

Mr. Machete lanced upward through Regis' rib cage, Mehira's hand smoking as it clutched the enchanted weapon's hilt. Heir Chop-A-Lot jumped in Lucy's hand as the machete blade slid across the sword's edge somewhere inside Regis' body.

"I believe in this," I said and held Killicutty high. Regis' eyes widened as I lunged and yelled "Sanctu Spitu!"

I plunged the large sword down through Regis' chest. The blade ripped through his body and stuck into the ground.

Regis' body twitched and wriggled but he still didn't die. Basnet and Foti sucked in deep breaths and dropped their hands as the holds on them dissolved.

Winters arose and steadied himself on his cane, "William, I believe your contract had been fulfilled."

"Bill," I said, "and thanks."

Regis' eyes widened as Lucy pressed her pistol against the base of his skull, "I believe in bullets."

She pulled the trigger. There were no magic tricks that time.

Chapter Forty-Two

The next thing I remembered was the steady beeping of a heart rate monitor and the distinctive odor of hospital disinfectants. I wasn't sure how long I had been out, but I had a strong case of cotton mouth and my eyelids felt like they had been glued shut.

I wasn't alone. I hadn't even opened my eyes yet, but I could tell. Someone was nearby, breathing softly. Doctors and nurses don't hang out quietly in patients' rooms. Whoever was in the room with me was being quiet. Out of respect, I hoped. Let the big guy have his rest. Right?

I wasn't feeling any pain, which was a little bit worrisome. I had taken a hell of a beating and I had used my power words to defer a lot of pain. I had borrowed from a lot of tomorrows. So, either I was paralyzed and unable to feel pain or I was seriously drugged up. Either way, I didn't take it as a good sign.

I didn't remember passing out after the fight, but I must have. I'd lost a lot of blood that night and the bleeding wasn't stopping on its own. I had pushed myself to the limit and about five miles past that.

I remember seeing Regis go down right before I went out. Without a host body, the demon would've been sucked back to Hell. That's how it worked with that kind of invitation. If the demon had come by way of summoning, the demon would have been free to wreak havoc once freed of its host body. That was all that really mattered now. The demon was gone, and no more innocent people had to die because of it.

It took some doing, but I managed to get my eyes to open. It also took some doing to get them to focus.

Like I guessed, I wasn't alone. There, in a chair next to my bed sat Lucille Red, her booted feet propped up on the edge of my bed frame, her eyes half-closed.

And, happy as a clam, sat Leo there on her lap. Lucy had no idea he was here. He'd gotten over his fear of her or the dark cloud he said he saw. I'd have to ask him about that sometime. I stifled a laugh.

He looked me up and down and nodded faintly and whispered, "You're gonna be OK." Then he touched a finger to his forehead in his customary mock salute, winked, then disappeared.

Lucy jerked awake then saw me, "Oh, hey. You're finally awake, you lazy bastard."

My throat was sore. "Water?"

She picked up a cup and placed the straw on my lips, "Drink slow."

I didn't. And I regretted it.

"You never listen to me," she chided.

"Old habits," I rasped.

"How are you feeling?"

"Don't feel a damned thing," I said.

"Good," Lucy said. "Winters and that White Lady worked you over pretty good before we brought you here. The doctor said you should be dead. Couldn't figure out how you survived."

"Not sure I did."

Lucy smiled, "You did."

"Winters is ok?"

"Technically yes," Lucy set the cup aside and avoided my eyes for a second, "He's pretty upset about Regis and of course Master Gosse."

"Gosse?"

"The fighting took a lot out of him," she said. "He didn't survive that cloud thing."

"Sorry." I didn't know the old wizard, but he didn't deserve to die fighting the likes of Regis and that demon. Nobody did. The collateral damage in this whole clusterfuck was measured in human lives.

"York?"

Lucy shrugged, "That guy's too much of an asshole. Hell didn't want him. And he refused the magic treatment, so he'll be in recovery for a long time."

I smiled. I didn't like the guy, but I had to respect him. He had taken on a minor demon without enchanted weaponry and survived. I had to give him props for that. I'd probably never tell him that to his face, but I'd remember it.

A lot of people had to dig deep in this ordeal, and some unexpected true colors had surfaced.

"Regis is dead?"

"Yes," Lucy stated without emotion. I took that as a good sign for Lucy's soul. She had put the wizard down, and she probably didn't enjoy it.

"How is Lucy?"

"All good," she said sharply.

"Liar," I rasped.

"I'll recover," she said seriously.

"That," I said between breaths, "I believe."

"Oh, and look." She pulled back a sleeve on her right arm to show off a fresh tattoo on her forearm, surrounding a recently healed scar, complete with some familiar looking runes. "I'm a freak like you now."

I laughed. Ouch.

Lucy leaned forward and spoke a little more quietly, "Seriously, though, Master Winters says the Nine-Fold Council owes you a huge debt of gratitude. You really went above and beyond."

"It's what I do," I tried to sound magnanimous, but I think I just sounded lame. And tired.

"Used to do," Lucy said. "Winters says you've retired."

"Finally," I mumbled.

Lucy averted her eyes from me. Hmmm. Guilt?

"My nest egg?"

"Yeah... about that," she said, studying a piece of lint on her pant leg.

I was too weak to sit up, but this was a moment where I would have liked to appear more menacing. After all I did. After all the shit I waded through...

Lucy finally met my eyes, "It was never gone."

"Huh?" I coughed.

"Well... Um... Master Winters might have cast a spell."

Son of a bitch.

"A suggestion spell," she went on, looking away from me again. "We never took a thing."

"Fuck me."

"Yeah," Lucy said softly, "You kinda just saw what you expected, based on what he led you to think."

"Based on what he implied."

She nodded meekly.

"So, all my money."

"Was always there."

"And all those useful enchanted weapons."

She didn't answer. She didn't need to.

In the end, things had wrapped up cleanly. No, that's not true, it was all a mess. But it all wrapped up with a with a certain finality.

Agent Charters and the young idiot Nestor became "permanent guests" of the Council. I wasn't sure what that meant for them, but the implication wasn't rosy.

Regis' death, though justified, sent shockwaves through the Council, both figurative and literal. Winters feared that it would result in lingering paranoia for some time to come. Gosse's death would be felt as well. Two vacant seats at the table would cast a shadow of doubt for some time to come. The remaining members of the Nine-Fold Council came together for another session while I was in the hospital. At that meeting, Lady Adda revealed that she was a high-ranking member of the Fae courts in the Otherside, and she had been sent to lobby for a treaty. Her position was part of why she was unable to fight freely in the battle. Diplomatic and magical agreements are dicey. Winters said my actions had served to convince the Fae and the Council that there were dangers on both sides of the veil and that few things were as black and white as previously imagined. In the end, the Nine-Fold Council voted to suspend monster hunting edicts for the time being. At least until a new agreement with the Otherside could be reached.

Mehira Fiodniagh slipped away in the chaotic aftermath of the battle, taking Mr. Machete with her. Apparently, Adda and the wizards were a little preoccupied with saving my life. Winters later told me that Mehira was a unique vampire in that she was Fae. I wasn't sure what to do with that. I didn't even know a Fae could be a vampire or vice versa. Lady Adda told him that Mehira had been exiled from the Otherside long ago and had changed considerably in the intervening years. I didn't know what that meant.

I had made a bargain with Mehira, though, and that suddenly became much more troubling. The Fae take bargains very seriously, and literally. Mehira had kept her side of the deal. I would have to keep mine. Lady Adda left one last morsel of information for me. Mehira Fiodniagh was a Baobhan'sith, and I could do with that information as I saw fit.

Winters sent me home in a limo.

After Lucy pushed me out of the hospital in a wheelchair—even though I could walk—and made a show of how strong she must be to accomplish such a feat, she joined me for the ride home.

It was a quiet ride, the most peaceful ride I'd had in several days. Neither of us spoke. We just enjoyed the brief journey.

The limo stopped on my street and Lucy hopped out to open the door for me. I'd been healed and mostly recovered, but my muscles were sore and stiff. I made old man noises as I climbed out of the vehicle.

"Come on Grandpa," she took my hand gingerly to help me out of the limo, as if she could hold my weight.

"I'll manage," I said, then added, "jerk."

Lucy smile and handed me a folded piece of parchment, "With regards, from Master Winters."

I took it without opening it, "You'll take care of yourself, right?"

Lucy rolled her eyes, but she was smiling, "If I'm not rushing headlong into danger, I'm not breathing."

I smiled at that, "You wouldn't be you otherwise."

"Enjoy your retirement, Bill. I think you actually earned it this time."

"Enjoy being a badass," I replied, "you've earned it too."

"Hell yeah I did," Lucy shook my hand and then climbed back into the car without looking back.

"You were a hell of a partner," I said as the door slammed shut.

I heard a faint "you too" as the limo sped away leaving me standing alone in front of my house and a vehicle blocking my sidewalk.

It was a mint condition jet black '69 Dodge Charger, with a big red bow on the roof. Wow.

I opened the paper Lucy had given me.

William,

Regretfully, I was unable to reacquire your car, as it had been irreparably damaged and subsequently demolished. Please accept this replacement by way of an apology for the deceptions suffered by my hand. You have my utmost respect and deepest gratitude. You are forever welcome at the Council Table.

Regards,

Master Winters

I ran my hand across the hood of the car, grinning like a kid on Christmas morning. Winters gave me a car! Of course, it wasn't an equal replacement for my Monte Carlo. It was immeasurably better.

"Apology accepted," I said quietly. "And it's Bill."

As I stepped around the car and onto my sidewalk, something on my porch moved. A large furry beast had been curled up in front of my door, waiting for me.

"Lady!" I said. The big dog sprung from the porch in one bound and met me in the yard. She jumped up into my arms and I staggered to keep from falling. She licked me all over the face despite my efforts to twist my head away from her. After a moment, I gave up trying and let her show her affection. Eventually, I just sat down on the lawn with her and hugged her tightly while she wagged her tail gleefully.

"I missed you too," I said and scratched her ears. Lady groaned and leaned into my chest, encouraging me to keep it up. I don't know how long I would have kept going if my phone hadn't buzzed, telling me I got a text message. I wrestled a hand free to check it.

Hey, this is Jesse... you got my number. Well, that angry chick gave me yours!

"Interesting," I smiled and put down my phone.

As I sat there in my yard, in the shadow of a classic muscle car, holding onto a giant dog who loved me unconditionally, I decided I didn't really need to go away and retire on a private island somewhere. This was close enough to paradise for me. I had earned a nice long vacation though. Maybe a week or two on a beach.

But first, I needed a good cup of coffee.

My name is Bill Kemper, and I am a retired monster hunter.

THE END

ABOUT THE AUTHOR

Jason Lankton was born and raised in Kansas, where he lives with a very old terrier.

He has been a newspaper reporter, a carpenter, an electrician, a truck driver, small town policeman, and a maintenance supervisor. When he's not doing the job that pays the bills, you may catch him heading for the mountains, making kitchen cutlery, riding a motorcycle, or searching for the next spark of inspiration. Sometimes, he writes books.

If you enjoyed The Hunter's Goodbye, please leave a review wherever you purchased this book. You can learn more about the author at www.jasonlankton.com. Drop in and say "Hi."